MW00640221

SARGASSA

SARGASSA

SOPHIE BURNHAM

DAW BOOKS
NEW YORK

Jacket design by Adam Auerbach
Jacket illustration by Rebecca Yanovskaya
Book design by Fine Design
Edited by Navah Wolfe

DAW Book Collectors No. 1968

DAW Books
An imprint of Astra Publishing House
dawbooks.com
DAW Books and its logo are registered trademarks of Astra Publishing House

Printed in the United States of America

Library of Congress Cataloging-in-Publication Data

Names: Burnham, Sophie, author.
Title: Sargassa / Sophie Burnham.
Description: First edition. | New York : DAW Books, 2024. |
Series: Ex Romana ; [1]
Identifiers: LCCN 2024016187 (print) | LCCN 2024016188 (ebook) |
ISBN 9780756419363 (hardcover) | ISBN 9780756419370 (ebook)
Subjects: LCSH: Rome--History--Empire, 30 B.C.-476 A.D.--Fiction. |
LCGFT: Alternative histories (Fiction) | Novels.
Classification: LCC PS3602.U7645 S37 2024 (print) |
LCC PS3602.U7645 (ebook) | DDC 813/.6--dc23/eng/20240412
LC record available at https://lccn.loc.gov/2024016187
LC ebook record available at https://lccn.loc.gov/2024016188

First edition: October 2024
10 9 8 7 6 5 4 3 2 1

For Zephyr and Isla—for the future.

I

779 POST QUIETAM

THE HISTORIAN

Alexander Kleios knows he has just minutes left to live. Even now, moving down the dark hall in long, brisk strides, the color is all but gone from his face and his hands shake all the more violently. Thunder rumbles somewhere outside in the distance, far beyond the handsome tapestries and marble sculptures here within the ancient institute he has long considered a second home.

No rain follows, not yet.

Just the promise of a storm.

No one is coming to help him. He knows this now, knows it as deeply and as true as he knows the furrow of both his children's brows, the rich deep warmth of his wife's laughter, the wine-dark swells of the Sargasso Sea. Even if his distress call reached the person it was intended for, she won't get here in time.

Time is running short, but his task is nearly complete. A cold sweat breaks out as he manages to close the grand oak-and-iron door behind him, alone now in his mahogany-lined office. Just him and the furious wind raging against the tall windows rattling in their clear-glass panes. Between the dim fire crackling low in its grate and the comforting weight of the curious little object clutched tightly under his arm, a sudden calm descends upon him. A calm he wouldn't have thought possible ten minutes ago.

In the shadow of the dark pre-dawn, he crosses to the far end of his office, over to where a row of quite unremarkable wooden panels line the wall. Second panel from the left where wood meets molding, he digs his shaking fingernails into the well-worn groove and *pulls*. A thin compartment slips free, and he slides the leather bindings from beneath his arm and into its depths.

There, he thinks, shutting it firmly closed again. *We are not lost yet.*

He's done all he can, and somehow the thought lightens his heart even as his hands shake beyond his control. A scrawled note slipped in his secretary's inbox some floors below, the only person in the world who knows this secret cache. He'll find it, and deliver it to his daughter's safekeeping. Years may pass before she learns how to read it, but it will not now pass into the wrong hands. It will not now be used to the wrong ends.

She *will* learn to read it someday, of that he has no doubt. He's taught her too well to consider the alternative. And perhaps, after all, the passage of some time and acquired wisdom will prove an advantage for her. He had not meant to burden her with this for many years to come. Not when she's too young to truly understand. Too young to avoid the same mistakes he's made.

But there's no value in regrets—though he has many of his own—and even less in worrying for a future he can no longer control. So Alexander Kleios sits at his desk, and he waits for the end.

THEO

Dawn arrives overcast and drizzling on the port of Luxana, salt winds blowing in violent, erratic gusts off the dark gray sea in the weak morning light. Anyone who's lived long enough in Roma Sargassa's capital city knows the signs of a hurricane on the horizon, and Theodora Nix has lived here all their life.

Not that the dangerous weather will put off the local street vendors. Nothing ever does. At barely six in the morning, the slate-and-brick Regio Marina neighborhood stirs feebly to life the same as always. Little girls with wheelbarrows in oversized oilskins and thick woven duskras, shouting out their parents' fresh eel and seaweed haul. The sizzle of acorn-flour on cast iron as men entice passersby with stacks of fried dappham from beneath dripping canvas tents. Rickets collectors, discount servae traders, hemp and spice and indigo merchants. They'll be here until the very last moment, the promise of one last sale too valuable to miss. Hurricanes can last up to a month in this part of the empires—empty stomachs can't.

Pulling their wool scarf tight around damp black hair, Theo makes their way down the wharf. Past the fishermen as they shout and haul in their catch, past seafoam-green shutters flung open for one last gasp of fresh air, past a splintering wooden underpass sheltering a pair of whispering lovers they'd be willing to bet never made it to bed.

Pa'akal and Avis are waiting for them with the cart at the northwest end of the Regio, hunkered over and grim in their oilskins. Izara isn't here, she's been deep undercover for months. Griff's not here yet, either, but that's no surprise, she's always the last to show up. Never mind that she's the one who called them here, but Theo has no idea what Griff actually *does* most of the time. None of them do, and that's as it should be. There's safety in ignorance. Not safety for themselves, but for the greater network of the Revenants across Sargassa. Cells in Halcya and Paxenos and Bostinium, all reporting back to their central base here in Luxana, and even so, Theo, who thinks they might be the closest thing Griff has to a friend, has no idea just how large the network extends.

What they know is what Griff allows them to know, and for Theo that means operations in Luxana, the political and cultural heart of Roma Sargassa. Infiltrating and collecting intel on the movements of the Imperium's fine institutions, the Archives and the Senate and the Institute Civitatem. Positioning themselves strategically for when the time comes—though the time for what, Theo isn't entirely sure.

Direct democracy. Independence from Roma. That's always been the Revenant goal. But where Griff's predecessor had looked to messy fixes and instant gratification—kidnapping a petty officer to interrogate him on naval defense, intercepting supply lines out to the legions, the sort of aggression that resulted in nothing but friends and fellow Revenants dropping at an alarming rate—Griff has always been cleaner than that. Seen the bigger picture laid out broad, and relied on subtlety to shift the tides of opinion.

"People aren't going to throw themselves behind chaos," she told Theo once over a late night mug of tazine, back before she was Griff, back when she was still quietly consolidating power. "That's too frightening. It's too much to ask. And anyway, it's too early for this sort of offensive strategy. There's no revolution without popular consent, so we need the rest of Sargassa if we're going to see this thing through. Before anything else, we need to open people's eyes to what's *possible*." Theo doesn't know if that's the moment she earned their loyalty, but it's what they thought back to, later on, when they shoved a knife in the old Griff's gut to make way for the new.

So no, Theo doesn't always understand why Griff asks what she does of them. They aren't privy to the master plan, what exactly Griff's waiting for while she moves her chess pieces into place. They believe in her all the same. Everyone in the Luxana cell does.

Pa'akal Zetnes is part of the old guard, been doing this for longer than Theo's been alive. Maybe even longer than Griff has been involved. Certainly longer than the seven years Griff has had command. He's the muscle, and a good humor exists beneath that bristly gray beard and suit of black tattoos extending from ear to toe. Avis

Tiago-Laith is a different story, mainly because Theo doesn't actually know him very well. He's new, and slight, and serious, and very, *very* green. If he hadn't mentioned remembering the Brushfires of '52, Theo would swear he's younger than they are. But Griff recruited him personally, and while Theo doesn't see much in him beyond his access as an employee to the Ministerium of Records, they trust their mentor's reasoning. They smile brightly at him. He's doing his best to hide his nerves. He's failing.

"Sorry to keep you waiting," a mild voice cuts through the squall.

Griff is an unremarkable-looking woman. Forty-something, maybe. Five-foot-something, maybe. Somewhat brown, somewhat thick. Not beautiful, not ugly. The kind of person you don't think to notice. Theo sometimes catches themself thinking of Griff as a mother figure, and immediately has to bring that line of thought to a screeching halt.

She's not a mother. She's a spider.

"Thanks for coming on such short notice," she continues, as if any of them would have refused. "Shall we?"

The cart clatters down the cobblestone from the Regio Marina into the Third Ward and the very heart of the city. The streets are emptier than usual, though still lightly bustling with people determined to complete their morning errands before the storm gets any worse. Plebs, mainly—the sprawling concra streets and trash piles of the Third Ward play home to the rabble, maybe the odd Cohort officer patrolling here and there, looking for trouble. As they approach the more upscale Seven Dials district, however, they're cut off the road by a sudden convoy of riders. Green uniforms mark them as Cohort Publica, but the wary-eyed rider in black bringing up the rear gives them away. Cohort Intelligentia. Blackbags. The not-so-secret police.

Avis goes rigid at the sight, and Theo can't help but roll their eyes. "Relax," they whisper. "Griff always manages to get them out of the way." He nods, stiff, and they feel a sudden stab of pity. They've been doing this since they were sixteen. Eleven long years. Enough time to forget how truly shit-your-pants terrifying this actually used to be. Avis may be older, but age is meaningless against experience. Theo squeezes his shoulder.

Through Seven Dials, then, to the Scholar's Gate and up into the Universitas District. All limestone townhouses and academic halls, though there's not a soul to be found from the famed Luxana Universitas out on the street. If the people who live here need to go out in this kind of weather, they can afford to send someone to do it for them.

If they were anyone else, their party would come up through Iveroa Promenade next—a wide pedestrian avenue paved in that same white limestone, dotted here and there with stone benches and manicured gardens for study and conversation, ending at last in the towering Imperial Archives. They're not anyone else.

The back entrance to the Archives is guarded by a single unlucky sentry. Unlucky to begin with, on shift during weather like this. Unluckier still as Theo draws one of their blades across his throat, silencing him before he can shout the alarm. Blood mixes with the rush of rainwater around cobblestone, and briefly they wonder at how much easier this has gotten. A clean slice through stubborn inches of sinew and cartilage requires an even measure of willpower and physical strength. Willpower they had from the start, a fury born from the same hellhole as their starved and malnourished frame. By the time they had built their body into something worthy of fighting back, fury had converted to something far more dangerous. Purpose.

Theo's never been inside the Imperial Archives before now. Most of their adult life has sidelined them to the shadows. Even if they had somehow managed to make their way here as a child, the sentries in their crisp, powder-blue uniforms would have taken one look at Theo's ill-fitting and filthy tunic and called the Publica.

There's a classic grandeur to the domed marble ceiling of the cavernous foyer, the brass paraffin lamps lit dimly in their sconces. Rich Anatolian carpeted hallways, woven in silver and crimson, soften their steps underfoot. Outside, the screaming wind and gradual build into torrential rain has kept the students and scholars and tourists away, dry and warm and safe. It's a stroke of luck, but Theo can't help feeling a twinge of disappointment all the same. They've been perfecting their cut-glass patrician accent—they were looking forward to taking it out for a spin.

Griff navigates them through the endless maze of corridors, meeting rooms, and lecture halls. One wide passageway doubles as a two-story library, shooting outward into row after row of shelves, and Theo finds themself rooted to the sleek wooden floor, gaping upward at the dark arched ceiling far above. The sheer number of books in this one room alone is easily more than they've seen in the entire course of their life. Harder to wrestle their mind around is the knowledge that within the Imperial Archives, the epicenter of all written knowledge in Roma and her client empires across the world, this must barely count as a library at all.

Theo doesn't ask how Griff knows her way around so well, just trusts in whatever muscle memory she apparently has of the labyrinthine Archives until the four of them arrive at the top floor, thirty stories high, and a long hallway ending in front of a magnificently wrought door of oak and iron.

Inside his office, the Imperial Historian is dead.

"Fuck," whispers Griff, bronze face bloodless beneath her scarf. "Frag it, Alex."

To all the world, the man could have just fallen asleep at his desk. But Theo knows poison when they see it. The tracks of lurid blue snaking down his neck would be enough of a giveaway, even without Griff delicately tilting his head to one side, revealing the milky cataracts formed over wide green eyes.

This was definitely not part of the plan.

This is a rescue mission, as far as Theo's aware. Griff had sent a message in the early hours of the morning—one of their own was in trouble, and that's all Theo needed to know. But surely she hadn't meant . . . *Alex?*

Either way, rescue or not, a dead patrician was *not* part of the plan. The Revenants aren't the mindless butchers that the Roman Imperium and their puppet Cato Palmar paint them out to be in their propaganda. Not even under previous, less careful leadership. Oh, they're killers to a one—the unfortunate sentry outside is proof enough of that—but it's never for its own sake. And they aren't *stupid* about it. High-profile murder is messy—questions and investigation and the Cohorts gone power-mad in the streets—and the Revenants are in the business of efficiency. Assassination's useless when the next patrician brat just springs up to take their parent's place. It's rarely worth the risk.

But this is what the Imperium does. Paints political dissidents as monsters, lest the general citizenry be allowed to think for themselves. They've been dancing to this tune for a long time now. Two hundred years, some say, ever since the first Revenant escaped the executions and slaughter that ended the Twelfth Servile War. Others say there have been Revenants as long as there's been a Roma, or a Roma Sargassa, or an end to the Great Quiet some eight hundred years ago. Others, Theo among them, say it doesn't fucking matter. They're here now.

Griff runs a hand over her face and says, "Right. That's unfortunate. But we move on. Pa'akal—guard the door. Avis, are you all right?"

The man looks like he's about to vomit, warily eyeing the Historian's dead body, and his voice is thin and strained when he responds. "Yes. I . . . I don't mean to be . . . It's just that you said we were going to the Senate."

"Really? That was careless of me."

Avis opens his mouth, like he's about to push the subject, then seems to think better of it.

"So who are we looking for?" Theo asks. This is a rescue mission, supposedly, but other than a corpse there doesn't seem to be anyone here.

Griff doesn't answer, not at first. She's still staring at the dead Historian, her face impossible to read. There's a slip of paper just peeking out from under his pale, bloated hand, something scrawled across in neat and elegant loops. Griff slides it out with two fingers, the divot between her brows furrowing as she reads. Then, with a slow but decisive finality, she crumples the paper into her palm, slips it into the pocket of her long oilskin coat.

Then she turns back to the Historian, slouched over at his desk in undignified death, and draws her own dagger. Theo frowns as Griff takes the blade to her own palm, squeezes it tight. A few errant drops escape her clenched fist before she places a bloody thumb to the

Historian's forehead. An old rite, older than Roma's rule over Sargassa, for those who fall before their time. Sentiment, Theo would put it down to, if Griff had a sentimental bone in her body.

"Let's move out," says Griff, and avoids the question in Theo's eyes.

Warning bells clang from the nearby city watchtower as they emerge out the back door with the rest. Either someone discovered the sentry's dead body and raised the alarm, or the storm is shaping up to be worse than anybody expected. In either case, dark figures of the Cohort Publica move in the rain-fogged distance, one of them shouting angrily as they catch sight of the four Revenants exiting out into the street. But the torrential storm provides a welcome cover of confusion, and they slip easily away through the empty streets of crumbling brick and stone, quickly putting distance between themselves, the Cohort, and the Imperial Archives.

In no time at all, they're back to the safety and relative anonymity of the derelict Third Ward. A flash of lightning splits the dark morning as Griff raises her hand, signaling their stop beneath a concra-covered overpass.

Theo bends over to catch their breath, a hand resting against the cool building. They tug the scarf down from around their face, gasping the free air and relishing the absence of oppressive damp wool sticking to their mouth. Somewhere to their left, Griff is murmuring quietly to Pa'akal, then moving to check in on Avis, who's currently barfing into a wheelbarrow.

"Holding up there, Shrimp?" asks Pa'akal, just low enough for them to hear beneath the howling wind. The nickname's an old one, an ironic holdover from darker days. Theo grins.

"You know me. Always."

"Glad to hear it," he says, and nods over to Avis. "Look sharp now." They frown but don't question it, just follow him over to where Griff is bracing Avis by the shoulder. She looks up as they approach, only for a moment.

"First time seeing a dead body?" she asks Avis, not unkindly.

He nods, still looking vaguely ill.

Griff squeezes his shoulder. "You did well in there." And for the first time all day, despite his shaking, despite the brewing hurricane and the Historian's death-still face and the smell of his own vomit, Avis smiles. Griff returns it in kind, gives his shoulder another little squeeze. Then she looks up again at Pa'akal and Theo. "Such a shame."

And all at once they understand.

Pa'akal seizes Avis, locking him in place. Theo draws their blades.

"I took the long way round past the Senate this morning," says Griff, still pleasant as a meridiem date. "The Cohort Intelligentia were waiting for us there."

Avis Tiago-Laith's eyes widen, realization taking hold at last. Theo has witnessed this happen before. It disappoints them now as much as it did then.

"I never tell a new recruit the real mark," Griff says, casually removing a dagger of her own from inside her overcoat. "It's been a good strategy so far."

II

AFTER THE STORM

Two weeks later

THIRD AMENDMENT TO THE IMPERIAL
CHARTER OF ROMA SARGASSA

Should a plebeian citizen violate the law of the land in such a manner as to take the life of another citizen, his or her life shall be forfeit. Should a plebeian citizen violate the law of the land in a non-lethal manner, his or her citizenship (as well as those of dependent legal minors) shall be forfeit, and they shall be contracted for the remainder of their natural life as serva non habet personam to whatever governmental institute, place of business, or private citizen may purchase a contract of their services.

D. 2 PQ

SEVENTH AMENDMENT TO THE IMPERIAL
CHARTER OF ROMA SARGASSA

Individuals born to any one servile parent (those verna non habet personam) may earn, but are not entitled to, a trade apprenticeship under the supervision of a qualified citizen. If their supervisor deems their work satisfactory after Imperial review, said verna shall be at age eighteen granted the conditional citizenship of a client plebeian. A client plebeian shall work under their former supervisor and remain a member of the familia to which they were born, owing rent and a yearly tax, as determined by their paterfamilias. Descendants of client plebeians shall enjoy the benefits of full plebeian citizenship.

D. 48 PQ

ARRAN

Arran was ten years old the first time he realized his father may have made a mistake. Most children fortunate enough to have good parents who love them would find it alarming enough to come by this realization in the first place, but Arran wasn't most children. He was the son of one of the most powerful patricians in the empires. It hadn't occurred to Arran before then that his father even *could* be wrong.

The long stretch of summer was just beginning, and already burdened by an oppressive heat that stuck heavy on his skin and clothes. His stepmother Naevia had taken to winding herself in cool strips of linen soaked in water and aloe before hiding in the tiled bathhouse with his little sister Selah, who was six at the time and still too little to be very interesting. And though she'd expressly forbidden him from going out into the sun, Naevia wasn't his mima, and Arran had slipped away to join the other boys from his elementary in the shallows that ran along the lush private shores of Luxana's Arborem district.

Nine boys in all splashed about the shoals, taking turns on a thin reed skimboard someone had brought, daring each other to go out farther to where the largest waves crested and broke. A few nannies sat here and there under the shade of the gray shale cliffs, calling at their charges *not to wander too far now, Valerius* and *I see you, Julian, don't even think about it.* Arran had been searching for a crab or a particularly good clump of muddy sand to slip down the back of Phineas Halitha's trunks, when somehow the conversation turned to their upcoming superior levels.

"I'll be going to Farrows Hall in September," said Val, who would of course be going into medicine like his father, and his father's father. "You too, Phin, yeah?"

Phineas, who was as stupid as he was mean—but would eventually replace his mother as the chairman of Luxana's largest private hospitium all the same—grunted an affirmative.

"Thank Terra we won't have to deal with those two at Laurium," whispered Julian, who had been his best friend at the time. Arran didn't say anything.

It wasn't the *wrong* assumption to make. Julian's family were scholars like Arran's, and it stood to reason that they would both be attending the Laurium School for their superior, like their parents before them. It was a great honor to go to Laurium, even among the patrician class. While Phineas and Valerian would be taught the ins and outs of medical business and maybe even how to hold a scalpel, he and Julian would learn something much more important than all that—the means and practice of scholarship itself. Because *scholarship* meant *knowledge*, and every single child in Roma Sargassa knew just how sacred that was. How much had been lost after the Great Quiet. How revered those were who dealt with the collection and preservation of the world's knowledge, or the translation and interpretation and pushing forward into new understanding. Resurrecting everything that had once been known, back before they had to rebuild again from the ground up. And *his* dad, Arran had thought with a burning pride in his chest, was at the heart of that. Kleioses had always gone to school at Laurium. Selah would go there one day, too. Only it had just occurred to him then that no one had ever actually *told* him he would be going there to study in the fall. It just hadn't come up.

"Don't be stupid. Laurium wouldn't take someone like *him*."

Phin had chosen that moment to find his voice. He sloshed his way through the high tide over to the pair of them, looming large overhead.

"Like hell they won't," Julian shot back, shocking everyone from the boys to the nannies with his low-caste language. "His dad's the Imperial Historian."

"Vernae get apprenticeships, not schools," said Phin. "Everyone knows that."

Arran felt himself go hot and red and knew it had nothing to do with the sun.

But that was wrong. He wasn't a verna. If he were a verna, he wouldn't live in a beautiful home in the historic Arborem. He wouldn't have a powerful father and a senator stepmother. If he were a verna, his parents would be servae like Julian's nanny—pleb men and women who had wasted their chance to be productive and useful members of Sargassan society, and now had to be told what to do instead. If he were a verna, he wouldn't be free. Not for eight more years anyway. And Arran Alexander had always been free.

His dad had just forgotten to talk to him about Laurium. That had to be it. He had so many other things going on at work that it must have slipped his mind. Disconcerting as it was to realize his dad was even capable of making a mistake like that, Arran reasoned that as Imperial Historian, he spent his days working on research projects and advising the Consul and other important members of the Imperium, and he had a lot on his plate, after all. Maybe he thought that Naevia had already done it, even though she was just as busy and important at the Senate. Maybe he *had* remembered, but assumed it was so obvious that there was no need to say anything about it at all.

Shaking off his momentary embarrassment, Arran took advantage of Phin's proximity to lob a handful of foul-smelling red seaweed directly into his face, instigating a battle that would become the stuff of legends. For the next three months, anyway.

When he returned home crusted over with sand and salt, Naevia gave him a dressing down about the dangers of direct sunlight this time of year, especially for boys with skin like his, then had the cook give him and Selah each a shaved ice with mint syrup. Sure enough, within an hour his normally pale skin had bumped up and turned a violent shade of dark pink. By the time he'd gone to bed that night in his large room with the bay window overlooking the sea, itching and burning to the point of frustrated tears, he had forgotten all about stupid Phin Halitha's accusations and his dad's harmless mistake.

Down in the sprawling Third Ward, market vendors hawk their wares in a cacophony of shouts and blur of bright colors. Salarypeople rush to their next meeting, harried aides and apprentices scurrying in their wake. Crowds are shoved aside by sentries to part the way for ornate palanquins. Tourists from Siracusa and Bostinium point at the turrets and spires of older stone and concra buildings that have somehow managed to stay in one piece over the many years and weather systems. Kids shout and play in the hurricane wreckage of those that didn't. And down on the low bank of one of the canals snaking through it all, a tight throng of plebs throw money at each other, shouting countering bets.

Arran's shirtless in the center of it, jav-and-honey curls damp with sweat, lip bleeding, one of his high cheekbones purpling already. Smiling through it all the same. His opponent's even worse for wear, but that doesn't change the fact that he's easily three times as wide. Good. Keeps things interesting.

He dodges the next jab just as easily as each of the ones before— that was one of the first things he'd learned in the legions. The camp prefect's voice rings in his ears like it's still the second day of basic training and not a good thirteen months after the fact—"Come on, boy, hit him like you mean it. You may be built like a beanpole, but you're damn fast. That's an advantage. Use it."

Arran circles his opponent, bare fists raised, and in the next half second thinks he sees someone from across the makeshift ring, arms crossed and gold glinting from dark braids, someone with his father's face who can only be—*Oof.*

A sickening crack as the other fighter catches him across the nose. And now that's bleeding freely, too.

Groans and cheers alike rip from the crowd—more cheers than groans, truth be told—but he's deaf to them all, too preoccupied with the stars ringing on the inside of his skull. It's only when the next blow doesn't come, when the tenor of the rising shouts around him begins to change, that he realizes something's wrong. Excitement giving way to panic. Jostling to pushing.

Frag it. The Publica are here.

This shouldn't be a surprise—gambling and street fighting are both illegal, technically, but it's the kind of thing the Cohort's usually happy to turn a blind eye to so long as they get cut in on the take. Not today, apparently. Green uniforms swarm the cobblestone bank instead, apprehending onlookers as they attempt to flee the scene, nightsticks out and clapping wrists in irons at will.

Arran scrambles to gather himself together, blinking furiously to shake the stars from his eyes so he can find cover, an alley to duck down or a shop to lose himself in. But it's too late. The hands that haul him to his feet are surprisingly strong for the small Publica officer they belong to. Short but stout, she wastes no time twisting his arm behind his back, and before Arran can get his bearings he's halfway up the bank toward the growing line of chained offenders. That's when he registers the cold iron clamped around both his wrists.

Oh shit, he thinks faintly. *Oh shit. This is bad. This is really, really bad.*

Because his dad is dead, and he has been for two weeks, and it isn't until this exact moment that Arran's truly appreciated this simple fact: that no matter how much else he'd resented Dad for, the protections he's taken for granted his whole life are now gone, too. The fight they'd had—the roaring argument barely a week after he'd returned home from his year away in the legions—it seems idiotic now, in the stark light of what's about to happen.

He is about to be arrested. Hauled in front of a magistrate who'll take one look at his conditional citizenship and take it away. The best he can hope for is that the news will somehow get back to Breakwater before his contract goes public. After that . . . his gut twists at the thought.

And then, clear and loud over the racket—"Kleios familia. And *that's my brother.*"

He hears her before he sees her, though he could have sworn he had caught sight of her in the crowd during that last round. Black braids piled high and messy on top of her head, a few wisps escaping to frame her heart-shaped face. Thick brows furrowed in that half-exasperated way. At twenty-two, Selah looks more and more like their dad every day. Arran doesn't know if that breaks his heart or makes him love her even more. For the moment, though, she's got her patent of identity raised, that unmistakable emblem of the eight-point Kleios sun mere inches from a tall Publica officer's nose, her other hand pointed straight at Arran.

The other officer—the one Arran's got the pleasure of dealing with—stops dead in her tracks. He says nothing as the officer digs roughly through his pockets, coming up with his own patent. She frowns. "Says here he's a client plebeian, ma'am."

"And I'm the Imperial Historian. Are you going to make me wait?" The effect is immediate. Spine stiffening, shoulders pulling back, and the officer's eyes go wide. And yet for all that, the hesitation's slight, but it's there. Bloody and bruised and shirtless and shining in his own sweat, Arran's the clear culprit here, the actual perpetrator breaking the law by brawling in the streets. Not to mention how distinctly *un*related he and Selah look. But there's no denying her authority, the weight of the title he's just heard her claim for the very first time, and all three of them know it. Barely ten seconds pass before the officer begrudgingly twists the irons free from Arran's wrists.

It should be a relief, and it is, but there's something darker twisting itself around the feeling. Dad may be dead, but the protections aren't. They're just Selah's job now.

He doesn't know why that realization is so ugly.

"I'd keep a closer eye on him in the future, ma'am," the officer says, pushing him toward Selah before moving on to help her fellow Publica with the rest of the straggling crowd. Arran watches her go through narrowed eyes, and spits a wad of blood out onto the cobblestone. But by the time he turns back to his sister, he remembers that it isn't her that he's annoyed with.

"Ma'am," he parrots, quirking a brow.

She punches him.

"*Ow*," he says, pointed. That was already going to bruise without her help, thanks. She glares at him. He glares right back. A standoff, her dark face mere inches from his paler one. Then—

He pulls her into his arms, and she clings on tight. Fierce. Holding on for dear life, never mind the sweat and blood he has to be getting on her dress. And for the first time since their father died, he regrets not going home. He already had the shitty room above a taberna in Paleaside where he'd crashed to cool off after the fight with Dad, and in the aftermath, knowing that the terrible things they'd said had been their last . . . well, it had felt easier, somehow, to stay away. Easier to just lose himself in the streets. But Arran has been gone in the legions for more than a year, and seen Selah maybe twice in the three weeks since he's been back.

"Hi," he says quietly, into her hair.

"Hi. I missed you."

Guilt curdles in his spleen. At twenty-six, Arran has lived enough of life to know that his father was never the infallible person his ten-year-old son once assumed him to be. Back before he learned he wasn't allowed to take his superior at all, never mind thoughts of Laurium School. Back before a lot of things. But that doesn't mean he has to take it out on his sister.

Selah was never far from his thoughts when he first left home. He could almost hear her voice next to him at the start—wry jokes about his fellow conscripts and the foreign desert heat of southwestern Fornia. But her phantom voice had faded eventually, replaced by new friends and an alien landscape. Arran had known from the start that his posting would take him far from the familiar salt air and oak forests of Luxana, once he'd finally accepted that military service was one thing his family couldn't get him out of. The Imperium learned a long time ago to stamp out any conflicting feelings in their ranks on policing their own, and always sent their conscripted twenty-four-year-olds to opposite ends of the empires. It was part of how the Imperium had survived for so long. So Arran had expected that. He hadn't, however, been ready for the sheer overwhelming beauty of towering mesas and plunging canyons, great cracks and ravines in the red earth that went on as far as the eye could see. He hadn't expected the locals to live so differently, their cities carved into the sides of canyons to escape the punishing heat, their cuisine formed around cacti and root vegetables that thrive below the ground. But what Arran had been least prepared for during his mandatory year in the military fort at Teec Nos Pos was to *enjoy* it.

Luxana is a small town at heart, and life in the patrician Arborem was never designed to take someone like him into account. It had been heady, disappearing into the regimented and anonymous life of a foot soldier, where no one knew who he was. Jarring, then terrifying, then abruptly, *wildly* liberating. No holier-than-thou once-overs, no smiles that never quite manage to reach the eyes, no murmurs of *freedman* and *no reason to inflict him on the rest of us* behind his back. He was just Arran Alexander, and that had been enough for doors to open. To tag in on a clavaspher pickup match that was down a player. To sneak out to a house party in the city with his new friends Enyo and Fagan. To be as good as he could find it in himself to be—with a spear, with his fists, with a tactical suggestion that earned the approving nod of his tribune—and actually see the rewards of that come back to him. And with each door that opened, he'd felt another brick in the carefully built defenses of showmanship and laissez-faire charm, built up over a lifetime, crumble to dust.

The return to Luxana hadn't been the easy slip back into his old life that everyone had been expecting. Arran had wanted to go back to the legions. Dad . . . hadn't understood that.

"You're an idiot," Selah is saying now, squeezing him once more before letting him go. "Is this actually fun for you?"

He shrugs. "Good way to make money."

"Uh-huh."

At least it's halfway true. She doesn't need to know about the other half, the half where sometimes he feels like he's going to spin right out of his skin until it breaks open and he can *feel* something. This, if nothing else, is grounding. Something he knows how to do.

"Mima's going to fully spin out, you do realize that."

"She's only going to find out if you tell her."

Selah raises a brow. "You sure about that? I think walking into Dad's viewing tonight looking like you just got beat to the Quiet and back might sort of give you away." He pauses midway through pulling his trampled shirt back on. "Are you not coming? Or did you forget?"

He absolutely did not forget. He just didn't know if he'd be welcome.

Dad's viewing. No one would miss him, no one that isn't Selah, but that doesn't mean he feels easy, exactly, about skipping out on Dad's final rites. Tonight will be for the masses, a chance for Luxana society to pay their respects to the late Imperial Historian—and to be seen doing so, obviously. But tomorrow they'll send him back to

All-Mater Terra, burned and interred deep in the catacombs beneath the city, and that's just for family. He doesn't know if he counts as that anymore.

He slaps on a lopsided sort of smile, the kind of thing he hasn't had to fake in months. "Of course I'm coming. Have to come make my new paterfamilias look good, right? *Ma'am.*"

"It's *mater*familias, actually."

"Oh, I bet the Arborem familias are going to love that. Unless that's the new fashion? I'm old. I don't understand youth culture. Is that a thing now?"

"I'm making it a thing."

He kisses the top of her head. "Always the trailblazer." And then he stops, the reality of the situation dawning harsh and cold. "Where's your sentry? You shouldn't be out here alone."

No one's been arrested or even claimed credit for Dad's murder yet, and though of course everyone assumes the Revenants are to blame, that doesn't explain the *why*. Until there's some explanation, some sort of logic and motive to track, Selah isn't safe. Not now she's the new Historian.

"I'm not alone." She shrugs. "I've got my scary big brother to defend me."

"You could've been murdered on the way here," he points out. "And then Naevia would've murdered *me*."

True as that may be, neither of them have ever been able to resist a steaming bowl of bastia cam, and so much the better if it comes from the stall on the corner of Fernsedge and Wilde. Arran's practically inhaled half of his already by the time Selah gets hers, midway through a diatribe on Dean Nija Thane's latest crimes against scholarship and academia.

"—and then she said, *I'm sure there are more important things that need your attention right now.*" Selah fumes, sloshing precious fish soup over the sides of her bowl. "As if I'm not *perfectly* aware of how fragging busy I am. The Archives are a bona fide madhouse right now. Every time I think I've got ten minutes to actually do something *fun*—" Because sneezing through dusty tomes on arcane medicine and long-forgotten harvesting tools is his sister's idea of fun. "—a staffer comes by with an admin issue or Gil tells me there's a senator who wants to know if the bill they're introducing violates some obscure treaty, and still. *Still*. I still took the time out of all that to come to *her* and her precious universitas, expressly because this is a priority."

"Maybe she was just talking about the viewing?"

"Like she actually cares about that," says Selah. "She just didn't want to have the conversation. She's fully scared of progress, just like anyone else in charge of anything. And now that I'm *important* or something she won't even have the decency to own up to it."

"She can't own up to it. The universitas needs access to the Archives, she can't vex you off."

"Well, she has."

"What did you propose, then?" he yawns. "Mobile libraries in Sinktown? Teaching missions to Arawaka and the Taino Territories?" Selah goes oddly quiet. "Was that it? Don't tell me that was it, that's fully and certifiably insane."

She shakes her head, cheeks flushed. Then, very quickly, she pulls out the sheaf of papers and stuffs them into Arran's free hand. He hands his empty soup bowl back to the vendor and glances down at the title of the proposal, neatly printed in Selah's spiky handwriting. It takes a moment to realize what he's looking at.

Servile Education Extension Program—Proposal & Curriculum.

"Oh."

"Yeah."

"Um," he says, clearing his throat awkwardly. "So she curbed it."

"Of course she did," says Selah, practically throwing her empty bowl at the stall and taking off down the crowded street in a huff. Arran has to jog to catch up with her.

"The universitas is a place of higher learning for all," she goes on, barely breaking stride, "but only so long as they're *citizens*. We have a bona fide wealth of untapped potential in the servile castes. How many of them might have cured our worst diseases? Written our greatest literary works? And they're slipping through the cracks because no one will give them a chance."

"You don't have to convince *me*," he says, reaching out to grab her arm. Because the answer to her problem is obvious. "Look, you have the Archives now, right?" he asks, jostling slightly as a gaggle of indigo merchants push past him, shouting angrily about the decreasing value of the ceres against the Aymaran neptos. Selah frowns and nods. He can't believe he has to spell this out for her. "So . . . let Nija Thane have her universitas. The greatest library in the world belongs to you. Use it."

"What, teach there?" She laughs. "You're spinning out."

"Am not."

"The Archives don't teach. We research and preserve."

"So do that, too. Servae know tons of things citizens don't, especially if you get a few Ynglots or other natives in there. Do you realize how much they could probably tell us about the outside lands off the Imperial Road? Set it up like that, an exchange that benefits the Archives, and I bet you'll have people lining the streets to sign their servae up."

It's not such an insane idea, now that he says it out loud. If only the right people would listen. And Selah *is* the right people.

Only she isn't listening. Not anymore.

The Publica are long gone, but a straggling line of criminals and debtors being walked along the street level above have caught Selah's attention instead, sunlight glinting off the new silver cuffs clasped to the ridge of each of their left ears. Servile processing. Something he's just missed by a hair. But he knows that intent look on Selah's face, and he knows what she's searching for, eyes flicking shrewdly down the line.

"She isn't there, Sel," he says, gently as he can, but it's been five years. Tair is gone. She isn't coming back. There are certain hard truths in life and this is one Selah's just going to have to learn to live with.

Selah angrily rubs at her eyes. "It's not about *her*," she bites out finally, and suddenly Arran thinks he understands.

Their father is dead, and it comes in waves. Sometimes he forgets. Sometimes he remembers, but it doesn't feel real, like an intellectual exercise. And sometimes the smallest thing—a dog barking, that certain shade of autumn sky—will set him off and he'll be useless for the rest of the day, head spinning and lungs heaving and utterly unable to keep his own mind straight. And sometimes he's angry. Angry that Dad had the unmitigated gall to get murdered without leaving Arran some kind of road map because he doesn't know how to *do* this.

There's no logic to this kind of grief. Small reminders of his mother don't do this to him. But he never knew her—postpartum depression saw to that—and he's lived with his losses for much longer than his sister has lived with hers.

"Come here," he says, and pulls Selah in again, his own solid weight settling against her as an anchor, letting himself sink into the steady warmth of hers.

"I miss Dad."

"Yeah, so do I," he says, and finds he means it.

FIVE YEARS EARLIER

774 PQ

*T*his isn't the first time she's snuck out at night. *Around the time she turned thirteen and realized how easy it was to navigate the secret internal passageways snaking through her ancestral family home, Selah Kleios had begun to do it practically every week for no reason other than because she could.*

She'd go on long walks down to the beachfront below Breakwater's gray shale cliffs, kicking off her boots to dig her toes in the warm sand, and wander the alleys near the universitas where student nightlife spilled out from the brownstone tabernas in music and strange lights. She had actually been brave enough to go inside one once, though she'd promptly been shooed out by the barlady for being so obviously underage. She had decided to ignore Tair when her friend pointed out that of course *the passageways in the manor are easy to navigate—they're not meant to be secret, just discreet enough for servae to avoid being seen. How else did Tair always win at hide-and-seek when they were kids? She's been using them all her life.*

So no, when Selah sneaks out one late summer night, it's not for the first time. But it is *the first time she's convinced Tair to come with her.*

The older girl's hand is clammy in hers, and she swears she can hear Tair's heartbeat pounding against her chest as they fly over cobblestone and concra in the dark. Tair on her cruiseboard, Selah on her bike, wild in the freedom of the night air. She can't help but thrill at the smooth warmth where their palms touch, pulses racing as they glide alongside one another.

One hour, that's what Tair had said when she finally gave in. Selah had shrugged, letting her take that for agreement, but there's no way the two of them will be home before sunrise. The fireworks, the dancing, the morning ocean vespers . . . she won't let Tair miss out on a moment, not when the Festival of Sol and Luna only comes once a year. Cultists may be slightly spun out—still hung up on worshipping intangible gods and deities instead of the All-Mater Terra beneath their feet—but they know how to throw one hell of a party.

The beach is already teeming when they arrive. Dancers thronging together to the music of the drum and steelstring band, decked out in gold streamers and moonmasks and archaic togas like the Caesarians of old. Groups of friends laughing and drinking and pushing each other into the soft, gray sand. Next to her, Tair has her arms crossed, pressing in against herself, and Selah sees what she's staring at. A small knot of middle-aged men, deep in their cups, wearing civilian clothes but easily given away by the green scarves poking out of back pockets—off-duty Cohort Publica.

Selah rolls her eyes. She'd bring Tair closer if she dared, press their foreheads against one another, let her know it's going to be all right. It'll be wonderful. She won't let anything go wrong. Instead, she grabs Tair's hand and tugs her toward the center of the crowd, kicking off her sandals and pulling her into a fast dance after the music's wild beat. A light grows in her solar plexus as the corners of Tair's lips quirk a begrudging smile, then a little laugh, until both girls are breathless, screaming and giggling to the point of tears. Out from behind her piles of dusty books and paper trails, Tair's deep-set eyes are alight with mischief, her close-cropped curls framing her face like some otherworldly halo, and Selah's heart bursts with joy.

"Seventeen tomorrow," Tair shouts over the music. "How's it feel?"

"Bona fide divine."

"What are you looking forward to more? Getting your hands on your trust fund—" Tair spins her around, "—or the look on those little boys' faces when you show up for class?"

"Reality drop. Those little boys are three years older than me."

"Exactly."

Her schoolfriends think she's completely lost her mind, but Tair of all people understands what it means to her, the accelerated course of study approved for her at Luxana Universitas beginning in two weeks. Years of rigorous training in her superior levels—paired with private tutoring by Dad's secretary Gil Delena—yielded exceptionally high scores in her entrance exams. She's earned that course.

When the song ends, the band strikes up a much slower tune. Selah thinks she knows this one, something Arran hums now and then. She can't be too sure. As much as her brother loves to sing, it's not one of his gifts.

Tair takes her hand and it's slower, this time. Closer. And suddenly Selah's not at all sure where to rest her eyes.

"One more month for you," she says, just to say something. "Eighteen. How does that feel?"

A shadow dances quickly across Tair's face—something conflicted, something secret, though she's never been much good at keeping her thoughts off her face. Not that this needs to be a secret, anyway. Selah is a patrician, but Tair is a verna. For her, becoming an adult means a different kind of freedom altogether.

"I honestly have no idea," says Tair at last. "It doesn't feel real."

"What's the first thing you're going to do?"

"Open a bank account."

"Boring. Maybe something that doesn't involve my parents holding your hands?"

Tair chooses that moment to spin her around and in, so that all at once she's wrapped up in her arms. She's suddenly very aware of how tall Tair is. She's very aware of her mouth, and its proximity to her own.

"I can think of a few things."

And Selah's heart does a small loop on itself. Maybe this is it, then. That thing they never talk about, but has gradually stretched out in the past year or so, making itself impossible to ignore. That thing she's coming closer and closer to acting on with each passing day, and she doesn't know why she's overthinking it like this, but she just thinks it would be so much simpler if Tair were the one to do something about it first.

"And you didn't want to come out tonight," she says quietly, willing her closer.

"I didn't not want to," says Tair, eyes flicking down to Selah's lips—briefly, just the tiniest moment. "I just didn't think it was a good idea."

"Still think so?"

The song continues and they linger there, the flush of that young, unspoken something sitting heavy between them. Selah could count each individual freckle of Tair's fawn-brown face if she wanted, the glint of that silver ear cuff just visible through the spray of auburn coils. Fireworks paint her face in reds and blues and Selah wonders if she should say something smart, or funny, or just say anything at all if it means that Tair will just do it, already, just—

Something knocks into her hard from behind.

A group of townies, their leader at the head, a cigarette hanging lazily from his mouth. They're dressed well, crisp tunics and shirts of yellows and blues and whites for the occasion. Not urchins, then. Just the kind of boys you might cross the street to avoid.

"Do us a favor, girls," says the straw-headed boy at the lead, smirk writ nasty even before he stops to wet his lips. "Take it some-where else."

Selah scrambles up off the sand, all righteous indignation, but Tair gets there first.

"You got a problem?" she barks.

"Yeah." He flicks the red-lit stub of his cigarette toward her. "Thing is, there's a certain level of class to the Cult of Sol and Luna. No one really wants to watch a couple serva crims going at it like bitches in heat. Unless there's an invitation to join."

Selah feels her face go hot with rage. How dare he? How dare he presume to teach them about manners and class? But even through her anger, she's aware of the subtle shift that passes through Tair on her left. Shoulders pulling back, she stands a little taller, even as her face goes neutral.

"The Boardwalk's public property," Tair says, calm and reason-able. "I'm allowed to be here." Her voice is sickening in its neutrality, because this boy has the kind of face that's asking to get punched.

Selah hates this. Tair may be a verna, but she's worth a hundred of these pathetic plebs.

"Not if I say different," says the boy, his friends laughing nastily behind him.

"Oh, and who are you?"

"What?"

"Well, you must be important to have a say in things like that, yeah? So who are you?"

"You giving me lip, serva girl?"

Tair shrugs. "Just making conversation."

The boy steps up into her face, and Selah can see Tair willing herself not to back down, even from the invasive hot breath mere inches away. "Take your little friend and fuck off now," he says, betraying his own caste with his careless vulgarity. "There's a nice pig pen a few streets over. It'll do for you and your crim slut."

"You're plebeian, aren't you?" Selah hears herself asking, and the boy's eyes snap over to her, alive with delight. But he can't hurt her, not the way he could hurt Tair, even if he doesn't realize who she is just yet. So she finds herself cutting in between them, both so much taller than her, a hand on each to push them apart.

All the same, she just barely stops herself from crying out when the boy grabs her wrist. The entitlement is bruising. No one's ever dared touch her like this before.

"Are you trying to make this worse for yourself?"

"Actually," she gasps. "I'm giving you an out. See that man over there?" She nods over some yards away toward a huge man she'd spotted earlier, six foot something of muscle on muscle. The boy's gaze follows hers. His eyes widen. Good.

"That's my bodyguard," she lies, privately screaming with gratitude that Dad and Mima let her study theater arts at her superior. "Horace. And you've assaulted me just now, so I'd give it another . . . I don't know, fifteen seconds before he comes over here and beats the living daylights out of you."

The boy glances back at her, then back to the huge stranger—who by some grace of Terra actually is looking over in their direction.

"Now, the way I see it," she says, "you talk like trash, which means you're a pleb. So you probably don't know who I am. That's not something that merits Horace beating the living daylights out of you, of course. But you are vile, which actually does merit him beating the living daylights out of you. So. Your choice."

She can see the wheels of the boy's mind working as the gravity of the situation bears down on him, the now-clear lack of cuff on her *ear ringing the alarms of his mistake. His hand around her wrist is a punishable offense. He could be stripped of citizenship for this, should she choose to press it to that point. Not that she would. But he doesn't know that.*

"C'mon, man," one of his friends says quietly, pulling at his shoulder. "Leave it."

The boy releases Selah's wrist, glancing nervously over at the fictional Horace again. "You're a patrician?" he asks, the word slipping from his tongue like a death knell. She doesn't deign to answer; a withering glare should suffice. His gaze shifts back to her, then over to Tair for the first time since Selah intervened. "That's disgusting."

Savage, she thinks ferociously as he shoves past her, disappearing back into the crowd along with his friends.

"We should go."

It comes from behind. Selah rolls her eyes and turns back to Tair, who doesn't look up at her. "No, it's curbed," she says. "They're just angry little boys looking for a fight."

But Tair is firm.

"This was a mistake."

THEO

The taberna by the docks of the Regio Marina is dark, and musty, and mostly empty this early in the morning. Only a few salt-worn sailors crowded around a table in the corner playing cards, making the most of shore leave, their laughter echoing loud enough to make up for the lack of other patrons. There's a reason this place is called Neptune's Folly.

Theo's contact isn't here yet.

Cloak-and-dagger intrigue is decidedly not the life they had envisioned for themself as a child, but to be fair, in those days they didn't tend to think much further than their squirming stomach. Even after Pa'akal put a blade in their hand, it had taken time to realize that sixteen years of want and shame had also given them the means to their own liberation. *Don't be noticed.* That one had been instilled in them early. Not by their useless father, but by older whispers and hard-earned experience. *Don't be noticed. There's nothing more dangerous for a serva than being noticed.*

It took some time, but as Theo became more proficient with their daggers—started putting on muscle and real body fat for the first time in their life, long since outgrowing Pa'akal's nickname *Shrimp*—they began to realize that they already knew how to wield their greatest weapon—dancing between the lines of what people expect to see. They've by no means come by it honestly, but they'll be the first to admit they're a damn good spy.

Resisting the urge to scratch at the long blond wig they're working with today, Theo feels as though they actually deserve a drink after all. But before they can make it over to the bar, a small commotion breaks out some ways down at the other end, and all thought of drinks and self-congratulations go out the window.

Una has got to be the worst canary in their ring.

Not that they'll ever tell Griff that. Recruiting Una was a coup, and Theo's coup at that, a serva right at the heart of the patrician

Kleios familia. Recruiting her had been the key to working their own way into the senator's circle of trust, using the information Una passed on about Naevia Kleios to place and present themself just right, ultimately—per Griff's instruction—securing a place on her senatorial staff. They couldn't have done any of it without Una, and they aren't in any hurry to let that debt go unpaid. Even if it means they now have to rescue her. Again.

There's a sailor who has Una pressed up against the bar, skin turned to leather from the merciless sun, the overpowering stink of sea and canvas and too much alcohol sweating from his pores. Theo heard the slap that Una dealt him before they saw her, and grits their teeth at the unforgiving hand the man has buried in her yellow hair, pulling at the roots while Una's eyes begin to water. Whether from the pressure or the stench, Theo doesn't know.

"*Oho,*" he's saying, eyes straying to the cuff around Una's ear. "Off on a little walkabout, huh? Who let a pretty thing like you off their leash?"

Theo is a good actor. They are good at weaving through the dark. But there isn't always a difference between efficiency and satisfaction, and they've never been one to deny themselves the latter.

"*I* did," they say, and punch the sailor squarely in the balls.

Despite being a terrible informant, frankly, despite being bullheaded and arrogant and all the things that Theo themself learned as a child not to be in order to survive, they have always liked Una. She was raised in the Ynglot clans beyond the Imperial Road, a godsdamn hurricane held captive now in enemy territory. Ynglots are native, insular, and tribalistic nomads who survive by way of raids on Sargassan settlements and traveling parties. At seventeen, Una had been part of a supply run on one of Luxana's outlying agricultural villages— always a gamble, you never know what sort of defenses you'll find yourself up against. The legionaries stationed in places like that are either the dregs of the barrel, too out of shape or just plain drunk to wield a sword, or fresh green conscripts on their mandatory year, eager to see some action. Whichever it was, Una's luck hadn't been with her that day. She'd been knocked out early, and woken up inside the Institute Civitatem.

"Una," she'd laughed bitterly over an illicit cigarette, back when Theo was still trying to gain her trust with well-placed questions and contraband gifts. "Creative, right? I was first in line for servile processing that day. Can't be having any uncivilized savage names in the jewel of Roma Sargassa."

She's never actually told them her real name.

Now, Theo sits languidly on the stoop just inside the abandoned apartment that passes for the movement's Regio safehouse, and rolls a dagger through casual fingers as the argument unfolds in front of them.

"But with the Historian dead, I thought—"

"Una—"

"I can do more than just pass on gossip," Una insists, her belligerence taking up the whole of the crumbling room. Griff, across the broken three-legged table, remains unfazed. "I'd be a better asset on the ground. I'm smart, I'm discreet, I know the city, I know the wilds *outside* the city, and you know you can trust me—"

"Which are all reasons why I need you where you are."

"But he's *dead*."

"And now there's a new one."

Keep an eye on the Imperial Historian, tell us what we need to know about the senator, and we'll get you free someday. That was the deal Griff had struck. Theo had been there, the day the promise of Una's freedom was made in exchange for information out of Breakwater. This, if nothing else, is the reason Theo's relatively confident that their aborted rescue mission to the Imperial Archives had nothing to do with saving Alexander Kleios from his fate. If he were one of theirs, there would be no need for a canary in his house.

Now, Una flares her nostrils in dangerous discontent, but Griff takes her hands in hers.

"Listen to me," she says, low and deadly serious. "What you're doing for us isn't just passing on gossip. I know it's frustrating, I've *been* there. But it's essential. You're the wheels that this entire operation rides on. I can find a blade for hire anywhere if the coin's right.

But eyes and ears who are already in the right places? That I already know I can trust? You have no idea how hard that is to come by. We *need* you. Just for a little longer."

Theo is a good actor, but Griff is a master at work. They watch the concern in her eyes, the conviction of spirit, the hand that seems to stretch out between her and Una as if to say, *You and I are one—and we are in this fight together.* They watch these things and know that Griff could not melt away Una's fury without that small, pure seed of truth sitting at the heart of it.

"How long?" Una whispers. "How long until we end all this?"

And Griff lets out a bark of laughter, though it doesn't seem to be at Una's expense.

"A year," she answers. "Fifty. Two hundred. Una, I don't know. The Imperium has had its grip on the world for millennia. If no one can remember a time before Roma, how are they supposed to even *begin* to imagine a world without it? And people *need* time. Time to get used to new ideas if they're going to help us achieve them. Force it on them when they aren't ready to accept it and we're just a new version of the old thing. But I've given over half my life to the Revenants, so if you can think of a faster way, I'm certainly listening."

Una slumps, as if giving in to a mother's weary warmth. "I can't spend the rest of my life like this. Not even half."

"You won't, I promise," says Griff, and now Theo knows for sure that she's lying. Without another reason, one that directly helps the movement in some tangible, actionable way, the Revenants aren't in the business of playing the freedom trail for every serva that asks for it. Collective liberation, after all, means individual sacrifice in service of the greater plan. Even Theo had to find their own way out.

"Now," she says, "about the viewing. Tell me everything."

Una may not be the best in the Luxana cell's network of canaries, but she's usually able to come through with something useful. This time, she's able to tell them about the notable guests who will be at the late Historian's viewing, how many servae and vernae are on staff, entrances and exits of service hallways, that sort of thing. What Una *hadn't* been able to tell them was anything that Griff or Theo them-self didn't already know.

"Happy now?" Griff asks, once Una has gone. "I told you she was a waste of time."

"Just wanted to be sure." Theo shrugs, and stretches luxuriously before climbing to their feet. "You know how much I hate surprises."

"That," says Griff, "is a bald-faced lie. Behave yourself tonight."

"Don't I always?"

"Such a liar." The corners of her mouth twitch, halfway to a smile, but there's something more to it. Something taut, like spooling ten-sion. Theo, who had been halfway out the door already, stops. That flicker of uncertainty, the chink in the armor.

This is what happens sometimes. Moments like this where it's just the two of them, when Griff suddenly ceases to be *Griff*—the idea, the figurehead, that impenetrable symbol of their collective strength undaunted—and for a fleeting, terrifying moment, what's left in her place is just a woman, flesh and blood and that string of purple-white shells she always wears around her neck. A woman with too many cares and concerns for one person to hold. This happens sometimes, when it's just the two of them, and Theo doesn't think twice about saying it.

"There's something else."

A moment of hesitation, brief, but it's enough. They slide the dag-ger back into their boot and wait. Griff purses her lips as she seems to make up her mind, and then olive fingers reach into the pocket of her overcoat to pass a crumpled piece of paper over into Theo's hand.

It takes a moment to place, but yes. They've seen it before, slipped out from under the lifeless fingers of Alexander Kleios during an early hurricane morning two weeks ago.

Selah—Ask Gil where I've left

It's not a complete sentence. Elegant loops and curves of the His-torian's penmanship shake violently where a poisoned hand had tried and failed to finish off the note.

But that's it. That's all there is.

That's not the part that has Theo frowning down at the unfinished letter. Because they've been undercover in Senator Naevia Kleios's office for a few months now—long enough to know the familia's major players, but not quite long enough to know why Griff wanted them there in the first place. They have a feeling that's about to change.

Selah.

They know that one. That one's easy. They've even spent a fair amount of time with her. They like the senator's daughter, or at least as well as one can *like* an ivory-tower patrician. She's amusing, at any rate, in the way that naive idealists sometimes are. Would-be saviors of the downtrodden who don't have the first idea how their world really works. Back when Theo was first hired onto her mother's support staff, Selah had tracked them down at the Senate and they'd humored her for a long meridiem break at a nearby jav, answering questions and making up stories about a plebeian childhood and education and career that belonged to some girl who didn't exist. It's sweet, really, the way Selah had been so enthralled, caught up in the exact sort of feel-good success story every liberal patrician wants to believe so they can live with themself. The two of them have seen each other a handful of times since, Theo easily charming their way into her good graces, though not so much since Alexander Kleios died. They're given to understand that Selah's a bit busy these days.

Gil.

That's another easy one, though they've never met the man himself. Anyone with half a brain and access to the senator's daily calendar knows that Gil Delena is her husband's secretary. Was, anyway, though he's still got to be around somewhere.

Theo looks up.

"Ask Gil where he's left what?"

A wan smile crosses Griff's face. "I don't know. Not for certain."

"But you have a guess."

"I do. A good one, actually."

"Why do I have a feeling it's the reason you wanted me getting close to the Kleios familia in the first place?" And all this time Theo had thought it was to do with the senator.

"Probably because we're having this conversation." Griff takes the slip of paper back from them, then stows it in her pocket with a surprising amount of care. Then, blunt as anything, "There's a book."

Theo blinks. "A book."

"Yes. We need it."

"That's frustratingly vague."

The corner of her mouth crooks up. "Then let me clarify," says Griff. "It's not just a *book*. It's a weapon."

At that, Theo can't help it. They snort. They've heard that sort of platitude before, from street orators and elementary-level mantras and that starry-eyed universitas undergrad they were fucking a few years back. *Print cuts sharper than swords* and all that. Elitist bullshit.

"They call it the Iveroa Stone," Griff goes on, ignoring them. "I can't explain to you how it works. Not now. But I *have* seen it with my own eyes. I know that it exists. I know that—Well. I know what it has the power to do. And more immediately, right now, I know that it was in the possession of Alexander Kleios last, and his mother before him."

"And now, what, his secretary has it?"

"If he hasn't already given it to Selah by now."

"So, what, you want me to *kidnap* her?"

Maybe it's stupid, the blunt instrument of that kind of methodology not like Griff at all, but Theo can't see what else she might be implying here. It wouldn't be hard, not really. An invitation back to the jav where they first spent a meridiem together, maybe, though Theo would probably never be able to show their face in public again. But that isn't Griff's way. Her plans are more calculated than that, wheels set into motion long before you can see how far they've actually carried you. It's why Theo supported her takeover. It's why Theo was her blade in the dark.

"Of course you aren't going to kidnap her." Griff rolls her eyes. "If anything happened to the new Historian, the city would go under full lockdown. The last few weeks have been bad enough with the ruckus her father's death caused. And anyway, I think we might've stumbled into a golden opportunity here with Selah Kleios. Alexander was a non-starter, too set in his ways. But from what you've told me about his daughter . . . I want you to keep doing exactly what you've been doing. And I want you to spend more time with her."

It clicks, then. Of course that's what this is.

"You want me to turn her."

Griff nods. "Idealism and a savior complex can be useful weapons, too."

It makes sense. It makes all the sense in the world. The initial reason why Theo was put in the senator's circle seems obvious now. More than just spying on the senator's movements, but influencing the future Historian toward their cause. Only it's come to fruition decades early. The sort of golden opportunity no one could have predicted or even thought to hope for.

Selah Kleios is wide-eyed and fresh to her position. Selah Kleios knows nothing about how her world really works. Selah Kleios comes with funds and connections, access to every higher institution and political body in the entirety of the empires, and—if what Griff's told them is true—Selah Kleios is in possession of some sort of book that's actually a weapon. One that the Revenants need.

"Griff, this Iveroa Stone . . . if that's supposed to clarify *anything*—"

"It's not. But I need you to understand the importance of what you're doing in that house." And this time it's Theo's hands that she grasps between her own, something raw and genuine shining in those gray eyes so unlike her act for Una's benefit. "I need you to gain her trust, influence her toward us, so that soon she'll hand the Stone over to us willingly. Because this . . . *this* is going to change things. This is the answer to expelling Roman rule from Sargassa. This is what I've been waiting for. We're ready and we're strong, but we can't do it until we have the Iveroa Stone in our possession. Theo, this is a Quiet-damned deus ex machina."

Vaguely, they're aware of the urge to laugh. Strong words for a couple hundred pages sewn together, unless those pages happen to be made of sharp steel blades—and even then Theo can't fathom how in the Great fucking Quiet a *book* could hold so much power. But stronger still is the ferocity behind Griff's gray eyes, and the indomitable strength of their own curiosity at such bold words. The laughter dies in Theo's throat.

The answer to overturning Roman rule in Sargassa. A deus ex machina.

It's been a long time since Theo believed in gods and fairy tales. They believe in Griff and the cause now, instead.

"How?" they ask.

"You'll know when the time is right. But first I need something. First I need Selah Kleios on our side."

SELAH

This is going to be a disaster. She can smell it the moment she and Arran walk through the door, alongside the scent of smoked bluefish and honey-roasted vegetables wafting up into the atrium from somewhere beneath her feet. Fabian will be down there conducting his kitchen staff with the precision of a concert symphony, and the majordomo Imarry is probably shouting at a scullion somewhere as the staff finishes setting up the manor's public rooms. The same last-minute energy that always heralds the parties Selah has spent her life attending.

Usually she enjoys those—even when she's stuck being pestered about her graduate studies by Mima's politico friends or Dad's centenarian colleagues, shocking them half to death over lobster and peas—of *course* granary workers should have equal shares, and no, the election process for the senatorial colleges is confusing and outdated, frankly. But this isn't a party, and her father isn't here. It's his viewing instead, and Selah already feels very tired at the prospect. There are only so many times you can politely listen to people tell you *just how really very sorry they are* and *what an excellent man he was* in that same terribly solemn voice before you start to become a little jaded by the whole thing and possibly say something completely inappropriate out of sheer boredom. Not to mention the lecture she's no doubt already in for as soon as she crosses paths with her mother.

She's just considering grabbing Arran and making a bid to escape upstairs when a voice cuts through the high atrium like a crack of thunder.

"*There* you are."

Selah winces, all plans of avoiding her mother thoroughly shot as she descends the sweeping atrium stairs. Mima is a commanding woman, even without the full mourning gold she's worn every day for the past fortnight, or the saltwater sea pearls woven through her tumbles of dense, tight-coiling hair. Selah may be paterfamilias now by law, the necessary continuance of familia lines demanding that inheritance pass to the next generation, but the idea of trying to pull rank on her mima is downright laughable.

"I nearly had a heart attack," Mima says, cutting her way through the bustle of staff. "I swear to Terra, the next time you sneak off from the Archives without telling anyone, I'm putting you under house arrest."

"Ice, Mima. I was just at the universitas. I had a meeting with Thane."

"No, I will not *ice*, Selah," she snaps. "You aren't *safe*. I need to know where you are. Not gallivanting around town getting into who knows what kind of trouble." And to prove her point, she gestures at the new bruising along Arran's face.

"What, these?" he asks, ignoring the way the cut on his lip seems to be opening back up when he talks. "Old news. Tripped in the bath."

Mima rolls her eyes. But then they soften, and she's pulling him in for a kiss on the cheek. "Thank you for finding her. It *is* good to see you." The hug that follows is brief, if only because Arran is quick to break away, smile slightly strained. Selah isn't the only one to notice.

"How are you?" Mima asks.

"I'm fine," he responds, and it's almost convincing.

"Arran."

"Really."

"*Arran.*"

"Naevia."

Mima fixes him with that look of hers like she knows he's lying, and then his smile relaxes—*truly* relaxes—into something Selah knows. Something a little sad. Something like sunlight finally filtering through the rain. They're right there with him.

"Tell you what, though," he says, "the second I need a fainting couch, you'll be the first to know."

But when he moves to turn away, she catches his hand in hers and says, "You know this is your home. It always will be." And Selah feels herself glow, because this is important.

She doesn't know why Arran took off almost as soon as he got home, not really. Oh, she knows how the fight started, over breakfast a few days after he'd come home from Fornia. His tribune had hinted at a promotion if he came back, and apparently Arran was actually considering it. But Dad had put his foot down, and of course Dad was his patron so he needed his permission to go. The two of them had taken it upstairs from there, and aside from the shouts that nearly brought Breakwater House down and then the silent fury of Arran's leaving, she doesn't really know what happened. Only that he didn't come home, not even when Dad was found dead the next day.

Tair had left, and then Arran, and then Dad, and Selah had been alone.

Arran has always straddled a strange line, she knows that, more at home following Gil around or bothering Lian the stablemaster or flirting with the house servae, but never entirely belonging there, either. Dad had been proud of him, though, educating him and including him like any patrician son, always making it clear he isn't just familia—he's *family*. Mima has always accepted that without complaint. She had to. Arran was here first.

So Selah knows what her mother is doing. This is an olive branch, a promise that nothing's changed. An offer to come back home, back to where he belongs.

"Yeah," says Arran, after a beat. "I know."

When she slips through the door to Dad's study, Gil is elbow deep in a sea of boxes, tawny hair sticking out haphazard in all directions, and Selah has to stifle a laugh.

"Brought you a present," she announces, setting the very large bottle of Gallia red down in front of him on the floor. "Thought you might need it."

Gil's head pops out of a particularly dusty trunk of old books and breaks into a gratified smile. "You have no idea. I loved your dad, Sel, but for the life of me I don't know how I let it get to this point without strangling him." He pops the cork, and is about to take a drink when he stops and glances up at her. "Sorry. Too soon?"

"Savage Quiet, no," she says, helping herself. "It's refreshing. Everyone's acting like someone died."

"Ha."

It's comfortable—comfortable, and normal, and she finds herself wishing that she could just hide away in here with Gil for the rest of the night. Let Mima deal with her guests, Selah's no politician. And even if she were, who could fault her for wanting some space right now? How in the savage Quiet is she expected to make polite small-talk about the Imperium's internal elections and the recent hurricane when her dad was just *assassinated*? But responsibility comes with expectations, and she's just going to have to swallow that.

She glances at one of the boxes of books and tries to shove down the thought of how much she'd prefer to spend the evening delving into them, helping Gil decipher the notes from Dad's latest internal research project. A definitive history of Terra worship, apparently, with particular emphasis on differentiating the fringe cultists who view the All-Mater as some kind of actual deity. Dad had planned on proposing a new national festival to the Consul, one that put emphasis on individual responsibility to the physical earth instead—which is what most sane people understand All-Mater Terra to represent anyway, but he'd thought it was worth the reinforcement. That's the project he'd hinted at, anyway, but Dad had still been in the note-taking stage and his chicken scratch is nearly impossible to decipher.

Speaking of.

"Were you going to ask how the Serv-Ed proposal went," she asks, "or were you waiting to see how long I could go without bringing it up?"

He glances up at her, sharp. "You didn't."

"Didn't what?"

"You actually proposed that to her? I thought it was just a thought exercise."

"Of course it wasn't. And Nija Thane, in true Nija Thane fashion, curbed me in about three minutes because she's objectively abject. *But*," she presses on, finger raised, eyes gleaming, "Arran, being the bona fide brilliant person that he is, figured out a solution."

"Arran's home?"

"Yeah, but *listen*. I have the Archives now. We can just set it up there. Solved. Done. It's happening." She claps her hands together, then frowns. "You don't look excited. Why aren't you excited?"

"I don't know . . ."

"What's not to know?"

"This isn't some school project. Things are different now."

"Yeah, I know," she responds, wondering if he had actually listened to a word she just said. "Now I've got the power to do this on my own terms. I don't need her permission. Or anyone's, for that matter."

It's sort of perfect, actually. Selah has spent the last five years feeling the sting of injustice, the obvious gaps to be patched, held up by the terminal slowness of committee and bureaucracy and protocol, and in the meantime all of the people who deserve so much more than what they get slipping through. But she has the means now. The power to build her own bridge right over those cracks.

Gil, however, just sets down the pile of papers and sits back, leaving Selah with the distinct feeling that she's being scrutinized, even as he considers and condenses and maybe thinks better of what he'd like to say. From anyone else, she wouldn't stand for it. But from Gil, with his soft-spoken voice and deadly edge to his humor, somehow she finds that she doesn't mind so much.

Then, quite abruptly, he says, "You won't want to hear this, I know, but there are two things you have to take very seriously now. The first is the political game."

Selah frowns. That isn't right. "The Archives aren't political," she tells him, though he should really know it already. Historians advise politicians on matters of precedent and such, make proposals and suggestions now and again, act as guides and consultants when needed, but they're not politicians themselves. And Gil, who's been her father's secretary since well before Alexander Kleios inherited his mother's position, knows that.

"Everything is political." He smiles wryly. "The universitas endowment's nearly half of our annual budget. Grad students make up a third of our research staff. Faculty and students get access to some of our resources in return for that, but if we start offering courses, too, you might as well cut out the middleman."

"Except that the universitas won't *let* these kind of students in, that's the diff—"

"Doesn't matter. That's how she'll see it. Thane will be threatened."

"Good," says Selah, a little more vindictively than she means to. "Maybe this can be a reality drop for her. Maybe being a little uncomfortable is exactly what she needs."

"Maybe. But the Consul may still have something to say about it."

She frowns. Logically she's always known that the Consul is just as much her father's direct superior as he is her mother's, but she's never given him much thought where the Archives are concerned. Mostly that's because she's hardly ever *seen* him. The Consul of Roma Sargassa—a stoic, old-guard politician called Cato Palmar with a very large mustache—spends most of his time on the island city of Paxenos, far on the western coast. The rare periods he's actually in residence here, he's usually busy enjoying the trappings of vacation— playing the Boardwalk tables and entertaining at his Arborem estate Belamar. A lunch meeting now and then is the closest he gets to doing any real work. Somehow she's always assumed that Consul Palmar never exercised that much control over Dad at all. It's almost absurd to think of, that waxmelt face storming into Dad's office to tell him he can't possibly use *that* loanword when translating an Aymaran weaving manual, *this* modulation will come far closer to the original meaning of Quispe's text.

"Why would Palmar care?"

Gil leans back, chewing his lip, as though unsure how to say exactly what he wants to next. Finally, he asks, "What are the Archives for?"

"Is that a joke?"

"It's not."

Selah rolls her eyes. The answer exists like a tattoo written on her skin. "The collection and safeguarding of the world's knowledge so the Imperium can rebuild and regain its lost progress after the Great Quiet."

"That's one definition."

"It's *the* definition."

"Maybe. Palmar might have a different one."

"Well, he shouldn't." The thought, frankly, is insulting. What does Cato Palmar know about the Archives anyway? He doesn't work there, surrounded by the richness of millennia upon millennia of human culture and innovation and potential. He doesn't even live in Luxana most of the time. "Anyway, what was number two? The other thing I have to take *very seriously now.*"

Gil ignores her mocking, but gives her a sad smile and says, "Time. How much time you actually have in your day, and what you choose to do with it."

"I'll have time for—"

"You won't. You'll think you will, but you won't. Your dad was the same, I watched him do it for years. He tried to make time for everything."

"I know," says Selah quietly. "It was the best thing about him." Suddenly she feels a burning behind her eyes again. *Stupid.* She blinks it back. *Stop doing that.*

"I want to help you with this, Selah," Gil says. "I do. But you're being asked to grow up faster than you were supposed to. You need to learn how to do this job first. It's not just your own projects. It's managing everyone else's research and curation, making sure resources are being properly allocated, securing relationships with the right politicians so the outside world remembers just how vital the work we do here is. You've *got* to be able to see the bigger picture. And I'm not nearly as well equipped as Alex to teach you how."

Maybe it's the hand on hers or something in the tone of his voice, but very suddenly Selah realizes that Gil must be just as overwhelmed as she is. Gil Delena has always been an invaluable asset to the Archives. He's the one who keeps the place running smoothly, who coordinates and organizes more or less everything from behind the scenes. The one who made sure Dad knew which appointments he was supposed to be at and when, and made sure he ate when he'd been too buried in work to remember. But he's not supposed to teach her how to do this. He's a plebeian, and a client plebeian at that. He couldn't have been privy to half of what Dad actually got up to, or best practices to do it. Yet here he is all the same, shoved into the role of teacher, as though it could ever be that easy. As though the patron he'd known and been friends with since they were both young boys wasn't inconveniently too dead to do it himself.

"No one's going to forget how important the Archives are," she tells him gently. "Or how important it is to rebuild the old world. That's just . . . something we grow up knowing, isn't it? I think I knew that before I even knew what the Great Quiet was."

"And you think that's by accident, do you?" He rubs the meat of his palm against his head. "You don't think that's by design? Or the deliberate, careful work of every Historian who came before? We're doomed to—"

"—*doomed to repeat the mistakes we don't remember*," she finishes for him, reciting the elementary-levels mantra by rote. "I know, Gil. I know."

FIVE YEARS EARLIER

774 PQ

"How is wanting to celebrate my birthday a mistake?"

Selah is infuriating. Not always, not often, but when she is it takes every ounce of Tair's willpower to remember why she loves her. Selah lives fast and loud and bright, and has the luck of birth to be able to wear her heart on her sleeve. Usually this is endearing. This is the Selah who needled her father into letting Tair have free rein of the Archives. The Selah who argues passionately at dinner with ancient scholars and politicians too stuck in their ways to see that she actually makes a good point. The Selah who runs in the streets without shoes because she relishes the sunbaked grit of the earth beneath her bare feet. But this is also the Selah who is blissfully unaware that her experience of the world isn't shared by everyone, and that's the Selah who is currently standing in Tair's room.

Her rickety wooden bedroom may not mirror the opulence and grandeur of the historic estate in which it sits at the top, but Tair loves it all the same. Wall-to-wall bookshelves. The small bed tucked into the alcove by the round window, a perfect reading nook. Tair is not a hoarder, thank you very much, but a keen and discerning collector, and a lifetime of trinkets and papers neatly cover the surfaces of the remaining desks and shelves. There's an organization to it. Her own form of organization, maybe, but an organization all the same. This bedroom is home, and what's more, it's hers, private from the other dormitories and shared quarters here at the very top attic of Breakwater House. It's cozy, generally, but the energy inside right now is anything but.

"It's not a mistake," she says, patience wearing thin. "But you should've gone with Arran, or one of your friends, not—"

"You are my best friend," Selah interrupts, annoyingly. "You. And I can't celebrate with you tomorrow, so Quiet forbid I wanted to tonight."

"Well, I *didn't* want to. One month until I can go and do whatever the frag I like. That's all I asked you to wait for, and you couldn't even do that. Just like you couldn't—"

No. Not yet. She'll have a lifetime to challenge Selah the way she's always wanted, to call her out on all the things she doesn't understand. But not for another month. Not until she turns eighteen. Not until she's an adult, and a plebeian, and a citizen, and free.

"What?" Selah snaps.

"It's nothing."

"*Like I couldn't* what?"

Tair shakes her head. Selah wouldn't see her punished for speaking out of turn, she never has. It's probably never even occurred to her that she *could*. But there are some things you just don't say. Not when you've worked this hard and waited this long for something that's almost within your grasp.

"Tell *me*."

"Is that an order?" Tair spits, and Terra help her since she clearly can't help herself. Selah, who gives her three orders a day without realizing it, at least has the grace to look horrified, the blood draining from her dark brown face. "Of course not."

She *does* this. Gets under her skin. Most of the time Tair thinks it's that thing, that unspoken thing she can never act on. It's easy to forget how fragged up it really is, this thing that exists between them, but moments like this remind her all too clearly.

Then Selah, who's never been able to help herself much either, keeps talking. "But I really wish you would tell me what's got you so vexed off, because I don't know how this somehow became my fault. We snuck out—successfully, I could add—and we had fun, and you're letting a couple of bona fide savages ruin the whole night—"

"You couldn't let it be," Tair snaps, every instinct screaming at her to shut up just shut up. "You never can. I was handling it."

And then Selah had barged in and taken over, power trip in one hand and savior complex in the other, as though she weren't capable of handling herself. Stumbling blindly into the promise of violence growing beneath those boys' gleeful smiles, blissfully unaware that there was a line Tair herself could never cross.

"*That's what you're angry about?*" *asks Selah, and has the nerve to look as though she might laugh.* "*That I stepped on your moment?*"

Tair could strangle her.

"*No! I mean yes, but not like—Fuck,*" *she bites out, taking them both aback. She never slips like that in front of patricians. Never.* "*You just . . . you can't see it.*"

"*Then* help *me to.*"

A sudden knock on the door jolts them out of the bubble of argument they've woven around themselves. Then it swings open and of course, of course *it's Una.*

"*Morning,*" *the older woman says with a terrifying calm.*

"*Frag,*" *says Tair, with acute and sudden awareness of the time.* "*Did we wake you up?*"

Una's raised brow exudes the air of an empress rather than a thirty-something serva with tangled blond hair. "*I think you've probably woken everyone,*" *she says, and Tair hopes to Terra she only means those on the attic floor.* "*But not everyone's as friendly as me, so I thought I'd stop by and tell you to shut up.*"

"*Sorry, Una,*" *Selah cuts in, and Tair grits her teeth because there she goes again. Speaking over her as though she isn't even there. As though she knows better.*

If Una is surprised to see Selah there, nothing in her face gives it away. "*Respectfully and all that, miss,*" *she says, with absolutely no respect at all,* "*you might get to sleep in tomorrow, but I'm up in two hours.*"

"*Right, really very sorry.*"

And then she's gone, taking the air out of the room with her.

Selah glances over. "*Do you think all natives are as mean as our Una, or did we just get lucky?*"

It's a bad attempt to cut through the lingering tension. Tair flops on her bed, suddenly incredibly tired. The spark's gone out and she just doesn't want to argue anymore.

"*She's not that mean, Sel.*"

Maybe because it's two in the morning and she's tired, maybe because Selah's at least trying to make peace, but somehow she finds that she doesn't actually mind so much when Selah sits down on the bed next to her. Or when Selah's fingers begin to dance along her wrist, tentative and slow, tracing the faint rising lines of the veins just under her skin. So soft and light you'd barely know they were there. Despite herself, she finds herself releasing into the feeling, the vulnerability of it. And Selah smiles that little smile of hers, the one that says Forgive me? *And Tair finds herself smiling back, finds it easy enough to forgive.*

It's not Selah's fault. She's been raised in privilege, and is both a remarkable and a remarkably kind person when she could so much more easily be neither. It's no one's fault. It just is what it is.

And then Selah strikes.

Fingers dig into the soft skin beneath Tair's ribs, and the spasm of tickles jolt her up off the bed screaming, "NO!"

Selah only cackles, and doubles down on her attack.

"You monster!*" she growls, managing to grab a pillow somehow and whack it across Selah's head, knocking her to the side. She grabs for her and digs an indignant hand through those careful black braids, and Selah's roar lands somewhere between a scream and a laugh as she launches herself at Tair once again.*

Somewhere in the scuffle, breathless with laughter, she's ended up on top of Selah because of course she has, their faces inches from each other. Second time tonight, *she thinks hopelessly, and hates the way you're supposed to know exactly what to do. Because Selah's face is tilted up toward her and the moonlight is in her black hair and Tair wonders how she's ever supposed to know what this* means. *Or if it ever meant anything at all. Because she's not brave enough for this. Knowing is one thing but acting on it is something else completely.*

There are things that are only allowed to exist in the abstract.

She lets it go.

Falling over next to her, breathing hard, Tair privately thinks that she just needs to get herself a nice pleb girlfriend and move on with her life. Like it would ever be as easy as that. Freedom for a verna is only ever halfway. She's been apprenticed to Gil Delena for nearly a decade, and even after she becomes a citizen she's going to be Selah's secretary for the rest of her life. There's no way out from her. She doesn't want a way out from her. Not when most days she knows the familiar weight on the bed next to her better than she knows herself.

"Where do we go first?" she asks quietly, looking up. She had pinned the map of the world to the ceiling above her bed on the night of her eleventh birthday. A gift from Gil, along with the silver push-pins she and Selah have dotted liberally across it in the years since, marking all the places they'll visit one day, once they're old enough to not need anyone else's permission.

It's a familiar dream, an old game. We'll go where we want, and eat what we want, and say what we want. And no one can stop us. Tair has never been allowed outside the city of Luxana, but Selah has her own constraints, the history and traditions of civilization itself resting on her shoulders. Both girls understand the importance of this, just as they both understand that a gilded cage is still a cage.

"Maghreb-Anatolia," Selah says this time, pointing upward at a land that exists in Tair's imagination as clear blue seas and spice towers and pilgrimages to Mecca.

"Why?"

"The food, the desert . . . the ruins of the Greco Empire's outposts. I want to ride an elephant. I want to go somewhere entirely different from here."

"Tin'buktu's different. No Imperium."

"And crawling with great-grandparents. No thank you."

Feeling a sudden recklessness, a flash of cabin fever she knows has been stirring for months if not years, she takes Selah's hand in hers so that their fingers are pointing together to the lower righthand corner of the map. The only quadrant with no pins at all.

"Pacifica?"

"Outside the empires completely," Tair responds, a sudden thrill running through her when she finds that she's unable to imagine anything at all. "As different as you can get."

"No Roma . . . no Aksum," says Selah, and Tair can hear sleep curling in at the edges. "No Imperium at all."

"Total anarchy."

Adrenaline pounds through her veins, heart beating fast at the thought, lips curling at the edges. Selah nuzzles her face into her neck and curls up to sleep, but Tair continues to stare up at the world above her, the dizzying array of so many sudden futures unfolding before her mind's eye.

"I can't wait."

DARIUS

Hooves clop over sweeping cobblestone. In the growing dark, the paraffin lamps that light the Arborem district's main avenue glow a soft orange against curling wrought-iron gates. Darius tugs the reins to slow his horse, allows a passing couple to cross ahead of him, and tries not to give anything of his impatience away.

He's running late. Not a good look, he knows, but there was a scuffle down in Paleaside and one of the junior agents thought the perp's description sounded something like Tiago-Laith—the living one, that is—and with the Chief General already gone for the night it fell to him to sort it out. Agent Oha had been wrong, of course, and probably knew exactly what she was doing, but by the time *Darius* knew that, he was far down in the lower districts and already running half an hour late.

Across the thoroughfare, then, and up the neat gravel road that twists away into Breakwater Estate. Stately, draping elms line the drive to keep prying eyes away, then open out past stables and greenhouses, past the sprawling lawn and far distant chimneys of clustered client homes, all the way up to the manor house itself. Gray shale and high arched windows, spires and balconies and chimneys, it sits atop a jutting peninsula on cliffs overlooking the Sargasso Sea. He's never been here before, too newly settled into Luxana for that. But Breakwater House is one of Sargassa's great historical sites, one of those names you read so often as a child it becomes familiar as myth.

Dating all the way back to the Great Quiet, the grounds rest at the very tip of the Arborem and sprawl out a good deal further than that into the Hazards—the wild oak and hickory forest marking Luxana's city limits. Great swaths of untamed land stretch between here and the outskirts of Siracusa, hundreds of miles away, with travel between cities so notoriously dangerous that the lower castes rarely chance it. Children are taught early to stay on the Imperial Road if they *do* have to travel at all—better that than chance a meeting with savage Ynglot raiders or noxious clouds that herald smoking fever, or any number of the other unknown dangers lurking in the wilds. Eight hundred years later, Sargassans are still discovering what strange savageries the Great Quiet left behind.

Low-caste superstition, Darius used to think, back before he'd made the journey himself. He knows better than that now. He's seen it for himself, that altogether unnatural *something* in the wild and oppressive dark of the woods beyond the Road. He isn't particularly keen to find out what's hiding in their depths.

Inside Breakwater House, the viewing is already well underway. Darius straightens the lapel of his black Intelligentia uniform, and ignores the flutter of anxiety sprouting in his gut. *Stop that.* He belongs here just the same as anyone else. He's earned it.

Turned out in resplendent mourning gold, the Kleios familia's guests make for an impressive sight. It's politicos, mainly. Old men and women arguing in tired voices, nervous young staffers too green to hide their awe at having been invited to something anywhere near this important. And beyond that, the usual suspects. The Halithas, the Everses, the Briagos. The pinnacle of patrician society. Here and there young men and women cluster together importantly, self-satisfied and luxuriating in their boredom. Middle-aged socialites gossip happily about friends who haven't yet arrived, or pick apart the latest tabloids—a famous actress's affair with a serva, racketeering in the Paxenos senator's office, some drug scandal involving a clavaspher player from the local league. The woman who invited him, however, is nowhere to be seen, and Darius has to stop himself from craning his neck to look.

"You're late," says a familiar voice instead.

There's a gold band wrapped around his left arm, but otherwise Quintus Kopitar looks the same as he always does. Salt-streak hair neatly combed back and a strong, broad chest despite his advancing age, ceremonial medals over a formal uniform marking him Chief General of the Cohort Intelligentia. That twinkle of stern humor behind it all, easy to miss if you don't know him very well. Darius, though, has known him for going on ten years.

"Business in the downdistricts," he tells him, taking a glass of wine from a passing serva's tray. It's not an excuse, but Kopitar understands the way things are. The job comes first.

"Anything interesting?"

"Not really. Agent Oha thought she had a lead on the Revs. She didn't."

"Shame. That girl could use a win." And Darius could use a day where the junior agents stop messing with him for their own amusement, but that isn't likely to happen, either. He keeps that to himself.

"Seen the senator yet?" he asks instead, taking a sip of the frankly excellent wine.

"From afar. Buried under a sea of well-wishers."

"Poor woman."

"Save your sympathies for someone who needs them, Miranda," Kopitar says, that knowing something like amusement. "For someone like her, this is a work event."

Darius frowns. On a night like this, somehow he hadn't imagined Senator Kleios would be feeling very social at all. Vague images of a subdued widow in mourning veils had come to mind, even through the latent nerves and how undeniably pleased he'd been to receive her invitation.

Something of the surprise must show on his face, because Kopitar leans in close. "Friendly word of advice," he mutters, caution caught between his teeth the way it might have been when Darius was still a junior agent fresh from the universitas, green and untested in the field, still in awe that someone like Kopitar had decided to take him under his wing. "Luxana society's a different breed. They've got claws under those duskras."

"You say that like you aren't one of them."

"Perhaps. But you're one of us now, too."

A bead of condensation slides down the glass onto his thumb, and inexplicably Darius remembers being thirteen. Frustrated and embarrassed to tears by some long-forgotten slight, he'd sat down at the shabby heirloom desk in the cramped bedroom he shared with his older brother Titus and written down a list. Well, more of a manifesto than a *list*, if he's being entirely honest about it. *Miranda's Fifty Rules for Success in the Course of One's Imperial Duty.* Quite the accomplishment for one so young. He'd imagined himself something of a prodigy at the time. He could see it very clearly, actually—stacks of books in store display windows and an induction to the Imperial Archives and important scholars debating its merits and, *"Did you know this Darius Miranda fellow is only thirteen years old? Impressive. Most impressive."*

It had never happened, of course. The pretentious piece of overwrought self-importance was altogether unpublishable in hindsight, though not for lack of trying. Instead, he's slashed it apart and amended it to the Quiet and back for his own personal use a hundred times since.

Academic goals and study methods tweaked over the course of his superior and undergrad. Philosophical musings on familial piety replaced with duty to the Imperium every time his father showed up drunk to a public engagement *again*. Additions about the necessity of marriage and children, the continuity of familia more abstract duty than anything to do with desires of the flesh. Having that one written down in stark black and white made it easier, somehow, knowing what would one day be required. Even if he'd never be the Miranda paterfamilias, it was only right.

A blanket ban on drugs or alcohol, unfortunately, had to go entirely. It was obvious after about five minutes at Halcya Universitas that you didn't get anywhere without the ability to have a social life. No one likes a bore.

No debts, though. That one will never change. Darius learned that lesson early and he learned it well, with humiliation burning in his cheeks every time his parents begged another loan off of wealthier plebeian neighbors. The Miranda fortune was squandered generations ago, with nothing left to show for the patrician name but the hereditary role of Ithaca's Chief General and a house they couldn't afford. Without assets or staff, Darius's childhood was one of worn-out hand-me-downs and snide remarks from classmates and being sequestered to only a handful of rooms in the sprawling old manor home. Paraffin is expensive, after all, and they could hardly keep servae to maintain the hearths beneath the floorboards. Darius's father had tried to rectify the situation through marriage, only to gamble and drink away each and every one of his mother-in-law's loans.

Inherited poverty is one thing. A man can do something about that. Flagrant stupidity, on the other hand, is something Darius finds impossible to forgive.

So he'd been smarter. He'd had to be. The youngest of four, he would never be paterfamilias, never inherit his father's job, but perhaps therein lay opportunity. If you worked for it. If you could figure out the rules to success. So yes, no debt. No complaining. Only the highest grades. Remember everyone you meet. Cultivate mentorships from those whose qualities you admire. Be worthy of their admiration in return. The Imperium, after all, rewards those who take responsibility for themselves. And it paid off, in the end.

At just thirty-one years old, Darius Miranda is now the Deputy Chief of the Cohort Intelligentia, down in the shining capital city of Roma Sargassa. It's the highest position he can ever hope to achieve. He gained the title decades before anyone ever expected him to. So maybe it shouldn't have come as such a surprise, being invited to the viewing of Alexander Kleios when he never met the man in life. Darius has only even met his wife, the senator, once. But the invitation had come from her office all the same, sealed with the Kleios sun and a personal note scrawled at the bottom of elegant vellum.

Please say you'll come. It would mean the world to me.

Darius hadn't shown anyone that part, not even Kopitar. No one likes a peacock. Still, he can't help it, the little thrill. He must have made an impression.

"Straight back, Deputy," Kopitar chides then, and with a flush Darius realizes he's half turned, craning without quite realizing it for a glimpse of Senator Kleios somewhere in the crowd. But instead of another reprimand, his mentor's thin lips press together in the obvious ghost of a smile. "Watch out for the claws."

"I don't—"

"On Terra, if that isn't Chief General Kopitar."

Darius turns.

Free at last from whatever mob of admirers she's found herself buried beneath, Naevia Kleios cuts a statuesque figure. Just as with the first time they met, Darius is instantly struck by how easily she might have spent her life relying on looks alone, had she been so inclined. Fast approaching fifty, recent widowhood becomes the legendary beauty uncommonly well. Gold mourning silk striking against the honey umber glow of her skin, the only trace of grief taking its toll lingering somewhere in the hard crow's feet about her eyes. And beyond that—the bold certainty of power. That wherever her footsteps land, she's sure to be welcomed.

It's not attraction, he thinks, that jolt in his gut. Not exactly. Not the way he's observed between husbands and wives. Still, Darius finds his shoulders pulling back.

"Senator Kleios," Kopitar greets, kissing the woman's cheek.

"Oh, none of that, Quin, you'll make me feel about a hundred years old."

"Naevia," he says, half-amused. "It's been too long. I wish it were under better circumstances."

"A beach in Aymara comes to mind. Summer of '55, wasn't it?"

"Don't start. You remember Deputy Chief Miranda."

The senator turns her gaze on him then, warm smile at the ready, and Darius straightens his back. "Yes, of course. How lovely to see you again, Deputy. I'd hoped our paths would cross sooner, but . . . well, life rarely takes what we want into account, does it?"

If this were a philosophical debate, Darius might argue that. In his experience, life takes exactly what you want into account, actually, so long as you're willing to put in the work to get it. But he knows a rhetorical question when he hears one, and he knows better than to expect pure logic from a widow in the throes of grief. Her husband has just been taken from her well before his time. The survival of her familia's continuity now passed down to her only child, a mere girl of twenty-two. It must be disorienting.

"I'm so sorry for your loss," he says instead, because it's the thing to do.

Her lips purse into a smile, one that doesn't quite meet her eyes. "Thank you." And then, turning to Kopitar, "Quin, do you know an Emilius Gainol?"

"Unfortunately. Pulled him out of a tight spot earlier in the year. Don't tell me you've invited him."

"Had to, really." She sighs. "But he's parked out by the bar telling passersby the more . . . delicate details about that tight spot. Not that anyone would believe it, of course, but I did think you ought to know."

"Oh, for the love of—" Kopitar slams his drink on a passing tray and disappears promptly into the press of the crowd. Darius is half a step behind him, no clue really what this Gainol's on about—not that it matters, not when some belligerent fool's threatening the integrity of the Intelligentia's reputation for anyone to hear—but then a hand darts out, elegantly snaking around his arm in a surprisingly firm grip.

Senator Kleios smiles up at him. "Walk with me?"

Somehow, it doesn't feel very much like a question at all.

It's only right to let her lead, the pair of them passing arm in arm through the crowd, and Darius in that moment can't help the pride of it swelling in his chest. Gleaming gold buttons on a pressed black uniform and a famous woman on his arm, the personal invitation here to the most important event happening tonight in the most important city in the world—outside, naturally, of Roma herself. If his father ever sobered up long enough to see his youngest son now, Darius hardly thinks he'd believe it.

Guests part like the sea as the senator steers him through, the rings on her dark hand gleaming in the candlelight. "How are you settling in, Deputy?" she asks. "You must be missing Siracusa terribly."

"No, not really," he says, and feels awkard the moment it's left his mouth. "I'm happy to go where the Imperium sends me." That's no good, either. He sounds like an ass. "That is to say—I'm originally from Ithaca."

"Are you?" She raises a brow, and he hopes to Terra she doesn't seize on that particular thread. "Well, even so. We're lucky to have you here now." And with a smooth turn left, she guides him out to the edge of the sweeping balcony overlooking the ocean below. Darius stiffens. Here, laid in state, is the late Alexander Kleios.

The former Imperial Historian, he's somewhat surprised to see, had been a robust man in his late forties. Without reason or opportunity to meet him in life, he realizes now that he had been imagining the stooped and frail sort of scholar who had taught at his superior—not this tall, broad-shouldered man with a full head of white-flecked auburn hair and the build of a clavaspher player in the prime of health. Aside, of course, from the fact that he's now dead. Body preserved with the alchemical use of balms and salts, and some effort has been made into rectifying the greenish pallor from the sunken face to garish effect.

He's seen plenty of dead bodies out in the field, but there's something peculiar about *this* one that sets his teeth on edge. The indignity of it, perhaps. That such a fine man might be laid so low. Darius runs a hand over his slicked-back blond hair, smoothing stray pieces into proper place.

"You never had the chance to meet him, did you?" asks Senator Kleios, gazing down at her late husband with a sad sort of fondness.

"I didn't, my lady," he answers, and wonders what in Terra's name else he's supposed to say to that. She saves him the trouble of working it out.

"A shame. I think you might have gotten along famously."

"Really?"

"Indeed. Masters of intelligence and information, the pair of you. You and Alex would have had much to talk about."

"I didn't realize the late Historian had such an interest in the law."

"Oh, Alex was interested in all manner of things. Law was more of an abstraction to him, I'll admit—his perspective was often more cerebral than practical, really. But crime thrillers always *were* his favorites at the theater."

"Forgive me," Darius laughs, "but those dramatizations hardly ever come close to the real thing."

"Yes, and he *really* could have used a friend who was willing to point that out."

White teeth flash in a sad smile, and Darius finds himself glowing warm at the idea, the sudden vision of what could have been. Drinks and conversation in a well-appointed study, he imagines something like leather armchairs and a fatherly hand on his shoulder. He's never had much use for scholars, not really, but he respects the work happening in the Archives as much as the next Sargassan raised to understand the weight borne by any who take on the Historian's mantle. Too much was lost during the Great Quiet, the progress of ages wiped away. That's why it has to be overseen carefully now, knowledge arcane and modern, delivered from all corners of the world to the central sanctum of the Imperial Archives where it can be preserved and kept safe.

For Darius's own part, the work he does matters. It's crucial, keeping the empire running in defiance of those who would risk its success with their own stupidity and laziness and simple malicious intent. It *matters*. Except that its importance doesn't permeate in the same way—it isn't drilled into schoolchildren across the empires, isn't a constant refrain of schoolyard rhymes and poetry. *Those who forget are doomed to repeat their mistakes,* and that sort of thing. But the senator *is* right. The Intelligentia deal in the shadows, their work the stuff of living knowledge to keep the empire running at its full potential. A practical arm of that same promise that keeps the Archives sacred at the Imperium's heart and soul. And if Senator Kleios thinks that her husband would have found common ground, who is Darius to presume otherwise?

The senator smiles then, something sad still tinged at the edge. "Oh, but you know, what Alex really loved was *people*. Their stories. How they came to be where they were. Which is why I think he'd have been particularly interested in *you*, Deputy. Youngest in history, a little bird told me—that's no small accomplishment. I'm sure he'd have loved to hear the story behind that."

Darius fights down the flush. Luxana may be hundreds of miles from where he grew up, but that doesn't mean the gossip's stayed behind. He's spent a lifetime with people talking behind his back, the name *Miranda* patrician enough to merit notice, shameful enough to merit scorn. He sees it in his junior officers' faces every time he issues an order, the hidden smirk and how very much they'd love to shirk his authority. So no. He doesn't believe for a moment that a woman like

Naevia Kleios is unaware of who he is or where he comes from. But before he can say anything to that, she smiles gently, the hand around his arm squeezing a reassurance.

"I, on the other hand," she says, "don't see the need to go prying into people's pasts. Not when I can see them for who they've clearly become. I'm a poor substitute, Deputy, but in lieu of the impossible, I *would* very much like us to be friends."

That smile again, and the twist around Darius's heart unclenches. Yes. Yes, this is right. This is the arc of the universe veering toward justice. "I'd like that, too, my lady."

"Good. So we are friends, then." She leans in, dark eyes belying some deep trust. "And I wonder if, as my friend, you might do something for me."

"Oh?"

"Quin and I go far back. Maybe a little *too* far back." She laughs, shaking her head in fond commiseration. "He and my older sister were *involved*, actually, once upon a time, but you didn't hear that from me. The problem, though, is that we go so far back it seems our trust ran out at a certain point. His did, at any rate, though I can't imagine what I ever did to warrant that. And I worry there might be something he isn't telling me."

"My lady, I'm sure that's not true. The Chief General—"

"Oh, I'm sure you're right. The unfounded paranoia of a widow. I do know I'm not in my right mind. But a widow whose husband was *murdered*, so can you really blame me?"

He frowns, not entirely sure he's comfortable with where this conversation's somehow gone. Naevia Kleios's hand around his arm tightens then, the crow's feet around her eyes somehow deeper than before. "Forgive me for putting you in this position, but Alex was assassinated two weeks ago and Quintus Kopitar has hardly seen fit to inform me on the progress of the investigation. And, forgive me, but I quite frankly refuse to believe that it's because the Intelligentia are so very incompetent that there hasn't *been* any."

Darius hesitates. The senator is right, of course. The hunt for the Historian's assassin has unfolded rapidly in the weeks since the man's death, but has for the most part resulted in little but dead ends. The

Revenants are the obvious culprit, terrorists with no aim other than to destabilize the Imperium and strike fear in the hearts of its law-abiding citizens. There have even been public announcements made on that front, street orators promising a reward for anyone who brings forward information about the anarchist group. But that doesn't mean the Intelligentia are any nearer to closing in on them than Darius is to willingly bringing Naevia Kleios in on the finer details of the case. Senator or not, she isn't Intelligentia. No one gets to know their inner workings. It's too delicate, too easily compromised for that.

"Senator . . ." he starts, and runs his hand back over his hair again. "Would it be enough to have my assurance, as a friend, that the Historian's murder *is* our highest priority?"

She closes her dark eyes, breathes in deep. "I wish it were, Deputy, I really do." When she opens them again, they're wet. Her hand fragile around his arm. "But if you could find it in yourself to keep me in the loop . . . What Quintus doesn't know won't hurt him, and it really would go so far to soothe a grieving widow's heart."

Women, in Darius's experience, have never made particular sense. It's been a source of annoyance and confusion both, something like terror in the darkest night when he really just needs to *go to bed already*, because things always look better in the morning. But occasionally, very occasionally, that particular blind spot tends to be a secret weapon. This, it turns out, is one of those times.

Because Darius doesn't understand women, not really, but he does understand *people*. And when he can close the separation between the two then he can actually see them more clearly than his fellow agents or older brothers, precisely *because* he lacks distraction. So Naevia Kleios looks up at him with her dark eyes, damp clinging to those long eyelashes, and Darius—who just five minutes ago had been so, *so* proud to be in her company, sharing in her confidence—feels nothing but contempt. He understands now, with a sudden and furious clarity, that this has been her plan all along. Darius doesn't wrest his arm away, but it's a very near thing.

"You're asking me to play the spy." It's blunt, not a question.

Naevia blinks. "Of course not. I'm asking—"

"For me to betray the confidence of my Chief and compromise the integrity of the Intelligentia."

She laughs, not that charming thing but a dump of breath that now seems to Darius altogether repulsive. "I'm asking for a friendly favor," she presses, "that's all. What leads you're chasing, that sort of thing."

"An informant. You're asking me to be an informant."

"That's dramatic."

No. No, it isn't. Not when there's a proper way to do things, an order and decorum at the heart of Sargassan values, order and decorum that demand respect because they *work*. Perhaps Naevia Kleios can't appreciate that, and Darius curses himself now because he should have seen this coming. Flattering words and a personalized invitation, and he should have *known* better.

The senator is a Dya'ogo by birth. An Aksumite, really, because the familia she was born to is only a generation removed from the independent empire south of Roma, and he should have *seen this coming*. She's already proven herself a snake, worming her way into one of Sargassa's most esteemed familias. Sullying Breakwater House with a lingering sense of foreign decor. He should have sniffed her out the moment he walked through the doors.

"I think," he says instead, and hands his glass firmly over to a passing serva, "that maybe it's time for us to speak honestly, Senator."

Naevia Kleios's eyes, by now, are entirely dry. Something shrewd and sharp in her gaze instead, something like a shark. Kopitar, after all, had warned him about this. "I wasn't aware we were doing anything but."

"This is a matter of domestic terrorism, my lady. Of course we presume the Revenants to hold some responsibility, that much has been made publicly known. But I'm sure you can understand—"

"I understand," she hisses, "that it's been *weeks* and I have yet to see any progress except for whining about some terrorists who haven't actually been active in years."

"That bridge in Bostinium last year—"

"Collapsed due to poor maintenance. You and I both know perfectly well that the Revenants have become a convenient name to drop whenever someone needs to save face. When terrorists actually want to cause terror, they claim responsibility for it."

"The Revenants are slippery," he tells her flatly, unimpressed. Kopitar was right. He was right, and Darius is a fool. He allowed the senator to play to his vanities, and he's a Quiet-damned *fool*. "And this leader," he goes on. "This *Griff*—he might as well be a ghost. But I assure you that—"

Abruptly, he stops. Because out of the corner of his eye, Darius notices something strange. A serva—the one he's just handed his glass of wine—standing in place, staring directly at him.

"Excuse me," he snaps. "Can I help you?"

The serva nearly jumps out of her skin, then promptly drops her eyes down somewhere in the vicinity of his clavicle, where they belong. Scraggly ash-blond hair, cropped short and neat like most servae. A prematurely lined face, late thirties maybe. Overall uninteresting aside from her nose, clearly broken. No, he's never seen her before. He'll certainly remember her now.

"Sorry, sir," she says, and moves on. Darius watches her go.

"Ynglot," Senator Kleios tells him, watching her impertinent serva disappear into the crowd of guests. "A native. Decades in service and still barely any manners. She'll be dealt with."

"I'm sure. But to the point, Senator. The Intelligentia, I assure you, are treating this matter with utmost gravity. I'd have you trust that we *will* bring those responsible to justice. And hope you might not ask me something like this again."

Her lips press together. "Of course." Then they relax, the sudden transformation back to a woman at perfect comfort, a queen amidst her court, like nothing of the last five minutes might have happened at all. "Well, tell me," she says, the very picture of a hostess at ease, "is there a Madam Miranda I should have invited?"

Darius smooths his hair into place once more. "I don't think there's very much I can tell you that you don't already know, Senator Kleios."

ARRAN

Kasari Ederan is three drinks in, just drunk enough to forget that she doesn't actually like to be seen speaking with him. That, or Selah's sudden ascension to power has made her rethink that particular stance. Others might see what they expect to see, but Kasari and Selah have been friends since their first day of undergrad at Luxana Universitas and she's smarter than most would give her credit for. She knows that working her way into Arran's good graces both gets her and *keeps* her in Selah's. Something that Kasari, the second-youngest child of Bostinium social climbers, knows the value of all too well.

He'd just begun feeling the familiar itch of out-of-placeness climbing into his skin when Kasari found him—three drinks in, and annoyed at being snubbed by Selah in favor of the truly ancient scholars monopolizing her attention. He'd chosen not to point out that his sister didn't look too thrilled about the arrangement, either.

"But if *you* tell her," Kasari is insisting now. The little alcove by the bar has become progressively more crowded as word spreads as to where the younger set is camped out, and by this point Kasari is practically sitting on top of him. "My parents' villa out in the country," she says, "is the epitome of max. I've invited Marcellus Evers for her especially, everyone who's anyone will be there, but Selah keeps insisting she has to *work*, the absolute nag. But I'm sure that if *you* tell her. She listens to you. And this is fully what she needs right now."

"Nah," he tells her. "Let's not mix motives here. What Selah needs right now is to learn how to do a job she wasn't supposed to do for another couple of decades. What *you* need is to escape your creepy cult parents for a weekend so you can get laid."

Kasari's eyes narrow, the crime of mentioning her greatest shame clearly warring with delight at such a scandalous answer. "Christianity," she says, finally, "is *not* a cult."

He declines to respond that it is, in fact, the very definition of a cult, and instead says, "It *is* fragging weird, though."

"Arran Alexander, I'm about to bona fide curb you."

"Well, that's not very Christian of you—*Ow*."

Prim as she can manage, drunk as she is, Kasari stands and heads off to join a couple of women she evidently knows, leaving Arran behind to massage the back of his head, the boys to his left eyeing him with blatant curiosity.

"She loves me, really," he tells them. "Not as much as she loves my sister, but beggars can't be—"

"Sorry," cuts in the younger of the two, not sounding sorry at all. "I must have misheard before. I thought Kasari said you were Alexander Kleios's son?"

"No, you heard right."

"Arran . . . Alexander, did she call you?" the other drawls slowly, an unpleasant smile spreading across his face. "A patronym, how fully odd. Almost like a freedman."

It's not a subtle dig, but neither is it particularly creative. And Arran has spent a lifetime deflecting, a lifetime observing and adapting the sort of casual arrogant grace his peers assume as birthright. They won't see the tightness working its way through his jaw.

"Like I said. Excellent hearing, both of you."

Putting some distance between himself and the boys as he approaches the bar, he lets out a breath he wasn't entirely aware he was holding. A year ago, Arran would have shrugged the whole thing off. Here and now, he'd like nothing more than to just deck the pair of them. But that won't work, not in the patrician social scene. *Freedman* may not be a particularly polite or politically correct term to call someone like him, but it's not the worst. Nor is it technically inaccurate.

"You get that a lot?" asks a voice to his right, and Arran turns to see a young woman with a spray of black curls and striking dark eyes standing next to him at the bar. Clearly she heard the whole exchange.

"What, get smacked by a drunk Christian?" he asks, smile back on. "At least once a day."

To his great relief, she laughs and extends a hand. He takes it.

"Theodora Arlot. Theo."

"Arran Alexander."

"I know," she says. "I work for your stepmother."

"Staffer?"

"Junior. Very junior."

"And how's that going?"

He signals for two drinks. Arran doesn't make it a habit of spending a lot of time around Naevia's office, but he thinks he would have noticed Theo before now. She must be a recent hire. He doesn't really make a habit of flirting with Naevia's staffers, either, but then again he doesn't actually make a habit of flirting with much of anyone in the Arborem. Not in any serious sort of way.

"Illuminating," she answers him, and leans against the bar. "Terrifying."

"She can definitely be both."

"Oh, not the senator," Theo says, bright eyed. "She's incredible."

"An inspiration to little patrician girls everywhere."

"Plebs, too."

Arran raises an eyebrow at that. He's met plebeians who work in government before, certainly, but almost always as aides or bagmen. Not that they're not *allowed* in higher-level jobs, per se, but while younger patrician children may not have a specific role to inherit, the very best of what's left is put aside for them all the same. There are just unwritten rules about that sort of thing. Suddenly the woman in front of him becomes significantly more interesting. More to the point, suddenly she becomes a great deal less out of his reach.

"My father's patron was a senator as well," Theo answers the obvious but unasked question. "He took a liking to me, made sure I got what I was worth."

Ah. There it is.

Always a catch.

It certainly explains a few things. Not only how Theo Arlot—and Arran racks his brain, thinks he remembers an Arlot Perrigam or Perrinal or Perri-something who's the senator of Veritanium—got to be where she is, but also why exactly Theo Arlot is speaking to him in the first place. She's a first-gen pleb. The child of a freedman. She can't be one herself, or she would still be working for another familia. It must have been a parent who earned the patronym *Arlot* upon becoming a citizen, a parent with a patron who works somewhere in politics and decided to give Theo a leg up. Even then, for their child to rise high enough to work as a senatorial staffer is practically unheard of.

"You haven't been in Luxana long, have you?" he asks, more resigned than annoyed.

"Couple of months."

"And you thought you'd rack up points with your new boss by befriending me? Common cause and all that."

Theo takes this in stride. "Are you always like this, or do you just not like women?"

He laughs, despite himself. "You're just not as good at this as you think you are."

"What, flirting?"

That gets her a wry smile, at least. "Okay. Reality drop," he says. "You're new in town, so you can have this one for free. People don't talk to me unless they want something from my family."

"Is that *bona fide*?" Theo asks, pitching her voice into a slightly more upper-crust patrician cant, making him choke slightly as he stifles a laugh. She grins. "It's an interesting theory. But there's a flaw."

"Oh, yeah?" he asks, coughing slightly.

"Yeah. I'm already on your stepmother's payroll, and I do like your sister but she's not really my type." She pauses a moment. "*Reality drop*. All I want is for a cute guy to order me a drink."

Despite himself, Arran finds that he is very, very into this girl. "You always get what you want?"

Maybe privy to some cosmic inside joke, the serva behind the bar chooses that moment to set two glasses of wine in front of them.

Theo takes a long sip from hers and says, "Usually."

Forty-five minutes and two drinks later, and for the life of him Arran doesn't know how they ended up here, tucked into an anteroom just off the courtyard, but he isn't going to be the one to end it. Theo squints at him for a long moment before deciding.

"Dare."

Challenge accepted. "That man by the bar," he says, pointing out the target through the door back outside. Boisterously loud and red in the face from drink, The Man by the Bar is hard to miss.

"What about him?"

"Get his drink."

Theo doesn't hesitate. She takes a determined sip of wine, and Arran's torn between amusement and finding himself deeply impressed as she saunters up to the man and snatches his glass of whiskey, leaving him open-mouthed and gaping in her wake.

She sets the glass down in front of Arran. "Your turn."

"Dare."

"No! You've picked dare every time!"

"Is there a rule against that?"

"Yeah. My rule. I just made it."

"Fine," Arran replies, rolling his eyes. "Truth."

A wicked smile grows as she muses on it for a moment. He watches the way her long pointer finger draws little circles on the wooden table as she considers the question, feeling warm and content in a way he certainly hadn't expected to tonight. He likes Theo. He likes the way she laughs when he speaks—not signaling the usual sense of safety in the accomplishment, but as if leading toward something else. Something bigger, maybe.

Finally, she asks, "What did you want to be when you grew up?"

Arran laughs. "What kind of a question is that?"

"The kind of question I can't ask anyone else." She tucks a loose curl behind her ear. "Literally. Architects' children become architects. Fishermen's children become fishermen. Plebs' lives are set out for us before we're even born. But you? That's gray area. You're lucky, you know."

"Spoken like someone who has no idea what they're talking about," Arran responds, surprised at his own good humor. He likes Theo, he really does. She's practically a stranger still, but in the last hour he's learned that she's scrappy and ambitious, and does exactly what she wants and when, and is utterly unafraid to speak her mind. More to the point, being with her is *easy*. Easy in a way he doesn't think he's ever been with someone he met in the Arborem.

"That's fair. I don't." She shrugs. "I never got to think about what

I *wanted* to do with my life, just what would happen anyway. How to move the needle, do something interesting in the field instead of getting stuck as a paper pusher in some bore of a bureaucrat's office." Then: "Answer the question."

"A sorcerer. But to be fair, I was about five at the time."

"Stop that," she snaps, surprising him into a laugh.

"Stop what?"

"That—*that*. Be real for five minutes, yeah?"

Slightly unnerved, Arran takes a long drink. She's treading dangerously close to territory he doesn't speak about, not with anyone— not with Fagan and Enyo, not with Selah, and certainly not with someone he met barely an hour ago. Only the once with Dad, and Terra knows how well *that* turned out. But where earlier in the evening his defenses may have been higher, the combination of alcohol and Theo Arlot's easy sort of irreverence have done their work well.

"When I was a kid . . . I actually sort of assumed I'd be the next Historian," he finally admits. "Then I realized two, uh, pretty important things."

"Which are?"

"I'm a premie client," he tells her. "Found that out when I was about ten."

Again, not exactly a politically correct term, but also not technically inaccurate. Just a tiny detail that's derailed his entire life. Because Phineas Halitha, that smug bastard, had been right all those years ago on that summer day at the Arborem shore. Children follow the mother when it comes to class. Someone's got to raise them, after all, or so the theory goes. So Phineas had been right.

Well, half right, anyway. Arran may have been born a verna, but he certainly wasn't one by the time Phineas said he was. And that, it turned out, had actually been a problem.

Vernae are apprenticed young so that they're ready to take on a trade and qualify for citizenship at eighteen, an escape from the life of service inherited from servae parents. But a verna boy whose patrician father pulled a few strings with the higher-ups to free him at barely two years old? There's a reason you're not supposed to do it. Arran now couldn't do an apprenticeship; those are for vernae only.

He could take elementary levels, but not superiors, and taking on his parents' trades the way a pleb would had always been out of the question. His mother had been a serva, and only a patrician like Selah could have Dad's job. Gil may have cobbled together something halfway between superior levels and Tair's apprenticeship for him, but that doesn't mean his haphazard education actually qualifies him to do anything aside from sit around and hope his family doesn't get sick of him. There's a reason the legions had appealed beyond his mandatory year, and it has nothing to do with the glory of the Imperium. It's the only option left.

"So," Theo says, evidently reading along the same lines, "basically you're fucked."

"Basically."

She raises her glass to that. He meets her toast, and her level gaze. It's not a moment of pity, for which he feels a rush of profound gratitude. Just the frank facts of life and two people headed toward something. When she puts her glass back down on the table, she lets her hand linger there, resting against his. Then she says, "So what's the second thing?"

"Hm?" he asks, enjoying the sensation of her warm fingers faintly resting against his and the feeling as though his heart's jumped up a few inches toward his throat, the way the candlelight plays in her hair. She bites her lip when she smiles.

"Why you can't be the Imperial Historian. You said there were two reasons."

"Oh. That," he says, and takes Theo's hand in his. "I'd be a really shit librarian."

FIVE YEARS EARLIER

774 PQ

*A*t the moment, Tair has exactly four legal rights.

Right to life, right to food and water, right to shelter, right to education. One right more than a serva, and even then the quality of that education has always been up for debate. Most vernae get the required elementary reading and writing and maybe some basic math, and after that their paterfamilias never even tries to find them an apprenticeship. She's lucky. Lucky to have been a loudmouth know-it-all by age six, even if it meant her perpetually bruised knuckles were a favorite target for the Mothers at the Servile Children's Asylum. Lucky that Gil picked her out from all the other vernae to be his apprentice. Lucky they got on so extremely well. Lucky that even if they hadn't, he isn't the type to have sent her back.

So, yeah, four rights.

In two weeks, on the day she turns eighteen and Alexander Kleios commutes her contract of service, making her a citizen of the Imperium, she'll have forty-seven. The same as that gang of boys they encountered on the beach two weeks ago. Only sixteen fewer than Selah. She's memorized them all.

"Tair Alexander," she hums into the empty spare bedroom of Gil's old tenant house, feeling something like she's stealing the name even when it's only a matter of days before it's hers. Part of her wishes it were going to be Delena—not for Selah's grandmother's sake, neither of them ever met the woman, but because Gil is the closest thing she has to family. It would be nice to share a name.

But sharing one with Arran isn't the worst second choice. They've shared enough as it is to make a certain kind of sense, and they shared this makeshift classroom for nearly ten years. Research projects and lively debates turning to shouting matches and surprising Gil on his birthday and pranking him on Terranalia. Converting it back into an empty, unused bedroom feels like sacrilege, erasing all that history. Like none of it ever mattered.

"How's it going up there?"

"Very slowly," Tair grumbles, loud enough to carry. She dumps the last of the chalkboard erasers into the box and sticks her head out into the little wooden hallway, the one she helped him paint palest blue. "Can't we get some staff in here to do this?"

Gil's laugh echoes from the kitchen somewhere below. "Careful you don't get too high and mighty up there, my lady. Servae don't clean my house, and they won't clean yours either."

Her house. Her house. This is the thing about getting closer to the day—things that existed in the abstract are suddenly becoming real with an alarming clarity. Somewhere in the back of her mind she always knew, of course, what becoming the newest client of the Kleios familia entails. Citizenship. Legal protections. A job. A house. A name. But now she can see it. Not just a bedroom to call her own, but a living room and a kitchen and a hallway all to herself, filled with all the things she will buy with her own hard-earned ceres. She wonders which one it'll be. She wonders if she'll be allowed to pick it out for herself. Out of the three tenant homes sitting empty at the bottom of Breakwater's winding gravel road, there's one that stands just next door.

Wooden stairs bypass creaks into outright groaning, announcing Gil's arrival long before he enters the room, two steaming clay mugs of spiced tazine held in each hand. Tazine first, always. Pleb families, she knows, each have their own private recipe. Patricians may have the security of familia name, but everyone else loses that each time someone cycles back down to the bottom. Tazine is all that most plebeians have in the way of lineage, and even that's a far cry from foolproof. Tair herself had been a foundling, named and raised from infancy by the Mothers at the Servile Children's Asylum before her contract was bought by the Kleios familia. She has no idea who her parents were, or if they had a recipe of their own. Gil's tazine— vanilla and black pepper, hints of sassafras—is the closest thing she has.

He stops short, taking in the haphazard stacks of books, the desks pushed crooked against the wall, the fine layer of chalk dust settled across surfaces and sparkling in lazy motes through the air. Tair's been up here all day, ostensibly converting schoolroom back to spare bedroom. She should be further along than this, and they both know it.

"Well," he says after a moment, "I don't know why I expected anything different."

"There is a system to—"

"I know, I know." He sets one of the mugs down before taking a long sip from his own, a furrow of concern growing in the divot between his brows. "Makes me wonder, though. You'll have to be organized where Selah's not. That's important . . . might have been an oversight on my end. Maybe it's best if we delay all this by a few more months—"

"You wouldn't."

He's joking. He is joking. He has to be. Alexander Kleios may be her paterfamilias but Gil Delena is her supervisor, and without his sign-off that her apprenticeship under him is at an end, citizenship will always be out of reach. He shrugs over his tazine, noncommittal, but there's an unmistakable spark of mischief in the slight twitch of his lips. Tair wants to hit him.

"You're the worst," she says, and takes her mug.

"Only because I know you. And I know what this is really about."

"Oh yeah?"

"Oh yeah. You're dragging your feet to get out of kitchen rotation."

That is, actually, exactly what this is about. It's not that she minds washing dishes, normally. But with two weeks left in service, Tair fails to see why she should be forced to put up with Imarry and her horrible moods. The majordomo's a terror on a good day but, apparently in mourning for loss of status over one of her underlings, she's been absolutely savage for the past few weeks. Tair had to sleep ass-to-the-air last night thanks to the welts Imarry dealt her for badly folded napkins, and she has a feeling she'll be doing the same for a few more nights to come.

"Can't you just tell her you need me instead?" she groans over her tazine. "I'll do his RSVP backlog for you, or—"

But Gil shakes his tawny head. "I'd never dream of crossing

Imarry. If you're on the grounds after six, she gets you. You know that."

He crosses his arms and leans against the crooked desk, looking to all the world like the stern taskmaster she'd assumed him to be the first time she'd lain eyes on him, a Mother hissing in her ear to behave—do you have any idea who his patron is? *That was before she knew better.*

"But," he continues, tapping a slender finger to his jaw and ah, there it is, "maybe there's a way you're not on the grounds."

"Oh?"

He plucks a book from the top of the nearest stack. "Mm. Syntax and Semiotics, Volume Eight. *Extremely important text. And, you know, now that I think about it, I believe our paterfamilias needs it at the Archives right away, actually. And as you can see*—" he takes a long, leisurely sip of tazine "—*I'm entirely too busy right now to do it myself. You'll have to go immediately."*

Tair grins and takes the book. "Immediately?"

"Immediately," he answers, utterly grave. "Can't keep the Imperial Historian waiting."

She could hug him. She doesn't, of course. It's just not what they do. Not that it really matters. Gil was the one who knelt down on overlong legs with a kind word for a frightened six-year-old he'd been told was intelligent, who might fit his needs. The one who sat at her bedside as fever burned through her body at age eleven, fingers sunk deep in her short, damp curls. The one who met her wry observations of the world with laughter instead of the strap. It doesn't matter that she'd like nothing more than to wrap her arms around his wiry frame, feel his scratchy sweater warm against her. She has enough of him as it is.

Tair is halfway down the groaning stairs when she hears him call her name. She looks up, half expecting him to have changed his mind. Instead, he's leaning against the rickety banister, a rare smile playing out across his pale face, and the perpetual dark circles beneath his eyes seem to somehow disappear in its wake.

"I'm proud of you," he says, and her heart could burst from the light.

It carries her down the gravel road, out onto the Arborem's main limestone thoroughfare, where she doesn't stop to worry about the scandalized looks she attracts on her cruiseboard, skating past stately coaches and promenading patricians. If they don't look too close in the gathering dark, she could be anyone at all. If they look too close, she's in for far worse from Imarry than what she's currently avoiding.

She's not doing anything wrong, mind you. Serviles just aren't supposed to be noticed.

If this is to be a long enough errand to justify getting out of kitchen rotation, she might as well do the thing right and take the long way round through the Boardwalk. Iron-curling gates and draping elms of the Arborem district give way to broad avenues of cobblestone, high-end hotels and lively string music spilling from bright-colored restaurants awash in the salt sea air. This is the domain of the merchant plebs and their hard-built fortunes, the well-to-do tourists out to dinner, the bored homemakers come to the sea for their health and the Universitas District museos. And on a late summer evening like this, Tair takes refuge from the growing crowds in the dark-lit glow of the Boardwalk's residential backstreets.

This, it will not take long for her to realize, is a mistake.

The mistake isn't conscious, and neither is it moral—turning left down the street when she could have just as easily turned right. Of course she'll find ways to blame herself for what happens, later on. She should have gone straight to the Imperial Archives. Shouldn't have tricked Gil into letting her skip out on chores. Shouldn't have let Selah bully her into sneaking out to the Festival of Sol and Luna two weeks ago. Should have stopped her before she barged into a situation she didn't understand and put a target on her back—a target that shifted over to Tair the moment it became clear that Selah herself was untouchable. She'll finds ways to make it her own fault, later on.

Right now, she's staring down the barrel of an empty backstreet at six boys, six horribly familiar boys lounging like a pack of satisfied cats across a white, paraffin lamp–lit porch. If she'd been walking, maybe, they might not have heard her. If she'd been slower, maybe, she might have crept by. But cruiseboard wheels have a habit of announcing themselves on cobblestone, and she isn't paying enough attention to see them in time to backtrack. As it is, she can already make out the fine-stitched detail of the nearest boy's linen duskra by the time she realizes where she's seen them before. Their leader, straw-headed and holding court amongst the empty bottles of hops, sets down his latest as his own recognition sets in.

"Hey, boys," he calls. "Look what's come to give us a hello."

Gleeful delight can barely mask the hard edge beneath. Selah made him look weak in front of his gang. Selah threatened his power over them, forced him to tuck his tail between his legs and slink away. But Selah is untouchable, and Selah isn't here.

The same can't be said for Tair.

The hairs at the back of her neck begin to rise, dormant animal instincts doing battle for a half-second too long. Flight kicks in first, and she could run. She could *run*, and she might even make it. But it's a long way back the way she came, and the way ahead is blocked now six boys across, edging closer.

"Couldn't stay away, gorgeous?" says one.

"Been thinking about us, have you?" says another.

"She's not bad for a crim," says their leader, bare inches away. "I've had worse."

Fight, then. That's the only other option.

But she can't. She very literally can't. Fighting them means attacking them, and attacking a citizen when she isn't one yet herself means breaking the law. And breaking the law isn't an option. Not when she's so close to having everything she's worked for.

That's what Tair would remind herself, anyway, were she not so utterly terrified. As it is, she can barely move, but for the sudden awareness of her cruiseboard, hard and sturdy and unyielding, solid beneath her fingertips.

They have her circled, now, and the straw-haired boy grabs her by the chin.

She lets him.

There's a place that Tair goes sometimes. It's small, and quiet, and lives in the deepest recesses of her conscious mind. It's where she goes when the world asks for too much. Where she can pull the physical bounds of her body in around herself like a secret, because what's *secret can never be taken from you. She just has to keep calm and go there now for a little while. Just has to keep calm. Keep calm and . . . let this happen. Let them do what they want, and let Alexander Kleios sue for damages to his investment later on. Let justice be done the proper way. There's a cold and comforting logic to it, but then a large, heavy hand wraps around her upper arm and something snaps.*

No.

It's a heady word.

A complete sentence.

Tair has said it out loud maybe a dozen times total.

No.

No.

No.

The fingers around her cruiseboard tighten in their splintering grip, and for the first time in her life, Tair fights back.

SELAH

This is not at all the first impression she'd hoped to make on Consul Palmar.

Selah doesn't blame Mima, who told her this morning there was no response to the invitation she sent down to Belamar. It's a great honor, of course, that the Imperium's supreme leader of Roma Sargassa would want to pay homage to the late Historian. And she's seen him before, in passing, but this is different. Now he's her direct superior. A little warning would have been nice, if only so he didn't have to witness her downing two glasses of wine in a row right before being introduced. Over his shoulder, Mima looks like she's about five seconds from downing her own glass in utter despair.

In Selah's defense, Arran disappeared ages ago and she's been stuck listening to a pair of ancient scholars drone on for over an hour. Something about insurgents in Lhasa protesting the removal of cult religious texts for safekeeping at the Archives. Theo Arlot had caught her eye from across the room at one point, mimed hanging herself in a display so fragging ostentatious Selah had barely kept herself from losing it right then and there. But even that hadn't been enough to escape.

"I suppose they have a sentimental point," Selah tells Palmar, after she finishes coughing long enough to thank him for coming, and decides it's worth at least trying to claw back some degree of dignity. "But actual, practicing Buddhists are far and few between. Most of the locals observe All-Mater Terra as much as the rest of us, so I do think the preservation of some obscure texts takes precedence over the hurt feelings of a few fringe cultists—and it'll benefit them in the long run, you know, in the event of another calamity. My father would agree on that."

"Indeed he would. I respected your father greatly," Cato Palmar says, positively grandfatherly with his enormous white mustache. "I certainly didn't agree with some of his more radical ideas, but he was a man of vision and scope."

"Radical?" She bites down the urge to laugh. It's not the word she would have used to describe him.

"Oh, yes," he says. "I remember when he first took office, all sorts of lofty ideas. Greater protections for the guilds. A forty-hour work week. Even argued for the abolition of vernae once, right at the start. Historians have no political sway, of course, but he certainly talked my ear off. Treaties and testimonies arriving at my office every other day, well, you can imagine."

She can't imagine, actually. She hadn't known that. But it makes a certain kind of sense. Mima hadn't married Dad yet, back when her grandmother passed and he took on the mantle of Historian. Arran couldn't have been more than a year old. But that still doesn't add up to what she's always known about her father. Alexander Kleios was a servant of the Imperium, and instilled in his children from a young age what that means.

We live for the many, not ourselves. We are cogs in the great machine. If nothing else, he made that clear enough the day she lost Tair.

Yet he must have found something in those books and treaties and testimonies that gave him pause. Something that made sense to him beyond the personal, because he'd never been a man to act on the whim of emotion. Or maybe he had just been young, preoccupied by the same haunting thoughts that have kept Selah herself awake on countless nights over the last five years, memories of a girl with deep-set eyes, fireworks on the beach refracting off pale brown skin.

"The whim of a young idealist," the Consul adds, dismissive.

"Is it, though?" She blurts it out before she can think about it, and immediately turns red.

"Selah, don't be rude," Mima snaps, but the Consul raises his hand almost lazily to cut her off.

"Oh, no, Senator Kleios. I'm delighted to get to know the . . . young woman I'll be working with." He turns back to her, smile not quite reaching his eyes, and motions for her to continue.

She ignores the warning in Mima's glance, ignores that Consul Palmar had clearly been about to call her a *girl*. Because he's right, after all, they *will* be working together, pride of place giving the Historian a direct line to the Consul on advice for implementing new discoveries or warnings when his office threatens to ignore the lessons of ages past—and Selah has no intention of curbing her opinions or intelligence for the sake of an old man's ego. Leave rhetoric to the politicians. This is a chance to show him that she isn't to be underestimated, twenty-two years old or no.

"I just mean," she says, "that there's no harm in taking a fresh look at *reality* where vernae are concerned. The natural arc of social reform. After all, it's been over two hundred years since the gladiator games were abolished."

"Perhaps," Palmar says, "but we're not speaking about mindless butchery, are we? The gladiator games slaked a thirst for blood in the citizenry that served precisely no one, and I daresay we're all the better for their absence. Vernae, however, fulfill their promise to the collective betterment of us all. They have good, comfortable lives, with education and training to become productive citizens and members of the imperial workforce at adulthood. Moreover, the existence of the vernae class severely diminishes that of the working poor."

These are classic talking points, the tired buzzwords and arguments that Selah's heard so many times throughout her life, and she knows better, now. She's known better for five long and painful years.

"But the working poor still exist," she insists. "Client plebeians still experience social stigma and, laws aside, vernae aren't *all* treated well by their familias. Or even able to become citizens when by all rights they should." That last point comes out sounding more like a bark, and Mima says her name again in that *way* of hers, because she knows this has ventured into personal territory. Selah takes a breath, willing herself calm again. "I just mean . . . it stands to reason that servae exist. If you commit a crime or fall into debt, that was your choice. Or a clear indication, at least, that you aren't to be trusted to pull your own weight. But why extend that to their children? Why treat *them* as criminals?"

"An interesting question," the Consul says, looking the furthest thing from interested and distinctly less grandfatherly now. "Where would you suggest these children go, then, after we take them from their parents? We could foster them, perhaps? With good familias who

might house and feed and educate them as their own until they come
of age? Unless I'm very much mistaken, we already *do* that."

Her skin burns hot, as she realizes she's fallen right into the trap
he laid for her. But she's never been one to go down easily.

"That's fair," she says, scrambling, though it's really, really not.
The scuffle at the canal comes to her mind then, the chained row of
onlookers to Arran's fight who will now spend the rest of their lives in
service for just being in the wrong place at the wrong time. "But
maybe we should look to alternate judicial punishment. Maybe service isn't the answer to *every* petty crime, and a tier system—"

"Did you know that, for a time, in the Ante Quietam, criminals
would be sent to penal colonies or long-term prisons?"

Of course she knows that. She's the Imperial fragging Historian.
She has to resist the urge to roll her eyes.

"And how did that turn out in the end?"

She hesitates. It's not that she doesn't know the answer to this,
too—she very much does, and that's what causes her to draw up
short. She doesn't want to play into Palmar's point. "It was an enormous strain on the annual budget," she finally admits.

"Precisely. The operation of a single prison required considerable—
no, *prohibitive*—funding."

"Even though it produced free labor," she can't help but snipe.

"Even though it produced free labor," Palmar agrees. "I hope you
trust me when I say that alternate justice is not a novel idea."

"Then why not stop looking at the symptoms, and look to the root
of the problem instead?" Selah finds herself asking the question before she's really thought it through. They're here, aren't they? They're
talking about it already. Maybe the Consul will back her. Maybe he
can become the ally she needs against Thane, if only she can make
him see that it's an answer to a long-unsolved systemic question. "Education. If we can give greater opportunities to—"

"This has been debated in the Senate time and time again for eight
hundred years. Just ask your mother. Without our judicial system in
place, our economy would all but collapse. The balance is delicate.
Upending all we have built is not the answer. It simply wouldn't work."

He didn't even let her ask.

"I do hope you'll pay me a visit at Belamar sometime, young lady," he continues, a firm end to the conversation in his voice, and something about the prim satisfaction of his thin, pursed lips making Selah's skin crawl. "I'll be in residence for at least a few more weeks, I should think. And this has been an all-too-enlightening conversation."

THEO

Arran Alexander's bed is the nicest they've ever been in. Theo luxuriates in the sensation of soft, clean linen against their skin, stretching out pleasantly to accommodate the new little aches and pops in their legs and lower back. They don't bother hiding their enjoyment—Theodora Arlot, were she to actually exist, would no doubt feel the same way.

The candles have burned low since the pair of them crashed through the door, breathless with giddy laughter, but the rising moon through the large bay window shines brightly, illuminating the dark Sargasso Sea far below. Lying head to opposite toe, Theo can make out Arran's face in the moonlight as he reaches over to draw a finger lightly down the underside of their foot. Jerking back, they aim a kick his way.

He laughs, then says, "Truth."

"Have you ever peed in a pool?"

"Obviously."

"Gross."

They throw a pillow at him. He bats it away before it hits his face. "Like you haven't."

"I don't have to answer that. Yet. Truth."

Arran takes time to consider, humming slightly as soft, questioning fingers trace the length of Theo's left calf, down along the ugly, puckered, jagged thing where shattered bone once poked through on both sides. "Where'd you get this one?"

"What if I said I was mauled by a coyote?"

"I'd say you weren't taking the game seriously, and I'd be offended."

"And I'd say you were being really insensitive about my childhood trauma." He laughs, and this time they actually do kick him, because it's the truth.

Much of tonight has turned out to be an exercise in the truth, actually—a turn of events that could have shocked no one more than themself. Theo hadn't managed a real conversation with Selah during the viewing, nothing beyond a brief moment where they briefly caught one another's gaze across the room, and Theo couldn't help but feel altogether sorry for the girl. The gaggle of important patricians and would-be-important social climbers had followed her around like a cloud of noxious smoke, ambition choking any real moment of personal connection that tried to slip through. But Theo had expected that. And they had a different target tonight.

The dead Historian's wayward son was an obvious mark. Theo hadn't known that he existed, actually, for the first month or so in Naevia Kleios's office. It was Selah herself who'd first mentioned him, obvious affection shining through.

"He'd have done so well at the universitas," Selah had told them over hibiscus tea at that meridiem jav, as if to explain the barrage of questions over Theo's own invented education. Apparently she was collecting ideas for some kind of reform scheme. Sweet girl, really. Sweet and so, so blind. "He'll be back soon, though," she'd added, brightening at the prospect. "The legions should have sent him home a month ago, so we're expecting him in a few weeks."

So, yes, Arran Alexander was the obvious mark, now that they know Griff wants Selah on their side. Get close to her half-caste brother, the one no doubt responsible for Selah's more liberal inclinations in the first place, and Theo's miles closer to turning both the new Historian and this weapon she has to the Revenant cause.

Except. Well.

Sleeping with him had been part of the plan. Actually *liking* him definitely had not.

"If you say so," Arran says now, sitting up, though he definitely looks as though he's going to laugh at them again. "Truth, then."

Theo's brain is feeling hot and stupid from drink and sex and the October heat. "What's your middle name?"

"Don't have one. I don't think. My mima named me and Dad just kind of went with it."

"So ask her."

"Yeah, I'd do that, only she's dead."

Well, shit. Now it's their turn to sit up, an apology ready on their lips, but Arran doesn't seem all that upset. "Don't worry," he says. "It's been a minute. Birth . . . stuff."

That, Theo thinks, *doesn't make it better at all.*

"I mean, she was nineteen, so . . ."

"She was just a kid."

"Yeah, but so was my dad."

As though that makes it any less messed up. Theo may not know the exact details of what might compel the son of a patrician familia to knock up a teenage serva, but they don't have to imagine very hard. They've known too many mothers to insist their child has no father.

Those children, however, don't usually come to their father's defense. Then again, those children don't usually grow up with every luxury in the empires thrown at them.

"He did what he could with me," Arran says, avoiding their gaze, and they can tell that their frown is making him uncomfortable, "but . . ."

"Parents from different castes never really get it."

Arran looks up at them, curious, and mentally they kick themself. Theodora Arlot has a history that he already knows something of, the daughter of a freedman rising to success out of her own hard work and sheer determination. Theo Nix, however, is a very different story. And their heart doubles over in their chest as they realize that they don't really want to lie.

"My dad," they tell him, fishing for the right words to find that seed of truth, "had all of these deeply rooted ideas that were just . . . so at odds with what I knew. I . . . he," they catch themself, "had a really damaging childhood, and that shit sticks."

He nods quietly, taking in their words. "Had?"

"Hm?"

"You keep using the past tense."

"Oh." They lie back down, the truth coming out more easily now. "Yeah. The old story. Couldn't assimilate to the new life. Drank a lot. Died young." So maybe Jarol had fallen from pleb to serva, not the other way around, but the end result was the same.

"I'm sorry."

"I'm not. Not really."

And that, too, is the truth. Jarol had been a mean and hopeless drunk, steadily sinking his family into debt and squalor, all the while refusing to see how he was in any way responsible for what ultimately became of them. The few bright memories Theo has of him—teaching them to restring a bow or enchanting a full mess hall with late-night tales of Ante Quietam heroes—are quickly overshadowed by the others. Starvation and beatings and the dark, endless choke of the underground. The unfocused eyes he'd looked at them through because there was nothing to be done. It was too late. He might be their father, but the Publica had come for them as much as him, because Theo was only three. Too little to be left on their own. So as much as they can tell themself otherwise, it was Jarol, really, in the end. His fault that their future was ripped away, replaced by a black brand and nothing but long years of service ahead. It had been a mercy for them both when he went.

Theo, however, has never been much good at self-pity, so they try smiling just a little instead into the comfortable silence that stretches out between them and Arran.

"My dad and I weren't talking at the end," he offers, after a moment, and they shift to look at him. Eyes gazing up toward the ceiling, his long, slender fingers running through messy brown curls, as though needing somewhere to put that restless energy. Anywhere but the words so clearly fighting to be let out.

"Why?"

He shrugs, flushing a little bit. "Ah . . . We said some things. He called me an *idealistic individualist*—which, trust me, was an insult coming from him. He said I was being *willfully overdramatic*."

"And were you?" they ask, poking him with a toe.

"A little, yeah. I, uh. I told him he should have just let me grow up verna."

"*What?*" Theo asks this a great deal more loudly than they had meant to, just short of a yelp. Because that has got to be the most insane thing they've ever heard anyone say. "Arran, that is so messed up."

"Yeah, I know," he says, having the decency at least to look embarrassed about it. "I was angry. I didn't actually mean it."

"Good. Because I'm with your dad on this one. That's the stupidest . . . the *blindest* thing I've ever—"

"I *know*," Arran says loudly, cutting them off before they can build up too much steam. "I'm not an idiot. I was just trying to . . . If I could have just grabbed him and shaken him and known it would've made some sort of difference, I'd have done that instead, but . . ." He breaks off, staring hard at the wall like the words he needs could be written on it somewhere if he looks hard enough. Theo watches with a level gaze, waiting for him to find them, and feels as though those words had better be good. It takes a very specific set of life experiences—or lack thereof—to even joke about something like that.

When Arran speaks again, his voice is calmer. "My dad . . . Terra knows how he did it, I never asked, but he got my contract commuted *years* before he was supposed to. And I *am* grateful for that, because I can't even imagine . . . But it's like you said, he never actually understood what doing that meant. From a practical standpoint."

There's a frank quiet in his voice, like if he can just put the words in the right order and get them out into the air between the two of them, then maybe Theo can comprehend their meaning without laying their own thoughts or truths over them. And Theo, who has never wanted anyone else's anger or pity either, finds themself strangely inclined to listen.

"The world isn't built for people like me to exist," he says, "so effectively I don't. This has been my bed my whole life, but it's not actually mine. Nothing is. And there's no way for me to change that or make my own money, not without joining the legions. So unless I do that, the rest of my life depends on how much my little sister *likes* me. And I don't want to be angry about that. I know how lucky I am. But I guess I always thought he had some sort of plan for me . . . and it turns out he didn't. What he did wasn't about me at all, just making good with his own conscience. So, yeah. I'm angry. And I have no idea what the answer to that is."

Arran stops, and Theo, for their part, feels their own anger abate. Though they still don't know if they want to hug him or smack him. Probably both. Because as much as they want to yell at him again for daring to complain when he lives a life that most can barely dream of, he already knows. And they recognize the hurt that wraps around him, a complicated wound to the soul that will never really heal. They wear it themself. By now they just know how to live with it.

"The worst part," he says, "is that I never knew if he did it out of love or guilt."

"You don't get angry like that with people you don't love," they tell him quietly.

"No, I know he loved me. But I don't know if he loved her."

The night creeps on and they find their way back into each other's arms again. The heat between them is thicker now, with Arran's fingers tracing the notches in Theo's spine as they ride him, hard and slow, against the linen sheets. He sighs into the curve of their body, and throws his head back, and they bury trailing laughter down his throat even as they fight to stay underneath his skin. After, he traces along the thick sea-green ridges of their tattooed back with quiet, questioning fingernails until he drifts away to sleep.

Theo doesn't sleep. They can't.

Instead, sheets pulled up around them at the foot of the bed, they count the dark beauty marks that dot his neck and milk-pale face, and pushes away the voice that can't help but wonder if they've made a huge mistake.

FIVE YEARS EARLIER

774 PQ

*C*utting through the sticky September heat, a thin trail of cold slides down her spine like an ice cube slipped down the back of her dress.

Selah is out of her chair before she has time to really consider her next move, much less the alarmed ornatrice she leaves behind in her bedroom, comb and extensions still in hand. Mima calls after her, but she lets the words slide away, already halfway down the carpeted third-floor hall of Breakwater House. She doesn't think her mother is lying to her, exactly. But she's certain she's been misinformed. She *must* be. There's no way Dad would let this happen.

The pounding in her ears and the icy chill down her neck carry her upstairs to the fourth floor. Past floral arrangements sitting in blown-glass vases, through intricately carved doorframes, to the door of Dad's study where the eight-point Kleios sun sits carved in mahogany wood. She doesn't knock. Not today.

If Alexander Kleios is at all surprised to see his only daughter burst into the privacy of his inner sanctum, hair half-loose, he disguises it remarkably well. He seems, if anything, to have been expecting her. Peering over pale steepled fingers from his wing-back chair, the grand desk of the Imperial Historian's home office draws the clear battle line between them.

"It wasn't her fault."

"Selah—"

"You know it wasn't her fault."

"Sit down."

"I don't want to sit down."

"Sit," he growls, and Selah nearly takes a step back. A far cry from the vaguely frayed academic of a father she knows, quiet consideration has given way to a stone wall of grave authority, and for the first time Selah can truly appreciate that her father is the Imperial Historian of all Roma's empires.

The Imperium had first appointed the title to their ancestor Antal Iveroa nearly eight hundred years ago, heralding the end of the Great Quiet and the beginning of the Imperial Age of Enlightenment. After untold centuries of darkness and chaos and war, the Imperium had regained control of Roma and her client empires, but so much had been lost by then. Knowledge that would never be restored—or, at least, not for an extremely long time. So Antal Iveroa was charged with the building and safeguarding of the Imperial Archives, the greatest library in the world, and the stewardship of the empires' collective knowledge. For nearly eight hundred years that sacred task has been passed down, from mothers and fathers to eldest daughters and sons.

This is what it must be like, then, to be one of Dad's clients, or a patrician neighbor vying for favor. Not to look at Dad and see Dad—auburn hair flecked with white, and how his eyes turn to crescent moons when he smiles—but something else entirely. Centuries of power and authority, and a staunch refusal to be pushed around. But Selah has always assumed it was a projection—that people see what they expect to see. She didn't know it was something he's aware of. Something he could intentionally activate, like one of his prize solaric lamps. She didn't know he was capable of changing masks so easily. It makes her skin prickle.

But this isn't about her. This is about Tair, who has no one else to be her champion. So Selah swallows her pride and her fury and her shock, and everything else that demands she stand her ground. She runs a conscious hand over her half-loose hair and, with as much dignity as she can muster, takes a seat in the handsome leather chair on her side of the battle line.

"Mima's under the impression that court didn't go in Tair's favor today," she says, calmly, *and watches him move to the black-lacquer bar cart in the corner. "But she must be mistaken."*

"And why is that?"

She could strangle him. She doesn't need a scholar right now. She needs her father. But this is her father. This is his way—forcing her and even Arran to work their problems out to a conclusion.

"Because I told you what happened to her," she answers through

*gritted teeth. "I told you she acted in self-defense. And I told you,"
and here Selah has to swallow her guilt, "that it was my fault. Those
boys never would have spared her a second thought if I hadn't vexed
them off. So I would assume you told that to the magistrate. What
good are the courts if the Historian's word counts for nothing?"*

*He doesn't answer right away, just turns and hands her a word-
less glass of whiskey and leans against his desk, glancing out at the
orange sunset. She doesn't touch her drink. She wouldn't have even if
he'd remembered she doesn't like the stuff. One of his ancient solaric
lamps sits on the corner of the desk, the bright, otherworldly glow of
its shining black bulb casting shadows across his face. Solaric technology has always made Selah uneasy, as with most things left over
from before the Quiet that have yet to be understood. Stick their
black irradium bulbs in the sun for an hour and they'll light up for the
next few months. No paraffin or beeswax necessary. And still, all
these years later, no one knows how.*

"Dad."

*He isn't ignoring her, she knows that, but this forlorn act is nei-
ther helpful nor inspiring much confidence.*

"Dad," she snaps, patience gone. "What happened?"

*Finally he sets his glass down on the desk and looks at her. "One
of the young men from the incident," he says at last, his voice betraying nothing. "An Isaya Jellene. He has a scratched cornea."*

The bottom of Selah's stomach drops away.

"But," she scrambles, "if it was self-defense—"

*"Self-defense doesn't exist for the servile castes, Selah, you know
that. Non habet personam—no persona, no self. One cannot defend
what doesn't exist."*

"But she's about to be—"

*"Whatever her justification, whatever she was about to be, it's a
moot point," he says, returning to his large wing-back chair on the
other side of the desk. "Tair harmed a citizen. Tair broke the law, and
that is all that matters to the magistrate."*

*"But you're the Historian," she explodes, bursting from her chair
again, unwilling to entertain that this is truly happening, that this has*

truly spiraled so far out of her or Dad's control. "You can overturn it. You can protect her. You've done it before, for Arran when—"

"Don't bring your brother into this." Dad's broad, pale face grows somehow dark, and the edge in his voice is back. "The situations couldn't be more different."

"How? Honestly, how is this any different?"

"For one thing, Arran has never broken the law."

Cool and quiet still, he does not rise to tower over her as he very well could, and if she were any less angry Selah might feel foolish standing there, the weight of his authoritative gaze shining steady judgment up at her like the brightest and harshest of solaric lights, leaving her exposed.

"Even if I did wield that kind of influence," he goes on, "the magistrate has made a decision. He has passed a sentence in accordance with her crime, and it is not my place to interfere. Just as it was not Tair's place to harm a citizen."

"You can't believe that. I know you can't believe that."

The Kleios familia is large and strong, and Selah has seen her father laugh with his clients and feast with servae on Terranalia, and he embraces Gil Delena like a brother. He knows Tair, and he knows that she is clever, and funny, and deserves to walk unharmed through the world. He knows this, and she can't understand why he won't fight for it.

But then he stands, and it's clear that this conversation is over.

"We all have our parts to play," he says, staring out again at the purpling sky. "We are all cogs in the great machine. Someday you'll understand that."

"Two weeks," Tair says, the dark golden sunset streaming from the small window of her bedroom to nestle in her hair. Sullen, sporting a bruised and swollen black eye, refusing to look at Selah. "Two weeks."

She stands there, unsure what there is left to say when the cold facts are these:

Tair assaulted a citizen. Tair broke the law. And so Tair, who was

meant to leave her verna life behind in two weeks, has lost her eligi-
bility for citizenship. Permanently. That was the magistrate's verdict.

"I'm so, so sorry," *she says, feeling even as she says it that it's a*
fairly weak thing to say.

Evidently, Tair agrees.

"Okay," *she says, half a numb and bitter laugh, and she still won't*
look at her. Selah's feet carry her across the small attic bedroom in
two short strides so that she can sit on the bed next to Tair and take
hold of her hands.

"I am," *she says, desperate for her to understand how very much*
on her side she is.

"And that helps me how, exactly?" *Tair spits, snatching her hands*
away. "I had twelve days left, and now it's just* gone. *But yeah, sure,*
it's okay, because you're sorry."

There are no words that can fix this. Selah looks for them anyway.

"Maybe . . ." *Her mind races toward Pacifica and Anatolia, and*
how maybe her parents won't actually mind Tair going so much after
all if Selah goes with her. How maybe things can still be normal, how
the line between verna and client pleb is a legal fiction, really, and
how maybe amongst themselves they can move forward the way
they're meant to. This is just a minor setback.

"Listen. What if we—"

"Leave me alone, Selah."

"No, really, maybe there's a way—"

"Get *out.*"

Selah doesn't know this yet, but this will be their last conversation.
When she wakes up the next morning, Tair will be gone, vanished
into the air. The Cohort Publica will search the city and surrounding
agricultural villages. Street orators will advertise rewards for knowl-
edge of her whereabouts. Gil will mourn her. And Selah will never
see her again.

SELAH

There's an unpleasant buzz beneath her skin, something that has nothing whatsoever to do with the decanter of Gallia red sitting between her and Gil, and everything to do instead with her disastrous introduction to Consul Palmar. Dad's study feels oppressive, the walls closing in from all sides. But she's entirely too alert and annoyed to go to bed yet.

She should let Gil go home. It's half past one in the morning and he's been at this all day.

"This is hopeless," she groans instead. Dad's handwriting is no clearer than it was when she finally slipped away from the party downstairs, notes allegedly on Terran motherhood cults in northwest Fornia turning to nothing but blurry lines. Selah drops her head on the desk.

Blearily, Gil looks up. "Right, that's it," he says, closing the journal he's been trying to wade through with a definitive snap. "Bedtime."

"No, you go. I can—"

"This will still be here in the morning."

Will it?

It's a stupid thought, she does know that. The stacks of notes, the bar cart, Dad's desk—*her* desk, now. They'll still be here in the morning, he's right. But for how long? The study still smells like Dad, the leather corner chair still imprinted where he sat. It's all hers now in name, but she doesn't *want* it. Not yet. Doesn't want to sit here and try to work out his handwriting, not if he can't read it out loud to her instead, green eyes wide with excitement and arms gesticulating dangerously in the midst of a particularly complicated thought. She doesn't want to go to bed. Not when it means she'll have to wake up tomorrow, and don her mourning gold again, and send him as ash into Terra's arms.

Selah turns—to what, tell Gil to stop? But before she can decide, a dark glint catches her eye.

The solaric lamps.

Her father's prize possessions.

Black bulbs of irradium stone, set on a base of copper, nothing like them exists on earth. Esoteric and rare collector's items, more myth than fact to most of the world. Slowly, Selah picks one up, the cool black sphere strangely heavy in her palm. At the bottom, set into the copper base, the eight-point Kleios sun glints, etched inside a circle. However old this tech is, her familia can trace their history just as far. These lamps don't work like paraffin, but she's seen Dad do this before. So instead of turning a dial to light the oil, she smooths her thumb across the circle and gently presses *in*.

The effect is luminous. Brilliant solaric light fills the shadowed study, so clear and clean it puts shame to sunlight itself. Seeping into every shelf and cranny, bouncing off peeling gold-lamé titles so she could read even the oldest of print if she really wanted. Gil looks up, the purple shadows under his eyes brought into startling relief as he squints, and for the first time in Selah's life she can see the small scar running along the rim of his ear. An involuntary shudder passes over her, raising small goosebumps down her arms.

She presses the sun again, and the room goes dark once more.

"You knew him the longest," she says then, quietly, and wonders how they've never talked about this before. They were children together, then stupid teenage boys, then men. He was born in this house, the same as Dad. His own father works in the gardens even now.

Gil nods, something sad behind tired eyes.

"Tell me something about him I don't know?"

The smile bursts out full formed. "I can do you one better," he says, and shifts overlong legs to rummage for something in his bag. When he emerges, Selah has to laugh.

"Not more *books*."

"Yes, more *books*." He places them carefully in front of her, two crumbling and ancient tomes stacked one on top of the other. Neither appear to have a title. "Books your dad specifically asked me to make sure got to you. He left a note. *Classified,* apparently." He winks.

"Oh?"

"Hid them in a special cache in his office and everything. Lucky for you, I'm the only person who knew where that was. We used to leave frogs in there for your grandmother to find when we were kids."

Selah yawns, smashing a cheek against one hand as she carefully opens the top volume's front cover. "What are the chances we get lucky again and these hold the code to deciphering Alexander Kleios's fragging abysmal handwriting?"

He laughs.

But then Selah pauses, halfway through idly flipping the delicate pages. She frowns.

"Gil," she says slowly, eyes fixed to the page. "What is this?"

"I don't know, I didn't exactly get a chance to ask."

"Come take a look."

The book on top, it transpires, isn't just a *book*.

It's an atlas. Map after meticulously drawn map, traced over paper so old Selah really does feel she should run and grab a pair of gloves. But that isn't what's strange. Gil moves around to her side of the desk, and she doesn't know whether to be gratified or disappointed to see an equal look of confusion come over his face.

"That's Aymara, right?"

"Well, I'd assume so," he answers, shifting the book slightly to get a better look at the particular map in question. "The general coastal shape is correct, but—"

"The internal landmass is all wrong."

The coastlines may not be exactly accurate, but it's still distinctly recognizable as Roma Aymara, the tropical client empire to the south comprising two major islands and several minor ones. But where ocean straits and rivers should be is nothing but a sea of green.

Selah's eyes go wide as she realizes what this must mean. "This is dated Ante Quietam, isn't it?" she asks, excitedly flipping through pages again, taking much more care this time. "From before the Great Quiet. Before proper cartography instruments and all that."

"It certainly looks old enough," says Gil, eyes drinking in the sight of inaccurate map after inaccurate map with just as much interest. "And I don't recognize this language in the least."

It's true, Selah realizes with another little thrill. Forget *language*, the rivers and mountains and notations scribbled in the margins are all written in an alphabet she finds utterly incomprehensible. Perhaps a relic of some pre-Roma civilization that once existed there.

Only that can't be it. Roma has been in Aymara—and indeed in Sargassa—since long before the Great Quiet, exploring and cultivating her client empires for hundreds of years before the world went mad and lost all contact. From Roma to Sargassa to Aymara to Serica, and even the Aksum Empire beyond Imperial control. Each had been well and truly on their own. A child of five could tell you that.

Natives, then. Perhaps this book—this *atlas*—is the result of their crude attempts at cartography. But who would bother to print it? She amuses herself for a moment at the idea of some Ante Quietam printer, a maverick by reputation, pressing and binding this atlas in the dead of night for a native friend. Or perhaps enjoying a period of relative peace, a pocket of time during which Sargassans both Roman and native had worked together toward prosperity. Selah knows of no such time. But there's so much that was lost to the Great Quiet, and the promise of an academic mystery curls pleasantly in Selah's mind, warmly chasing away any lingering unpleasantness from the viewing and her encounter with the Consul, temporarily easing the yawning gap of grief that Dad left behind.

"This is a bona fide major find," she says. "Why wouldn't Dad have donated this to the Archives? Or at least shared it with us?"

Gil shrugs. "Maybe he thought it was a fake."

"Maybe . . . but that doesn't explain why he wanted me to have it. Or why he said it was classified."

Careful of its crumbling spine, she shifts the atlas to the side. The volume beneath is equally old, though kept in infinitely better shape. Soft leather bindings worn but strong, and Selah is about to flip that open, too, when Gil tries—and fails—to stifle a massive yawn.

Frag. She'd meant to send him home.

"You're right," she says, and she swipes a thumb over the leather cover. A final, undiscovered piece of Dad, something that will still be here for her in the morning. "Time for bed."

They part ways in the atrium, where the candles in their sconces have nearly burnt out and the handsome grandfather clock declares it to be nearly two thirty in the morning. Selah isn't tired, though, as she watches Gil's lanky profile slouch down the hill toward the semicircle of small houses where most of her father's clients live. *Her* clients. That's going to take some getting used to.

She passes from the atrium out into the open air of the long colonnade, and is just thinking of sneaking out down to the beach to be alone with her thoughts and the salt air when she notices a familiar figure ahead. Out where the courtyard juts into a balcony overlooking the far ocean below, Arran looks down upon the now-shrouded body of their late father. Too far away in the falling dark to read what's written across his face, yet it's immediately clear to Selah that she's stepped into something she wasn't meant to see. There's a cursory attempt to backtrack, but a scuff on the tile gives her away. Arran looks up, sharp, then breaks into a smile.

"You survived."

"No thanks to you." She punches her brother on the shoulder as he approaches, not hard, then wraps her arms around him. "Saw you talking to Theodora Arlot. Dick. I wanted to introduce you."

He shrugs. "Got there first."

But there's something uncharacteristically awkward about it, something spread across high cheekbones that if Selah didn't know better she'd say was a *blush*. She can't help it, the dump of laughter. "You *didn't*."

Arran just shrugs again, and doesn't even look all that embarrassed about it, actually. Not that he should, Theo's a perfectly nice girl. Smart, competent, perfectly inspiring in her defiance against the odds to make something of her life. If Selah's being completely honest, she was actually hoping that Theo and her brother would become friends. Quiet knows Arran could do with some. She just hadn't really imagined it would be anything more than that.

He *would* pick someone up at their Dad's viewing.

She punches him again.

They end up out on the dark lawn, formalwear loosened and dis-carded as they sprawl across the great hill behind Breakwater House. Out ahead of them, the lawn spills onto the expanse of the estate, disappearing into the Hazards beyond. New-cut grass between their toes, stars laid out far above their eyes. Selah hits the very end of the spliff while Arran rolls another.

"Terra's beautiful saggy tits," she exhales deeply, the weight of the day's anxieties going up in smoke as the gentle slope of the earth wel-comes her ever more deeply. "You cannot get plant like this in Luxana."

"No, you can't. Next time I go to Fornia, you're coming with. No excuses."

"Like they'll ever let me out of the city again. I'm bona fide chained to a desk arguing with old men for the rest of my life." And it's not the ancient scholars that come to mind. Plenty to learn from erudites, if you can stay awake long enough to listen. No, it's the pale and sag-ging face of Consul Cato Palmar that sets her teeth on edge.

"Worse fates," her brother says lightly. "But hey, call it a work trip. All you have to do is visit a museo and you're gold."

"They have those out there?"

He shrugs, finishes rolling the spliff, and lights it. Selah frowns as she accepts it from him, and wonders if the question is worth asking. *Worse fates*. She thinks she already knows the answer, but she would rather hear the truth of it from him. Dad certainly hadn't been willing to talk about it.

Arran lies down, his familiar weight bumping up against her and giving her the boost of confidence she needs.

"Hey, Arran?" She passes the spliff back and stares up into the dark sky.

"Hm?"

"Why did you leave?"

She hears him exhale slowly, then—"Nah, it's boring."

"I know you and Dad weren't . . . happy with each other. At the end."

To that, Arran doesn't say anything at all, and Selah feels a flush of embarrassment. There is nothing the pair of them haven't willingly shared with one another since she came into the world. Childhood toys and friends and teenage adventure, yes, but also the quieter moments, hopes and fears and dreams. There have been fights, of course. Four years is a tricky age gap to navigate, and certainly there were times when he didn't want her trailing after him and his friends, or she had screamed at him for patronizing her and calling her a brat. But those are fleeting moments compared to the nights like this one when they've stayed up late together, the secret worlds they built in the Hazards as children, the way they know how to navigate each other's moods and tempers. Arran has never once coddled her, always knowing exactly when to come to her defense and when to let her take a loss. It's always been the two of them, really.

When she lost Tair, he's the one who was there for her. Not just because he was Tair's friend, too—he was, Selah gets that, it's just not the same. And sure, Gil had been there, too, in his way, in mourning because he loved Tair like a daughter. But Arran was different. Arran was there for her in a way no one else ever could have been, because he was the only other person in the world who understood what it was like to be let down by Dad.

Which makes it all the harder to acknowledge that maybe, this time, it wasn't her place to ask. She can't imagine that the brother she knows so well really could care that much about returning to the military legions, not after their family had tried so hard and failed so spectacularly to keep him out of mandatory service in the first place. But a year is a long time, and more than enough for a person to change. Maybe it really is as simple as that.

She's about to apologize or say it doesn't matter, actually, just forget it, when he lets out a long smoky exhale and says, "You know what the last thing I ever said to him was?"

"What?" she asks, quietly surprised, as though anything louder might cause him to change his mind.

"Fuck. You."

Silence.

And then she can't help it. What Dad's face must have looked like. The sheer *idea* of it. Selah bursts into laughter. The plant catching up with her, utterly stoned and bubbling up from deep within, but then Arran's joining in with her and the two of them roll around in the grass cackling with belly-deep laughter until tears stream down their faces, the release desperately welcome. They don't settle for a long, lovely moment, until they do, his arm nestled around her.

"He left you an allowance, you know," Selah says into the comfortable silence, suddenly feeling a little more charitable to their father, who had loved and disappointed them both. Maybe he wasn't a perfect man but he had, after all, tried his best to make things right at least for Arran in the end.

"Yeah, I do know. The estate doesn't want to let me have it. Naevia's getting involved, some loophole about Patron-Client Willable Assets."

"Sounds made up."

"Probably is."

She laughs, unconcerned. Mima's a force to be reckoned with when it comes to taking care of her familia, and there is no doubt in Selah's mind that she can get Arran whatever he's owed. "Thought about what you're going to do with it?" she asks.

"Well, I was planning on spending it all on booze and loose women—"

"Naturally."

"—but then I remembered that mooching off your little sister your entire life is considered impolite and sort of embarrassing. So I should probably save up."

Selah falls quiet for a moment, frowning, while he plays with the ends of her hair with one hand, almost a little kid again. It's not what he's said—Arran is notorious for not taking things seriously, and she's more than used to that by now. No, instead it's the memory of something they had spoken about earlier in the day, although it feels much longer ago than that.

"Do you seriously think I'd just leave you out to dry?" she asks him.

Though she can't see his face, lying like this, she can practically feel him rolling his eyes. "It was a joke, Sel," he says. "I know you wouldn't."

She sits up, all business. "I'm not talking about money." Because the savage Quiet take her but Gil is right. She can't do this on her own. And neither is she about to lose another member of her shrinking family. "You're the smartest person I know, and I'm not letting you waste that. Frag the legions, come work with me."

"That's funny," he says, and this time she actually sees him rolling his eyes.

She hits him. Because she isn't trying to flatter him. Arran is *smart* and *capable* and if the world had just let him *be* someone, then maybe he would believe it, too. "Jokes in a time of crisis are your thing, not mine. I want to hire you."

"Yeah, but you can't. *I* can't."

Arran hits the spliff again. She knocks it out of his hand.

"*Frag*, Selah."

"If I have to be paterfamilias now," she tells him coolly, "then I say you can. You have to. Because, Terra bless him, Gil's doing his best, but I don't know what the frag I'm doing and I *need* you. And since *apparently* I won't have the time to do it myself, I'll need someone to head this new extended education initiative."

Selah watches it happen, the moment it dawns on him exactly *which* extended education initiative she's talking about, and then the ghost of a smile creeps onto his face.

"I thought you were going by *mater*familias now," he says finally, and it takes Selah a split second to realize what he's talking about. Then she grins, and knows she's got him.

"One battle at a time."

Arran sits up now, too. He looks at her searchingly for a long moment, the green-gold eyes they share so like Dad's, set in a stranger's pale face so very different from her and Mima's. Then he says, "You know what I think?"

"What?"

"I think . . . that you're very high."

Selah nods, solemn. "That's true. But I'm also very serious."

They might have stayed like that, eyes boring into one another, until the plant took over again and another bout of laughter came bubbling up. But it's a loud clatter that breaks the moment, instead, followed by a stifled cry.

Both she and Arran instantly snap their attention up to the manor in the near distance.

Something is hanging out of a fourth-story window, and Selah's eyes narrow as she tries to focus on what it is. Then they go wide as she realizes. It's not some*thing*. It's some*one*.

"Savage Quiet," she whispers, and hears Arran beside her mutter, "What in the . . ."

She's already on her feet. Her brother shouts behind her as she races back up the hill toward Breakwater House, but she ignores him. Someone is about to fall out of a fourth-floor window. Someone in her familia, the one she's now responsible for. Never mind that it's three in the morning, she has to raise the alarm.

But then something happens that causes Selah to pull up short. Up at the manor, still a ways ahead, the person hanging from the window begins to scale their way down. She can't see precisely how from here, but whoever this person is seems to know exactly what hand and footholds to look for, and all too soon is landing neatly on the ground like a cat. A chill goes down Selah's spine. This was no accident. Perhaps they hadn't meant to fall, but they had definitely meant to exit through the window. And anyone who intentionally leaves through a fourth-floor window is almost certainly not meant to be there in the first place.

A light goes on in the first floor, and though the intruder is hooded and cloaked, Selah catches sight of a thin leather book clutched tightly under their arm.

She knows that book. She was running her fingers over it not even half an hour ago. Not the atlas, crumbling and delicate, but the other unknown tome, the one she hasn't opened yet, the other classified volume that Dad left behind in her care. The thief looks up, face still shrouded by their hood, locking in on Selah for a half beat before tearing off in the other direction toward the Hazards.

Oh, absolutely *not*.

Ignoring Arran's shouts of alarm, the new light now spilling from the manor out onto the dark lawn, she doesn't hesitate. She races after them—across the massive grounds, into the forest beyond.

It's another world in here. Dappled moonlight finds its way through the oaks and birches and maples above, casting an otherworldly glow on the forest floor beneath. Lungs pumping, Selah crashes through branches and over roots, her hooded quarry flickering every now and again into view up ahead. They've got good ground on her, but Selah knows the Hazards like the back of her hand. Every creek, every clearing, every break in the battered, healing earth. A childhood of playing in the shadow of these trees has taught her well. No man-made paths exist here, but she knows precisely what she's looking for as the thief ahead of her arcs a wide path around a deep ravine.

Abruptly Selah peels off to the right, focusing on nothing but the sound of her breath and the crushing darkness and the crunch of dead leaves underfoot, gathering speed until she races across the fallen oak over the gaping crack in the earth. And then she barrels straight into something solid. A body. The thief.

The two of them are sent tumbling down beneath the low branches, dirt and sticks flying and tangling in her hair. She comes to a rolling stop with an unpleasant *thud*, then looks wildly around as the thief scrambles back to their feet. Selah tries to follow suit, but trips over something lying in the underbrush and crashes back down hard, cutting her lip on her teeth. The book. The thief dropped it where they fell, and now the front leather cover lies open in the dirt and autumn leaves—except.

Except it's not a book at all.

Where pages should be glints instead an impossibly smooth rectangular stone of pure black, sleeker and shinier than any onyx or tourmaline. Selah stares at it for half a second, unsure of what she's looking at, exactly. But before she can do anything else, the thief's hands shoot out to snatch it back up. Their hood falls down around their shoulders, and Selah's heart catches somewhere in her throat.

Ocher-red hair grown out long, twisted back into thick ropes, wooden beads and glimpses of gold and blue flashing here and there. Stark black lines of keloid tattoo wrapping around lean, well-muscled arms. There's a scar over her left eyelid that, though faded, hadn't been there before. Five years older and five years rougher, yet Selah would know that face anywhere. It's the same one she sees every night when she closes her eyes.

She opens her mouth to call out her name, to tell her to wait, just to say anything at all. But her voice catches.

Tair—and it *is* Tair, beneath it all—gives her one last look. And is that panic? Regret? Or something else entirely? Then she hoists the hood back over her head and disappears once more into the dark woods.

III

MERIDIEM IN THE DROWNED CITY

All in all, we're doing shockingly well. Yuyan, that most excellent woman, has been holding out on me—after last year's fire season wrought such devastation, she sent the majority of the valuables to the Lhasa house, and has had it perpetually stocked and prepared to move in ever since. And myself not a word the wiser! The moment we saw the flames on the horizon, she had the servants hitch up the horses and off we two went, nothing on us but for a few coins and the clothes on our backs like the Caesarians of old. We likely won't return. Lhasa is lovely this time of year, and I really can't think of something I'd rather do less than face the headache of rebuilding again. You see, we've had word that the entire estate was razed to the ground. I do hope the servae thought to free the horses from the stables. How awful if they had burned.

—Translated excerpt from the private correspondence of Imperial Historian Dyan Kleios, sent from Consul Tzu Sulima of Roma Serica.

Dated 293 PQ.

Editor's Note: This letter is of particular historical interest, being the first known personal address to an Imperial Historian without the Iveroa name. For further reading on the scandal and political fallout of Dyan Iveroa and Martius Kleios's marriage—despite being two patres familia in their own right—see more from this author's text, *Suns and Swallows: The Scandalous Joining of Two Dynasties* (604 PQ).

Don't go down to the Sinktown-way.
If a crim catches you then there you'll stay.
They'll put you in a pot
And gobble you up hot
Stray too far and now you're lunch.

—CHILDREN'S RHYMING GAME, POPULAR IN LUXANA
AND SURROUNDING AGRICULTURAL VILLAGES C. 730 PQ

TAIR

Light spills in through green slatted shutters, piercing the cool darkness. It creeps in red over her eyelids until she has no choice but to open them, sore and spent and utterly exhausted as she is. Tair rolls over in her narrow bed with a groan, and right onto something that squishes beneath her with an odd crackle. Still not entirely awake, she reaches down to unearth an oat and raisin roll. Ibdi must have gone already, the absolute mother hen. Squinting into the stucco apartment's morning light from beneath Terra-twists hanging in front of her face, she tears off a chunk and frowns, the previous night flooding back in exhausted waves as sleep falls away.

Breakwater. The Hazards. *Selah.* Savage fucking Quiet, that wasn't supposed to happen. Running into Selah had always been a risk, but Tair had been certain she could remember her way around Breakwater well enough to avoid being seen. Only she had forgotten about the slightly longer drop down to the first foothold below the study window, and *that* is entirely on her. As is the very real possibility that the Publica will now be swarming the streets looking for her, stolen property in possession of more stolen property. Five years of distance and relative peace had lulled her into a dangerous sense of security, and now Tair might have to go underground again. Great.

Pushing the woven blanket away, she stuffs the rest of the roll into her mouth and grabs a pair of Ibdi's leggings off the floor. Scoops up the strange leather-bound stone slate and stuffs it into her bag. All this for a piece of rock.

The first message came in the middle of yesterday afternoon, delivered through a little boy she sometimes sees at the Sisters' free breakfast. When she'd asked him who had sent it, he'd just shrugged and said, "Some lady." Well, whoever *some lady* was, the message in the note was clear:

I know who you are. Bring me the Iveroa Stone, or I will expose you as a fugitive, a terrorist, and a runaway.

There had been more to it than that. What, exactly, an Iveroa
Stone even looked like and where it probably was. Details from Tair's
own life—how she had left Breakwater, and the people who helped
her do it—things a stranger couldn't possibly know. And, of course,
the threat of exactly what would happen if she were to ignore her instructions.

The second message had been verbal. Egeria from across the way
had flagged her down as she was arriving home after dark. "Some
man wanted me to tell you to 'do it tonight'? And that he'll meet you
in a week."

"A *man*?"

A shrug. "Could've been thremid. They said you'd understand."
Then, with a suggestive sort of smirk, "Tair, what *are* you up to?"

Truth be told, she has no idea. She just knows that the moment
she's exposed, the Sisters of the First go down with her. And there
isn't a chance in the Quiet she's about to let that happen.

Dawn broke hours ago, she realizes, stepping out onto the ledged
pathway three precarious levels high over the Kirnaval's main thrust.
She's slept in way too late. Down the uneven stairs, then, where she
hops over a pile of waste and shouts a greeting over the canal to Egeria
and Wes and Iris, sharing in a final cigarette before they head off to
bed. The prostitutes, friendly as always, wave a hello back before Tair
joins the throng, her cruiseboard gliding easily through the packed
towpath, eyes on the alert for telltale uniforms of black or green.

But the Publica haven't bothered with the Kirnaval yet this morning. They'll be here later, with their bullshit reasons to stop-check and
arrest whoever they like. They've never left the slums alone before,
but lately it's just getting out of hand.

Diluvoside, they call it. Sinktown. No broad avenues of white
limestone here, no cobblestones or even the packed-down dirt and
straw of Paleaside and the Third Ward. No, the Kirnaval flooded a
long time ago—that, or its denizens were left with no choice but to
build out into the bay. No one can really remember which came first.
Levels on levels of once-colorful wood and stucco, built up precariously high over crumbling jetties and waterways, and with each storm
and hurricane sinking steadily deeper into the Sargasso Sea. Home to

countless thousands, the low-class rabble. A district to be set aside and ignored, only to be bothered with when one of them steps out of line. It's a good place to disappear. A good place to become someone else entirely.

With a well-practiced grace, she maneuvers her board through the crowd. It's a deliberate, if not obvious, zigzagging pattern, making it difficult for any plainclothes Cohort who might be following to keep track of her for very long amidst the colors and shouts, the narrow bridges and canal-side alleys, the press of bodies and the smell of salt and manure and crispy fried smelt. This was one of the first things Ibdi taught her, back at the start. It's come in handy any number of times since then. The Sisters of the First aren't criminals, and their work isn't outside the law. That doesn't mean the Cohorts are fond of them, exactly.

Up the side path and around the corner, across the cement bridge to the small plaza where old men play chess and stallholders shove dead fish and squares of hemp at passing barges and pedestrians, then down a narrow flight of steps into another alleyway as she stops on her rounds. To the children's home to pick up Oyeli's practice universitas entrance exams. To the apartment shared by Elissa Stinam and her rowdy gang of siblings, to make sure the poppam fever hasn't taken a turn for the worse. And finally, at the very end of Naqvi Row, to the cramped, unassuming headquarters of the Sisters of the First.

"Got your beauty sleep in all right?" Ibdi needles her, plump olive arms spooning out helpings from a vat of baked beans when Tair arrives at their side, nudging a place for herself amongst the other morning volunteers. Tair piles some beans and two seaweed dappham onto a plate, hands it to the preteen boy who's next in line. Then she turns and punches Ibdi in the arm, hard.

"Why didn't you wake me up? I was late for rounds."

They shrug, handing over another plate. "Revenge, mima."

"Revenge."

"Yeah. You didn't invite me with wherever you went last night—*Hey,*" they bark out suddenly across the long buffet table, dangerously brandishing a ladle. "You two better not be. Put those in your mouth or get out and stop wasting my food."

A boy and girl, no older than nine, look over guiltily from where they've been pelting beans at one another, and promptly begin eating them instead. The round table where they sit is one of about ten cramped inside the first-floor community center, every one of them packed with kids. Elementary-level children mostly, but here and there a few older teens who can prove they haven't dropped out of school yet.

Smirking at the pair of troublemakers, Tair flicks a bean in Ibdi's face and says, "I'll make it up to you. Tomorrow. Flip night at the Bitter End. I'll buy."

"Bet?"

"Believe."

"Tair."

Artemide Ekagara stands in the entrance to the stairway, arms crossed over his broad chest. The chairman's hair and beard are more salt than pepper these days, but his black, unwrinkled face gives him an ethereal, almost ageless quality.

"Morning, Art," she says, and he tilts his head slightly, beckoning her to follow. She looks at Ibdi for some kind of hint, but they only shrug. So she flicks another bean at them and follows Artemide up the stairs to his third-floor office.

There's a kettle steaming away in the corner, and Tair perches on one of the rickety wooden chairs crammed into the office as he pours a mug of tazine for each of them. Tair breathes in the warm spices as Art takes a long sip, then gets down to business.

"So. The Watchers."

Ugh.

"What about them?"

"Don't give me that," he says, leaning against his desk. "Jinni needs you."

"Jinni doesn't *need* anyone. She's frighteningly self-sufficient."

"Tair."

"I told you already I don't want to. I'm happy in Education."

"It doesn't matter what you *want*," he tells her, and it's not harsh. Just true. "It matters where you're needed. And it's done, so enough

with the face. You've done a lot to turn the Education Corps around—
we've more than doubled our retention rate since you joined. But let's
face it—you're not the most patient teacher, and the Watchers is where
you can do the most good."

"So why didn't you put me on there to start?" she asks, feeling
disgruntled and more than a little ornery. Maybe he's right, maybe
the Watchers *is* where she can do the most good, but being reassigned
to them will put her out in the open, dangerously exposed.

"Don't be cute. You were holding out on us and you know it.
Quiet only knows why. You told us you could read, but you didn't say
a thing about calculus. Or history. Or politics and rhetoric and law.
That came later."

Tair flushes, because it's true. She's never told the Sisters where she
comes from—but, to be fair, they haven't asked. It was enough for
them to know that she was running from something, that she needed
anonymity and protection, and eventually came to believe in their
work enough to join them in it. Guilty as she feels knowing that Ibdi
and Artemide and the rest are clearly under the impression she was
fleeing an abusive home life, Tair can never tell them the truth. It
doesn't matter that they've laughed and eaten and mourned and
worked together for years. It doesn't matter that she and Ibdi share an
apartment. In fact, it makes it all the worse. To knowingly harbor a
fuga would put their life's work at stake, never mind their liberty.

It's why she didn't tell them at the start, knowing they would have
turned her away. It's why they can never find out.

Which is exactly how she's found herself over the last month in
this ongoing argument with Artemide over joining the Watchers—an
arm of the Sisters she can't deny suits her perfectly, gives her the
chance to use her mind in ways far beyond tutoring schoolchildren.
There's great value in that, of course, but he's right—she doesn't have
the temperament for it. Half the time she wants to strangle her students, unable to see how they could miss what's so clearly in front of
their eyes. Gil used to call her a prodigy, and Tair had taken pride in
that. She knows better now. People only call you that so you're stuck
living up to their expectations.

But the Watchers turn the tables. They're accountability in action. Most advocates won't touch the people the Watchers work with—plebs skimming either side of the poverty line, the lost causes. But citizens are allowed to represent themselves in the courts, and *that's* the loophole that the Watchers work within. Preparing defendants to defend themselves. It's rare, practically unheard of, for someone to actually manage to get themselves free and clear, but the Watchers ensure that they at least don't go down without a fight. They arm their charges with the facts and the words they need to make it clear to anyone with one working ear and half a brain that no justice is being served that day. They stand watch in the background during court proceedings, reminding the magistrate that they're there. They have seen everything. And they will remember.

Of course, there's more to it than that, or Tair would jump at the chance to join. The problem is street patrol. The Watchers aren't just legal aid. They offer lessons in self-defense, and they go out in shifts, every day and every night, ready to stand witness to Publica brutality and raise Quietfury in the district prefect's office whenever an officer gets overenthusiastic. That's the part that worries her.

In Education Corps, at least, she can stay safely out of sight.

"I—" she says, then stops. How to spin this in a way that isn't a lie, exactly, but could be something that Artemide will accept? "I can't—" she tries again, and he raises a brow. "You're right. It's a good place for me. And anyway, I lied before. I'd like to be a Watcher. But I *can't*."

"And why's that?" he asks, draining the last of his tazine.

She stares down at her own mug, little motes of resin and spice swirling to the top. "Someone in the courts," she says finally. "They'd know me."

This is the truth, in a technical sense. Whether the magistrate who sentenced her is still active in the courts system, she doesn't know. Nor would she be willing to place so much as one ceres on him remembering her face in particular amongst the countless other vernae lives he's undoubtedly ruined. But such a public-facing role as the Watchers has the potential to put her in direct contact with any number of people who *would* know her. And if it makes sense to Artemide to assume that it's a specter from her past who would drag her back into the mire of her old life, well. He's not wrong about that.

He takes this in, regarding her as he leans back slightly onto the desk, one hand on his gray-flecked beard.

"I remember the day Ibdi brought you into the clinic," he says at last. "Half-starved, living on pigeons and rats. Shit fully kicked out of you."

"More like fully covered in shit."

They hadn't been kind, those two months before Ibdi had quite literally tripped over her, exhausted, tucked into the alley behind a bakery, trying to steal a moment's sleep. The Kirnaval hadn't been the obvious place to disappear, not at first. But weeks of looking for work in Seven Dials and Paleaside and the Regio Marina had only resulted in closed doors and pitying looks. It wasn't long before she was sleeping in gutters, avoiding both Publica patrols and Egeria's comments whenever she passed the brothel that *it isn't that bad a job, really*, and all the while trying not to think that maybe she had made a huge mistake.

"My point is, I don't know that girl anymore," says Artemide. "She's not in this room, anyway. She didn't speak her mind as freely as you do. She didn't *fight* like you do, that's for damn sure. You've worked hard and given over a lot to become the person you are now. But all this time it's been clear to me you were never running toward something. You've been running away."

He stands, and crosses around to the other side of his desk. "You can't run from shadows forever, Tair. You're no good to anyone if you don't turn and face whatever's haunting you at some point. No good to yourself, and definitely no good to us. I know I don't need to remind you of all people that we're not a charity. You're only as good as what you can give back."

The finality in his voice leaves no room for argument, and she keeps silent, eyes fixed on the darkened spot of stucco to the left behind Artemide's head as he rummages through sheaves of paperwork. There's nothing *to* say, not without edging closer to the truth, and for Tair that's just not an option.

"Here," he says at last, and hands her the folder he's been looking for. "Give this to Pio. It's for his Ontiveros case, the Seven Dials girl. Tell Jinni I sent you." And, off her mutinous glare—"Cheer up. She won't put you out in the field, not right away. Not until you're ready."

The Watchers may not be doing anything illegal, technically, but they *are* the arm of the Sisters that verges closest to what the Cohorts would consider criminal activity. As such, they keep their headquarters separate from the rest. Better to be safe, in the event of a raid.

The sun has nearly reached its high point in the clear blue sky when Tair steps back out onto the jetty, and the normally crowded bustle of the Kirnaval has thinned out accordingly, its denizens retreating into the cool respite of their homes and shops for the crushing, dangerous heat of meridiem. Sticking close to building walls to escape the searing sun, she cruises her board quickly down the cement towpaths and back across the plaza, uneasy thoughts guiding her way.

Tair turns the corner to a side alley and doesn't notice the enormous man heading her way. Not until she's skated directly into him, barely catching herself before she ends up eating the bite of hard grit cement.

"*Oof*—Terra, sorry." Then she notices who it is exactly she's crashed into, and with considerably less empathy says, "Oh. Hi. Bye."

Without missing a step, Pa'akal Zetnes leans a massive arm against the wall, neatly blocking her way. She glances up at all near-seven feet of him, then tries to go around the other side. He blocks that way, too.

"What?" she snaps, any remaining pretense of niceties gone.

"Boss wants to see you," says Pa'akal, and Tair's laugh is hollow.

"Maybe you missed this while you were busy flexing in the mirror, but I don't work for her anymore."

He shrugs, unbothered, acknowledging the truth of it. Pa'akal isn't the type to exert himself unnecessarily, she knows this. Not the kind of man to be cruel or get angry without good reason. Still, he's dangerous, so when he reaches to close a hand around Tair's arm—and whether it's to frog-march her out to wherever the Revenants are hiding these days or to throw her over his shoulder like a sack of potatoes, she neither knows nor cares—she moves on pure instinct.

There's a combat knife a hair's breadth from his groin before he's so much as shifted weight. Pa'akal may be bigger—an understatement, if ever there was one—but she's faster, and she knows how to use that to her advantage. Glancing down, he grins, and doesn't attempt to conceal a hint of pride. Theo taught her well, once upon a time.

"Fair enough," he says, and releases her arm. "But for old time's sake—why go home?"

So they know. Of course they know. It's the only logical reason for Pa'akal to be here now, bothering with her for the first time since she joined the Sisters. Perhaps some small part of her had hoped they had written her off, but even in thinking it Tair knows it doesn't work that way. She owes Griff her freedom. No doubt the Revenants have had tabs on her since the moment she left them, one eye on her as she begged and starved and lived on the streets until Terra sent Ibdi her way. Biding their time, waiting for the moment she became useful to them again. Or got in their way.

The high noon sun beats mercilessly down on the both of them, sweat gathering in Tair's palms as she grips her knife all the more tightly.

"It's not my home," she tells him, ignoring the question.

"Not anymore, maybe, but it was," he says, not remotely bothered by the large blade edging closer to his valuables. "Maybe you were feeling nostalgic. Felt like taking a trip down memory lane. Thought maybe, for the right price, you could go back. Have your comfy rooms and nice books again and all that."

Tair blinks up at him, and has to resist the urge to laugh. So they know she was at Breakwater last night. They know that much, but they've clearly misinterpreted the reason why. They have no idea what she was really there to do—and Terra, how *easy* it had been. She'd fully expected to have to tear the room apart, but the Iveroa Stone was just sitting there on the Historian's desk like it was waiting for her all that time. So the Revenants have no idea. Savage Quiet, they probably have no idea what an Iveroa Stone even is. *She* certainly doesn't. All they know is that she's capable of telling Selah—and, maybe more alarmingly for them, Senator Kleios—plenty of information that would bring their little revolution to a swift and decisive end.

Like Tair would ever be petty enough to risk her freedom for that.

She returns her knife to its sheath, concealed in the inner pocket of her coat. "If Griff has questions for me," she says, "she can come and ask me herself. She's not a queen. Not yet, anyway." And with that, she pushes past him and cruises on.

DARIUS

There's a pressure point in his temple that's been threatening to turn into a headache for what feels like a week, though it's really only been since he woke up.

Quiet-cursed Naevia Kleios, he thinks, and not for the first time today.

"Have fun last night?" asks Claudia Oha, and he winces at the *thud* when she drops a stack of files on his desk. He gets the distinct impression she's done it on purpose.

"Oodles. What's this?"

"A list of every merchant in the city authorized to sell water hemlock, blueprints of the Imperial Archives, and an invoice for reparations on a morning of my life that I will never get back."

"If you want a raise for doing the bare minimum of your job, take it up with the Chief."

It's not his fault Agent Oha is still a junior grunt, and not a very good one at that. He knows her gripes well enough, taking orders from someone a decade her junior with a name she considers beneath her. They aren't his problem. His attention's needed on the case in front of him instead, tracking down the Revenants, not least because it's their mandate from Consul Palmar. But while Darius isn't averse to the idea of being the one to finally eradicate a centuries-old terrorist cell, there's something about the case that doesn't sit right with him.

Alexander Kleios was murdered, there's no disputing that, but it's the *manner* in which he was murdered that presents more questions than answers. Why use parcae, a notoriously slow-acting poison distilled from water hemlock, when a blade to the throat could have ended things so much more efficiently? The only conclusion: The assassin wanted to draw it out. Wanted him to suffer. Wanted him to *know* that he was dying.

The methodology, the bizarre and savage blood ritual left behind at the scene . . . all of this, when combined with the simple fact that there's no obvious motive, points to an incentive more personal than political. Not assassination, but murder.

And now there's Naevia Kleios.

It's a distasteful thought, one that Darius hadn't wanted to entertain. It goes against every belief he holds, everything he knows about duty to familia and to the Imperium at large. But Naevia Kleios had wanted to know where the investigation was taking them without the Chief General knowing, and Darius can't quiet the voice in the back of his mind that wonders if there's more to it than the simple nagging curiosity of a widow who's suffered a terrible shock.

He has no idea how to broach this with Kopitar. The idea is horrendous. It leaves a disgusting taste in his mouth. It's far from the behavior of a patrician lady. But then again, Naevia Dya'ogo Kleios is hardly *really* Sargassan.

Claudia coughs. He looks up from his desk.

"Was there something else?"

"Yes." She turns back toward the door. "Tiago-Laith's husband is back in the city. Stakeout clocked him entering his apartment this morning. Kopitar said for you to meet him out front."

"When?"

She glances at the clock. "Five minutes ago."

Cunt.

Leks Tiago-Laith is handsome in a generic kind of way, soft brown hair and a self-deprecating smile. The sort of extremely tall man who seems perpetually confused by his own height. Or has, at the very least, shrunk back into himself at the sight of two Intelligentia agents standing in his tastefully furnished, if rather small, Ecclesmur apartment. Darius glimpses a corner of the made-up bed through a door to the bedroom, and quickly looks away.

That bed. The matching set of blue ceramic mugs. The wedding sketch framed in pride of place. Darius's skin itches.

The man's husband Avis, he remembers, had been slight. Nervous. A junior undersecretary in the Ministerium of Records, just the kind of easily ignored paper-pusher who makes the perfect mole. Except, of course, that he'd fed the Intelligentia bad information, that day of the hurricane two weeks ago, sending them to the Senate instead of the Archives where they might have prevented this murder happening at all. Tiago-Laith himself had been found rotting in a back alley three days later, taking with him the mystery of where his loyalties really lay.

"I've got no idea where he is," Leks is saying now, hands shaking slightly as he busies himself with the kettle of tazine. "When he didn't come home . . . I figured that was it, he'd finally left me. Suspected for a while Avis was seeing someone else, but I thought he'd at least give me the chance to *fight* for us."

"So you had to get out of the city for a time." Kopitar nods along. "Cool off, clear your head, that sort of thing?"

"Yeah. Went to see my sister . . . Is Avis in trouble?"

"Why don't you just answer a few more questions," Darius cuts in, and tries not to let the man's fingers touch his as he accepts a cup of tazine. Kopitar wants names, locations, any trail that might lead them to the Revenants now that their informant's too dead to do it himself. Darius, for his own part, just wants to get the Quiet out of here. "You thought he was having an affair," he goes on. "Has he been unfaithful before?"

Tiago-Laith shakes his head, but there's a growing frown on his face despite his nerves. "No," he says. "But we weren't . . . happy. Terra, that's the cliché, isn't it? Stressed about—well, everything, really. Money. Work. He'd been passed over for promotion at Records twice and, well . . . I mean, actors don't make much money even when we're working."

He pauses, a little embarrassed. "I don't know, it just got to be that we were snapping at each other all the time. Hadn't, you know, really . . . *been* with each other in months. And then he started staying out all the time, not coming home after work. It seemed pretty obvious to me at that point that Avis had gone and tried to find happiness with someone else, because Terra knows he wasn't finding it with me."

Darius glances at Kopitar, who gives the most imperceptible shake of the head. He's inclined to agree. The man's too skittish, too earnest, wears his thoughts too openly on his face. Darius can't help but hope he's never subjected to a play in which Leks Tiago-Laith is performing. In any case, it seems unlikely he knows that his husband is dead. Or that Avis was a double agent in the employ of both the Revenants and the Intelligentia. That doesn't mean he can't still be useful.

"Did you ever ask him about it? Did he ever make excuses, give reasons for why he was staying out so much?"

Tiago-Laith shrugs, clearly bewildered by the line of questioning but not withholding. People rarely are, when faced with the Intelligentia uniform. "The sort of thing you'd expect, I guess. He had to work late, he was meeting up with some friends—"

"What friends?"

"Coworkers, mainly. Sometimes he said he was going to Neptune's Folly, but I know that was a lie. Showed up to surprise him once, when I still thought I could save our marriage, only he wasn't there."

"Neptune's Folly?"

"Bar down by the docks. It's an absolute dive, but *Terra*, their deep-fried clams. We found it on our third date."

Kopitar tears a piece of paper from his notebook, sets it on the table. "Where else?"

"Shouldn't we have told him his husband's dead?" Darius asks fifteen minutes later, when they step back out onto the streets of the exasperatingly aspirational Ecclesmur neighborhood and, for the first time in half an hour, he feels like he can breathe.

"No," Kopitar answers, taking the reins of his horse from the waiting attendant. "A fresh widower's a liability, and we may need to question him again. We need his thoughts as clear as possible, not mired and unfocused by grief."

"Not to mention," Darius says, sweeping his gaze across the street, "he could be a better actor than he wants us to believe. Might run to warn his Rev friends the second we're gone."

Kopitar swings his leg over the horse. "Good thinking. Put two plainclothes agents on this apartment day and night. In the meantime, start knocking on doors."

"Sir?"

"Every establishment Tiago-Laith mentioned. We'll sniff out the Revs, one way or another."

It's a good plan. A solid lead. Despite himself, Darius hesitates anyway.

"What is it, Miranda?"

He wasn't going to tell him. He'd decided that last night, after he'd extracted himself from Naevia Kleios and found his superior again in the crowd. He wasn't going to say anything. If Kopitar and she really did go as far back as the senator suggested, there was no point in sullying the Chief General's good opinion of her. Not when the matter had been so thoroughly laid to rest. Not when Kopitar has been such an important mentor to him for going on ten years and doesn't deserve unnecessary suspicion planted in his mind as thanks.

And yet.

There's that voice again. The one in the back of his mind that won't stay quiet. The one that says there is a *reason* why Darius has managed to work his way into the office he has, and that it's only halfway to do with hard work and duty. Those can be learned. But a sense for danger, a nose for when something's out of place? That's sheer instinct. It can't be taught. And what he smells right now is *rancid*.

So he says, low, "I may have a different lead."

The furrow of Kopitar's brow divots hard. "And you're only mentioning this now?"

"The lead only showed up last night. And I wanted to be sure. . . . It's delicate." Darius swings his leg over his own horse, a roan beauty he's become particularly fond of from the Intelligentia stables. He places a hand to the beast's neck, as though he might subsume her quiet strength, and presses on. "Senator Kleios made a request last night. She asked me to report on the details of this case. What leads we're pursuing. She asked me to keep it from you."

If he'd expected shock, he doesn't get it. Not shock, nor outrage, nor the sort of blank stare he might have anticipated at the news of such an underhanded move. Instead, Kopitar actually *laughs*.

It's short, practically a bark, but unmistakable. Kopitar shakes his head in baffling amusement, strong jaw dimpling in a rueful grin. "I presume you turned her down."

"Of course. I would never—"

"That's what I've always liked about you, Miranda," he says, and doesn't bother keeping his voice down. "I'm surprised it took her so long, to be honest. Naevia's office knows better by now than to test the loyalty of my men. You, though, you were a new and unknown variable. I'm sure she was thrilled at the prospect of making you her creature. Oh, no, but you've got *integrity*. Good man."

"But," Darius insists, because the Chief clearly doesn't understand the real weight of what he's just said, "if she's asking for intel on *this* case, specifically, then don't you think it's at least worth taking a closer look—"

"Her husband's died, man, of course she has an interest."

"Or she wants to stay a step ahead of us."

A long moment passes then, and Kopitar isn't laughing anymore. "I hope," he says at last, "that you aren't implying what I think you are."

Darius takes the Chief's horse's bridle in hand, as if the act alone could impress upon him how very serious he is. "Alexander Kleios was poisoned," he says, low again. "Parcae. That's intimate. Planned. A person needs *access* for that. And yes, of course, the Revs hardly need a reason for their senseless chaos, but isn't it at least worth *considering* a personal motive?" He breathes in hard. "I'm not suggesting the senator herself is at fault, but she could be protecting someone. Making sure we stay off the scent. Even if it's only to protect her familia's reputation. A disgruntled client, maybe, or the Historian's verna bastard—for Terra's sake, her own daughter gained—"

"Enough."

It's glacial. A hiss. And for the first time in the ten years he's known him, one look in Kopitar's eyes and Darius's blood runs cold.

"That is enough," Kopitar says again, hand clenched around the roan mare's bridle now, so close Darius can feel his breath on his cheek. "I like you, Deputy, so I'll forget about it this once. But if I ever hear so much as a *whisper* of you slandering a good familia's name again—never mind that of the *Imperial Historian*—I swear I'll have you packed up and shipped back to that hovel in Ithaca so fast you won't even have a chance to dismount your horse."

He releases the bridle.

Darius sits frozen in place, heart pounding furious against his chest. Casework and common sense has never been met with this sort of ice-cold stone wall before. It goes against everything he's ever known. And Ithaca . . . his lucid mind can barely comprehend the threat as real. Kopitar has never once spoken to him like this.

"Consul Palmar wants us to focus our attentions on the Revenants," the Chief General goes on then, easy, like nothing of the last minute happened at all, "and I'm inclined to agree. Start knocking on those doors, Deputy. We're on their tail now."

SELAH

It takes her the better part of the morning, but Selah finally slips free of her overbearing new sentry Linet, blending seamlessly into the crowd of the Universitas District as she hurries along. Three days she's been trying to shake off Linet, and three days Linet's been shadowing her on Mima's orders like an overenthusiastic guard dog.

She understands her mother's worry—Dad's dead, and no one wants Selah to be next. More likely, no one wants her to get any ideas and go looking for his murderer herself. She'd be flattered, if she weren't so insulted. Even Selah can admit that she's impulsive, but she isn't stupid enough to think she can take on a dangerous crim like that all by herself. That's what the Intelligentia are for. Unfortunately, having Linet as a second shadow hasn't exactly been conducive to the sudden and alarming fact of Tair's reappearance.

So it takes her three days and the better part of a morning, actually, but she's finally broken free. She had been in her new office, high at the top floor of the Archives, elbow deep in backed-up access petitions from various research groups and all the while completely distracted by archaic atlases and stolen black slates and *TairTairTair* when the thought occurred. Her sentry, after all, had stayed out in the hall guarding the door. And her sentry, after all, was too new to know about the secret passage, the one with a private attollo running directly from her office all the way down to the basement stacks. So it's only with a tiny stab of guilt for abandoning her work that Selah turns toward the Scholar's Gate, the sun on her face and a bag jostling against her hip, and for a moment she could be any other student rushing off to her next class. Only she's not. She has an altogether different mission, and access petitions can wait.

Because it *had* been Tair in the forest, she's sure of it. Tair who had taken the strange stone tablet from the manor, the *classified* one that Dad had left expressly for Gil to put in Selah's care. Tair who had disappeared again into the night. Tair who hadn't offered so much as a word of greeting or explanation for where she's been all these years.

Selah hasn't told a soul. Not even Arran or Gil. And honestly, she struggled with that. It would be easy enough. One word from Mima— one word from *her*, she realizes with a jolt—and the Cohort would be deployed to every corner of the province, the full weight of the Publica searching streets and homes and tabernas and wagons. An all-out circus that Selah's sure would do nothing but drive Tair even deeper into hiding, and then she'd lose her for good.

No, much better to search her out herself.

A moment's hesitation at the Scholar's Gate, and she turns eastward toward the sea. Not up to the broad paved limestone boulevards of the Arborem or the soft sand beaches of the Boardwalk, but south. Down to the tang of brine and the song of a hundred different languages flying through the salty sea air as sailors and travelers from every corner of the world hustle to and fro down the cobblestone streets. Or so Selah imagines. She's never actually been to the Regio Marina before. But at the intersection of so many voyagers coming and going, she feels confident it's a good place to start looking for someone who doesn't want to be found.

She smells it before she sees it, and the moment Selah steps foot through the Sailor's Gate, she knows she's miscalculated. The streets here are cramped and crowded, and she finds herself overwhelmed by the drudgery and sheer *normality* of it all.

People with lined, weather-beaten faces carrying on conversations in booming voices more like barks. A sweat-stained laborer who stops shifting blocks of debris to wipe his brow, only to catch her staring and shoot her a wink. Selah practically jumps out of the way as a group of girls around her own age burst into shrieks of delight. Clacking her teeth, a new determination sweeps over her. She's being stupid. People are people. She can talk to anyone she wants.

Only they don't seem to want to talk to her. A bowed and ancient crone sweeping her front stoop waves her off impatiently when she approaches, as do a pair of crabbers loading wooden crates into a cart. The clerk at the harbormaster's office listens for a moment or two, but soon grows impatient when Selah refuses to provide him with a name.

"I deal in *records*, not faces," he finally snaps after five minutes of her increasingly desperate descriptions of Tair, turning pointedly to the man behind her in line. "Next!"

By the time the sun sinks behind the city's western skyline, Selah is hot and frazzled and dusty and so, so tired. She's taken a winding route with no real sense of direction other than toward the next semi-friendly face, so that by the time she thinks to look around and get a sense of her bearings, she realizes with a thrill of dread that she has no idea where she is.

All sounds and bustle of the nearby harbor are gone, and somewhere deep in her heart Selah knows she's strayed far from the Regio Marina and into the unknown heart of the city. Towering rows of faded stucco built steep on top of each other line the dark, cramped street, the smell of brine and salt joined by manure and some spice blend she can't quite place. Here and there, lights twinkle from the tall buildings with an air of vague foreboding as twilight descends.

Shivering in spite of the warm October evening, Selah stops and looks up. The sky is vaguely lighter up ahead and to the right, indicating the western inland. If she wants to return home before nightfall, she'll have to turn around and zigzag back northeastward. But how could she even think of returning now? Her search for Tair has led to nowhere, but she may never get another chance at this.

A slew of abrupt shouting wrenches her from her thoughts. A small squabbling knot of people gathered a short distance down the street, spilling out onto the cement in a flurry so fierce that Selah thinks at first she must be watching a taberna fight gone out of hand, and instinctively she presses herself against the stucco, into the shadow of the high wall. But then, through the gathering dark, she can make out several men and women clad in the telltale green uniform of the Cohort Publica. She edges along the wall to get a closer look, only to stop short when she realizes what she's actually seeing.

A man—a boy, really—curled up on the ground, legs tucked up in the fetal position and arms clutched protectively over his head in a feeble attempt to stave off the officers' blows. This is no fight. It's a beating.

On instinct, she scrabbles in her bag for her patent of identity. It isn't there, she realizes with a jolt. Linet was carrying her wallet.

"Stop!" Selah shouts anyway, struck with horror, pushing herself out from the shadows before she can think twice about it. She does not care that there are four of them and one of her, or that she's short and bony. All that seems to exist in the world are the young man's cries and the satisfaction on the officers' faces. "*Stop it,*" she shouts again, reaching out to grab for an officer's club. "Can't you see he's just a kid?"

Suddenly her wrist is caught in a bruising grip, and the hand it belongs to *twists*. Selah lets out a yelp, and then she's being thrown back against curb and pain is searing through her ankle, caught beneath her falling weight.

She can't stand, but she's desperate for them to stop, for someone else to help. Someone stronger. Where *is* everyone? As soon as the Publica had descended, the few pedestrians out and about on the winding street had melted away as swift as daylight. She's the only chance the poor boy on the ground has, injured as she is. Gritting her teeth, she forces herself to her feet, but—

"Marcus Croziar, as I live and breathe."

The officers stop, and so does Selah. Back up the way she came stands a small throng of people, fifteen or so in all. Men and women, stone-faced, all carrying the same kind of wooden staff ready in their hands or strapped against their backs. At their front stands a well-muscled, heavy-set woman with a paunchy, moon-pale face and hair buzzed down to the scalp. Authority in her stance and grim determination in that of her followers, and Selah knows on some animal instinct that their being here is no accident. On the ground, the young man moans in pain.

One of the officers, a red-faced man, stiffens at the sight of them. "Keep it moving, Jordan. This is Publica business."

The woman called Jordan makes no move to leave. She casually flips her staff over her shoulders instead. "I'd never interfere with

Publica business, Marky. We just missed having you around, is all, wanted to give you a proper Kirnaval welcome back. How're the ribs?"

"How dare you presume to—"

Jordan flips her staff back into the offensive position with such speed and vigor that the man called Croziar jumps directly into the officer behind him.

"Go on, don't let me stop you. How dare I presume to what now?" she asks, mild, though the smile has now vanished from her face. Croziar opens his mouth, then closes it.

"Imagine," Jordan says. "Being afraid of a little walking stick." Some of the others behind her shift to hold their staffs with just the slightest bit more conviction. Preparing.

Finally finding his tongue, Croziar mutters, "Come on, we're leaving."

Jaw working furiously, he bends down to peel the young man off the cobblestones, but a sharp tap of Jordan's staff against cement stops them short. "I don't think so," she says quietly. "He needs a medic. We'll take him off your hands."

Croziar glares at her a moment longer, before dropping the man unceremoniously back to the ground and disappearing with his squad into the night.

In a moment, the group is upon the boy, checking him over to see what's broken, to work out where they can grip him that's likely to do the least additional damage. Selah tries to take a step forward, but collapses again. This time, a pair of strong arms break the fall. She glances up, and finds herself face to face with Jordan.

"Hi there," says the older woman. Her voice is lighter now, more genuine in its low-caste patois, but there's still a brusqueness to it that Selah suspects never quite fades. "I'm Jinni Jordan. Who are you?"

Selah gapes, then says, "Se—Theodora," because it's the first name that comes to her mind. It's a good cover, she thinks. A good person to emulate here. Someone who knows both worlds. "How did you *do* that? Make them leave."

"Oh, that wasn't anything. Marky and I've got history," says Jinni

Jordan, helping Selah to sit down on the curbside. "He knows better than to challenge the Watchers anymore. What *you* did, on the other hand, was very brave. Stupid, but brave."

"They were going to kill him. They were *enjoying* it. What did he even do?"

Jinni laughs, though it comes out more like a bark. "Hard to say," she says with a hard half-smile. "Could've stolen some food. Could've looked at one of them wrong. Could be he just fits the profile. But he's definitely guilty, best believe that. Guilty of living in the Kirnaval."

And Selah feels the blood drain from her face, suddenly remembering Jinni's words from before. *A proper Kirnaval welcome.*

"We're—" she starts, then licks her lips, aware that they're suddenly very dry. "We're in *Sinktown*?"

"Yeah, the part that ain't sunk yet. You didn't know?"

"No. I'm . . . I think I took a wrong turn . . ."

She's heard stories of the Kirnaval, of course, along with the sorts of crims and degenerate savages that make their home there. Rapists and poppam addicts and child-eaters. Only now that she's here, there doesn't seem to be anything particularly frightening about the place at all. Nothing beyond the disturbing actions of the Cohort Publica, at any rate, and the stories never mentioned *them*. She's seen them in action before, of course she has, doing what they have to do to keep the peace. But never without a reason. Never like this.

Abruptly she becomes aware of Jinni's curious eyes on her, and nods toward the staff-wielders—Watchers, did she say?—carrying the bruised and bleeding boy up the street. "Where are they taking him?"

"The Sisters have a clinic nearby. We'll take care of him."

Selah hasn't got the first idea who the Sisters are, but this seems reasonable enough.

"Now you, Theodora," Jinni continues, suddenly all business. "You took a wrong turn, and now you're lost in the Kirnaval with a bum ankle. Are we taking you to the clinic, too, or is there somewhere else you best be?"

Selah hesitates. But Jinni Jordan, hard and prickly and low-caste, is also the most helpful person she's met all day. "Well, I *was* looking for my sister," she says, latching back onto the lie she's been peddling. Tair is lighter than she is, with ruddy clay hair and oddly contrasting freckles covering her face, but they've still been taken for siblings more often than she and Arran ever have. And it's an easier story than the truth. "I don't even know if she's in this district. She's been gone a long time."

"Try me out," says Jinni. "These parts are a haven for runaways, and I got a knack for remembering names."

"Tair. Her name's Tair."

ARRAN

Selah's missing, and Arran's not sure what the worst part about that is.

It might have been the moment Linet came to tell him that Selah had disappeared from her office, and the floor dropped out from under him. It might have been her once-stoic face, now a wild mix of worry and insistence and fear, as she begged him in quiet tones not to tell Naevia just yet, to please just give her a few hours, she can bring Selah back.

"My children," she had said, not looking at him. "They're at the Institute Civitatem."

So maybe the worst part is how quickly the words "Yes, of course" and "I'll help" had come tumbling out of his mouth. Or maybe it might be knowing his sister too well, knowing that Selah probably just gave her guard the slip, and is running around the city on a lark with no idea or care for the alarm she's caused.

It might be the possibility that she isn't.

Whoever killed Dad left no demands. No credo. Not even a message claiming credit after the fact. Just some arcane blood ritual whose meaning is either lost to the Quiet or just too obscure for the average Sargassan to make sense of. So until they know who the assassin is and what they want, Selah is always going to be in danger. And now she's missing, and the weight of a small boulder seems to have taken up residence at the pit of Arran's stomach, the tight alarm of his lungs threatening a panic attack at any moment.

It's ridiculous, the guilt. The churning of his stomach that says he should have gone after Dad's killer himself. There are no leads, nothing from the Intelligentia aside from the predictable announcement that the Revenants are suspect number one. No obvious clue where to start. Still, it's there, something angry rising in his gut the other night, as he stood behind Selah while Terra's priestesses set Dad's rotting body to ash. He'd stood there, the heavy stone of grief overtaking anything else even if just for that moment. He'd stood there, and Selah reached back to grab his hand. She didn't look back—couldn't, even if she'd wanted to. The pyre demanded witness. But she had reached back to hold his hand, and as the priestess's wailing song rose and echoed about the catacombs, grief had given way to something else. Something harder to define, but within it was the absolute certainty that whoever murdered their father could *not* have his sister, too.

And now she's gone anyway.

They part ways almost immediately, with Linet off to the western gates to head off anyone who might be trying to smuggle Selah out of the city. Arran finds himself veering east before he can really make a conscious decision about it, jostling through the crowd toward the Boardwalk. He knows his sister, knows her moods, and knows where she would go to be alone.

But Selah isn't walking the north-end beach or the stone breakwater, or sitting inside any of the Boardwalk javs. Nor is she at the Purgatory Chasm overhang or the abandoned Amphitheater Messalina, where she and her friends from Laurium threw parties in their superior. He changes tack, racing through the Arborem with as much decorum as he can muster, ignoring the scandalized looks thrown his way. But Selah isn't at the Swan and Sailor taberna, or at the Topiary Gardens, or even with Kasari Ederan when he tracks her down to a private open-air bathhouse in Ecclesmur of all places.

A few hours past meridiem, Arran doubles back to the Universitas District, and by now he's beginning to feel well and truly panicked. There's nothing else for it. He'll have to go to the Senate, have to tell Naevia what's happened so she can call in the Cohorts. She'll be absolutely furious with him, but he can deal with that. Selah's safety is more important. And Linet . . .

His heart sinks at the thought of the sentry and her children. The Institute Civitatem has borrowed her out to Breakwater, and they hold the power to assign her children anywhere at all for however long they choose. They could sell their contracts outright. With a mark this black on her record, would she ever be allowed to see them again?

That's not on you, a treacherous voice that sounds disconcertingly like his own whispers in the back of his mind, and he's out of breath somehow despite standing perfectly still. *Go to Naevia now or put it off until later, Linet's fate is set. You can't save everyone. But act now and there might still be time to save Selah.*

Arran pushes a frustrated palm through his sweaty curls in an attempt to steady himself, to shove out the pounding of his heart in his ears, to stave off the way his vision is suddenly going fuzzy around the edges. He is not having a panic attack right now. He isn't. He just has to make a *decision*, damn it. Right. Okay. Focus.

Feeling slightly ill, Arran turns around and walks straight into Theodora Arlot.

"Shit!"

"*Ow.*"

"Sorry!"

"Oh, it's you."

Arran tries not to take too much offense to that.

Theo had still been there when he climbed back into bed in the early hours of the morning the night of Dad's viewing, but she certainly hadn't been when he woke up the next day. He hasn't heard so much as a word from her since. Too embarrassed at having slept with the Kleios familia accident to give him the time of day. He gets it. It's far from the first time it's happened. Except that *this* time, he'd been stupid enough to think . . .

Well. It doesn't matter now.

Almost immediately, though, Theo backtracks. "Oh, not like *that*. Sorry. I didn't mean—I just wasn't expecting to see you . . . uh. Here."

"I can see that."

Out and about on what he can only assume is her day off from work, Theo presents a far cry from the polished young politico he met three nights ago. Her once-loose hair has been coiled into dozens of tiny buns, and she's traded in her neat mourning dress for a cheap olive-green duskra and heavy work boots. It's remarkable, the way she slips between worlds like this with easy confidence. Though Arran might be more inclined to appreciate this if he weren't in the middle of a Selah-induced crisis.

Theo bites her lip, one corner of her mouth tugging upward slightly in a sheepish grin, and says, "Hey, listen, about the other n—"

"Sorry, I don't really have time to talk right now," he says, and pushes past her. He knows he's being rude, but he's still having trouble coming up for breath and he's running short on time. Despite having spent the last three days thinking about Theo and wondering where exactly he'd gotten it wrong, this is definitely not the moment to pile on another rejection.

"Wait, hold up—*Arran*." She grabs him by the wrist, though he yanks it back out of her grasp just as fast.

"I don't have time for this," he tells her, a little more aggressively than he means to, but the pounding in his head has yet to fully subside. "I'm sorry, but. My little sister's gone and I don't know where she is and I've wasted *hours* looking for her because I didn't want to get her Quiet-damned sentry in trouble and now she will be anyway, so if you don't mind? I have to go destroy a family because my own couldn't fucking keep it together."

Theo blinks at him.

He flushes, but before he can turn on his heel and get the savage Quiet out of there, she asks, "Your sister's . . . gone?"

"Missing, yeah."

"Selah?"

"Only got the one."

"Okay, then," she says, suddenly all business. "Let's go."

"You don't have to come with me to the Senate," he tells her, annoyed. Even if it were any of her business, he'd prefer Theo of all people not to see this. Although maybe having a witness isn't such a bad idea. Just in case Naevia ends up murdering him.

She shakes her head. "We're not going to the Senate."

"Yeah, *I* am."

"No, you're not," she says. "Honestly, I didn't really understand half of what you just said, but it sounds like Senator Kleios finding out about this puts more than just your pride at risk. So I'm helping you search."

"I've been looking for her all day. I can't find her anywhere."

"Sure you can't. But that's because you didn't have me."

Having Theo Arlot, it turns out, means having access to places he never would have considered searching. Arran's confusion as she leads him along the narrow jetties running parallel to the Kirnaval's waterways turns to outright gaping when she stops at the door of what's clearly a brothel, then steps confidently inside.

Furtive, he looks around at the main parlor, dark sunlight fighting through the gauzy curtains, empty of life this early in the afternoon but steeped in a liberal heavy perfume that fails to mask the unmistakable scents of poppam and various bodily fluids. This isn't exactly the kind of place that Selah would go, a thought he's about to share out loud when a reedy voice from somewhere behind them abruptly snaps, *"Out!"*

The voice, it turns out, belongs to a sallow-faced, pockmarked, middle-aged man with badly dyed black hair that only serves to make him look ill. Watery eyes narrowed at the pair of them, he stands arms akimbo in the doorframe, back to the little entrance hall, as though preparing for war. "Out," he snaps again, eyes fixed on Theo. "I've told you, Nix, I have *warned* you. I run a business, not a social hour."

Far from being taken aback by this less than friendly welcome, Theo smiles and says, "Of course not. I only need to borrow Wes for a minute. Five tops." And with that she neatly places two bronze ceres on the wooden side table between them.

The proprietor snatches up the coins, weighing them in his palm momentarily before telling her with a sneer, "It's off-hours. He's sleeping."

"So wake him up." She shrugs, and tosses him a third ceres. "I'm a paying customer, Vorndran."

Satisfied with his cut, the man called Vorndran tosses her a final glare of deepest dislike before disappearing back down the hallway, calling out behind him, "You know the room."

"Stay here," Theo tells Arran quietly, and before he can argue, or ask why Vorndran called her *Nix*, or demand to know what on earth she's up to in a Kirnaval brothel of all places, she's disappeared up the stairs and into the depths of the crumbling building. Slowly, he takes a seat on the edge of a fraying couch, and tries not to think about where its various stains came from, and tries instead to make some sense of what's happening here. Because he's been in places like this before.

Arran's never seen the appeal of brothels, even as an awkward teenager trying to keep up with Julian and his other childhood friends, following after them in a desperate bid to prove he was still worth spending time with. He'd have done anything, naive idiot that he was, but he'd been fifteen and in that house in Paleaside for all of five minutes before turning around and leaving. Maybe it would be one thing if prostitutes were servae, stripped of choice in a way that's clear and easy to define. It would be simpler then to explain his disgust. Easier to rail against. But by and large the women, men, and themed working in a place like this are citizens at the end of their rope. Forced into it by the invisible hand of a poverty the Imperium has the fragging nerve to call choice. Except that the other side of that choice is presenting yourself to the Institute Civitatem to be processed as a serva, and that's no choice at all.

In the end, Theo doesn't need a full five minutes upstairs with whoever Wes is. She comes clamoring back down the wooden staircase after barely three, wearing a broad look of relief across her dimpled face.

"What was that?" he asks when they step back into the dusty sunlight, the bustling throng of the Kirnaval enveloping them back into its tumult.

Theo cuts a path across a dangerously tilting plaza, hand firmly wrapped in his to keep from losing each other in the crowd. "She's not being held for a bounty. At least, the rickets haven't gone out, so we can effectively rule out that possibility. Which is good. That was the most likely scenario for unfriendlies."

"Wha . . ." He gapes, and realizes he's been doing rather a lot of that today, at least where Theo's concerned. She sounds more like a member of the espionage legions than a politico. "How do you know that?"

"Vorndran's an idiot. Wes doesn't sleep," she says, though that feels like a distinct non-answer. "Come on."

Next, she leads him to an elderly woman sitting outside a make-shift shelter beneath a bridge in the Third Ward, then they hop a rickshaw to a clerk with a severe middle part who berates them soundly for daring to approach him while at work in the Financial Quarter prefect's office. Both of them—including the clerk, in the end—consent to a hushed conversation with Theo, leaving her increasingly satisfied that Selah's managed to avoid some grim fate. Evidently Arawakan pirates haven't been seen in Luxana since before the hurricane, and there's no word of grumblings loud enough from the colleges or guild halls to suspect a kidnapping for ransom. She may as well be speaking a foreign language.

But as the afternoon wears on, Arran finds his chest loosening as he becomes increasingly less terrified for his sister, and increasingly more intrigued by Theo's inexplicable network of underground connections.

"One more box to check off, then I think it'll be pretty safe to say Selah's just out meeting her secret lover or something," she tells him, nudging his shoulder with hers as they exit the alley behind the prefect's office.

"Who *are* you?" Arran laughs, the once-idle wheels of curiosity in the back of his mind now working overtime. "Seriously, you've only been in town for a few months and you already know more about the . . . *underbelly* of the city than I ever have."

"Well—" she shrugs, but gives him a knowing sort of smile, "I wouldn't be much good at my job if I didn't."

Of all the answers he thinks she might have given, *that* most certainly isn't among them. Arran blinks at her for a half second before his brain catches up with him. "Naevia . . . knows about all this."

"Of course. Why do you think she hired me?"

"You said you were connected. Your dad's patron—"

"I *am* connected. So is every kid trying to climb the ladder, and their connections are significantly more impressive than mine. But I also have my ear to the ground, and Senator Kleios is the kind of politician who values that more."

Arran's blatant confusion must be clearly written across his face, because she takes one look at him and laughs. "How much does she actually talk about her politics at home?" she asks, leading him sharply left down yet another twisting street toward what he thinks is vaguely back in the direction of the Kirnaval. It smells like garbage, and the sea.

"She's popular with the plebs."

"That's true," Theo says, nodding. "And as long as Senate floor sessions remain closed and plebs don't know how their government actually *works*, she'll stay that way."

"Yeah, you've lost me."

"Happy to explain, but you have to promise me something."

"What?"

She stops in the middle of the cobblestone street and grins. "You won't get me fired."

Arran stops too, the warm glow of three days previous nudging its way back in. Something in that easy humor, and how she actually listens, and the way she knows she's the smartest person in the room but won't hold it over you. It's enough, almost, to forget the way it abruptly ended.

He sticks out his hand. "Deal."

She takes it.

"The Senate's a sham. Completely for show," she says conversationally and continues down the street, as though she weren't casually spitting abject treason for anyone to hear. "Its power exists to the extent that the Imperium *allows* it to exist, but by and large any motions passed by the Senate are rigged from the start."

"Don't you think that's overly—"

"The Imperium may feel far off across the ocean in Roma, but they're here. They've got their fingers in us. All those Imperium officials swarming the Plaza Capitolio on any given day are just the messenger hawks bringing senators their instructions."

If he were anyone else, he'd say she sounds cracked. Like a conspiracy theorist. A pseudohistorian. One of those oddball fringe pamphlets that gets printed now and again, distributed for a brief time before the blackbags shut it down. By now, though, Arran knows better. Back in Teec Nos Pos, this sort of talk was just daily conversation when Fagan and Enyo were involved, holding court at the far end of camp, safely out of earshot from the prefect and legates. And there's something in the matter-of-factness of her words, the way she doesn't so much as hesitate in her stride, that gives him pause. In Theodora Arlot, Arran's beginning to get the sense he knows what he's dealing with.

So he raises a brow and says, "That sounds . . . simplistic."

"Oh, yeah?"

"Yeah. The college system is definitely corrupt, I agree. But the Atticus College has Naevia on at least five different committees in addition to her day-to-day. Ethics panels. Project boards. I'm sure you know more about it than I do. That's a lot of pointless busywork for someone sitting around waiting for orders."

"Yeah, it would be," Theo grants him, barely breaking her stride, "if the colleges didn't represent what's really important to the senators."

"And that is . . . ?"

"The colleges—all their committees and foreign relation bureaus . . . well, they're social clubs, aren't they? Birds of a feather with the same outside business interests, all jostling for the Imperium's favor, trying to make sure they come out on top."

"Let's say that's true," he grants her, the way he might have over a pint of hops in a Fornia taberna. "Why have elections at all, then? Or a Senate? It'd be way less effort for the Imperium to just set Cato Palmar up as dictator."

"Yeah, but they wouldn't want to give him any ideas, though, would they? And anyway, the illusion of self-governance is a powerful thing. It keeps us happy. We're a lot bigger than Roma. There are a lot more of us than there are of them. *And* we're pretty far away. Putting down a rebellion over here wouldn't be much fun for them, so it's just a whole lot easier if we think there's nothing to rebel against in the first place."

Yes. Arran knows exactly what he's dealing with. He backs off. "Well, that's cheerful."

Theo shrugs. *You asked.*

"So what does that have to do with you and Naevia?"

"Well," she starts, "if being a senator and *staying* a senator isn't about actually shaping the world for the better, then naturally it's about shaping the world to your own advantage." She stops outside a large, nondescript building and turns to face him, the low October sun glinting off her black hair. "That's all politics are, really. That's the game. And Senator Kleios found a different way to play it. She doesn't bother with bribes to stay in power. She makes the masses think she's listening to *them*, that she's on the Senate floor every day fighting for *them*. But in order to do that, she needs to actually speak their language."

"And that's where you come in. To translate."

"Ding ding. Not to mention, bringing a pleb into a senior-tracked role is a good publicity stunt. Endears her to voters."

He knows something about that. Arran remembers the moment he himself realized the cachet he lends to Naevia's public persona by the simple fact of just existing. He remembers wondering if it was something that Naevia herself was even aware of. Looking back now, he wonders how he could have been so naive.

Theo, maybe mistaking his disquiet for silent disapproval, is quick to add, "Don't take all of this the wrong way. I like your stepmother. She's a brilliant woman, and she knows how to use optics to her advantage. I'm learning a lot from her."

"Is that why you left?" he asks suddenly. It comes out without meaning to. He wasn't going to push it, wasn't going to bring it up unless she did. But it's out there now, and he can't take it back. "The other night, you left before I woke up. Afraid of what she'd think?"

She barely bats an eye. "More or less," she says, smiling ruefully as she leans against the gray stone wall. "I was afraid for my job, honestly. I hadn't intended to . . . I woke up in the middle of the night and suddenly realized how it was going to look to her and kinda spun out. Savage Quiet, *you* thought I was using you to get in her good graces when we first met. Of course she was going to think that I had, I don't know . . ."

"Seduced me?"

"Something like that, yeah."

"Yeah, that makes sense," says Arran, and he can feel his heart thumping away so hard he half expects it to burst right through his chest, though he's suddenly very aware of his hands and not totally sure what to do with them. "So. You don't, uh, regret it, then?"

Theo raises a single brow, looking at him as though he's grown an extra head, and shifts incrementally closer to him. "No. Why, do you?"

"No," he says, and his heart flips on itself. "Should we do it again sometime?"

"I'd like that."

"Preferably with the, you know, talking part, too."

"Well, yeah. I sort of assumed that was part of the package."

TAIR

"*B*ut," says Tair, pulling the pencil out of her mouth, and impatiently blows a stray twist out of her face. "But that *presumes ill intent by definition*, so then the whole thing will fall apart because she can't sound like she's accusing the Publica of a cover-up. The defense *has* to stay focused on the one officer as a bad actor."

Sticking the pencil behind her ear, she slams the massive legal dictionary closed against her legs.

"Tair," Ibdi answers wearily from across several beds. "Get outta my ward."

She ignores them, flipping open on a sudden inspiration one of the many files she's spread across the little corner of the clinic she's claimed as her office.

Artemide was right. Jinni didn't put her in the field, not right away. Instead, she's got her doing legal support work for the other Watchers, and Tair isn't naive enough not to know that this is a test. Not of skills or intelligence, but of temperament. The ability to look a lost cause in the face and give their case everything she's got all the same. No amount of preparation or research can help someone who has actually committed a crime, no matter how petty the infraction or absurd the law broken. Which is a fucking shame because half these cases could be turned over *easily* with a well-placed argument—that is, of course, in the kind of world where Tair's allowed to stand in court and argue a case at all.

She flicks that impossible wish away, and barely notices Ibdi until they're towering right over her, arms folded across their chest. "We've got an apartment, you know. Quiet spot. Big table. No vomiting or amputations or—"

"*Too* quiet. I can't get anything done. Anyway, you're my best sounding board."

"You're annoying my patients."

"You have no patients."

It's true. Amidst the shelves of medicinal herbs and cheap blankets, a single person currently occupies the beds of the clinic's upstairs ward. And Mihrimo Jens—peeled from the stoop of a taberna to sleep off his drunken stupor for the third time this week—doesn't count.

Then the door to the tiny ward slams open, and a small rush of people bearing a barely conscious body comes pouring in. Ibdi, consummate fucking professional that they are, doesn't even bother gloating. They don't bother with Tair at all. Game face on, they've got a medical emergency to tend to, immediately barking at people to back up as they stride down toward the milling throng at the other end of the ward.

Clocking bo staffs and a familiar face or two, Tair sets the files onto the bed and moves to follow Ibdi. There's a dour air about them, but that's no surprise. Even before joining their ranks, she's always known the Watchers to be a fairly grim bunch, especially after returning from patrol. But as Tair approaches, she catches sight of the young man they've set on the bed nearest to the door, and lets out a small cry of dismay. Because it's not a man at all.

It's Oyeli, who looks like they've been run down by a stampede of horses, cut and bruised and bleeding and cradling an arm bent at a gut-lurching angle. Oyeli, who Tair has tutored for the last two years because the matron at the children's home makes her charges work for their room and board instead of attending school. Oyeli, who registered for their universitas entrance exams just this morning.

"Get her out of here," Ibdi says to no one in particular, barely glancing up as they methodically cut the ruined tunic from Oyeli's battered chest.

Tair ignores them, shrugs off the calm hand that reaches out to rest on her shoulder.

"What happened?" she demands, glaring from face to stoic face, feeling anger rise as she meets each of their eyes and finds only pity there. *Hysterical,* they seem to say. *Still too green for the field.* Well, frag that—she never wanted to be put out in the field in the first place, but she certainly isn't hysterical.

"What," she repeats, *calmly,* "happened?"

"Guess the Publica thought they fit a profile," says a brusque voice somewhere to her left, and Jinni's eyes hold no pity in them as she meets Tair's. "Someone reported a Kirnaval panhandler in the Universitas District this morning. Know a tune to that song?"

"They weren't panhandling. They were registering for entrance exams."

Jinni shrugs. "I know that. The Publica knows that, probably."

And she feels her rage die. Jinni has *opinions* on folks who stand out. It makes her job harder. Luxana Universitas holds two places open for plebs every year, though they usually go to the highest bidder. Perfect grades or no, Oyeli's chances were never high to start. But this isn't Jinni's fault any more than it is theirs, and misplaced anger is an agent of catastrophe. It was one of the first things Tair learned when she first left Breakwater, and no matter what else she feels about Griff and Pa'akal and Theo and the rest, she takes it with her as a promise to herself. That at the crux of catastrophe and change, rage brings the former and focus brings the latter, and that she will always choose change.

"Okay," she says, willing herself back to stillness as she inhales deeply through her nose. Focus. Change. Actionable steps. "How can I help?"

"You can't. No case here, we sent them off. Which is lucky for you. I'm sure you've got your hands full as it is."

"Um." Tair slides slightly to the left, obscuring the mess of paperwork and law texts sprawled across the empty bed at the end of the ward. Jinni raises a brow, but doesn't give any other indication at having seen it.

"Lucky you're here," she says instead. "I've got someone downstairs asking around for you."

Well, that can't be good. Her only friends are, as a general rule, all fellow Sisters. People with the clearance to just walk upstairs and find her if they need. Apart from that, she can only imagine Pa'akal back with another missive, or an agent of Breakwater who's tracked her down, or . . . surely not another go-between demanding she turn over the Stone? They're not supposed to meet for another four days.

"Oh, yeah?" she asks, in a voice she desperately hopes passes as casual, heart thumping inconveniently loud.

"Yeah," says Jinni, turning back to the bed where Ibdi is now pressing their fingers gently along Oyeli's side to check for broken ribs. "Found her wandering around updistrict picking fights with the Publica. Someone called Theodora ring a bell?"

There's only one explanation for this, Tair reasons from outside the door to the second ward five minutes later, cruiseboard tucked under her arm. A thousand alternate scenarios had run through her mind on the brief jaunt down the stairs to get here, each more unlikely than the next.

Stupid. She'd been stupid to think that Pa'akal would be the end of it. Whatever Griff wants from her, assurances that she hasn't been tattling on them to the Kleioses or no, Theo Nix is just about the last person she wants to talk to about it. Not after what she said to them five years ago, stuffing her bag with rations in her hurry to get away.

I don't want this. I'm done following orders without knowing the reason why. Maybe you're happy to trade one master for another, but I left for a reason.

Theo had punched her in the face.

She takes a deep breath, then another, pushes the door to the second ward open, and then goes very still. Because the young woman sitting on the edge of a neatly made bed, ankle elevated and wrapped with a compress, is most definitely *not* Theodora Nix.

It takes all of three seconds for her to look up, and Tair—caught, trapped in the squeaking doorframe—feels a hot flush rippling down her skin even as she wonders if she's been turned to stone. No part of her body feels entirely real, because this is it.

This is how it ends.

This is how everything she's built comes crashing down.

Dimly, stupidly, she wonders if Jinni and Pio and the rest will be able to make sense of her case notes without her there to explain them.

"Hi," says Selah, quietly, and Tair lets the door close behind her.

She doesn't know what else to do. Every corner of her subconscious mind screams with instinct she has to clamp down hard on because those instincts are *badmadwrong*.

No one else is there. Either it's a quiet night at the clinic on the whole, or this is all some kind of setup. The dramatic staged conclusion to Selah's wild gull chase to track down her errant verna. The climactic scene where she gets to vent her fury and sorrow and frustration before dragging Tair back to Breakwater or sending her off to the Institute Civitatem for reeducation. But no, that's not the Selah she knows. Dramatic, yes, but never cruel. Then again, five years can change a person. They've certainly changed her.

Suddenly she feels very tired.

She sits down.

"Hi," she responds, and laughs.

She can't help it. It bursts out of her like spit-up, a burbling giggle so unlike herself because how is this happening? Selah—*here*—with some sort of anxiety and joy written across her face like she wants Tair to reassure her that it's okay that she's *here* that she's *won* that they've *won* that Tair's *lost*. And she slams the bony backside of her knuckles against her mouth because it's ridiculous to be smiling and then she decides she doesn't actually care. She might not get to decide much of anything for a while after this.

Selah's still looking at her, like she's concerned for her maybe, but honestly that's fair. "How—how are you?" she asks tentatively, her long neck thin and brown, and Tair laughs again.

"Good," she says, and they could be out on a meridiem date. "How are you?"

"I twisted my ankle."

"I can see that." There's a tear in her trousers where skin peeks through at the knee.

"I was trying to help someone . . ." Selah trails off, and Tair wonders if she's looking for some kind of congratulations. "A boy. The Publica attacked him. They brought him in with me but I haven't seen—"

"Not a boy."

Selah flushes. "Sorry, a man—"

"Not a man." And at her look of confusion Tair tries not to be too annoyed. Thremid is considered too backwater Sargassan to be recognized by the Romans and their rigid sense of gender binary, but that's no excuse for ignorance when Selah has full access to a first-rate font of global knowledge. Thremed live undefined outside gender roles and concepts, and outside of the Arborem and Pantheon Park, they're as common as the brick foundations of the city.

Tair, however, says none of this.

She's suddenly very tired again, and aware of the energy in the ward in a way she hadn't been sure she would remember. But the body knows. The body remembers. Remembers how to anticipate change. Remembers how not to fill the space, as if doing that would mean filling herself with too much to hope for. Remembers to be small. Remembers how to walk into a room and immediately case it, determine who's there and how to put them at ease and walk the line of least danger. Remembers to discard that particular ineffable thing she once knew to carry only in private.

So she doesn't laugh and she doesn't say anything impertinent and she doesn't look at Selah because the veil of a good dream is being lifted and she's returning to the waking world. The body remembers.

It remembers more than that.

"Why?" Selah asks, quiet.

She does this. *Asks* things. Wants to get inside her like it's the most natural thing in the world. Like she doesn't have to be invited in.

One syllable, a simple enough question. *Loaded,* certainly, but Tair doesn't need to meet her gaze or ask for clarification to know the full weight of its meaning. She doesn't answer, either. She just shrugs, gaze fixed on one of the larger freckles of her own left hand, because her tongue is still too heavy and unpracticed for anything but the truth. And the truth isn't small.

The silence drags on, and Tair wishes that Selah would just say whatever's on her mind and be done with it. She'll have to sit there and listen to it either way, stubbornly ignoring the way her heart is doubling over on itself, and she can sense Selah's restlessness, her frustration and her hurt and betrayal. She wishes she'd just spit it out already.

But instead Selah says this: "Jinni said this clinic is run by the . . . Sisters of the First?"

Now it's not just her heart but her stomach that lurches while two universes collide. Abruptly, she finds her voice.

"They don't know who I am," she tells her quickly, urgently, the full implication of Selah's words crashing down. She knows Jinni, by name. She knows the Sisters, by name. "Not really. They didn't know they were harboring a fuga. They do good work here. You can't— Please don't turn them in."

She expects this to be met by anger or disappointment or even some measure of satisfaction. Instead, Selah looks vaguely sick.

"I *wouldn't*," she says, horrified, reaching across the space between beds to take Tair's hands in hers. Tair doesn't pull them away, a sudden hot familiar pulse shooting up from where skin meets skin, but neither does she make any motion to grasp Selah's in return. In spite or perhaps *because* of this, Selah squeezes them tighter. "Tair, I would *never*. You know I wouldn't."

"I don't know that. You'd be within your rights. You own me."

So then it's Selah who releases her hands like a shock of static pulsed through them, and maybe she takes some degree of rotten enjoyment in that.

"I don't *own*—" she begins, but Tair cuts her off, all thoughts of self-preservation out the window after the fashion they tend to go when Selah's involved. That, she *had* forgotten.

"Your father died," she says, and there's no heat in it. It's just true. "You're paterfamilias. You inherited me. You own me—*fine*, whatever, you own my contract, it's the same thing. And if things hadn't gone tits up I would have been your client and you still would've fucking owned me, all niceties aside. So can we stop debating semantics?" And off her stunned face—"Oh, I'm sorry, did that hurt your feelings?"

Tair gets the distinct impression that Selah's fighting to swallow the first response that comes to mind, and patiently waits for the second.

"Do you . . ." Selah starts. "Have you always felt that way?"

"No," she responds, because she's probably getting dumped at the Institute Civitatem as soon as they leave this place anyway. She might as well get it out now. "No, I haven't. Things were supposed to be different for me, you know? *I* was a verna. *I* was an apprentice. I was going to be a client, and a citizen. And I wouldn't have to ask anyone's permission after that, not for anything."

Selah shifts slightly on the squeaking bed, uncomfortable. Good.

"We both were," she points out, and although she isn't eighteen anymore, Tair remembers that, too. *We'll go where we want, and eat what we want, and say what we want. And no one can stop us.*

"And wasn't that such a polite little lie. So respectable. You wanted to know the reason I left," she says, standing again because she can and Selah can't, ankle busted as it is, and the lack of space between them is too much. "It's because I played by the rules. I did everything I was supposed to. And it still wasn't enough. So I decided I was done."

She can feel the tenor of her voice rising, and finds that she doesn't much care. This anger is not pointless. It is not misguided. These are the lessons she had learned, long years and several lifetimes ago:

That she is the product of failure, last in a line of laziness and ingratitude and inability. That she, and she alone, is responsible for proving herself better than those who landed her at the bottom of the food chain. That if she is quiet and disciplined and polite, and keeps herself neat and clean and presentable, she can earn an apprenticeship. That if she applies herself in vigorous work and makes herself an asset and strives for no less than perfection, she can one day earn the freedoms of a client plebeian.

These are the lessons instilled in her through gentle words and harsher hands, and they are not the tools of survival and betterment she'd once been taught to believe by the stone-faced Mothers at the Servile Children's Asylum or even by Gil Delena's warm, approving smile.

Chains, all of them, cloaked in the lie of personal accountability. The tiniest slip and she was written off, because the truth is there *is* no difference. Vernae, servae, it didn't really matter so long as patricians' lives were easy and comfortable. She worked herself to perfection and *still* she wasn't worth half the dignity and respect Selah takes for granted every day of her life.

"You know, the incredible thing," she goes on, because now that she's started it's difficult to stop, "the amazing, *awful* thing I figured out after leaving . . . is that it's more of the same out here. There's freedom as a pleb, but it's the freedom to work and fight and scrape your way to a better life, and yeah, you might manage to build some wealth, but you'll never be patrician, and eventually *someone* down the line will mess up. Families keep cycling back down to rock bottom every couple generations, it's just what happens. So even if things worked out the way they were supposed to, I was never special. I was just feeding the cycle."

"That's not true," Selah sputters. "You deserved everything you worked for, you're a fragging genius—"

"And that makes me better? Worth more?"

Selah opens her mouth to respond, then closes it just as abruptly.

"The Sisters of the First, this place . . . we fight back the best we can with education and food and housing and whatever else people need, but it's not *enough*. The Imperium should be providing them with all of this, but they *aren't*. Of course they aren't. You people can only be tall when you're standing on our necks, and one cog's as good as the next as far as the great machine is concerned, right?"

It's cruel, maybe, to mock Alexander Kleios's oft-spoken words to his daughter when he's so newly dead, but Tair can't particularly bring herself to care. The man who owned her had been kind and soft-spoken, and her eyes are wide open.

If Selah takes offense, she makes no indication of it. Instead, she shifts, as if wanting to stand, to go to her, then realizing her twisted ankle can't bear the weight. Tair doesn't offer to help. Doesn't notice the way she bites at her chapped lips.

Selah frowns at her foot for a long moment, then nods once sharply, evidently to herself. "I didn't come here to bring you home," she says, and gone is the soft, tentative voice she's used since Tair walked through the door. It's firm. Decided. Tair's been expecting this, even before she decided to start yelling. She's already resigned herself to several upcoming months of reeducation and half convinced herself that the horror stories she's heard can't possibly be true. What she isn't expecting, however, is what Selah says next.

"You can stay here."

"What?"

She sits back down.

Selah shrugs, though her voice is strained. "Or leave. Do what you want, I don't care. I mean, I *do*—of course I do—but I won't tell anyone I've seen you and I won't . . . visit . . . if you don't want me to. If that's how you feel."

Tair gapes at her, certain this can't be happening. "What's the curb?"

"No curb," says Selah, and now she's the one who won't meet Tair's gaze, eyes locked firmly somewhere around her knees. "I just wanted to . . . see you. And ask what *that* is."

She nods toward the frayed messenger bag set against Tair's hip, the soft leather of the Iveroa Stone's bindings just peeking out over the top. For the third time in an hour, Tair feels the floor drop out from under her.

"Just a book," she says, shoving it down farther into the bag.

"Tair, you're a terrible liar. I saw it."

"Okay, fine. But I have no idea what it is. I'm just the middleman."

The Stone had been exactly where the note had said it would be, looking exactly as described. *A stone of deepest black and purest cut, two hands long and one hand wide, the depth of half a fingernail, and bound in old brown leather.* It's a curiosity, certainly, perhaps a relic of old Sargassa, before the Great Quiet. Tair doesn't particularly care. She has other worries where the Stone's concerned.

Only Selah's looking at her now like *she's* the one who's lost the plot, and Tair has to hold back a slight laugh. "It was in *your* study," she tells her. "Sitting on *your* desk. You're telling me you don't know what it is?"

"I'd only gotten it that night. I hadn't had a chance to look at it yet."

"Selah—"

"No, really. Gil had only just given it to me. From my dad. He . . . he wanted me to have it." It sits between them, heavy, and Tair refuses to let herself feel bad about this. Then Selah musters herself. "If you're the middleman, who hired you?"

"Well, I wasn't exactly *hired* . . . More like blackmailed."

"By who?"

"No idea. They use go-betweens. Always different. But they know me. Who I was. Who I am."

"What do they want it for?"

"Well, if I have no idea what it *is*, I can't really know that either, can I?"

"Terra, I forgot you're annoying."

"Not as annoying as you."

"Rude."

"Reality drop."

Selah flashes her a wicked grin, and the dam breaks. For a moment Tair is seventeen again, dancing on a crowded beach with steel-string music and moonmasks and a warm shared pulse between their bodies pressed together. But it passes quickly. Neither of them are young anymore.

Selah holds out her hand, palm open. Expectant. Tair stares.

"I did mention the part about blackmail, right?" Maybe she should be treading more carefully here, but somehow the solid compartment she'd managed to store Selah in with *Them* for so long has been cracked wide open. "I'm not giving it back."

"What's he got on you? This blackmailer."

"Just my life and liberty." She doesn't mention her time—however brief—spent with the Revenants. "Other people's, too. I'm supposed to hand it over in four days."

Tair takes a steadying breath, looks Selah square in the eyes as she hasn't the entire time they've been sitting here. She has to realize how serious this is. "Whoever this is, whoever's blackmailing me. They know who I am." She leans forward into the space between the two beds until she can see the gold flecks in Selah's eyes. She smells like salt and road dust. She smells like tazine. "They knew I could get into Breakwater without being seen. That I could get this for them. *They know who I am.* And if I don't give them whatever this thing is, they're going to expose me as a fuga, and *that* is going to destroy this place and everything these people have built. And it'll be my fault."

It's a leap of faith, because Tair doesn't trust Selah with the whole truth. Not yet. Maybe not ever. But now that she's here in front of her, and the animal instincts of fear and defeat and anger have passed over, Tair can remember who Selah is. The girl who runs barefoot in the streets. The girl who loves her brother. One of them, but not yet one of Them.

She's closer now, but she can still come back.

Selah can't know about Una, who spirited her away from Break-water in the early hours of the morning as the fog crept in off the sea. She can't know about Griff and Pa'akal and Theo and Izara, who hid her and trained her and counted her as one of their own for two months, until she opened her eyes and realized that the bad taste in her mouth wasn't the violence or the creed that came with being a Revenant, but the blind obedience where their leader was concerned. Selah can't know about any of that, or the link Tair creates between the Sisters of the First and the enemies of the state she left behind. How one word in the right ear and both the Revenants and the Sisters would be finished.

So, no, Selah can't know these things, but maybe she doesn't have to. Tair doesn't trust Selah anymore, but she remembers who she is. The person who needs to save everyone else. She's counting on that.

It takes a moment, a long stretched-out thing in which all those heavy truths sit between them:

One. Selah still holds the power here, could still change her mind.

But two. Selah still loves her.

Tair can see it, has seen it since the moment she stepped foot in the second ward. Proprietary, she had first thought, before Selah opened her mouth and reminded her who she is. Theirs is a history of stolen whispers and secret jokes and girlhood friendship grown into an all-encompassing ache. At seventeen Tair had thought that this could work—that she would rise in the world and neither would ever marry if they couldn't cross caste lines and they could make this work. This, too, had been a polite, respectable sort of lie.

She deserves more.

Selah may not understand that. But she loves her, and Tair knows it. She uses it.

"Okay," says Selah, as she knew she would. Only then—"Can I at least look at it?"

"Why?"

"Because I'm smart. And you're brilliant. And between the two of us, I bet we can figure out what it is. Maybe even who's blackmailing you. If you hand this over blindly, that won't stop them coming back around the next time they need something from you."

Tair hesitates, but she can't drown out the voice in the back of her mind telling her that Selah's probably right. And while she hasn't spent much time looking at it, just wanting to hand it over and be done with this whole mess, she can't deny there's a part of her that's been drowning in curiosity. The black stone is a mystery—as is its purpose, if it even has one. Aside from the perfect cut and the fact that some time ago someone thought to bind it in soft leather, the simple fact is that it's otherwise unremarkable. It just doesn't *do* anything.

Slowly, carefully, she slips the Stone from her bag.

SELAH

Selah takes the leather-bound tablet, its soft bindings worn and newly familiar beneath her fingers. She flips the cover open. Its surface is just as she remembers, dark and ominous and just reflective enough that she can make out her own murky profile in its depths. There's a small circle carved at the bottom, another rune within—the eight-point Kleios sun, just the same as the one stamped on her patent of identity, or on the solaric lamps sitting in Dad's office.

"This is irradium," she says quietly, a little jolt at the realization. "Solaric technology."

Tair nods. "It's called the Iveroa Stone."

That, at least, explains the sun. It belongs to the Kleios familia, but they did, after all, used to be Iveroas once upon a time.

She runs the pads of her fingers along the black, gleaming Stone, worrying her nails over the grooves at the edge. It's a curiously cool and heavy thing, and Selah rests one hand beneath the soft and supple leather, runs a finger down to the sun etched at the very bottom, brilliant and delicate and fine. She's all too aware of Tair, cross-legged on the rickety bed across from her, leaning forward into the space between them, and the air in the room goes thin and tense as it had been in the minutes before they achieved this uneasy truce.

Dad wanted her to have this, specifically. He made sure Gil kept it secret, the same as the old atlas now safely hidden away in her bedroom. He said that it was classified. There has to be a reason why.

So it isn't instinct. Not exactly. If anything, it's a recent muscle memory of black irradium just like this, those lamps in Dad's study that he prized so deeply. She draws her pointer finger down until the pad catches in the little circle, secure and *right* and a perfect fit, somehow, just nestled in the center, and she lets it linger there for just a moment. Then she presses *in*.

Nothing happens.

Selah frowns and presses again, jams her pointer against the black stone. Nothing.

The air around them seems to slump.

Tair leans back with a disappointed huff, while Selah lets out a breath she wasn't entirely aware that she was holding. Chewing at her lip in frustration, she flips the Stone over, but there's nothing but battered leather. She doesn't know what she expected to happen, exactly— the vibrance of solaric beams washing the little clinic ward in artificial sunlight, probably, for all that the Iveroa Stone bears no resemblance at all to the bulbs in Dad's office. She flips it back over, irradium-side up.

"Give it up, Selah. It's busted."

Tair sticks out her hand, expectant, to take the Stone back. Selah ignores her. "Solarics can't die," she points out instead.

"Yeah, but they do need exposure to the sun to work. That thing's probably been sitting in the dark for too long, ran out of whatever makes it tick."

That is, to be fair, a good point. Selah idly flips the Stone over once again, the turning of it in her hands half curiosity, half a measure against frustration, but this time her thumb catches on something new at the base. There, impossibly small and etched into the thinnest side of the irradium stone, barely a quarter inch tall—a single word. Well, what looks like a word, anyway.

Squinting against the ward's dull light, Selah can't make out what it says. Or perhaps, more to the point, can't make out what it means. As far as she can tell, it's a string of some sort of glyphs, and certainly none that she recognizes or understands.

"These mean anything to you?" she asks, handing the Stone back over.

Tair smooths a thumb across the glyphs etched into the stone, staring hard. "No," she admits at last. "Never seen anything like it before."

"Well, there has to be *something*," Selah says, frustration ripping from her center in waves she'd hardly realized were building there. "Otherwise it doesn't make any *sense*. Someone's threatening you over this and we need to know *why*."

"Gods, Selah, it's okay—"

"No. No, it's not okay. It's not okay at all." She didn't quite realize how upset the idea makes her, not until this moment. Because she understands loss now, in a way she never could before, and she'll be damned if she's going to lose Tair for good this time. "Give me three days."

Tair frowns. "What?"

"You have to hand over the Stone in four, right? If we can figure out what it does, why my dad gave it to me, why they want it before then . . . just give me a few days to poke around."

"And what if you end up finding something that changes your mind?" Tair slides the Iveroa Stone back into her rucksack, quickly like Selah might grab it from her hands.

"If so," Selah says, forcing herself to look into Tair's eyes so she can see that she's telling the truth, "then we decide how to move forward. Together."

There's a long, stretched-out moment in which Tair leans against the bedpost, critical gaze still landing hard and inscrutable on Selah in her red and gold duskra. An owl hoots faintly somewhere in the dark outside beyond.

At long last, she nods.

"Okay," Tair says. "We can start tomorrow."

"We?"

"We," she confirms, and a treacherous burst of warmth spreads through Selah's chest as a wry smile grows across Tair's face. "You really think I'm letting the Stone out of my sight?"

It isn't hard, getting back to Breakwater. Selah waves off Jinni Jordan's offers to stay the night, knows Mima's going to rain down Quietfury on her as it is for having snuck away again. Instead, she accepts the cheap wooden crutch the medic Ibdi offers and hobbles slowly out of Sinktown, awkward on her wrapped ankle. A straight shot north through the narrow end of the Regio Marina gets her into Seven Dials, and from there it's easy enough to catch a litter back to the Arborem.

There's a large rotunda on the estate grounds, built white and tall and columned to imitate antiquity. It sits just off the peninsula, right up against the shoreline where high shale cliffs shoot down to the rocks below. On a clear day you can see for miles. Right now, there's nothing but the all-encompassing dark, tiny pinpricks of light from Breakwater House shining up on the peninsula ahead. But she can't bring herself to return to its suffocating walls. Not just yet.

The cigarette between her lips flares hot and bright in the black sea breeze.

Tair is alive. Tair is alive. Tair is *alive*.

There's no reason this should surprise her this much, except that Selah had half begun to believe she'd been seeing things. That night in the Hazards, blood pumping, leg muscles seizing. She had been thinking about Tair all day. Her mind could have easily tricked her into seeing what she wanted to see.

But it didn't. She knows now that it didn't. She had the tangible proof, barely an hour ago, sitting mere inches away and bombarding her with all sorts of accusations of *ownership* and *you people*. Desecrating the sacred memory of an entire joint childhood, as though Selah hadn't been there, too, hadn't been there with her for every cruiseboard fall and every dressing down from Gil and the first time the two of them got supremely, spectacularly drunk off contraband whisky from Dad's liquor cabinet—and she *knows* this isn't fair. Tair can't suddenly decide that no, *this* actually happened this way and *that* wasn't actually okay, because Selah knows how it happened. She was *there*.

It's not just the words. It's the bitter taste enfolding them.

She's never heard Tair sound like that. More than anything, this is the reason it hasn't hit until now. The anger. The confusion. The way she would make it make sense if she could, how Tair is both still so herself yet someone else entirely. Loyal to a fault. Razor-focused in the meticulous choosing of her words. Still unable for the life of her to keep her thoughts off her face. All the familiar shadows Selah knows to look for, contained inside a woman who has long outgrown the girl she once was. Faded scars and grown-out hair is nothing compared to the black tattoos that now snake up along Tair's arms, a challenge saying, *Look at me. Look at the history etched in my skin. I am here. I exist. What do you know about the complicated and unpredictable agony of being alive?*

Everything. She knows everything about it, because she was there, too. She was there the day she came between Tair and those boys on the beach, barreling into a delicate dance of power and ego without the slightest idea of how far that ripple effect would stretch. She's put herself on trial every day since, trying to do better, trying to make up for the random chance of her own privilege. She isn't the same person she was five years ago, either. And Tair hasn't been here to see it. Tair *left*.

It's unfair, that thought. She does know that. Tair doesn't owe her anything, least of all a congratulations for doing the bare fragging minimum. It burns in her chest all the same, hot and thick, flaring and twisting and ugly and bursting to get out.

She takes another drag of the cigarette.

Selah hears them before she sees them, and she's really not in the mood. Emerging from the dark, the day's dust sits in Arran's hair and clings to his boots, the real Theodora Arlot's hand held loose in his. Vaguely, Selah thinks she probably shouldn't be as surprised by that development as she is. Given the . . . well, *everything else* of the last few days, she'd completely forgotten about that. Or maybe just hadn't assumed it had a shelf life longer than the one night. Arran's never been the type for actual relationships.

He stops short at the sight of her. "You've got to be joking."

"That," she answers, and exhales a long furl of smoke, "is your job. Hi, Theo."

"My lady," Theo says, brows raised high. "You gave us a good scare."

Arran, on the other hand, says nothing. He stomps straight up into the rotunda, grabs the cigarette from her mouth, and chucks it into the night. Up close, she realizes that he is *vexed*.

"What the frag, Arran?"

"Where have you *been*?"

It's harsh, a bark, and Selah blinks because she doesn't think Arran's talked to her like this since she was about eight, trailing after him and Julian Aleida with plaintive appeals to *please* let her come, too. But she made a promise and she's not going back on it, no matter how conflicted her feelings may be. She's not going to tell anyone about Tair. Not even Arran.

"None of your business," she mutters, and slides off the ledge.

"Actually," he replies, "it *is* my business. It's absolutely my business. Because I just spent all day looking for you."

"Well, no one asked you to do that, so . . ."

His nostrils flare, and immediately she knows she's made a mistake.

"Dad is *dead*, Selah." Each word is low and clearly enunciated, as though he is speaking to a small child, as though this is somehow brand-new information. "Do I really need to spell that out for you? He's dead, *murdered*, and we don't know why. So when you go missing like that, people are going to worry."

"I just needed some space, all right?" There's a testiness growing beneath that flick of annoyance. A warning. Arran, of all people, isn't someone who should be lecturing her about responsibility. Theo, she notices, has by now disappeared back into the night. Probably the smart move. Theo and Arran may have gotten themselves involved somehow, but this is family business. This is private.

"You could have been kidnapped, or killed, or *worse*—"

"Fragging *ice*," she snaps. "You sound like Mima. You're all *crowding* me. All the time. I can't hear myself *think*. I can't even *breathe*—"

"You are so unbelievably selfish."

Selah laughs. There's no humor in it. But the irony is too good. "Oh, right," she says, leaning against the rotunda pillar because her ankle *hurts*, dammit. "So when I do it, I'm being selfish, but when *you* take off for two weeks without so much as a goodbye, we're all supposed to nod and understand and 'give you the space you need.' Right. Got it. That's totally fair."

"Fuck what's fair." Arran's voice echoes around the rotunda, and Selah takes a shocked, unintended step backward. "If I take off, no one gives a shit and you know it. But *you* . . . savage Quiet, you have *no* concept of accountability—"

"Get off my dick, Arran."

"—and you have *no* idea what you almost did tonight."

"And what was that? Keep you from getting laid?"

He looks like he could slap her. Good. She's done with people standing around pelting her with unfounded accusations of what a terrible person she is, when all she's done for *years* is try to do better by them.

But he doesn't touch her. He doesn't say anything. Doesn't even look at her. And vexed off as she is, Selah thinks she understands.

Once, when she was twelve and Arran sixteen, they had gone to the cliffs overlooking Purgatory Chasm. Tair hadn't been allowed to come. Summer was in its first, glorious hour, and the Arborem's teens had turned out in full. Arran had broken off from her immediately to go sit with Julian and the other boys, even though Mima had asked him to watch her. But Selah hadn't cared. She was *twelve*. She didn't need a nanny. She'd spent the day with her friends, drinking cold fizz and challenging each other to handstand competitions and trading taunts with the Boardwalk kids over across on the public side of the chasm. Then Cassia, her then-best friend when Tair couldn't be there, had suggested they make their way down the sloping rock face toward the open water's edge. Selah had done her one better.

She hadn't thought that the jump down into the chasm would be so short, or the water within so shallow. Dark blood blossomed in generous ripples from her ruined shins as screams rang out from the teenagers high above, echoing down along the narrow crevice in the earth to where she flailed in searing pain. And then nothing. Darkness. The next thing she knew, Arran was hauling her up the sloping rock face, and then he was yelling at her like he had never yelled at her before, tears indistinguishable from salt water.

That night, huddled together beneath his heavy blankets, he admitted to her he'd thought she was dead. That Mima would blame him for not watching her. That she'd think he had done it on purpose.

So she understands that this isn't anger. Not really.

"You're not responsible for me," she tells him, still hot, because he's her big brother and she loves him for it, but she's an adult now and he is *overreacting*. "I understand why you went looking, but that was your choice. Not mine."

Arran still won't look at her. He works the muscle in his jaw, shakes his head like he's holding back what he wants to say, and Selah wishes he'd just *say* it so they can be done with this already. Savage Quiet curse her ankle for not letting her walk away.

The corner of his lip curls, and it's not a smile. "You had a sentry."

"What?"

"Linet. Your sentry."

"Yes. I know. What about her?"

"Linet, who we borrowed from the Institute Civitatem."

"I *know*."

A growl of frustration escapes Arran, almost disbelieving. Selah doesn't think that's entirely fair—of the two of them, *she's* not the one talking in cryptic circles, and for the life of her she can't see where this is going.

"If something happens to you," he asks, "what do you think happens to her?" The slow, deliberate way in which he's speaking to her—like she's a child, like she's *stupid*—makes her want to scream. All the more so because he isn't wrong. Not in theory, anyway. Selah's actions still ripple, the same as they did for Tair, and she *knows* this.

"Well, nothing did happen to me," she says, because even if it did, she has the power now to protect the people under her roof. Linet will be perfectly fine.

"Yes, but *if*—"

"I *know*."

"You can't be this irresponsible. You're head of the familia now, that means—"

"Yes. I am. I am head of the familia." He has to stop, she *needs* him to stop. Arran isn't Gil, and he's not their father, and she *knows*, she *does*, she knows it better than any of them could ever comprehend. "I know what it means," she hisses. "So *stop lecturing me*. You don't get to do that anymore. I'm paterfamilias, and you're a fragging client. I'm in charge. Not you. *Me*."

She regrets it the second she says it. The petulant little sister that never really went away came back to rear her bratty head, to grasp at whatever she could to make him *stop*. But what she had grasped was ugly, and true, and there's no way to take those words back. No way to undo the way that Arran pulls back from her as though just seeing her now for the first time—struck dumb for that one awful, dragging moment before the shock and hurt is neatly put away behind a smooth, blank canvas.

Raw guilt curdles in her spleen. "I didn't mean . . ."

But he shakes his head. *Don't.*

There are shouts coming down from Breakwater House now. Flickers of lamplight growing closer. Someone—*someones*—are coming this way.

"Yeah, you're right," he says, throwing her one last look. "You're in charge. So act like it."

ARRAN

Naevia is off the divan the instant they enter the parlor, descending on Selah with a sharp cry of relief. For a brief moment, Arran can appreciate that she must have been terrified to know that her daughter was missing. Certainly he had been.

It's too soon, the voice had said, the one in the back of his mind, ridiculously. Too soon for the cold blue anger that came with the letter to tell him that Alexander Kleios was dead. *Not Selah,* said the voice. *Not this again.*

But then Naevia turns her gaze on him and there's nothing there but fury. "What were you thinking?" she snaps. "She could have been *killed.*"

"Well, she wasn't," he snaps right back, to his own surprise as much as anyone else's. "She was never in danger. Just running off in her own daydreams like she always does."

"You should have come directly to me."

"Linet and I had it handled."

Naevia laughs, but there's no mirth in it. "And what a fine job you did. That fool sentry let her charge, the *Imperial Historian,* disappear from her sight. That is dereliction of duty. That is failure of the highest degree. At least she had the decency to find me and own up to it eventually." This is news. Arran feels himself go cold and stiff. But Naevia isn't done. "You, on the other hand . . . I thought you knew better."

"Mima—"

"Be quiet, Selah."

"Mima."

"I'll deal with you later."

"*No,*" says Selah, and pulls away from her vise grip. "You'll deal with me now. Because, like it or not, daughter or not, I'm also your paterfamilias."

Pulling rank on him is one thing. Pulling it on her mother is another entirely. Arran's brows shoot upward, but Naevia's face betrays nothing at all. "Very well, then," she says, low and calm, and he wonders if Selah can sense the danger she's wading into. He doubts it. "Paterfamilias. What do you have to say for yourself?"

Selah glances at him, just for a moment, before squaring back to her mother. "I'm sorry for worrying you," she says, the ghost of some impassive, authoritative thing taking over. "It was irresponsible of me, given the circumstances. But Arran isn't my keeper, and I'll thank you to keep your tone civil. Your anger's with me, not with him."

If she actually thinks that, she's more naive than even Arran realized. He'd find it sweet, if he weren't too busy being angry.

Mouth quirking with the unsaid, Naevia looks like she wants to laugh again. "Selah," she says instead. "You may be head of the familia now, but you will always be my daughter. I will never stop worrying about you."

"Fine," says Selah, with a cool clarity to match Naevia's. "You're entitled to your feelings. But you're not entitled to take them out on people who don't deserve them. And you're not entitled to have me followed anymore. No more curfews. No more bodyguards."

"Your father's assassin is still at—"

"I will *tell* you where I'm going. And that will be enough."

For a moment he thinks Naevia is going to slap her. She doesn't, but he can see the pain of struggle behind the decision. Nothing is more important to her than familia, and the structure it draws around their lives. Nothing. Not even, apparently, her own pride in the face of her only child's newfound power trip. So he watches her struggle, and watches her curl her lip, and watches as at last she curtly nods.

He should leave, if he has any sense of self-preservation, now Selah's made him so firmly the villain of Naevia's night. But anger is still bubbling in his spleen, and they aren't finished here. Whatever Selah may think, he knows who the real authority is in this house.

"What about Linet?" he makes himself ask.

There's annoyance in Naevia's face when she turns back to him, but surprise is writ there, too. "Who?"

"The sentry."

"What about her?"

His nostrils flare. "Where is she?"

"The Institute Civitatem, of course." She shrugs, and the bottom drops out from his stomach. "I sent her back."

Enyo Dietrik had told him, once, about what passes for reeducation in the civic centers, and the floggings and the rapes don't even begin to cover it. Humiliation. Sterilization. Lack of food, lack of sleep. Medical experiments. Servae who come out of reeducation are never fit for much more than unskilled labor, the barest hint of who they once were and who they might have become. He hadn't asked her how she knew this, but her father is a praetorian prefect at the Ministerium of Defense, and the way her face had gone hollow and gray was enough to know that it was true.

So the bottom drops out from his stomach, but it's Selah who sucks in a sharp breath. "Mima, you *didn't*."

"Of course I did. A sentry who fumbles her duties that badly has no place in this house."

Selah says nothing to that, just flits her gaze over to him, and Arran finds no satisfaction whatsoever in the low horror he finds there behind her eyes. He shouldn't have had to tell her. She should have already known.

Then the horror shutters, giving way to something dull and blank, and without so much as a word Selah turns on her heel and leaves the room.

He really, *really* should leave, too.

"You have to bring her back," he grits out instead.

Naevia looks unimpressed. "I don't *have* to do—"

"Tell them it was a misunderstanding." A muscle is working in his jaw, and he doesn't care that his voice is steadily rising, on the brink of crossing the tenuous line he's never dared approach.

Arran has never raised his voice at her before. She's his stepmother, yes, but that doesn't mean any actual parenting was ever hers to deal with. That was on Dad, or Gil. She took his monkey antics in stride when he was a kid, and more often than not ended up on his side during stupid arguments over new plays or the local clavaspher league. But if their relationship looks easy from the outside to someone like Selah, it's only because Arran has never given Naevia a reason for it not to be. He never wanted to find out what would happen when he tested the boundaries of her patience, and he never thought anything would ever change that.

Nothing could, except the iron blood coursing through his veins. Nothing, except the way it pounds now between ribs and heart, something wild rising in his chest, something swift and dangerous that's been percolating since the day Dad sat him down at ten years old, sunburnt and expectant, and explained exactly what it means that he is familia but not family. Nothing, except standing here and knowing that to someone like Naevia, Linet and her children are more faulty tool than fully human, and the only difference between him and them is the accident of who his dad decided to fuck.

A master politician, Naevia betrays nothing in the face of insurrection. "It's done. Even if I wanted to bring that crim back into this house, she's been turned back over to the Imperium. I have no more say in what happens to her—and neither does Selah, before either of you get any ideas."

"They'll destroy her. Take her kids away."

"And in all likelihood those children will be better off for it."

"She made a *mistake*," he says, sharp and loud enough to echo up to the arching beams, because his ease in this house has always been a carefully cultivated act. "A mistake that wasn't even really hers— Selah ran away because she got bored. That's on her. But you're the senator of Luxana. If you actually wanted to help her, you could. If you actually gave one shit about—"

"Enough."

Her voice is ice-quiet, and despite himself Arran finds his feet rooted to the floor, jaw slammed shut. Some habits die hard deaths, and Arran has always kept his habit of self-preservation well-nourished where Naevia's concerned.

"Now, you and I have always had an understanding, I think," she says, quietly crossing the room to where he stands. She doesn't even seem angry, and that makes it all the more chilling. This, apparently, is what happens when you cross the line. "I always welcome honest conversation. But you are having an attitude right now that I can't allow. I may not be your patron, but with your father gone, I realize it now falls to me to steer you, because Terra knows Selah's not going to do it. To identify where he allowed sentiment to muddy the waters. It's kinder in the long run, and better for everyone when there's no confusion about who they are. This *is* your home. We all abide by a social contract within these walls. Your part in that is unorthodox, I do realize that, so I feel it's important right now to make clear that you may *not* question my judgment. Ever. Not mine, not Selah's. A broken social contract creates danger in a home. Do you understand that?"

Arran keeps his gaze fixed somewhere in the vicinity of her right shoulder, twisting his mouth, the words caught in his throat as he breathes deeply through his nose. In, then out.

He should say yes. Give in to that habit of self-preservation. Keep his anger to himself, where she can't find it. Tell her that he understands, that even though he has his father's jaw and his father's eyes and his father's height, that despite all this he understands that everyone has their place, and he knows where he belongs.

"Arran. I'm telling you this for your own good. Tell me you understand."

He should say no. He doesn't understand. Doesn't understand how she can't see it.

But of course she can't. Who would willingly see something when their entire way of life depends on never seeing it at all?

"Yes," he says, and finally meets her eyes. "I understand completely."

DARIUS

The uniform is a help, most of the time. Does half the job for him. One look at crisp black folds and shining gold buttons generally has backs straightening to comply, and whether that's out of respect or fear or just some bone-deep understanding of the natural order of things, it doesn't particularly matter in the end. But that's in the orderly mid-districts, Ecclesmur and Seven Dials and the tiny, oft-forgotten Fourth Ward. Down in the Kirnaval, Darius knows better than to think the Intelligentia uniform will get him anything but belligerence and a stone wall.

Even then, he's got his work cut out for him. Dirty work boots and a duskra belonging to his housekeeper, and still the proprietress of this particular establishment barely gave him the time of day. "Order something or clear out," she'd finally snapped, apparently immune to flattery and flirtation, like she's got the first right to be there herself. Granted, the long line growing behind him probably had something to do with that, too, but Darius still feels the flick of annoyance. The Publica should have shut this makeshift taberna down ages ago, with its illicit slick-tack tables and chairs spilling out at sundown to perch precariously on the crumbling steps between two Kirnaval tenement halls. He'd have a word with the district prefect himself if it didn't mean erasing a lead.

So that's a problem for a different day. In the meantime, if the Revs *are* using this as a meeting place, he'll have to sniff them out a different way.

Darius sets himself at a table with a pint of watery hops, ignoring the suspicious sticky patina covering its surface, ignoring the ugly bubble in his gut that says this is a waste of his fragging time, and tries not to let his distaste show. This is the last on Leks Tiago-Laith's list, and not *one* of them—not the taberna by the Regio Marina docks or the mid-tier Ecclesmur bathhouse—have yielded so much as a whisper of Revenant activity. Three days of this and it's become abundantly clear that either Avis Tiago-Laith was deliberately misleading his husband about his whereabouts, or he was never as far up in this *Griff*'s esteem as his messages back to the Intelligentia made out.

A waste of time. A waste of resources.

But it's pointless even to think it, because both Kopitar and Consul Palmar's instructions were explicit. The threat behind them even more so.

If I ever hear so much as a whisper of you slandering a good familia's name again—never mind that of the Imperial Historian—*I swear I'll have you packed up and shipped back to that hovel in Ithaca so fast you won't even have a chance to dismount your horse.*

Kopitar is a good man. He is. Darius has reminded himself of this time and time again over the last couple of days, because he can't shake the memory of harsh words and the blood running to ice through his veins. Kopitar is a good man, with good instincts, and moreover he is *good* at his job. Aided and guided Darius for ten years in a way his own father certainly never bothered, and never once led him astray. He's only trying to protect him, Darius knows that, because he isn't stupid enough not to understand the repercussions if he gets this wrong. He'd only thought the Chief might quietly give him leave to pursue it a little further if he asked.

He hadn't, though, and Darius is trying to make his peace with that. It isn't worth losing everything he's worked his entire life to gain.

Instead, he's knocked on doors and followed the fast-vanishing ghost of Avis Tiago-Laith's trail. Which is how he's somehow ended up amidst the stinking, indecorous rabble of Sinktown. Half of them probably don't have two ceres to rub together, and still decide to spend the one on booze. It's hard to feel anything but disdain.

He'll have to get over that, though—or pretend to, at least. Darius casts another glance around, looking for someone likely to strike up a friendly conversation. Someone who looks like they might be a regular, might have seen something or, with any luck, actually know the name Avis Tiago-Laith. The rowdy table of eelwomen, that's an obvious mark. Or there, just a little ways up the steps from them, two old men deep in silent concentration over a battered game of chess. Or—

His heart doubles on itself.

No.

There's no way that's . . .

But it is. Black curls and honey skin, wide and curving in a cheap green duskra. He doesn't know her name. But he knows her on sight. There's a jav in the Plaza Capitolio he likes to frequent during meridiem, sheltering from the hot sun under the relief of cool blue tiles with a cold glass of hibiscus tea. She spends her meridiem hour there, too. And that's hardly something notable, just another face in the crowd of regulars—capitol staffers and politicos all—but there's no mistaking her now, and there's no honest reason he can think of for a decent young woman like her to be *here* of all places.

Darius doesn't believe in coincidence. And, all threats of demotion and banishment aside, he doesn't believe in ignoring his gut. He hasn't spoken to her once in his life, knows her by sight alone. That doesn't mean he isn't perfectly aware of whose senatorial office she works in.

"This seat taken?" he asks quietly.

Dark eyes flick up, then go wide. "Deputy," she says, and he doesn't know whether to feel guilty or not at the obvious shock. It doesn't particularly surprise him that she knows who he is. She gestures to the empty chair. "By all means."

He sits.

So. She knows him on sight, too. That follows easily enough—he's sure the Arborem mimas make it their business to know when someone new and unattached comes to town, then make it their children's business, too.

"I'm afraid you have me at a disadvantage," he says with a pleasant smile all the same.

The woman—mid-twenties, maybe, something clever in that sharp grin now she's gotten over the shock—laughs. She actually laughs, and Darius can't help but be slightly discomfited by how quickly she's moved past the surprise of him being there. She really should be much more worried than she is.

"Theodora Arlot," she tells him instead, extending a hand. "But you have to call me Theo."

"Why do I have to?"

"Well, all my friends do."

He takes the hand, despite himself, suspicion still percolating. There's just no earthly reason for one of Naevia Kleios's staffers to be at a suspected Revenant nest. "Theo, then," he says. "Forgive me, but this doesn't seem like one of your usual haunts."

"And you know all about my usual haunts, Deputy Miranda?"

He'll give her that. He didn't even know her name until thirty seconds ago. "Fair enough. You could forgive a man for being curious. This isn't the sort of place I'd expect to find a nice patrician girl."

"No, I wouldn't either," Theo says. "Then again, I don't see any of those around. Do you?"

Darius stares. Pieces falling into places.

"Arlot," he says at last. "I'm not familiar with the name."

"No, you wouldn't be. It's new. Given by a family friend." And then she winks. She actually winks.

Outrage at Theo Arlot's sheer audacity wars with shock at the realization of what she's implying. What this means. That this woman is a plebeian, and not just that, but the daughter of a freedman. One who somehow climbed her way up the ladder high enough to merit a position in the Greater Senate of Roma Sargassa. And yet, for all the shock and outrage, what ultimately wins out in Darius's chest is something like *relief.* The nagging voice shutting up again. The ordered universe returning to rights. Theodora Arlot came from this rabble, so at least her being here isn't the obvious incongruity he'd taken it for, nor is it further damnation against Naevia Kleios. He slumps back in his chair, suddenly tired again.

"So, what," he asks, "this is old stomping grounds?"

"No, I'm not from Luxana. Updistricts are a lot, though, and I don't . . ." She hesitates, something rueful at the edge. "I don't always feel entirely welcome, to be honest." There's something about Theo Arlot, something he can't quite put his finger on. Something where he thinks his own annoyance might otherwise be for any other low-class pleb, except. Except that she's crawled her way out of the gutter, same as him. "Sometimes it's just nice to get away."

"I know something about that," he tells her, taking a long drink. "But you know, it wouldn't be the worst thing in the world to get yourself some distance from this crowd."

"Oh, yeah?"

"I mean you're obviously smart, and ambitious enough to end up where you have. You don't want anyone else holding you back."

Darius learned that the hard way. There had been a time, if he's perfectly honest with his own memory, that he thought he could do both. Keep the needle moving, rise above what had been given to him at birth, but still keep his family close. Not his father, of course, or his idiot brother Aulus, the familia heir. But Titus and Florian, his mother . . . Well, it doesn't matter now. His mother turned to religion when the rest of her life became disappointment, half-stoned on incense burned at the altar of a woman meant to be some Terra idol. Florian's a drunk. And Titus never managed to amount to much, still riding on the Miranda name and hope that the meager fact of just being patrician will somehow be enough to sustain him once the money runs out completely. Darius doesn't like it, but he understands the way the world works, the slights and passing-overs that come along with a family as embarrassing as his. The very material consequences that come with the shame of association. He'd had to cut ties completely.

Now, that rueful something plays at the corner of Theo's lip. "I'll remember that," she says. He wonders if maybe there are already people she's left behind. "All right. Your turn."

He pauses. "Me?"

"Mm-hm." She sips at her hops, waggles a dark brow. "What's your excuse? Wait, no, let me guess. You're meeting your secret lover."

Darius rolls his eyes despite himself. "Hardly."

"All right, not that. Must be some top-secret Intelligentia business, then, if you're down here in *that* getup."

"What's wrong with my getup?" Darius blusters, glancing down at the dirtied duskra.

"Nothing, nothing." She laughs. "It's just . . . different from your usual look."

"I could say the same for you."

"Yeah, but we already covered me. Now spill."

Darius hesitates. Obviously he isn't going to tell her the truth. Not the full extent of it, anyway. Even if Theodora Arlot didn't work for the senator, wouldn't report back what she'd learned in an instant. Which she will, no doubt. Ambition and loyalty make for a powerful cocktail. But there's something easy about her, something that makes the frustration of the last few days bubble up, demanding to make itself known, and *Terra*, Darius's head hurts.

He doesn't have to tell her the whole truth, after all.

"You're right," he says, and downs the rest of his drink. "It's Cohort business."

"Any luck?"

"Like I'm going to tell you that."

"Fair." She grins. "Well, if it helps at all, I haven't seen anything suspicious since I sat down. Except for an Intelligentia agent trying to blend in, of course."

"Ha. Ha."

He raises his empty pint in mock salute. She bangs hers against it, an aide of no importance who he'll probably never talk to again after this. A kindred spirit, even then. Someone who's clawed her way up. Terra knows why that's what does it. Days and days of unsteady ground. He buries his face in his hands with a groan.

Theo's brows shoot up. "You okay?"

"Not really." He wishes there were more in his pint, watered-down shit that it is.

"Must be a hell of a case."

"I'm not *telling* you," he says, a laugh punctuating the exhaustion despite himself.

This is ridiculous. What is he *doing*, talking like this to one of Naevia Kleios's staffers? He only even came over here to make sure she wasn't up to anything she shouldn't be, and, having sufficiently determined that she *isn't*, he really should get back to work. And yet . . . he's tired. That's the truth. He's really, really fragging tired.

The voice in his mind saying Kopitar's *wrong*, it's never said that be-fore. It's the one that chimes in when Darius knows the right thing to do, the right path to follow, and never once has it diverged from what's prescribed as *duty*. The misalignment of the two sits ugly in his gut.

"Have you ever—" he starts, unsure, faltering because if there's anyone who's ever been in this position before it might very well be the woman sitting with him at this table. He tries again. "Have you ever felt like there were two options, and one was right, but one was . . . I don't know, the *done thing*?"

Theo stares at him, incredulous, one brow raised. "I'm first gen," she says. "You think me being on Senator Kleios's staff is the done thing? You think *anyone* wanted that to happen?"

"Fair enough."

It was a stupid thing to ask, anyway. He respects what she's achieved. It's admirable, the dream of Sargassa laid out. But it's not the same, not really. People can talk and make snide comments about her all they like; that doesn't mean she's ever directly disobeyed a su-perior to get to where she is. Only then Theo's looking at him in that *way*, the one that says she's been exactly where he is, and says, "I'm going to tell you what I think."

"Oh, yeah?"

"Yeah. I think you're looking for the Revenants."

Darius doesn't choke, but it's a near thing. "I'm not going to *tell*—"

"You're not going to tell me, I know, I know. That's why I'm guess-ing. And if I'm completely off base, then you get to ignore me and go back to the Ministerium of Intelligentia and laugh about this with everyone, but in the meantime that's what I think. Everyone *knows* your office is after the Historian's killer and the street orators already announced that the Revenants are your prime suspects. Not exactly a leap of logic."

Darius opens his mouth to—what, correct her? Deny it? He can't, because she's right.

"But you know what else I think?" she says, and leans in close over the sticky tabletop. "I think you have a different idea of who's done it. And I think you want to chase that lead."

Darius presses his lips together, giving nothing away, even as his heart hammers double time, and he's beginning to get a sense of how, exactly, Theodora Arlot rose so high so fast. She sees the things that other people don't. Same as him. They understand each other, this pleb girl and he. Terra knows how, but they do.

"If," he says slowly, "and that's a big *if*—but let's say that were true. And let's say that I had been . . . discouraged from following that other lead. What would you do?"

Dark eyes shine in the cheap paraffin light. "I'd ask for forgiveness instead of permission."

"Do that in the senator's office a lot, do you?" he asks, and tries to ignore the way that it's a deflection from the traitorous rise in his chest.

Theo smiles. "All the time."

His heart still bangs against the cage of his ribs, but even for that he can't help but welcome the wave of fresh clarity. If it turns out there's really nothing more to Naevia Kleios than a politico pushing in where she has no business being, well. What Kopitar doesn't know can't hurt either of them. But if there's more to it than that, if Darius can bring him hard evidence—or, even better, *the perpetrator himself* . . . Forget demotion or banishment back to Ithaca, Kopitar will probably give him a fragging medal.

Darius breathes in hard, and steels his nerve.

THEO

Theo isn't actually all that hungry, which is convenient. In the event of real hunger, Zabele's taberna is probably the worst place they could have picked to rectify the situation. The limp stack of acorn-flour dappham was cold when it arrived, and the severely watered-down hops isn't much better. But Zabele herself is easy on the eyes and always good for a laugh, with her trashmouth humor and wild gold lion's mane, so Theo's never all that annoyed about meeting Griff here for their weekly debrief.

Darius Miranda, though. That was a surprise.

Any vestigial hunger they might have had vanished the second he approached their table, livery duskra and oysterman's boots clashing ridiculously. It didn't matter that they'd never spoken before, Theo had known him on sight. Even if they weren't a spy, didn't have a vested interest in keeping tabs on the top-ranked Intelligentia's movements, that's just how life in the Regio Capitolio *works*. Eyes open and ears perked, aware of who's who and how, precisely, they can be used to further one's own career if and when the moment presents itself. Two days undercover in Naevia Kleios's office was all it took for Theo to know that, when it comes to lies and deceit, the Revenants have got *nothing* on politicos.

They watch Miranda leave the taberna through narrowed eyes, and send a silent thank-you to whoever's listening that they'd been here to intercept him. It doesn't take a genius to put the pieces together—someone's clearly tipped him off that Zabele's is a common Revenant meeting place. And it had been easy work, getting rid of him, encouraging him to abandon their trail and sniff out whatever half-baked theory he's come up with instead. So now the question left spinning in Theo's mind, unsettled and disquiet, is how in the savage Quiet he knew to look here in the first place.

Gods, they need another drink. Today's been a fucking ride.

No sooner do they think it, though, than Griff is sliding casually into the empty seat across the table. Floral duskra and native-style trousers of sturdy, faded blue cotton twill, she looks to all the world like any other nice, middle-aged dear out for a drink at the end of a long work day. Theo isn't fooled. They set down their unfinished dap-pham, but take their time chewing the last mouthful of onion-tomato pancake.

"Griff."

"Theo. Those any good?"

"Not really."

Griff nods, then gets down to business. "Arran Alexander."

Theo looks up sharply. That, they hadn't expected. They didn't even know Griff knew Arran's name. Although maybe by this point they should stop being so surprised by the true extent of just how much Griff knows. "What about him?" they ask.

"You two spent the day together."

"What, are you having me followed now?"

Griff rolls her eyes, smacks them fondly across the arm, not hard. Like they should know better than that. "Please. Pa'akal saw you two coming out of Vorndran's."

"Yeah. We were looking for his sister. Selah went missing."

And hadn't that been a terrifying development. Not only for the girl in and of herself—and Theo had tried very hard to separate that, done their level best not to imagine the very worst scenarios their mind could conjure when it came to Selah's fate—but for what it could *mean*. The simple fact that Griff needs her, alive and whole and willing to wield some esoteric weapon for the cause, and *still* Theo doesn't understand how a spoiled patrician girl could possibly be so important.

They don't have to understand. All they needed to know was that, so far as Griff was concerned, Selah Kleios was *their* responsibility. And they needed to find her before someone else did. Before someone else got their hands on her and this Iveroa Stone, if it's really as pow-erful as Griff claims. And what had concerned Theo the most out of all the rest was that little voice in the back of their head reminding them that the Revenants still have no idea who really killed Alexander

Kleios, either. Theo had done their best to put that whispering voice out of their mind and focus instead on just *finding* Selah.

There's no alarm on Griff's part, no sudden moment of surprise, but Theo knows her well enough to recognize the slight widening of her eyes, the way she sucks in her cheeks in just that way. "Missing?" she asks, a hush.

"Yep. Don't worry, we found her. Safe and sound and cozy in her big mansion."

"You should have checked in with me first."

"Probably," they acknowledge. "But there's no harm done. Selah's fine. As for Arran, she loves her brother, so honestly making friends with him can only help if you really want her to trust me."

Friends. That's one word for it. Theo isn't completely sure when they stopped being an open book with Griff, only maybe it's something to do with the fact that this is new and unexplored territory.

They've fucked plenty of people before. They've used that count-less times as a means of getting closer to what the Revenants need— information on sentry changeover at the Ministerium of Defense, the key to a pawnbroker's shop in the Financial Quarter. This was sup-posed to be a means to an end. They've never known what it's like for it to be more than that. They weren't entirely sure they wanted to find out, actually, and had resolved not to. That was before they quite literally ran into him again in the middle of the street.

"Friends," Griff repeats, quiet, and Theo doesn't know if it's para-noia on their part or just the natural consequence of those unwaver-ing gray eyes. "Maybe so. But the problem is, Theo, he's not the only friend you've made today."

And Theo draws up short, dread pooling somewhere in the pit of her stomach, and the unbidden image of Darius Miranda's pale face comes to the fore. So Griff saw them. Of course she saw. Vaguely, Theo wonders just how long Griff was there, waiting in the shadows of the Kirnaval tenement alleys as they laughed and drank with him. It had been an act, of course. It's easy with men like that, letting the blackbag see whatever he needed to in them so long as it meant get-ting what they wanted in the end.

They open their mouth, intending to say as much, but then they feel it.

The blade's edge is subtle, but unmistakable in its presence just inside the crook where their hip bends beneath the table. The slightest nick to their femoral artery and they'll bleed out—and sure, it'll take a few minutes, but they'll be immobilized in the meantime, unable to seek help without collapsing, while Griff walks away with no one the wiser. Theo would know. They've done it themself enough times.

So it's with a deep sense of awareness that Griff could, and very much would, go through with it if she doesn't like the answers she gets, that Theo leans forward to meet her gaze.

Not a mother, they remind themself, heart pounding. *Not a mentor. A spider.*

"Yes," they tell her simply, quiet and calm as they can. "Darius Miranda approached me. He recognized me from the Senate."

"You two looked cozy. It didn't look like the first time." Griff's voice is low now, too, and laced with something utterly dangerous. Theo's skin prickles with it, heart spiking.

"Well, it was. He wanted to know why I was here, that's all."

"And you said—"

"*Nothing.* I said *nothing.* He's got no idea who I really am." Someone laughs at the table next to theirs, and Theo wishes they could take a moment to appreciate the irony.

"I'm yours." They will themself not to blink as Griff's searching gray eyes seem to see right through their own. "*Yours.*"

And then they do something completely suicidal.

Reaching down, they place their hand gently on Griff's—not the one resting on the slick-tack tabletop, no, but the one holding the small paring knife bare centimeters from their own hot, pumping blood. They lay their hand atop Griff's and ever so lightly *press.* Blades are Theo's specialty, as subtle and simple as people. So while they don't apply enough pressure to break the skin, they can practically feel as the surface fibers of their sturdy canvas trousers slice away under the knife's edge.

Griff's eyes widen slightly, then narrow in, as she registers Theo's meaning.

She is the spider that holds the strands of the Revenants' webs together, and she is the spider that plucks them as needed. Her unquestioned judgment is more important than one life. People are expendable, even the ones you value, even those the most devoted to you. People are expendable. Revolutions aren't. And if Griff decides the strand that is Theo is a threat to the health of the web, then so be it.

Of course, Theo really, *really* hopes this display of trust means that she won't. They're staking their life on it, actually.

A long moment passes, then two, then three. At the next table, the drunk woman lets out another shriek of laughter. A sound like the crack of thunder goes off somewhere in the distance. All around them, Zabele's patrons carry on drinking and dining and shouting, oblivious to the fact that Theo's short life could end right here at this table.

It doesn't.

Instead, a shrewd sort of smile extends across Griff's mouth, and she lifts the blade away. Theo barely registers their exhale of relief, the cold sweat trickling down the back of their neck.

"Sorry, but I had to be sure," Griff says, pleasant as a meridiem date once again, pocketing the knife into some unseen sheath within her outer tunic. "I didn't enjoy that."

"Trust me, neither did I."

"So. Tell me about Darius Miranda."

Theo breathes a steadying exhale. "Well, I'd put him early thirties. Average-ish height. Blond, which is a frankly criminal hair color for a person to have, in my op—"

"Theo."

"Poor idiot's in over his head."

"Don't tell me we're feeling sorry for blackbags now."

Theo laughs, more a dump of breath than anything else—the necessary exhale of all that fear and determination built up behind their teeth finding some sort of release at last from tension. "No chance," they say. "But we can't use Zabele's anymore. He knew to look for us here."

"How?"

"Great fucking question."

Griff frowns, that divot of worry in the center of her brow, and Theo has to stop themself from giving into the bizarre urge to squeeze her hand. This is what they do. This strange dance where Griff could easily threaten their life one minute and still Theo's right there the next, a shoulder to lean on when she needs. They curl their hands back into their lap.

"Anyway, he didn't seem fully convinced that tracking us was worth his time," they say instead. "I may have . . . encouraged that line of thinking. So that's the Intelligentia off our backs for a minute."

"You're sure?"

"Pretty sure. Miranda's definitely a threat, we shouldn't discount him. But I think he's ambitious, too. And way too convinced he's right. Whatever he's doing now, he won't let it go in a hurry, but you should have someone keeping an eye on him in case that trail goes dry and he starts looking for us again."

"I'm guessing he wasn't kind enough to tell you *why* he was tracking us."

"No, but did he really have to?"

"Mm. The Historian."

"The Historian."

Griff smiles, grim. "Good catch."

That ease is back, the one Theo usually feels with her. Like the last ten minutes never happened. But they did. They *did*, and it's enough to remember that they've never gained ground with Griff by being anything but honest. Even if it means reckoning with themself.

They like Arran. They do. There's something endearing about him, something in the coaxing out of honest reactions through the mask he's so carefully constructed. A personal triumph in every genuine smile, every blank look of shock, and the way his slender fingers tap along his collarbone when he's considering something Theo's said. They like his laughter—the real kind—and they feel nothing but guilty about that, something rotten at the center of delight.

They don't want to give that up. But they also don't want to lie to him.

There's the truth.

They don't want this to be a means to an end.

"While we're on the topic of my *excellent* foresight," they say, fortified in their resolve, "we should talk about Arran Alexander." Griff stops mid-sip, then continues to drink. "I want to bring him over."

This time, Griff actually sets down her pint.

"You've never recruited anyone before," she says—not accusatory, exactly, but definitely somewhere to the left of neutral. "Only canaries."

"Always a first for everything."

"Why him?"

"You want Selah Kleios, right? They're close. Closer than you'd think." And here Theo takes a breath, leans in, and plunges on ahead. "If I can get Selah's brother, then I'm a hell of a lot closer to getting her loyalty, too. Fuck, he'll probably do it for me."

Face still as glass, it's impossible to get a read on Griff.

"Anyway," they plunge on, "I tested him some today and he seemed open. Didn't go screaming for the blackbags, anyway. And he seems . . . ready for a change. No surprise, given his background. He was talking about going back into the legions, but it definitely wasn't out of patriotism. I think he's a perfect candidate."

"And that assessment has nothing to do with your personal feelings?"

"Of course it does," they reply coolly. "My personal feelings always affect my personal judgment. And I think you'd agree that my judgment's usually on point."

It was Theo's judgment, after all, that got Griff to where she is today. They don't think it'll help their case much to throw that in her face. It sits there between them all the same.

"You like him."

It's not a question.

"I do. *And* he'd be a good asset. Those aren't mutually exclusive concepts."

When Griff leans back in her chair, there's something akin to pity in her eyes. Theo isn't used to being annoyed with her, but after a near-death experience they think they're allowed an exception or two.

"What?" they ask, an uncharacteristic snap pulled out from a long, drawn-out moment of Griff saying precisely nothing.

But she just shakes her head and says, "You're so young."

And they feel the heat rise in their cheeks—not from embarrassment, but bitter irony. Young is a matter of perspective, and Theo has not been young for a very long time. They're not an idiot. They're not a small child. They didn't have the luxury of that even when they *were* a small child, not since their life was stolen from them for the crime of being Jarol's family. And they don't appreciate being treated as anything other than clear-eyed and prepared to do what needs to be done to prevent the same thing happening to another innocent person—as they've proven to the Revenants time and time again. As they proved when the previous Griff made as though to surrender to the insurrection, and it was only Theo's quick thinking that stopped him from slitting the new Griff's throat instead.

They weren't young then, the man's blood running in rivulets down their blade and wrist, and they certainly aren't young now.

"Your judgment of character is a thing I depend on, Theo," Griff says quietly. "More than I should, probably. You backed my leadership in the overturn. You thought Avis Tiago-Laith was weak. You trust Pa'akal and the others. But we all came as part and parcel of the cause to you. You have clarity where we're concerned because you didn't bring us to this danger. What happens when this boy joins us? What happens when it's his life or the cause? Will you be able to set your personal feelings aside when the moment demands it?"

"Ten minutes ago I was ready to bleed myself out for the survival of *your*—"

"There's a difference," says Griff, with an unmistakable edge of finality, "between sacrificing yourself and sacrificing those who matter to you." Unbidden, the image of Alexander Kleios and the bloodmark Griff left to honor him swims in Theo's mind, and the breath hitches in their lungs. "I don't think it's a good idea. I'm sorry."

Theo's heart sinks. "But—"

"The plan stays the same. You're in place for a reason. Close in on Selah Kleios and the Iveroa Stone. Let me know if there are any new developments. And whatever this is with Arran Alexander, end it. End it now."

IV

THE MINUTES AFTER
MIDNIGHT

We came upon it in the night. Great fallen towers overgrown with weeds, twisted with vines and grasses and moss, tall and terrible and gray. Rusted. Ruined. A dead city. A cursed city. Sizzling pockets of foul air that burnt at my eyes and brought bile up in my throat. Smoke, and simmering, and shadows that lingered just out of sight, their edges unfinished and shifting—spirits or natives, I don't know. Afiona had not wanted to leave the Imperial Road. She was frightened of natives lurking in the woods. But brigands had descended upon our travel caravan the week before, leaving us empty-handed and alone. We were desperate enough for food that I might have handled any natives that gave us trouble, had we not gotten so lost. But there, in that decaying and warped place we stumbled upon in the deepest, quietest wilds, we were undone.

—EXCERPT FROM AN INTERVIEW WITH XENIA WILDEN,
CONDUCTED BY DR. SORREL NAEVIUS OF PAXENOS
UNIVERSITAS. DATED 338 PQ.

Editor's note: Xenia and Afiona Wilden were eventually found and recovered to Paxenos, where the story caught the public's interest and popular imagination. A series of expeditions were launched along the north Fornian coast in the late 330s and throughout the 340s to find their "dead city." Each was unsuccessful, and the sisters' claims have since been largely discounted as a hoax. Afiona Wilden died of smoking fever in 339 PQ.

SELAH

Arran isn't speaking to her, and Selah can't blame him. She wouldn't speak to herself either, if she could.

A child, he'd called her. Irresponsible. Selfish.

And he's right, because this is exactly how she lost Tair in the first place. What in the savage Quiet is *wrong* with her?

Linet was in charge of her safety, but to Selah she'd just been an obstacle. She hadn't spared a single thought to how giving her guard the slip would put her in harm's way. Would see her punished, sent back to the Institute Civitatem, her children sent away to various assignments outside the city, never to come back. Savage Quiet, she hadn't even considered that Linet might *have* children. She'd never asked. And now Linet is gone.

She learned this lesson five years ago. Didn't she? That grand revelation, a sudden break in understanding about how power moves through the world. Some fissure that opened her eyes about the responsibility she has to make the world better, lit a fire in her gut to force that march toward *progress*. For Arran and Tair and Gil and all the people she loves, who deserve so much better than this.

But she didn't love Linet.

She'd barely even noticed Linet.

And the simple fact of that had, in the end, sealed Linet's fate.

The horror had sunk in slowly, then all at once. The realization of what, precisely, she had done. Selah had still been stupid in that moment, stupid enough to think that a message from the Imperial Historian would be enough to reverse the course Mima had set into motion. It wasn't. There's strict protocol surrounding reeducation, and the Institute Civitatem is, after all, an Imperial institution. Once a serva enters reeducation, there's no having them released. Linet and her children are gone, and it's entirely Selah's fault.

The queasiness pools at the bottom of her stomach as the night drags on, and it's no more than she deserves. Because that, too, was a lesson she thought she'd learned five years ago. Maybe it was what Dad was trying to teach her all along, that the mere act of throwing her power around could be ineffective at best, a dire mistake at worst. So she sits in it, and she wonders what the point of being paterfamilias or even just patrician at all *is*, in the end, if you're only going to get people hurt without holding any real power to intervene. She sits in it, and feels it bubble up in her chest, the near-hysterical notion that there *has* to be a better way than this.

You people can only be tall when you're standing on our necks, and one cog's as good as the next as far as the great machine is concerned.

And.

You inherited me. You own me. And if things hadn't gone tits up I would have been your client and you still would've fucking owned me.

She sits in that, too, Tair's words ringing an echo in her ears. She hadn't understood, not really. Not then. It had been too much, too harsh, too filled with an anger she couldn't make herself come to terms with, too at odds with the collective responsibility Sargassans are taught since childhood. Only that, too, is cracking open. Horror and guilt oozing in at the seams. She sits in that, too. She sits in it right up until the moment she wakes in the early hours of the next morning to find Tair, fully dressed, sitting cross-legged at the end of her bed and examining the Iveroa Stone's sleek surface.

"You're here," she blurts, the fog of sleep rapidly rolling back.

"Apparently," Tair responds, casual, as if her sneaking into Selah's bedroom at four in the morning is a thing that still happens on a regular basis. Her gaze is calm and intent, almost unnerving, and suddenly Selah finds it almost impossible to look at her.

Because they were supposed to know each other. In the vast, confusing, too-quickly-changing world, they were Selah and Tair, and that was supposed to stay constant. Even when one of them was no longer around. She had spent years searching for ghosts, for a glimpse of red hair or sun-browned freckles in a not-quite-so-brown face, the missing piece that made her whole. Selah and Tair, or *Selah-and-Tair*, as they'd been. Whispers in the other's mind, equal parts caution and encouragement to the other's worst impulses. Two souls in equal balance. On a fast current toward something more. Something that was always there, waiting.

The idea that was Tair, anyway. The real thing is here, now, and stood in front of her last night with words like a flinch, and Selah doesn't know what was real or imagined anymore. What was *them*, and what was Tair just trying to survive.

"Any luck poking around?" asks Tair, now.

"Not exactly," she says. She's been a little distracted. "But I did have a thought. Can I have another look at the Stone?"

There's a thrill she finds sometimes in the depths of a research project. A sudden bright spot of clarity that doesn't leave her with a final answer, exactly, but *does* open up an entirely new avenue of inquiry she hadn't previously considered. She's grateful for the distraction now, even if it's not nearly enough to permeate the ugly roiling in her gut that means she just wants to bury herself in blankets and rot.

She slips out of bed anyway, ignoring the sharp twinge in her still-healing ankle, and crosses over to the abalone mother-of-pearl vanity where she nearly fell asleep looking over the old atlas. The other half of the strange duo Dad left behind. It lies open to where she left it— one page depicting an island off southern Fornia that she's fairly sure doesn't exist, the other a wall of illegible, incomprehensible text. She'd wondered about that last night, because Dad had wanted her to have this, too, after all. That can't be coincidence.

A quick glance is all she needs to confirm her suspicions.

Selah hands the atlas to Tair, watches as she takes it with an unmistakable air of interest, because of course she does. From six to eighteen she was raised by Gil in the shadow of the Archives' hallowed halls, and you don't emerge from that without a healthy respect for books. When Tair flips it open, her gentle handling of the worn spine and peeling bindings is nothing against the awed light that grows in her brown eyes.

"What is this?" she asks, reverent wonder creeping into her voice.

"Look at the alphabet," Selah says, holding up the Iveroa Stone to give Tair a clear view of the string of glyphs etched into the thinnest edge, the same ones she recalled last night in a momentary flash of insight, then the certain realization that she *had*, in fact, seen them somewhere before. "It's the same thing."

Day breaks slowly over the Sargasso Sea's far horizon, the blue-black sky shot with pink and gold that refracts against the dark clouds. The glimmer of a rising sun dances across Tair's drawn and stubborn face as she perches on a nearby rock.

Selah tries instead to focus on the surprisingly sour apple in her hand, on the eddies and whirls of salt and silt in the tide pools between outcroppings of rock. Tries to push down the nagging voice that wonders where Linet is now. Tries not to notice her once-friend's delicate fingers as they scan the pages of the atlas, or the blue veins beneath the soft skin of her wrist. It's rude, frankly, the way Tair bites her bottom lip in concentration, and Selah sets her gaze on the crashing waves instead.

It wasn't easy work, getting down here. Her twisted ankle isn't especially bad, but Tair—begrudgingly—had had to help her down the sloping dirt path, packed smooth by years of foot traffic with only the odd root or spiny crabapple bush for handholds. After, one hand resting on Tair's shoulder, she'd felt the prickling heat where skin met skin, the lines of tension in her old friend's body as they moved one step slowly after the next down the little stone staircase, crude gashes carved into the cliff's face by some forgotten someone long ago.

But they'd needed privacy, and time, and no doubt some scullion downstairs was already awake lighting the fires, so Selah had shoved a note about where she'd gone under both Mima and Arran's doors and braved it down to the gravelly shore's protected cove. Tair's set to work some yards away, muttering under her breath as she examines the signs and symbols written down on the arcane maps. The Iveroa Stone sits quietly on a nearby rock, cover open, soaking in the warm morning sun.

"Anything?" Selah asks, after several more minutes of itchy quiet.

"Be a lot closer if you stopped asking," comes the curt response, and she winces. Tair's already snapped at her twice for interrupting.

Only then she lifts her head and says, "Nearly done. Look." Unceremoniously she tosses her notebook over, and Selah fumbles to catch it,
almost ripping out a couple of pages in the process.

Tair was not, evidently, taking down notes on the atlas's alphabet
after all. What Selah sees instead when she looks down at the notebook are crudely drawn lines twisting this way and that, some in
curves and others straight, here and there little labels affixed.

"Uh. What am I looking at, exactly?"

Begrudgingly Tair gets up from her rock, then plops back down on
the sand next to her. Selah doesn't know whether to shift over to give
her more room or not.

"Luxana," she says, trading her the notebook for the atlas, thumb
stuck to keep it open to one page in particular—a city. She rips out
the sketch, lays it atop the city map. "This one's Luxana."

It's an absolute mess of a rendering. Now that she points it out,
Selah can decipher within Tair's rudimentary sketch the familiar city
streets and neighborhood quarters of their hometown. All the same,
she raises a skeptical brow. Because the simple fact is that when the
thin notepaper is laid out on top of the atlas's map, Tair's drawings
and squiggles in no way match up to depict the same city.

"Uh," she says.

"You were coming at it from the wrong angle," says Tair, a slight
edge to her voice that can't be anything but annoyance, only it's the
kind that seems to say, *You're smart enough to have figured this out
on your own.* "If you can't read the language, you've gotta read the
landscape. I recognized Seven Dials—see here?"

She points to the very center of her sketch, a minuscule roundabout from which seven thoroughfares disperse in an even spoked
wheel, the smaller streets between them twisting and curling to connect. A perfect match to the black lines poking through the notepaper
from the atlas underneath. Selah's mouth drops open.

"And then there was the Plaza Capitolio—" her finger moves to a
square formation some ways northwest "—and the Archives . . . the
intersection of these two cross streets—that would still be around the
Universitas District, I'm pretty sure—and . . . well, Breakwater."

It isn't possible. Selah hasn't spent much time with this map in particular, it's true, but she's read this atlas back to front and failed to identify so much as a single city or town. They've all sat in the outer wilds or on the ghosts of other urban centers she knows to be there instead, but not a single one has actually been *real*. In fact, she had begun to suspect that the places in this book never even existed at all, that this was some kind of urban planning scheme that had never taken off, an ambitious dream forever left unrealized. How could her own home have been here the whole time, unknown to her, warped and alien and labeled under a foreign tongue?

"But," says Selah, still trying to wrap her mind around the impossible, staring at the ancient little dot that marks her house. "*How?* Luxana's only—"

"Eight hundred years old, I know," finishes Tair, taking the atlas back into her lap. "But places are built on top of each other all the time. Maybe there was something here before that. Something before Luxana. Or Roma."

"Like what?"

"I don't know. Something else."

"Roma was here before the Quiet."

"Maybe something else was, too."

They stare at each other for a long moment, the weight of her words lingering heavy between them. Something before Luxana. It's possible. The Great Quiet took so much from them, and left behind so little. But before *Roma*? You might as well say before human civilization itself. Selah can hardly conceive of such a thing.

But this atlas was in Dad's possession, and so was the Iveroa Stone, with its etchings in the same, archaic language. Perhaps it's just coincidence. Perhaps this goes deeper than even Selah can comprehend.

"Tair . . ." she says slowly, alarm bells beginning to sound in her head. "What if this is all connected?"

"What do you mean?"

Selah shoots to her feet, all at once incapable of staying in one place. There's a sudden itch where the pleasant mystery of academia once was, and she doesn't know if it's just the spillover of her own rotten guilt clawing toward something else, but it feels dark. It feels *wrong*.

"These both belonged to Dad," she says. "My dad, who asked Gil to keep them secret and give them to me, who thought it was important enough that he asked him to do it while he was *dying*. It was the only thing. And now someone's blackmailing *you* to get the Stone. And the Stone is in the same language as this atlas, a language neither of us have ever seen, and we're probably some of the best-educated people in the fragging province." She's talking in circles, she's very much aware of that, but that's because this *is* a circle. "It just . . ." she finishes lamely, "it *has* to be connected. It just has to be."

Tair is staring at her, still inscrutable, and very suddenly she's unsure what to do with her hands. Her mind is still going a hundred miles a minute, and just standing here talking about it feels so profoundly not enough.

"You think I'm spinning out," she says.

"No," says Tair. "I just think it's none of my business."

"*What?*"

"Oh, don't give me that," she snaps. "So someone's blackmailing me, big fucking deal. I have more than just my own skin to worry about."

"Exactly," Selah says, voice rising to match Tair's. "That's exactly my point. What if this is bigger than you and me? My dad was custodian of the Imperium's knowledge. So *maybe he knew something.*"

There's a long moment of silence between them. Selah had forgotten about this part, the way that they can get under each other's skin like no one else. But she also knows that look on Tair's face, the one that says she's intrigued despite herself. Selah holds her breath, stops herself from pushing it over the edge. She needs the Stone. She needs Tair's *mind*. She needs her for so much more than that. But she isn't going to push. She holds for what comes next.

At last, Tair pushes her red hair back with a groan, and Selah's gut flips on itself. "Does the Neutra Ward still have a section on solarics?" she asks.

Selah nods.

"All right, then," says Tair, brushing sand off her wrap pants as she stands. "If we're going to get this thing working, then we should see what the experts have to say."

TAIR

The journey from Breakwater to the Archives takes an hour by foot, forty minutes by carriage or wagon, and just about half that by cruiseboard. Tair would know—over the course of twenty-three years, she's done them all more times than she can count. So she's prepared for the long haul, made even longer by Selah's rolled ankle. What she isn't prepared for is the way her once-friend lights up when Tair pulls out her cruiseboard from the bush where she stashed it, and she's definitely not prepared for a detour behind the stables to pick up Selah's bicycle.

Eyebrows briefly meet hairline, but—"If I can walk, I can bike. Remember?"

And Tair does. For her, it's always been about getting from one point to the next, the freedom to go where and when she wants, the wandering in between. But Selah spent her childhood pushing the boundaries, pushing herself—going farther, faster, *wait, check out this trick, I can do it*—and this isn't her first fall.

They take the long way round leaving the Arborem, gliding through empty backstreets in the weak dawn light, hoods pulled down once they reach the high street, just in case any servae or early risers are taking in the new day through a window. Nothing suspicious to see here, just two young ladies out for a sunrise cruise down the thoroughfare. Once they pass out of the Arborem into Pantheon Park, though, it's hoods up and a direct route south, the unnerving weight of the Iveroa Stone nestled in the messenger bag at her hip.

This is probably a mistake.

The city comes to life in scents of jav and tazine and salt and shit, birds crying overhead and the early shift sharing a quiet smoke while grocer boys unload their haul. Tair carves wide, winding arcs through upscale neighborhoods and financial centers and southways down toward the inner city. Selah fast and steady at her side, it's all at once the most unnatural and the most natural thing in the world.

This is *definitely* a mistake.

Tair was ready to go right back to hating her, to gritting her teeth and just doing what needs to be done if it means quelling her own unwelcome conflict over handing off the Iveroa Stone. Because Selah's right. There's something at work here, something she doesn't understand—strange alphabets and blackmail threats and cities that shouldn't exist. But *what if*s are nothing compared to what *is*. Keeping the Stone or giving it back means putting the Sisters at risk, and that's a compromise she just isn't willing to make. But she wasn't prepared for Selah's . . . whatever this is. Remorse. Self-awareness, or something.

She's still half-waiting for the other shoe to drop, the same way Selah's eyes flick away whenever Tair looks over, as though afraid to be caught staring. If Selah doesn't know what to say, doesn't remember how to talk to her, that's her problem to figure out. But then Selah flashes her a sun-soaked smile and leans her weight onto her bike's back wheel, or trackstands a loop with a gleeful shout of laughter, and Tair can't help but tilt her head back and give herself to the wind.

The last few years have been hard. Hard earned and hard lived, with every day and every choice the difference between life and death, starvation and survival, freedom and bondage. She wouldn't give up those years or the woman they made her, not for anything, but it's the way the coming home feels. Because home was never a place, and she can give herself this, just for a little while. The simplicity of it, Selah racing along in the periphery. Like pulling on an old sweater and losing yourself in its familiar smell.

The center of Seven Dials is, creatively, also called Seven Dials—although, to be fair, that name almost definitely came first. A cobblestone roundabout out from which wide main streets shoot off in opposing directions, like a child's drawing of the sun. And at the center, a tall obelisk of dark gray granite stands sentinel. Otherwise, the intersection itself is entirely unremarkable. A perfectly ordinary little corner of the world. Brick townhouses. Cypress trees, neatly planted in plots of green between each home. Colorful potted ferns and flowers set along one stoop. A one-eared cat yawning serenely beneath a window. Tair steps off her cruiseboard when the cobblestones become too uneven.

"*Hey*. You!"

And then there's that.

Tair turns to face the approaching Publica officer, shoulders squared. "Problem, officer?" she asks, and of course there is. Seven Dials is a respectable neighborhood. No one with her hair and her tattoos and her clothes has any business being here, not according to the Publica.

"What are you up to here, girl?" he asks, nightstick in hand.

"Just out for a walk."

"A walk," he repeats, as though it's the most insidious lie he's ever been told, and his eyes narrow in on the cruiseboard beneath her arm. "Riding one of them's an infraction in this quarter."

Sure it is.

"Yeah." She shrugs. "That's why I was walking."

Meaty fingers clench around his nightstick and, Terra, she can see how badly he wants to use it. "And *you?*" He rounds on Selah, then stops short, because he clearly doesn't know what to make of this— Tair, with her roots in serious need of tightening, black-line swirls and geometrics snaking up both arms, wearing a pair of oversized wrap pants she's almost positive actually belong to Ibdi. Selah, with her gauzy muslin duskra and gleaming turquoise rings and sleek black braids and clear authority of someone who has never asked permission for anything in her life.

"Is this girl bothering you, miss?"

Just like old times. Tair doesn't need to hear it. Doesn't need to see it, the way Selah hands him her patent of identity. She's heard it all before. Lived it all before. Been stopped damn near two hundred times since finding her home in the Kirnaval, never mind the countless moments Selah had to step in to defend her over the course of their childhood. Justify her right to exist. This is routine, by now.

And then Tair gets angry.

Because she shouldn't be here. She shouldn't have agreed to this. This was a mistake. And it's only now in this moment with her hair grown long and the Regio Marina so close she can still smell the sea air that she's remembering—*really* remembering—that she doesn't *have* to agree to this.

Except. *Except.*

Except that Selah isn't handing the officer her patent. She isn't smiling politely, or winning him over with a smooth, cultured voice or that calm expectation of authority, or doing anything at all, actually, except for leaning forward on the front handles of her bike, eyes caught meaningfully on Tair's as if to say, *Your move.*

There's an opening up ahead, one of the dials delving deep in the other direction. A moment to decide, then Tair nods her chin toward it, the sense-memory echo of a hundred times before when the pair of them didn't need anything as overcomplicated as *words* to know what was on the other's mind. The corner of her mouth tugs up despite herself when Selah raises a brow. Affirmative. She sees it.

So Tair nods again, firm.

Now.

The Publica officer is surprisingly fast, but on their respective bike and cruiseboard, the two of them are faster. Selah shrieks with glee at her side, the rush of thrill coursing through Tair as the officer's angry shouts fall further behind. She throws a finger up for him until they make it to the end of the dial, turning a corner to disappear into the tangled backstreets.

By the time they make it to the Universitas District, her laughter's practically turned to tears. Selah skids to a stop next to her, gasping for breath, and Tair doesn't stop herself. She doesn't even try. She pulls Selah in, wrapping her in a hug, warm and familiar and heart so full she can ignore the way the other girl goes stiff, put aside all the rest for just this moment, because she *missed* her.

That's the truth.

It's not much. But it's something.

But when she lets go, there's a strange flicker of doubt behind Selah's green eyes, some hesitation, and it's been a long time since Tair knew how to read her moods. She doesn't have to, in the end.

"I'm sorry," says Selah, and Tair blinks.

"For . . . ?"

"You know."

"No, I don't." Not stepping in? There's no need to apologize for that. Privately Tair thinks Selah deserves a fucking medal, actually. But the pain behind her eyes is something else completely. Tair has to stop herself from reaching out.

"For what I did to you. I don't know how much that's worth anymore, but I'm *so* sorry for—"

"Savage Quiet, Selah—"

"No, please, just let me get this out. I'm *sorry*," she says again, like this has been building behind her teeth, and Tair feels frozen where she stands. "I'm sorry for never noticing, for thinking anything about the way we were brought up was . . . normal. Or all right. Because it's not. It's just. It's just *not*. But I thought I knew everything back then, and I was so self-absorbed, I didn't understand. . . . I shouldn't have made you come with me that night, to the beach. And I should have just let you handle those boys, and I'm not looking for absolution here but I need you to at least know how much I think about what happened that night, and—"

"We were kids."

"I was seventeen. I should've known."

"How?" It comes out harsher than she meant it to, but it's there all the same. Tair breathes in hard through her nose. "How were you gonna know? No one was going to tell you. Not even Arran."

"Then maybe I should've just opened my fragging *eyes* instead."

Selah's bottom lip is swollen where she's bitten down, but Tair forces her gaze to stay steady on her face, heart hammering all the while. Because she never thought she'd hear anything like this coming from Selah. She can trace so many moments back through the years. So many times she was spoken over. So many times she was spoken for. So many scoldings from Gil for being late to class because of something Selah wanted to do instead. So many smacks round the ears from Imarry because the familia is suddenly hosting *important guests* tomorrow and where is Tair to be found when it's all hands on deck? Stayed late at the Archives, of course, *reading*. Justified, every single one of them. Every time. Every hit. Every look of disappointment and disapproval. Her fault, and she knew it. For losing track of time, for being lazy, for thinking her opinion mattered. Five years have gone a long way to unlearn that kind of thinking, but she never once expected Selah to walk the path of unlearning it, too.

So Tair breathes in through her nose again. "Don't do that," she says at last. "Don't apologize, we're not doing that."

"But I shouldn't have—"

"We're *not* doing that. I didn't have to go to the beach with you that night, either. I could've said no. But I didn't want to, and *I* decided to go even though I knew it was a bad idea." Selah looks like she's on the verge of arguing that, but Tair's already ahead of her. "I made that choice. Not you. And if you stand there and try to take that away from me, then that—*that's* where you and I are gonna have a problem."

She needs to get this. Tair *needs* for her to get this. They have to rise above the past, metamorphose into something better, because otherwise this just isn't going to work. They can't see each other again after this. And despite everything, despite every intellectual, logical bone in her body screaming out in favor of reasonable self-preservation, there's still that small, selfish part of her that desperately hopes for Selah to come through.

"It means a lot," she goes on, "that you . . . *get* what happened. It kind of means everything. But I was never set up to win in the first place, even if we both did everything different. So stop apologizing. It isn't helpful. Just . . . do better next time."

Selah twists her mouth, like she doesn't quite believe her.

"Simple as that?" she asks.

This close, Tair can see the flecks of gold in Selah's green eyes. Something more unsaid behind them. Something like regret.

"Simple as that."

SELAH

It isn't forgiveness. Not really. Not from Tair, and not from herself. It doesn't help Linet, and Selah knows already that she's going to carry the weight of that forever. Vague memories of wiry muscles and worried eyes, forever lost. But she thinks she understands something else now, something that she didn't before.

I was never set up to win in the first place.

For as long as Selah can remember, she has been taught that everyone has a part to play. A collective responsibility to the whole. And after Tair vanished into the night, she was so, *so* sure that the world was broken. That something had gone terribly wrong. That it had failed in its responsibility to her friend. She had thought it was her path to fix that, through reform and through education and through all the other resources she has at her disposal. She understands better than that now.

Nothing's broken at all. The world works exactly how it was built to. She just has no idea what to do with that.

Tair can't get within ten blocks of the Imperial Archives without someone recognizing her, both girls can agree on that. She was a constant fixture there for twelve long years, well known to all as Gil's apprentice. So Selah leaves her at a jav on the district outskirts, makes her way alone up the gleaming limestone Iveroa Promenade. She knows better than to try using the front entrance. She won't get three steps inside without being waylaid. Not by *actual* work business, of course—researchers in residence and admin staff alike know better than to try going around Gil to get to her—but any change in the status quo brings on the vultures, and Selah's spent the last two weeks dodging the flock of well-wishers and rubberneckers camped out in the marble atrium, all hoping to catch her ear. She sneaks in through the back.

The Neutra Ward's in one of the private science libraries, up on the fourteenth floor. Access to the level is heavily restricted, but Selah is one of two people in the building with free rein to go wherever she likes at any time. She steps into the attollo, dials the brass signal to the correct floor, and is about to close the grate when someone slips in beside her.

"Stalking me?" she asks as the attollo begins to rise, a rush of fondness pulling in all the same.

"That's my job," Gil responds, quirking the corner of his lip. "You're in early."

"Am I?"

There's a brass-gilt clock on the wall of the attollo reading six fifty-eight in the morning. She'd completely lost track of the time. "Couldn't sleep," she tells him, and it *is* the truth. Sort of. "Figured I might as well get a head start."

Selah doesn't like lying to him, not even by omission. She likes lying to him about Tair, sitting at a javhouse only a mile from here, even less. She's got to do it anyway.

"I have a handwriting expert coming in later," Gil tells her then, the first in what she already knows after three weeks is his *your-agenda-for-the-day* voice. "That's your three o'clock. See if we can't get Alex's notes on the Terra project figured out. Already ran a background check, but I assumed you'd want to interview her, too."

"No need. Get her started when she comes in." She trusts Gil's judgment, and anyway, she has a feeling she may not be in the building very long.

"Of course." He makes a note in his ledger. "Also, the Shikibu team are asking for a meeting."

"Which one is that again?"

"They're translating *The Tale of Genji* out of Nipponese."

Selah rolls her eyes. "Haven't they already asked to see the original something like six times? They know they need to go through the petition process. And they *know* I'm going to say no, same as Dad did. They were given copies for a reason. The original's too fragile."

"I don't think that's it. Word is they want to fire a member of the team."

"If it's a personality thing, they can—"

"It's not a personality thing." Gil hesitates. "One of the translators told me privately they've been having issues with this one from the start, they've just been trying to handle it internally. Apparently he isn't happy with the more . . . Imperialist framing the translation's shaping into."

Selah frowns at that. When it comes to translation, a shift in narrative construction is normal. *Edits* are normal. That's why Dad handpicked each member of the team himself, to ensure the right version was told. That's a good half of the Archives' work, after all. Safekeeping and restoration, yes, guarding the central hub of Imperial knowledge. But then they release it back into the world as needed, shaping and counseling progress in the course of people's best interest. So why does she suddenly feel so uneasy about it? That little tendril of nausea like some shade of Linet—though the truth is, she doesn't remember what the woman's voice sounded like—asking who gave her the right to decide what's best for everyone else?

Savage Quiet, she needs some fragging jav.

"It's your call, of course," Gil goes on, "but if you do fire him and the translator—Jankara—decides to make a thing about it, that's going to bring down a world of annoyance that you do *not* want to deal with."

"Tell the team no. For now. But I want to meet with Jankara privately."

"Tomorrow?"

"Preferably."

Gil glances at the dial then. "Fourteen?"

"Mm-hm. Palmar wants to install attollos in some Paxenos Imperial buildings," she lies, quickly casting about for the nearest thing. Mechanics, too, are on fourteen. "Apparently they're still living in the 600s over there. I promised him the schematics to take back."

"We should think about taking those out of fourteen. Not like it's *really* classified information. Anyone with half a brain and the extra manpower can rig a pulley system."

Selah frowns. "This is manual?"

Gil raises a curious brow and nods. "Of course. Servae work the pulleys in teams."

At that, her heart skips a beat. The attollo rattles steadily upward beneath her feet, and with a sinking, ugly roil in her stomach she wonders how in the savage Quiet she never thought to wonder about that before. The lift system that operates day and night to carry scholars and researchers and students and visitors up and down the vast expanse of the Imperial Archives' thirty floors. The little brass dial, signaling which one. And somewhere deep below the ground, if Gil's to be believed, teams of servae laboring and sweating, heaving and pulling, to get them all where they want to go. There's twenty attollos in this building alone.

Selah sets aside the ever-growing nausea, that whisper of Linet, an iron clamp of resolve taking its place instead. *Do better next time.*

The Neutra Ward is small, at least compared to the soaring libraries of the first and second floors. A low-ceilinged room at the far corner of the fourteenth floor, creaking wood and cozy leather chairs. The domain of unproven scientific method and quackery, interesting in theory but potentially dangerous in irresponsible hands. The section on solaric technology comprises two books, both relatively new. *An Introduction to Solaric Technology* and *Oddities of the Sun: Notable Curios of Solaric Origin.* Selah shoves them both in her bag.

By the time she gets back to the javhouse on the district outskirts, the sun is well above her head. People out and about, the Universitas District fully woken up for the day. But she takes one look at Tair, sitting out front, and rather than feel any sort of worry for how exposed she is, Selah just laughs. "You look ridiculous," she says, and plops down in the chair next to her.

Tair shrugs, and somehow manages to take a sip of jav. "I *look*," she corrects her, "like a fundamentalist."

"They let their women drink jav?"

"Well, now you're just being offensive." And Tair slaps a hand over Selah's mouth, like they're ten years old again or something. Selah licks a broad, salty stripe up her palm. Tair yelps and pulls away.

She has no idea, actually, what constitutes offense where the most extreme of Christian cultists are involved. But she does have to admit, when it comes down to it, that the heavy green veil Tair's unearthed from somewhere is a *genius* disguise. Nothing remains to give her away but deep-set eyes.

"All right, all right," Tair gripes, the shadow of a smile in her gaze. "What did you find?"

"The vast array of the Imperium's knowledge when it comes to solaric tech," she responds, and thumps both books down on the tiled table. "I'm getting some jav."

But even caffeinated, there's nothing helpful in either text. Nothing that connects to unusual glyphs or strange maps that match Luxana's topography if not its infrastructure. Nothing, actually, except for theory and speculation, and the basics of solaric knowledge that both Selah and Tair already knew full well. *While the interior mechanism remains unproved . . .* and *Rumors persist of private Ynglot knowledge . . .* and Tair is taking furious notes, but Selah feels half a sentence away from screaming.

"This can't be all there is," she groans. Tair barely looks up.

"Did you miss a volume?"

"I didn't miss a volume."

"Then this is all there is."

"You know what would be bona fide helpful?" she asks, leaning on the back legs of her chair with a groan. "If this Ontiveros lady actually knew what the frag she was talking about."

That, for some reason, is what gets Tair's attention. Her head snaps up at once.

"Who?"

Selah turns *Oddities of the Sun* to its back page, the little blurb and sketch of its author. "Dr. Diana Ontiveros," she reads. "She wrote the other one, too. Listen to this—*Dr. Diana Ontiveros, DSc., is the foremost expert in Roma Sargassa on solaric technology. She completed both her undergraduate and higher-level studies at Luxana Universitas under a self-directed course. Currently Dr. Ontiveros resides with her two children in the Seven Dials neighborhood of Luxana.*" Selah snorts. "Foremost expert, my ass. More like the only one. Still, if she's all we've got, we should probably go talk to her ourselves.

There's a *very* good chance she was censored from publishing all of her findings. Not to mention that these are about a decade old. She might have broken ground since then."

Tair stares.

Then she stares some more.

And then, quite suddenly, she slams shut *An Introduction to Solaric Technology* and dives instead for her shoulder bag, pulls out a file, and begins furiously ripping through the disorganized papers inside.

"Uh," Selah starts, honestly a little unnerved. "What's happening?"

Tair ignores her, just keeps flicking through page after page until she finds what she's evidently looking for. It's hard to keep up, her face covered as it is, but there's something in the tell of her dark eyes going wide. Wide, then narrowed, like she's found what she needs but it's not particularly good news.

"I knew I'd heard that name before." She sets the file down on top of Dr. Ontiveros's textbooks. "She's not in Seven Dials right now."

"How do you know that?"

"Xochitl."

"Come again?"

"Xochitl Ontiveros," Tair repeats, as though she's speaking obvious, perfect Sargassan Latin. "Diana's daughter, if my notes are right. Which they are. This case I'm working on with the Sisters, this girl, Xochitl—she got picked up by the Publica the other day for allegedly threatening an officer. Total bullshit. But there isn't an advocate in the city who'll help her with the case, so Pio and the Watchers are doing it. I've been helping build a few legal defenses, including hers."

Selah frowns. Something doesn't add up. "But why wouldn't an advocate help? If her mother's a well-known scholar—"

But Tair shakes her head. "I told you, Diana's not in Seven Dials right now. She's—wait. Bear with me a sec, this is . . . So there's Xochitl, right?" she says, drawing a Publica intake sketch out of the file. "But this really starts with the brother, Diana's son—Miro." A second sketch, this one from a clavaspher pamphlet. Both Ontiveros siblings have wide, dark, intelligent faces framed by long black braids.

"Miro Ontiveros, classic underdog story. Local kid gets recruited to the city clavaspher league after a scout sees him play in some pickup game. Doesn't lose a single match his first season. Makes MVP as a rookie, gets a patrician sponsor, looks like he's tipped for the Imperial League. Rags to riches. People love it. Only then . . . he dies. He gets caught up by the Publica in a poppam bust down in the Kirnaval. He and his mother both."

And here Tair pulls out the third sketch. Dr. Diana Ontiveros. An older woman, the same wide face and long braids twisted up into a bun. The very same as the author portrait in the back of both her texts. Selah feels her heart sink. "So she's dead."

Tair hesitates. "Maybe."

"You said—"

"*Maybe.*" Tair's eyes flash beneath her veil. "Look, Diana was a pleb, but she was a pillar of the Seven Dials community. Not the type you'd expect to get pulled down by drugs. So Xochitl's upset. She wants answers. She goes after the Publica officers involved in the bust. Corners the one she thinks is responsible for killing them. Threatens him with a knife. The officer barely escapes with his life. That's the official story, anyway."

"It isn't true?"

"Not according to Xochitl. Or the forty-eight witnesses who say the poppam bust never happened."

Selah frowns. "How do you get forty-eight witnesses for a non-event?"

"Publica records put the poppam trade at Inanto Way, about six canals down from the Sisters' clinic," Tair says with a humorless smile. "Problem is, that entire jetty's just one big children's home. Bunch of tenements linked together. So even if they got the street number wrong on the report . . ."

". . . it couldn't have happened there."

"Mm-hm. Someone would have noticed. Kids tend to do that."

"But then," asks Selah, mind racing, "what actually happened to Diana and Miro?"

"Yeah," Tair says, grim. "Exactly."

She slips an envelope from the case files. Sleek, pure white, containing a single sheet of scented vellum paper. Selah takes it from her and reads the neat, looping print of the letter's contents with a jolt of startled incredulity.

"Cato Palmar."

"Yep."

"Why would *Cato Palmar* invite Miro Ontiveros and his mother to dinner?"

"Patrician sponsor, remember?"

"Yes, but . . ."

"What sponsor would actually bother hosting a pleb?" Tair offers, humorless. "I know. It's weird. Either way, Miro and Diana went to his house for dinner, and they didn't come back. Next thing Xochitl knows, she's being told they died huffing poppam ten miles away, on the other side of town."

Selah stares at the envelope. She can't do anything else, because it makes no *sense*. Well, no, it *does* make sense, the pieces falling into place with alarming clarity, but even so she knows that a couple days ago she wouldn't have *let* it make sense. Cato Palmar, who should be a paragon of the law. Cato Palmar, implicated in breaking it. She wants to shut her eyes, push away what this *means*, but Linet's voice is conflating now somewhere with a phantom Tair's.

Do better next time.

"Pio thought he had this case figured out," the real Tair goes on, here in the light of day. "We took for granted that Palmar's behind whatever happened to Miro, which obviously presents all sorts of its own problems. But we've been so focused on Xochitl and Miro, I never thought about Diana as anything but collateral damage."

A long moment passes, and Selah rubs her temples hard. Of all the people to get caught in the crosshairs, it had to be Cato Palmar. "I'm guessing the Publica didn't question the Consul about any of this."

Tair snorts. That's enough of an answer. Of course they didn't, even with the evidence of the invitation in hand. Palmar knows something, but Palmar is untouchable, and the Publica are covering it up.

So Selah drains the last of her jav, and despite the jarring shift of her reality upending itself even further, manages to find a modicum of genuine optimism in this mess. Linet is gone. There's no saving her now. And this can never absolve her of that, but Tair was right, her guilt and apologies help no one. What she can do now, what she can do *better*, is help this family who might still have a fighting chance.

"All right," she says, taking a breath. "Well, it seems to me like we might be able to kill two birds with one stone. We find Diana, and maybe she can tell us something that's actually *useful* about the Stone. We find Diana, and Xochitl's defense also falls into place."

"And where—" Tair laughs, an empty thing, "—do you suggest we even *start* to look for her?"

Selah doesn't roll her eyes, but it's a very near thing. They've done this a thousand times, traipsing through the Hazards in the dappled sunlight, waving fallen branches like Caesarian crusaders and looking for edible mushrooms and ferns to forage. Weekend afternoons in the little attic room as the rain pounds down on the roof above, bickering about the finer points of Homer's influence on Peletor's *Sargasseia*. Tair hanging upside-down off her bed, pointing out some unsolvable problem and Selah insisting that economics are just made up anyway, *okay?*, before a pillow hits her face. There's a rightness to this, like something clicking into place. It's the familiarity—that determined, slightly manic gleam of a challenge in Tair's eye as she lights on the threads of an idea.

So she begins packing their research away. "For a start," she says, "we talk to Xochitl."

ARRAN

When he wakes—so early the birds have only just begun to sing—his mind is set, and he needs to be anywhere but here.

Tell me you understand.

Naevia's voice rings in his ears.

Yes. I understand completely.

The bed that's his but isn't his screams at him to get out. The curtains and the Anatolian rug and the big bay window look all wrong, distorted in the early morning light, an accusation, how dare he presume, and every shirt he throws on is itchy or oversized or makes him want to throw up. There's no faintly growing buzz hovering behind his ears, no sense of impending doom, and isn't that curious? Arran is as clear-headed as ever, and he needs to leave.

So he throws on his clothes from last night without thinking anymore about it.

He walks.

Through the dim manor house slowly coming to life, ignoring the morning greetings Una and Kalinde call out to him. Outside, where the dark fog presses in around Breakwater House, hanging so low and thick it transforms the peninsula into an otherworldly island all its own. Down the long gravel road, the cold salt air crisp in his lungs, and with every step away from the house his lungs breathe a little easier.

He walks.

It takes over an hour to walk there from the Arborem, and the sky is growing light. The sentries at the Senate don't recognize him, and why would they? But they recognize the seal on his patent of identity, the eight-pointed sun of the Kleios familia. Naevia isn't in yet, but her secretary is—and it should be harder, conjuring a smile to ease him in, when every step away from Breakwater has loosened the vise grip on Arran's heart, making room for something bigger. Rage. But it's easy, pretending it's not there. It's always easy. He has too much practice for it to be anything but. So the secretary sees a man who is all dimpled smiles and empty of anger, and he blushes, and is only too happy to give Arran the address he needs.

A half hour later finds him outside a modest apartment building in the Fourth Ward, one of the scrappy little neighborhoods squeezed between Seven Dials and the Financial Quarter that he somehow never thinks to remember. It looks like the kind of place that should be quiet on a normal weekday morning such as this. Families, bakeries, children on their way to school. Awake, but content.

It's not.

Shouts and disgruntled mutterings waft over from a small crowd where an amateur orator in his orange robes is riling up the Fourth Ward's residents. He passes a small throng of angry middle-aged women talking animatedly about rent hikes and overeager Publica officers and *should have at least given her a few days*. Tension crackles in the air, and it does nothing to quell the riot already roiling inside him.

No one answers the blue-painted door when he knocks, and it occurs to him that she may have already left for work. But as he's standing there, feeling the ocean inside his chest swell to a point he doesn't think he can contain for much longer and wondering where else he could go now and when did his hands get so awkward and heavy and useless—

Theo turns the corner up ahead, half a dappham sticking out of her mouth.

"Sorry," he says, suddenly realizing how weird this is. "I'm not a stalker, I promise."

"Let me guess, you were just in the neighborhood?"

She lets him in anyway.

Theo's apartment is a small studio on the third floor. He knows enough to keep quiet despite the prickling of his skin—at least until she's poured two cups from the steaming kettle and handed him one. Her tazine is nutty, almost herbal. This, at least, feels right.

"Sorry," he says again, after taking a sip. "You probably have work."

She shakes her head. "Day off."

"Oh. Right." He takes another sip, and wants to open his mouth, to tell her everything, to rid himself of this bone-deep itch that has him coming out of his skin. But the words won't come. They're too new. Too big—and what if he's wrong about her? Altogether more frightening, what if he's *right*?

Instead, he nods to the window, to the shouts of the street. "What's all that about?"

"Pina Bema."

"'Scuse me?"

"Pina Bema. She owns the corner store. Well, she did. Publica arrested her for being a day late on rent."

"Feels like I'm hearing stories like that a lot these days," Arran says, eyes fixed on the ceiling.

Theo frowns. "You all right over there?"

"Yeah. Why wouldn't I be?"

"Arran," she says, and when he looks up she's staring straight at him. As if she already knows. "Why are you here?"

He hesitates, just for a moment, then says, "I'm gonna self-immolate."

"Sounds excessive."

"Yeah, probably."

And then it all comes pouring out. Because his mind is made up. He's made his decision. But first he needs her to understand *why*.

It's not just Naevia, but Selah, and Linet and her children and how it was his family's fault because they *did not care*. He doesn't mention Naevia's threats. To shut up and play nice and swallow down every hurt and injustice for the sake of keeping the peace—to get on board or get out. He doesn't tell her about that. He doesn't have to. It infects every word that spills from his mouth.

Theo listens quietly as he rails, unfurling crescendos of all his long-held frustrations and the deep-seated guilt of knowing—*knowing*, and looking the other way. She says nothing as he paces the length of her apartment and back again, needing to get this out before he can stop and overthink the way he sounds like a petulant kid just beginning to have his image of the world ruptured by toxic reality. It's not. This is not new. But between Dad dying and Naevia's threats and actually experiencing a life outside the rancid bubble of the Arborem, and then Theo suddenly existing and showing him a way out, he can't swallow this down anymore.

So he talks and he talks, and she stays silent all the while until he's talked himself quiet. It's only then that she uncrosses her plump arms from where she's leaning against the closed window shutters. "So," she says, "what do you want me to do about it?"

Her eyes are dark. Her face drawn, impassive. He's making a mess of this, and suddenly it becomes abundantly clear that coaxing her into revealing herself is not going to work. So he takes a breath, and he takes the plunge.

"I know."

"Know what?"

"Theo." He holds her gaze, steady in his. "I *know*. I know what you are."

A beat passes, then two, and for a moment he thinks he's maybe miscalculated. Then she goes very, very still.

"I'm sorry."

That, Arran hadn't expected. It's completely disconcerting. He's right—he's *right*, and now what is he supposed to do with that? But Theo doesn't apologize to anyone. Not for anything.

"You—" he says, uncertain, but there's something steady beating against his chest alongside his heart, fighting to get out. "You're not gonna deny it?"

"What's the point? You'll tell the senator the second you get home anyway. Not sure why you haven't already, to be honest."

"Because—because I don't want to. Because I want to be one, too."

An incredulous crease grows between her brows. "That's not the way it works. It's not something you *want*. You either are or you aren't. You know or you don't. It's not like playing dress up."

"I *want* it, okay?" he snaps, and grabs her arm, because semantics be damned but she's not listening to him. And she's not panicking, and she's not denying it, and she's not asking why, or how he figured her out, but she also hasn't gutted him with the kitchen knife he clocked on his way in, so it feels like there's still a way in here. And if she wants him to prove that he wants this—that he *needs* to do this—then he will.

"I know this isn't a game," he says. "I have to do something. And I thought maybe that was going back into the legions because at least there I'd have some kind of *trajectory* or, or some way of knowing that I was actually living. But it's more than that now. I need to do something that actually makes a difference, because this doesn't *work*, and no one is listening, and I can't sit on the sidelines anymore."

Theo blinks at him, then down at his hand clasped around her forearm, over the rough ridges of keloid aqua swirls and abstract geometric lines he knows run their way across her back. And then, as if on the brink of laughter, as if she hadn't been annoyed with him thirty seconds earlier, she asks slowly, "What are you talking about?"

The drum in his chest skips to an unsteady halt. "What . . . what are *you* talking about?"

This time, Theo actually does laugh, a small chuckle that radiates the length of her body, and she looks down at her long, steepled fingers for a drawn-out moment. Then she looks back up, fixes Arran with a clear gaze and says, "I'm not a girl. That's what we're talking about, yeah?"

"You're not a . . . ? Obviously you're not a girl. You're a woman."

Her dark eyes hold his, almost amused. "Nope. Try again."

Oh. *Oh.*

"Oh."

"Yeah. Oh," she—they, *they*—repeat, and Arran suddenly feels like a world-class idiot.

"I'm sorry, I didn't—"

"I didn't think you knew, it's fine. Just don't tell your stepmother, yeah? Turns out I like my job."

"I won't. And I won't tell her you're a Revenant, either."

THEO

Whatever they could have expected Arran to guess at, it was just about anything but the truth. Theo breaks into an incredulous laugh.

"Sure," they say, rolling their eyes. "Big scary terrorist, that's fully me."

"Isn't it?"

"Yeah, totally." It's not a seed of truth they have to dig for here. It's the whole damn bushel. "Skulking in alleys, slitting throats, you know me."

"Theo—"

"I'm actually late for a rendezvous at our super-secret headquarters just now, so if you don't mind me kicking you out in a few—"

"Theo," he barks. "Stop it. I know. I've known from the start."

And the laughter dies on their lips, because Arran isn't joking. But he isn't yelling for the Publica either, or flushing red with anger at the lies, or any of the things they might have expected from a well-bred young man facing a marked enemy of the state.

What in the actual fuck.

Theo runs through the various hiding places they've stowed their knives, just to be safe, then asks, quiet, "How?"

"I told you," he says, and it's not an accusation, "the very first night we met. No one talks to me unless they want something. I know when I'm being used."

"I wasn't—" they start, but that's a lie. That is such a fucking lie. They *have* been using him. They've been using him since the start. They used him with the full intention of getting closer to his sister, and they were preparing to turn him to their side just so they could make their peace with that. Before, of course, Griff put her foot down, and Theo's stomach quickly turns at that, the thought of what Griff would do if she knew that Arran were here. That he's forced their hand. That he *knows*.

"My canaries," they realize. "Yesterday, looking for Selah in the downdistricts. Overkill?"

"Just a little. And then there was that man who called you *Nix*. Confirmed my suspicions more than anything, but I had a hunch from the moment you snuck out of my room."

Of course he did. Of *course*.

Arran's half-caste, and he had to grow up quickly. Had to learn how to read rooms. How to sense danger, and the undercurrents that no one else would ever think to notice. He had to, if he wanted to survive. To endear himself to a hostile world. Theo knows this, because they had to do it, too. They should have known better than to assume he wouldn't be equally skilled at weaving through the facades of other people's perceptions, and that includes their own. People see what they expect to see. And Arran expects to be used. But Theo had been so caught up in their own schemes, so caught up in showing off, that they hadn't noticed him noticing them.

"I'm sorry," they say, and this might be the first time in their entire life that they've actually meant it.

"Are you?" His face is impossible to read.

"Yes. I'm sorry for using you. Sorry for lying. Even though a lot of it *was* the truth . . . I'm sorry you got caught up in all of this."

"Well," he says with a shrug, "I'm not."

And it's the way he's looking at them now. With a barely-there smile. Like Griff and the senator and dei ex machinis don't exist. Like it's them and him and nothing else in the world in between. Theo can count on one hand the number of times since joining the Revenants that they've been at a loss for words. This marks one more.

"You—you're not?"

"I'm not."

"You're not."

"I'm *not*." A small burst of laughter punctuates the word. "I'm done trying to fit in where I was never meant to be, and this—*this* is what I'm meant to do. Can't you see it?"

"Arran . . ." they start, heart sinking just a little, because Griff said *no* but Griff may have had a point. "Do you know what that actually means?"

This still isn't like playing dress-up. This is even less of a game.

Arran sets his jaw. "I do."

"No, I mean, do you understand what we're really after? The Imperium calls us terrorists, but most of the shit they pin on us, we had nothing to do with. We're not, you know, *anarchists*. We just want Roma to *leave*. We want a democracy of our own. One that actually works."

"I *know*," he says again. "I told you about my friends in Teec Nos Pos—"

"Fagan and Enyo, yeah. Kids playing at revolutionaries."

"Revenant informants. For the Fornia cell."

"I—*what?*"

Cells report back to Griff, deferring to her as the spider at the center of the Revenant web, but they have to have a certain amount of agency to operate on their own. Communication and travel between cities is just too slow and unreliable on the Imperial Road for anything else. Theo knows that the head of the Fornia cell is a man called Chirag, but that's the extent of it. They don't have the first idea who else is under his command.

"They didn't know I knew," Arran says then, and that grin is back. "Figured that out on my own. Amazing what you start to notice about a person once you start sleeping with them."

They don't ask which. They don't care. Their heart is racing, because Arran wants to join the Revenants and he's had time to think it through. Griff said no, but he knew all along and he knows what's at stake and he *wants* to join.

He wants to join, and he saw them from the start.

He *sees* them. He always did.

"Canaries," they say, licking their lips.

"Come again?"

"Not informants. We call them canaries."

He sees them. He knows their name. His mouth is red where he's bitten down on it, and Theo could crash their lips against his. They could, and so they do.

They fall onto the bed, scrabbling at each other's shirts against the backdrop of seagulls and children playing in the broken-tiled courtyard somewhere below. His hand splayed across their hipbone, he trails an urgent hum down their throat, follows that column to their navel and down *down* until they're bowing their head and biting out something that's half hiss, half laugh. Theo wraps their arms around him, after, buries some murmured thing into his hair as he folds his head beneath their chin, touches their ribs one by one until the buzzing under their skin subsides.

When they come alive to the world again, it's the height of meridiem and there's little point in doing anything *but* take their time. They roll over to play a hand idly through Arran's hair, his green eyes hazy with want. He makes a halfhearted attempt to roll out of bed but they pull him back, kissing away the protests that try to escape. By the time they actually do push back the sweat-sticky sheets, the noise from the streets below is reaching a peak. Shouting carries over the wind faintly from somewhere in the distance.

"They're gonna get themselves arrested doing that," Theo notes dryly, pulling their trousers back on. "I'm starving. You getting up?"

"No, I live here now," he says, and Theo sees his point. There's no reason to move, not even for food, not when the bed is comfortable and Arran's cheeks are flushed with the linger-fading meridiem heat, and Arran knows. Arran *knows*.

"Fair enough." They shrug, and splay back down onto the white sheets.

Theo closes their eyes, enjoying the soft glow of midday sun that plays across the inside of their eyelids, the cool breeze sweeping in from the open window, the clatter of wooden shades. They lie there and try not to think about how to present this to Griff, try to focus instead on the pads of Arran's fingers skimming along the path of their ink-packed tattoo scars.

"Can I ask," he starts, halting. "If it's not too personal."

They raise a lazy brow, and decide not to point out that the two of them are both naked for the second time this week. They think they're a little past *personal*.

"Except," he goes on, a little awkward, "I know it's sort of . . . all-encompassing. Thremid."

Oh. Right. That.

"Means something different for everyone," they tell him with a shrug. They've never really had to put it into words before. "The world sees whatever it wants to see. Just means I know who I am."

Arran nods, brow furrowed in thought, and seems to accept it. Maybe because he knows something about that. "Theodora Nix," he says into the October air instead, and the sound of it is enough for their heart to turn pleasantly on itself. "*Theodora.*"

"Theo."

"Never Theodora?"

"Mm, maybe. If you're nice to me."

"Theo*dora* . . ."

They punch him in the arm, hard. And then they hesitate. "Arran, listen. About Selah . . ."

They haven't planned this far ahead. Their hopes for bringing Arran over to the Revenants seemed dead on arrival after Griff's order to end things. Well, Arran had shot that plan to the Quiet and back by being far more observant than Theo had given him credit for, but now that leaves them in the unfortunate position of improvising where to go from here. They're already going to be in deep shit with Griff as it is. They really don't want to make the situation any worse by misplaying their hand. But if Arran wants to join the Revenants, *really* wants to join them, then he deserves to know exactly what he's getting into. And Theo needs to lay a foundation of trust.

He's watching them, waiting expectantly for whatever comes next. Theo goes with their gut.

"I was at the Archives the morning your father was murdered."

Arran's eyes go wide. "You—"

"He was dead when we got there," they cut in, preempting whatever assumptions he's no doubt making even as they speak. "I swear. I *swear.* If anything, it felt like maybe we were there to help him, but got there too late. Griff didn't say as much, obviously, but—"

"Griff," he says, brows raised.

Oh, right.

Griff is the most wanted person in Roma Sargassa. Enemy number one. The bogeyman parents warn their children about to keep them from wandering into seedier parts of town. The very real criminal turned to myth, not least because the name keeps getting passed down. Theo can't imagine how strange it must be for Arran, to hear her dropped into casual conversation like that. Myth made flesh. Better get used to it, though, he'll have to meet her sooner rather than later.

Theo is one thing; it's up to Griff in the end whether he gets to join them, and she's already made her opinion on the subject clear. Theo ignores the way their gut flips.

"Griff," they confirm instead. "Anyway, it felt . . . I don't know, something was off about the whole thing. The Historian was dead at his desk when we showed up, and we didn't even leave with anything to show for it."

"You said this was about Selah."

"It is."

Arran is sitting up now, frowning down at them. They follow suit, and want to take his hand, but maybe they'd better not.

"There's a reason Griff wanted me in Naevia's office. Beyond just passing information. I didn't know why until after your dad died, but she . . . she wants me to get close to your sister. She wants Selah to join us."

Arran goes stiff.

"Griff wants access to the Archives, I think, among other things. And she wants . . ." Full steam ahead. No turning back now. "She wants something that Selah has. It's called the Iveroa Stone. It's . . . well, I don't really know what it is, actually. I *think* it's a book, but Griff says it's some kind of weapon. Something big. Something . . ." They trail off, unsure how to phrase this. Arran may understand the Revenants' functional reason for being, but beyond Theo and his canary friends, he hasn't met them. He doesn't understand what it's really like.

"Right now," they continue, "this isn't a war. This isn't even a fair fight. Every time the Revenants change leadership, we get someone with different ideas and different tactics—so then whatever progress that last leader made, we're starting from scratch all over again. The last Griff was too chaotic. He just wanted to watch the world burn. But *this* Griff . . . she believes that the only way we'll ever be independent from Roma is if every single person in Sargassa collectively *decides* to be. And I believe in her. So it's a long game, even if I can't always see the pieces the way she can. But the Iveroa Stone . . . Griff seems to think it's powerful enough to make that game a hell of a lot shorter."

Fuck it. They grab his hand. "I like Selah. I do. I'm not trying to drag her into something dangerous here. I don't believe in a magical solution that's automatically going to win us a revolution. But if this is real, and there's a way to see some actual progress, some actual *freedom* for Sargassans before I die . . . then it's worth it. It has to be worth it."

Arran has stayed quiet all this time, as Theo's looked to explain the complicated reality of what he's asking to be brought into. He hasn't flinched, or taken his hand away, but he hasn't really looked at them either.

"I think," he says finally, and pushes the sheets off the bed, "it's time you introduce me to Griff."

DARIUS

Seven Dials is a red herring. Darius, upon first arriving in Luxana, had figured that one out fast. The quarter's streets might be narrow, twisted things, all cramped storefronts and cobblestone, but they hide a proud history. Residents who can trace their homes and livelihoods back hundreds of years, passed down from generation to generation—some to the very end of the Great Quiet itself. Newcomers tend to be seen as interlopers, regarded by their neighbors with an air of suspicion or assumptions of overreaching themselves. But this sort of ferocious pride results in the plebs of Seven Dials comporting themselves with a stronger sense of propriety and duty than most in the lower castes, and Darius can appreciate that.

Maybe that's why, of the seven merchants licensed to sell water hemlock within Luxana's city walls, he's picked Persie's Apothecary and Compounds to investigate first. The people of Seven Dials may not be the type to get caught up in schemes and murder, but that's exactly what would make them such a good cover.

The list wasn't hard to get his hands on. Water hemlock's a regulated substance, the basis for all kinds of illicit and toxic brews. The clerk at the Ministerium of Records knew better than to ask what he wanted it for, and Darius tries to shake the queasiness in his stomach at that as he turns his uniform collar up. Tries to shake the feeling that he's doing something wrong. Using his office to get into places where he shouldn't be.

He isn't.

He *isn't*.

Kopitar told him not to investigate Naevia Kleios or her familia, and he isn't. Not yet, anyway. He's following his gut a different way. Because parcae was the method of Alexander Kleios's murder, and he's allowed to look into its source.

The apothecary's an unassuming brick storefront, squeezed between a textiles shop and a townhouse. Impressively dilapidated, it has the distinct air of having been in business for an extraordinary number of years. The little bell over the door tingles when he enters, and when the bored girl at the counter looks up from her book, she goes pale at the sight of him.

"I'm looking for Tobin Persie, is he in?" he asks, glancing around. The girl's eyes widen, but she hops off her stool at once, disappearing into the depths of the shop.

Just as narrow as the storefront would suggest, the apothecary shoots down so far it's almost impossible to make out a back wall amidst the clutter. Row upon row of tiny stoppered vials, bunches of herbs hanging from the ceiling, enormous jewel-toned bottles of witch hazel and echinacea and marshmallow root—and at the center of it all, a jacquard couch of faded mauve and small rattan table, set with a steaming ceramic pot. Tazine, probably. Darius can't stand the stuff. There should be a standard recipe, at least—you never know how it's going to taste.

The girl reappears then, beckons him to follow.

"Persie can come to me, I think," he tells her.

She bites her lip, a hesitation, then proceeds to flap her hands about in a bizarre series of motions. Darius can't understand what she could possibly mean by it, but he understands at once that questioning, almost hopeful look in her eyes. "You're a mute."

It's not a question, but the look of relief that breaks out across her face is an answer all the same. It rankles, being ordered around by a defective girl of no more than fourteen—and a serva at that, he notes as she tucks a lock of hair behind her ear—but they're also wasting valuable time. Going rogue doesn't come with an open-ended time frame. There's only so long before Kopitar catches on that he isn't following the Revs' trail anymore. So Darius lets her lead the way through the twisting labyrinth of tinctures and tonics, barrels and shelves. A large tank of live lizards sits at the back of the far wall when they finally come to it, next to a closed door that the serva girl motions him through.

Persie's backroom is significantly more ordered than the front, and

Darius thinks he understands. The shop retains an aesthetic of organized chaos to create a desired impression for customers, but a man's
workspace must function foremost for the sake of utility.

"My apologies," calls a smooth, fruity sort of voice, sounding out
from somewhere to the left. "We don't often entertain new clientele.
Our customers generally know Janet and her limitations, and she
them and theirs. By and large most of them don't mind storming back
here shouting for me if they must."

The man at the workbench is enormous, his girth sheathed in a
giant apron, protective goggles strapped over his eyes. Small burns
run the length of his forearms, well-muscled despite advancing age.
He doesn't turn around, bent intently over a mortar and pestle as he is,
although the serva Janet signs out a new message to him, pressed directly into the palm of his hand.

"And yet," says Darius, as Janet exits the backroom, shutting the
door firmly in her wake, "*you* don't seem to have those limitations."

The apothecary adds more seeds to the stone bowl. "No, I don't,"
he says. "Again, I'm very sorry, officer, but this tonic is . . . time-
sensitive in nature. Active ingredients, you know."

"Mm," says Darius, and pushes down his annoyance. "You *are*
Tobin Persie? Owner and proprietor of this establishment?"

"Guilty as charged."

"You must do well for yourself here, to employ a serva. Albeit a
defective one."

"What Janet lacks in speech she makes up for in a keen mind and
a delightful sense of humor," he responds, voice easy as ever. "It's not
my niece's fault that her mother is a fool who lost everything."

Well, that would explain it. Darius's regard for the man, already
tenuous, plummets in an instant. So much for the hard-working plebs
of Seven Dials. Persie adds a dash of yellow liquid to the powdered
seeds.

"Have you had any break-ins recently?" Darius asks, deciding
they've wasted enough time on pleasantries. "Anything stolen?"

"Not that I recall."

"How about that you don't recall? Something you might have
noticed . . . skimmed off the top?"

"Can't say there's been anything."

"I'd understand," Darius presses, leaning against the wall, "if there *had* been—and it was a regulated substance—why you wouldn't want to report it to the Publica. Something like water hemlock, maybe?"

"Water hemlock?" And there's nothing in Persie's voice that betrays nerves or even false surprise, just curiosity. Still, he hasn't so much as made eye contact, and it's starting to prickle unnaturally at the back of Darius's neck. By now, the remedy's turned to a brown paste. "No, nothing of the kind. Why, have there been other incidents? Should I be worried?"

"If there had been, it'd hardly be the Intelligentia looking into it."

"I suppose that's true. Must say, that's a relief. Water hemlock's one of my best sellers."

Darius blinks. That, he hadn't expected.

"Excuse me?"

Persie just hums a nod, leaning all the more intently over his work, and Darius has no idea what to do with that. He's seen the books. He's *seen* them, in the Ministerium of Records. "But you haven't sold any in three months," he says. "Water hemlock's regulated, the Imperium requires—"

"The Imperium *requires* that I report purchases of regulated substances in excess of *reasonable need*. In the case of water hemlock, that means two ounces and above. I'm afraid that, were I required to inform the Imperium about purchases of any quantity smaller than that, my bimonthly report would fill the pages of a very large book." There's a thread of laughter in Persie's voice at that, but Darius is the furthest thing from amused.

"'Reasonable need.' Is that a legal term?"

"It's the Imperium's term."

"What reasonable need can a person have to distill parcae?"

"*Parcae?*" Tobin Persie all but laughs, squeezing drops from a pipette into the decanter and watching the curling fumes. "Great Terra, no. Most buyers are just looking for a quick fix the day after an unprotected . . . night of passion, if you catch my meaning. A pinch steeped in tea takes care of the whole situation, with no lingering health effects to the woman or threm—well, the woman."

Darius stares at the apothecary's enormous backside, the pieces falling into place, and not at all in the way he'd hoped. "Birth control."

"Just so. Most of my customers in the market for water hemlock are just young ladies feeling a little foolish. Or their servae. They're not *murderers*."

"I think it's *my* job to decide that," Darius snaps, annoyance flaring again so bright he almost forgets that he's trying to keep Persie at ease.

This was a waste of time. Chasing the thread of water hemlock at all is a complete dead end, if what Persie's telling him is true. There could be hundreds—no, *thousands*—of people in this city alone with built-up stores, acquired in small doses over time. And the pressure in his temple starts to mount again at that, the realization that if he's going to do this, *really* do this, really defy the explicit instructions that Kopitar—and, more alarmingly, Consul Palmar—gave him, then it's time to go to the source. It's time to investigate the Kleios familia properly, delving into the family's movements and opening up servae case files and—

And.

Servae.

"These small purchases," he says, the sudden flash of a new thought. "Do any of them come from patrician familias? Anyone who buys on a regular basis?"

And for the first time, something other than jovial serenity percolates under those safety goggles. Discomfort. "Oh," says Persie, decidedly less at ease. "Well . . . I mean. This apothecary has been in my family for a very long time. A very, very long time, and we enjoy the patronage of many who value their privacy as a matter of discretion. . . . I wouldn't like to say . . ."

"Well, I'd like you to." He doesn't bother masking the ice there. Persie clearly responds to authority over friendly questioning, and anyway, Darius's mind is already seven steps ahead.

"Yes," Persie responds. "Yes, of course. . . . But please understand. Water hemlock is a crucial ingredient to a wonderful variety of at-home remedies. Migraines, ear and sinus infections, a means to mitigate the pains of menstruation and post-natal—"

"Have you ever sold water hemlock to the Kleios familia?"

A long moment passes. Then, setting his jaw, the apothecary nods, tight. And Darius's gut flips. That voice in the back of his mind whirring, saying *closer, closer.*

"How often?"

"Monthly. They have a standing order."

"And who comes to pick it up?"

"A serva. The majordomo puts the order in."

Persie removes the decanter from its flame. *Closer.*

"What's his name?"

"Who, the domo? We've never—"

"The serva. The serva who collects water hemlock for Breakwater."

"Oh," says Persie, removing his protective gloves. "Well . . . gracious, I wish . . . I don't know. I've never exactly had a chat with her, you see."

"A woman. What does she look like?"

"Most unfortunately, Chief General, I couldn't tell you that, either," he responds, lifting away his goggles and finally, *finally* turning around to face Darius. His pale brown eyes, however, covered in milky cataracts, linger somewhere just above his left shoulder.

Blind. A blind witness.

This has got to be some sort of cosmic joke.

"So," says Darius, icy disbelief hardening around his gut. He's so close. He's so close he can fragging *taste* it. "A strange woman who you don't know and can't see said that she was a Kleios serva. She does this in order to purchase a regulated substance from you on a regular basis, potentially accumulating enough over time to eventually distill a deadly poison, and you just . . . believed her."

The smile that grows on Tobin Persie's face is not patronizing, and it's not arrogant, but it *is* unmistakably condescending. As though Darius should really know better than that.

"Give me a little more credit than that," he says, bafflingly kind. "You've just watched me concoct flumene whilst being interrogated, a serum that if mishandled might have caused a minor explosion, and all without missing a step."

To drive the point home, he plucks a tiny bottle from the row to his left, stoppered and filled with the same pale blue liquid. Flumene. Truth tonic. Red-code regulated and hardly permitted in the hands of a common pleb. But there on the little label, identically affixed to each tiny bottle, is the unmistakable seal of the Imperial Consul of Roma Sargassa. This is no common pleb, but an apothecary under the protection and patronage of Cato Palmar himself.

Persie winks at his dismay. "I know my way around an authentic patent of identity," he says. "I wouldn't have survived very long if I didn't." And then he turns and shouts, *"Janet!"*

In all of half a second, the serva girl—Persie's niece—is back, pressing another series of hand signs into her uncle's palm. They go back and forth like that for a moment, and Darius doesn't know if he should interrupt the flow of conversation.

But then Persie smiles. "The serva you're looking for is in her late thirties," he says. "Maybe early forties. Pale skin, blond. Ynglot, Janet thinks. Looks like she might have a broken nose."

Darius feels it then, lighting somewhere in his solar plexus. *There.* A lead. The thrill of the chase. He knew there was something here. He was *right.*

"Thank you," he says, already halfway out the door. "Thank you so much for your time."

Only, then—"One minute, officer. Janet has a name. The serva you're looking for is called Una."

TAIR

Tair's newfound optimism lasts all of fifteen minutes, about the time it takes her and Selah to enter the Seven Dials prefect's office, realize that the line snaking up to the clerk's desk isn't moving anywhere fast, and promptly cut to the front.

"Suicide," she repeats, again, frozen to the spot.

"Yes. As I've said. A sorry affair." The clerk shuffles his papers importantly, and doesn't sound sorry in the least. "Now, if there's nothing else that requires such immediate attention that you cannot wait your turn to be called upon, I really do insist you return to the back of the queue and wait your—"

"I've *been* waiting. Xochitl Ontiveros did *not* commit suicide."

The prefect's clerk—a prim, fussy thing too well maintained to actually live in the district where he serves—blinks up at her, clearly unused to being contradicted, then draws himself up. "I assure you, miss, she did."

Tair, already braced against the tall desk, takes full advantage of her height to stick her face up to the narrow service window, landing it six inches from the clerk's.

At her side, Selah's hands sit squarely on her hips, lips pressed in a worried thin line. "Where's her body now?" she asks, and her voice is soft but firm, and furious as she is, Tair *does* see what she's doing. "We want to see her."

It's not a takeover. Just a gentle nudge. A reminder about what gets results.

"I don't know where the body is," he sniffs, barely sparing Selah a glance. "Not at this precise moment. Perhaps if you both were to wait over—"

"What is even the *point* of you?" Tair hisses, taking her cue from Selah, low and deadly calm even as her back straightens and her chin rises in haughty arrogance. She's spent a lifetime watching entitled patrician women get what they want, and Selah's not the only one who can put on a show. "Get me someone who knows what they're doing."

"I hardly think—"

"Get me. The prefect. Now."

Danger lives in her eyes, somewhere to the left of primal, a hair's breadth away now from the clerk's nose, but it's probably more that no one's ever spoken to him this way before. Either way, the clerk winces back in fear, then slumps off his stool and disappears through the door behind his desk.

Tair is vibrating, trying to keep her anger in check until the facts have been laid out to ascertain, trying to ignore the way her hands are shaking.

It makes no sense.

Xochitl, who had people working to get her free. Xochitl, who still thought Diana and Miro were alive somewhere. Xochitl, who knew something.

It makes no sense.

An assassinated Historian. A stranger in the shadows, blackmailing Tair for the Iveroa Stone. An ancient atlas and a quiet piece of solaric technology, both bearing the same unknown code. A missing alchemical scientist, who might be the only person alive who could plumb the Stone's depths. And her daughter, the only lead to her disappearance, now murdered.

It makes no sense.

It makes all the sense in the world, if you let it.

A light touch lands on her upper arm and she flinches away, buzzing too far out of her own body for it, but Selah isn't offended. Brow set, hands back on her hips, she's in this fight, too. Dimly, Tair is aware of the growing murmurs around the cramped and humid lobby—the long line of visitors and petitioners catching wind of their business here, turning from annoyance and frustration at having been cut in line, now buzzing with the shock and disbelief and that certain cold thrill as the gossip chain travels.

Xochitl Ontiveros, dead.

Ontiveros? Like that clavaspher player?

Supposed to be getting a trial next week!
Orators all said—
Killed herself, that's what the clerk *just said.*
Bullshit.
It doesn't take a genius. The murmurs are growing angry.

If the prefect of Seven Dials is at all alarmed to walk into his lobby and find the hostile shifting of a waking beast, he doesn't show it. Maybe he doesn't even realize yet. Disdain, that's the first thing she sees on his face when he comes through the door, his clerk wilting behind him. Disdain, and that snappish, brutal gait like he has better places to be. He's a bulldog, she can smell it, sent here to beat them down until they know their place.

Tair pushes away from the desk as he comes around to her side. She wastes no time.

"Xochitl."

"Pardon?" So inquisitive, so polite, but everything from his looming stance to his pristine navy duskra says *you gotta be out of your Quiet-cursed mind.* Maybe she is. She's here anyway. He'll have to reckon with that.

"My defen—my friend," she catches herself. She can't be a Sister here. Definitely can't be a Watcher. "Who killed her?"

The prefect raises a single brow. "I'm afraid," he says, lip curling, and savage Quiet he is *enjoying* this, "that I don't have the first idea what you're talking about. If you'd like to report a crime, the Cohort Publica are right next door. Now, I presume you have seen the good people behind you patiently waiting their turn, but Gaius here tells me you see yourselves above such petty rules. Surely you don't think yourselves better than your neighbors?"

"No, I—"

"And surely you don't need a quarter prefect to take time from his very busy schedule to school you in basic manners and decency?"

"You don't—"

"And surely you didn't think that threatening said prefect's clerk would get you what you wanted?"

"*Xochitl Ontiveros,*" Tair snaps, finds her in, since she can't take the Iveroa Stone out of her bag and use it to smack the patronizing smirk off the prefect's face instead. "She died in your custody last night. Less than a week before her trial. *Surely* you remember that?"

For a moment she thinks he isn't going to answer. But then his pinched expression smooths out into one of understanding. "Ah, yes. Of course. A terrible tragedy."

"Your clerk, he said it was suicide."

"Yes."

"Hung herself."

"Nasty business."

"So I assume that whoever just *happened* to leave a rope in Xochitl's cell is being suspended without pay while a full inquiry is being launched."

The packed lobby is, by now, anything but patient, and she has to raise her voice to be heard over the din. But the prefect's smile is back, small and nasty in its approximation of solemn understanding. "The general public, I'm afraid, aren't privy to the internal workings of the Cohorts or the prefecture," he tells her. And then, snapping around to his clerk—"Would you *please* see to this commotion?"

A jagged sort of shout from outside. People are starting to gather. The clerk hurries off—next door, probably, to corral the district Publica captain—and the prefect tries to sweep away again to wherever that back door leads, but Selah gets there first. One hand resting firmly on the little swinging gate between the lobby and the space behind the clerk's desk, she stands firmly in his way.

"Is that really what you want to do, girl?"

Selah just shrugs, and cocks her head around the prefect at Tair. *Your move.*

"Xochitl's trial was next week," Tair says, and every word is aimed precise and razor sharp. "She was mounting a strong defense. She wouldn't have killed herself."

The prefect turns back to face her, clearly still deciding if he cares to take on two half-grown women by himself. With people spilling out now from the building into the street beyond, shouts and yells and the patter of dozens of frenetic footfalls, no one from the Publica is coming this way to give him a hand anytime soon. All the same, he sneers.

"I know what you are, *Watcher*," he says, all pretense of snide contrition gone. "And if that girl had so little faith in the defense you people concocted for her that she fell into despair and took her own life . . . well. Whose fault is that, really?"

Tair does not remember having ever been this angry. Her skin is on fire with it. When the boys from the beach cornered her in that Boardwalk alleyway, that had not been anger. That had been panic and fear as she lashed out, then a willful ejection of consciousness from her body until they were done with her. When Gil came to tell her the sentence handed down by the court magistrate, that had not been anger either but a numb acceptance. Eighteen years had taught her well not to feel, not to rage, to instead go inward to that place where no one could ever touch her. Where what was secret could never be taken away. Five years of hiding her body as well as her soul was not enough to undo those lessons. Turns out that a single prefect *is*.

"You motherfucking piece of shit."

Vaguely, she's aware of Selah behind the prefect, eyes wide in awe, half caught agape in terrified elation at her words. Mostly, though, she's zoned in on the prefect himself, that little smile on a pasty white face as if to say, *Yes, that's what I thought. A savage, uncouth crim.*

No. You have no idea who I am.

"Are you proud?" she's asking, but she's floating somewhere three feet above, every inch of blood and flesh and bone and sinew ringing with sound and fury. "Are you the big man now? Did they let you into their little club?"

Selah is dragging her away, dragging her toward the door.

"Bet they didn't, did they? And after you were *so* nice, making sure the nasty little girl stayed quiet. Making sure she wouldn't tattle on your big friends."

The prefect watches her struggle, that condescending smirk a fat fly she could slap right off his face. Savage fucking *Quiet*, Selah is stronger than she looks.

"How'd it feel, huh? Trading in an innocent woman's life for some pointless clout?"

"*Tair.*"

They're at the door. Tair is screaming.

"It must have been the best moment of your pathetic *life*!"

Outside, the crowd is buzzing, shouting overhead, gathering and dispersing as the Publica move through with their batons and swords, reforming once they've passed. *Xochitl Ontiveros,* some say. *Murdered.* Not some riffraff from the Third Ward or Sinktown, this is one of their own. A good girl from a good part of town. They're furious. Not as furious as her. She wants to march back inside, to take advantage of the Publica's distraction as the crowd turns to punch the prefect right in his perfectly manicured face. But Selah throws her arms around her.

"Let me go."

"No."

"Selah, let me *go.*"

From the moment the prefect's clerk told them about Xochitl's fate, Selah has let her take the lead. Stayed out of her way. This is *not* the moment she wants to go back on that. Now that Tair's anger has been unstoppered, there's no putting it back in. She's out for blood.

But Selah doesn't budge. "Listen to me—*listen to me,*" she pants, straining to hold her back. "Xochitl's dead, Tair. She's *dead.* You can't do anything more for her now."

"Bet? I can make him pay. I can make him feel *pain,*" she growls, and means it.

"And get yourself caught? Sent to the Institute Civitatem? To reeducation?"

"Worth it."

"*No.*"

Selah pulls her around the corner, away from the growing mob, down into the trash-strewn alley that runs alongside the prefect's office. She pins her there against the wall, a surprisingly strong hand braced against each upper arm. It's bruising. Urgent. Tender.

"*Tair,*" she breathes, an inch away, and Tair tries to focus on the anger, tries not to notice the way her heart flips double on itself to be this near to touch to *smell* and she wants to scream something hoarse and primal, it's all too much and it *hurts*. Fire crackles beneath her skin.

"She wouldn't want this—" A gasp pulls out from nowhere, deep within her chest, and Selah's grip loosens on her arms. They leave white fingerprints in their wake. They leave a chasm. "Okay? Xochitl *would—not—want—this*."

Tair is shaking, cold and bereft and sinking fast to that secret place she knows too well, curling inward to where no one can touch her. "You don't know that," she says, and it comes out half a sob. "We didn't know her."

"No, we didn't. But I still know what she would want you to do." And then—"You can't save Xochitl. Okay? I'm sorry, but you can't. But you can still find her mother. Her brother. You can still help them. You can *still do that*."

"How do we do that now?" she asks, and hates how hopeless it comes out sounding. How empty. "Xochitl's *dead*. She's dead, and she's the only person who knew anything."

"No, she wasn't," Selah says, solemn. "We have to go see Cato Palmar."

"Are you spinning out? He won't tell you—"

"No, I know. But if he really is behind what happened to Miro . . . if there's even the smallest chance that Miro's still alive . . . Miro's our best bet to lead us to Diana. And if he's alive, then that means we need to go see the Consul."

ARRAN

Whatever he was expecting, this isn't it. The woman who stands in front of them is about a foot shorter than Theo, and at least twenty years older. High cheekbones, slightly curling black hair, a dusk-warm face dotted with beauty marks and lined by laughter and worry both. A strung necklace of white and purple shell around her neck. Something about a hand resting on each hip, however, and the shrewdness in her gaze gives Arran the impression of being surveyed by a very small, somewhat stout hawk.

She's nothing at all like the hulking shadows that swarmed his imagination when Theo told him they were going to meet the Revenant queenpin herself, but still somehow he can't help but feel like a badly behaved child, standing shoulder to shoulder here with Theo in this bizarre below-ground shelter, waiting for the elementary schoolmaster to decide his lunchtime fate.

Griff purses her lips, then says, "Theo. Go."

"Let me exp—"

"You disobeyed a direct order," says Griff, and her voice is hoarse and low and lilting, like the ocean against gravel sand.

"I *didn't*," Theo snaps. "I didn't tell him a thing. He figured it out on his own."

"Did he?" she asks, unreadable, attention lingering for a moment on Arran in a way that makes him feel distinctly naked. "Interesting." And then she's back on Theo. "Wait outside."

They look like they want to protest again, but Arran catches their eye and shakes his head. Griff will never respect him so long as he lets others fight his battles. One last, lingering look, and Theo disappears again up the stairs and back out through what Arran had initially thought to be a cellar door.

If this is a cellar, it's the strangest one he's ever been in. Set deep in the earth at the bottom of a winding staircase, past a series of solid locked doors of not-concra and not-stone. And here, inside—a few mismatched pieces of furniture. A rickety wooden shelving unit stocked with meager supplies. And, strangest of all, solaric lighting overhead. He's seen solarics before, of course—those prized lamps Dad kept in his study. Solarics are eccentric collector's items, highly regulated by the Imperium. Not something you find in a place like this.

Arran would linger on this longer if it were anything but his life hanging in the balance.

"Here," says Griff, gesturing to a folding wooden chair. "Sit."

He does, and is aware of his heart hammering in his chest. Aware of the wooden chair and Griff's plusher one, and the two blue mugs and pot of tazine sitting on the table. He's not stupid, and he knows how this could go. He knows about Fagan and Enyo, reporting to her Fornia cell on the inner workings of the fort at Teec Nos Pos and Enyo's father at the Ministerium of Defense. He knows about Griff and Theo, and that they've got their sights on this Iveroa Stone, whatever in the savage Quiet that actually is. The point is, if Griff really doesn't want him here, he'll never leave alive. He knows too much. And even if she decides to let him live, he still has a gamble of his own to make.

So he takes the opening gambit on himself. "You're not what I expected."

"No?" She pours, and doesn't look up. "What did you expect?"

"I don't know. I just thought you'd be . . . different."

"Older?"

"Meaner. Scarier. Ugly face. Maybe a couple warts."

Humor is a familiar friend for unknown ground, but he isn't expecting Griff to honest-to-Terra *laugh*. Something in Arran's solar plexus doubles on itself from the thrill of it, as the most wanted woman in Roma Sargassa hands him a cup of tazine. The drink smells of wild mint and almond. It's thick and warm and tastes of spiced oats. It tastes familiar. Like something he might have had a hundred times before, only it's really just been once. It's the same as Theo's tazine.

"So," says Griff, setting her cup down. "Let's be honest about this. I don't want you here, and Theo knew that when they decided to bring you in all the same."

"They must've known that once you met me in person, you wouldn't be able to resist my winning qualities."

"You're funny. Theo didn't tell me you were funny."

He tips a salute. This might actually work.

Might.

Griff leans back and peers at him over steepled fingers, again leaving him with the distinct impression of being assessed. "So they've put me in a hard place here. I *could* kill you, but I try not to be in the business of murder when it's avoidable."

"And my father wasn't?"

There it is. A suicidal move. Out in the open, and impossible to take back. For a long, drawn-out moment Arran just stares at her over his mug of tazine, knowing that if she owns up to it, their business here is done.

Theo said it wasn't them. They said it wasn't Griff's way. They said that he was dead when they arrived at the Archives that first rainy morning of the hurricane. And he doesn't think they're lying to him, exactly, but he also knows enough to understand that Theo isn't always privy to the big boss's plans. So he needs to hear it from the woman herself.

There's no way to read the expression on her face. Considerate, maybe, but mostly just blank. And then—"I didn't kill your father, Arran."

"The Intelligentia think you did."

"The Intelligentia are poorly named."

"Theo told me you were there, that morning. When he died."

"And did they tell you he was already dead when we got there?" Griff's voice lowers dangerously, and Arran's spine meets the back of his chair. "Parcae," she says. "An awful death. I was there, I admit that much. I was first on the scene. But I did *not* kill him. And I didn't order his death, either. I wouldn't have done that unless I had no other choice."

Arran should stop, he knows this. But he can't help the challenge in his voice. "If you didn't do it, then who did?"

"I have absolutely no idea." Her voice is light again, but forcefully so. The finality of someone not used to having her status questioned nor her orders rebuked. It reminds him of Naevia.

Arran's heart is still hammering in his chest, a million new ques-

tions running through his mind, but Griff is already moving on.
"Now that we've cleared that up," she says, picking up her tazine
again. "It's not *you* that I'm against, per se. I don't even know you.
But I fear for your distraction. Yours and Theo's. But we're beyond
that now—you're here, and I see no reason to kill a willing volunteer.
So I have one question for you." She peers at him across the small table, piercing gray eyes dark as a storm. "Why?"

It's a fair question, but he swallows hard, because he never expected to get this far.

Why, indeed.

He's not a radical—hadn't been, anyway, until this last year or so
when Fagan and Enyo stormed into his life and made him realize just
what was possible. He'd never been allowed to be, before that. Never
had Selah's luxury of jumping in defense of what she believes is *right*.
The only time he'd even come close was with his father, the very last
time he saw him alive, when Dad was refusing to let him reenlist. But
that had been personal.

I belong to the familia, but I don't belong anywhere else.

How do you explain something that no words have been created for?

You belong to the Imperium. That's what Dad had said. *We all do.*
We live for the many, not for ourselves. I've taught you this, so I can't
see how this sudden streak of willful individualism is my fault.

At least verna have a future.

It was a truth they'd avoided for years. Dad's face had stormed
over.

You really think you'd have preferred that?

Maybe. No. I don't know. I just—

The difference is more than a legal fiction, Arran. His voice had
been terrible and rising as he had never heard it before. *If you think I*
ever would have allowed that. . . . My son. My firstborn. In my own
home— ·

You allowed his mother.

It had taken Arran less than an hour to pack up and leave.

So there was that. His first foray into admitting what he has always known to be true, and simply felt too small to do anything

about. That his father was wrong. That under the Imperium, no one lives for the many. Patricians live for themselves, in this playground they've built over the course of three thousand years. Anyone else is just existing for their benefit. He *knows* this. He's always known it. So he opens his mouth, and he tells her exactly that.

Griff says nothing, not at first. Then she stands, and Arran stiffens again, because he's good at reading people, but this woman is impossible to get a handle on. This was a test, and he has no idea if he passed it.

But then she's walking over to the corner of the small cellar, to a second door he'd briefly noticed when he first came in. She unlocks the door and pulls it open with a heavy creak. "Come with me."

It's another staircase. Going down. He takes a breath and follows, descending into the dark.

Winding and twisting left, then right, then left again, and Arran thinks that maybe other landings shoot off here and there, but he can't see a godsdamn thing. He's keeping balance with one hand solid against the concra wall, but from the steady pace of steps ahead of him he thinks that Griff must know this place like she knows the lines of her own hands. Finally, they come to a stop in front of another solid door, and he wonders if maybe this is where she kills him.

She knocks once, quiet but firm, and then twice more. A man's voice answers, hushed and harried. "What do you want?" he asks. "Who is it?"

"A friend."

The room within is dark, and cramped, and smells of burnt flesh and orange peel. Arran only just stops himself from gagging, eyes watering as they adjust to the scene at hand. Candles and incense account for the dim light and scent of citrus. Aside from him and Griff, three others occupy the room. A dark-skinned woman lies facedown on a long, sturdy table at the center, sweat and tears running in mingled salty tracks down her cheeks. A man sits by her side, her brother maybe, holding her hand. And the third . . .

Another man stands over the woman, deep in concentration, the searing-hot metal rod in his hand chiseling thin lines into the delicate flesh of her skin. The whole room seems to inhale as one as he lifts it away, before quickly dipping it into the jar of crimson red ink at his elbow, then tapping it neatly into the wound. He sings as he works, voice soft and low and rich, and somehow just for her. And in spite of the smell, in spite of the pain, Arran feels that he's intruding on something very private. Something intimate. Something he hasn't earned the right to see.

He glances at Griff, but her gaze is steady on the tattoo process before them, and he senses that he's meant to watch. So he does. Watches the way the woman's brother bends his head to murmur something in her ear, and she can't help but smile through the pain. The way the tattooist seems to breathe in on the lift of the heated rod, beginning a new phrase or stanza of his song in tandem with a new line of burning ink. The way the woman's breath synchronizes in with her tattooist's, in then out, as though they could have been one being.

It's only when the woman's hand goes limp in her brother's, finally passed out from the pain, when the tattooist glances up at them and nods, that Griff speaks.

"Ever seen a singer work before?" she asks Arran quietly.

"I—a what?"

"A singer. More than an artist. More than a medic. Someone who can guide you through the pain of the process. Ody here is one of the best."

"No," he admits. "But I don't see why you'd bother doing it this way. It looks excruciating."

"Sometimes a little pain is the price you pay for avoiding more. You haven't spotted it?"

This time, Griff's already looking back at him when he glances her way, smiling in that vaguely knowing way, and his stomach flips. She nods him toward the woman on the table, and now that Arran knows to look for it, everything about this place makes sense.

The brand at the base of the woman's spine is tiny—barely noticeable, really. An encircled X with three dots below. Long since healed, it bumps up along the skin of her lower back, the customary place for such a marking. But sitting just above is a second brand, slightly larger this time, and definitely uglier—a crude, geometric eye.

Arran doesn't know who these sigils belong to, but he knows

as well as anyone what they mean—that she's been contracted more than once in her lifetime, bad news to begin with, and should she try to run away the Publica will know exactly where to return her. Ear cuffs are easy to take off, if you have the right tools. Brands less so. But while the singer Ody hasn't made it down to her lower back yet, Arran can only imagine that the cauterizing effect of the burning ink will be enough to do away with the history etched in her skin.

"It's not a bad precaution for plebs, either," says Griff, as though he were shouting his thoughts instead. "Harder to get nabbed off the street when you're covered in something that says you already belong to yourself. Makes you a bad target for Publica looking to turn a couple ceres on the side."

"So," he says, quiet, "this is where servae go to disappear."

"Vernae, too. Your friend Tair was on that table a few years ago."

"She—she was?"

"Of course she was."

Arran feels ill. He had always liked Tair. She'd been Selah's friend. Gil's apprentice. His own schoolmate for a handful of years. He had known, on an intellectual sort of level, that Breakwater's servae staff must bear the familia sigil. But he hadn't known that she, a verna, was branded. *He* certainly wasn't. The thought is sickening, but he has to let himself sit in it. The idea of the Kleios sigil—that eight-point sun, so cleanly sealed on his identification card, the proud, rich lineage of all that knowledge and history and *his father*—burnt into the flesh of his own skin . . .

And then he remembers something else. White linen sheets and the bronze length of their bare back, warm to the touch as he drew his fingers along ridged paths of abstract aqua.

"Theo," he says. "Theo's been here, too."

"Mm. Took them ages to agree to go underground again. Would've taken me longer. Nine years down there, it's a wonder they're so damn cheerful all the time."

"Underground?" He frowns. "Wh—"

"That's not my story to tell."

"Then why are you telling me any of this?"

"You asked."

"No, why all of *this*?"

The woman on the table, Ody the singer bent in dedication over his work. Tair. Theo.

"Because," she says, ripping her gaze from Ody and his charge to level Arran with steady dark eyes, and the gravel in her voice is more like grit, "if you're really with us, there's a cost. You can't be fighting for yourself. Or for Theo. Or for me. This is bigger than any one person, and if you don't commit and fight just as hard as that woman on that table is fighting right now, then you're useless to everyone."

It's not unkind, somehow, and he does understand. *Cogs in the great machine. We live for the many, not ourselves.* Dad taught him how to do that.

And here's the thing. Arran had come down here with every intention of bargaining his way into this fight, but he had one final concession for Griff to make.

Leave Selah out of it.

The instinct screaming out to protect his little sister hasn't shut up since Theo first said her name. Selah's twenty-two, paterfamilias, the Imperial Historian. Irrelevant. She's still a kid, basically, and Arran isn't letting her anywhere near the danger inherent wherever the Revenants go. Because he knows her. He knows the maddening combination of justice, ego, and loyalty that drives her every action, more often than not without waiting to think the consequences through. Her forays into equal-opportunity education at Luxana Universitas and the Imperial Archives are child's play compared to what Theo and Griff want her to do, and given half the chance, he knows that she'll say yes.

They want access to the Archives? He has that. He can get whatever they need. This Iveroa Stone, whatever it is, he can find where Selah's stashed it and take it for the Revenants himself. She never has to be involved.

That was the plan, anyway.

Standing here, next to Ody the singer, with Griff's shrewd gaze upon him and her words ringing in his ears, he realizes now how selfish that plan was. The words die before they have the chance to reach his lips.

"Well," Griff says. "Now that you can make an informed decision, I believe the options were clear?"

They certainly were. Join the Revenants and maybe die, or turn her down and definitely die. Arran breathes in, then out, and it's not about hedging his bets, because he wants this. He's wanted this since the day he realized the meaning behind Fagan's scrawled missives littered in code at the bottom of the bunk's wastebasket. Since the first time Julian Aleida pretended not to know who he was. Since the moment he learned his mother killed herself rather than raise an unwanted child. He wants to do this because this is right, and he's not afraid of death.

At least now he has a reason to live first.

"Good," says Griff, grasping his hand in hers. It's warm and calloused, and there's a strange grim light in the depths of her eyes as they seem to search across his face. Despite himself, Arran shivers.

SELAH

"This is a bad idea."

"This was *your* idea."

"Was not," Selah shoots back, one eye keeping watch on the open road. "*I* wanted to go alone. This—this is a risk, and *not* a necessary one."

"Beg to differ on that," Tair pants from some ways behind her. "I've got more skin in this than you. I want to hear everything he says, exactly how he says it."

She's about to argue, but a jumbling clang of overturned trash echoes up from the alley somewhere behind her, followed by a loud string of highly creative swearing, and Selah can't help but smother a laugh even as her eyes stay fixed on the broad cobblestone street. But then Tair steps out from the nook in the alleyway and taps her on the shoulder, and she has to swallow a breath of shock.

"What d'you think?" Tair asks, piling her long hair into a black scarf high atop her head. "Suit me all right?"

Vernae don't wear uniforms, mostly. Their ear cuffs indicate status well enough. So Selah's never actually seen Tair like this—in basic service blacks stolen off a laundry line in Pantheon Park—and no, they don't suit her in the least. Selah wants to rip them off. Burn them. But they suit the role, the insane role Tair's insisting on taking upon herself despite the danger, despite every instinct in Selah's body screaming at her that this is a *bad* idea, that she needs to stay *safe*.

They've had this argument already. Tair may be convinced that no one ever looks at servae long enough to really notice them, but if she gets caught, Selah will never forgive herself.

Catching her disquiet, Tair takes hold of her wrist, gentle but firm, and says, "Hey. My choice, my risk."

There's no room for argument in Tair's eyes, but she knows a test when she hears it. She can give Tair that. She has to, actually.

"Yeah," she agrees. Then, hating it: "You're missing something."

Tair frowns, and Selah reaches up to the tiny red wisps escaping her scarf before thinking better of it. Barely an inch away, she pulls back, and pulls at the soft ridge of her own ear instead. Grim understanding sets itself along Tair's jaw, but she nods all the same. She reaches into her pocket and pulls out that old, familiar glint of silver. After all these years, Selah doesn't ask her why she kept it.

Belamar sits farther inland than Breakwater, contrary to what the name might suggest—pristine white columns and floor-to-ceiling windows tucked neatly into the rolling hills. *New money,* people had sniffed, back when it was first built a scarce century ago. But its up-keep had proven too much for the original owners to handle, and no one could remark on the Palmar pedigree when the familia made it their Luxana residence.

The atrium smells of rosewater and cloves, and some unidentifi-able cloying smell that manages to somehow be both stale and sour at the same time. Selah barely manages to keep from coughing when the doorman lets her in, and her eyes are still watering by the time she's shown into the parlor. She wants to glance back at Tair, trailing a few paces behind—to see if she's faring any better, to roll her eyes in that way they have, the one that says, *Is this place for real?* But she can't. Not if they're going to pull this off.

She studied theater arts, once upon a time in her superior. She can act the role. She has to.

Cato Palmar smiles wide when she enters the room, a predatory thing beneath his enormous mustache, and savage Quiet but how had she ever thought he looked like someone's kind grandfather? Sunlight filters in through high windows so that the parlor itself is almost blin-dingly white, all marble and dried flowers, and that smell like old potpourri wafting across in sickening waves.

Reclining back in his chaise like the emperors of old, the Consul clearly likes to surround himself with beautiful things. Intricately painted tea tables. An afternoon jacket of Songket brocade. And each serva—of which there are *many*, a display of living statues—fine-featured and clad in dark, draping cloth that amounts to little more than wisps of silk. It's not *inappropriate*, per se, just not what Selah would ever have called service blacks. The whole garish sight makes her stomach turn.

She's never been inside Belamar before. Her parents never brought her along on one of their rare social calls whenever the Consul was in town. She realizes now that may have been deliberate.

Biting down her disgust, she forces herself to stand a little taller, chin lifted slightly, willing that alien sense of status to overtake her. Cato Palmar is a lecherous old man, but *she* is the Imperial Historian. They're colleagues, now.

"Lady Historian," says Palmar, in that smooth voice, and Selah has to force herself to take his outstretched hand in hers, to tamp down the shudder that wants to run through her when his lips brush an old-fashioned kiss to the soft skin there.

He thinks he's being charming, playing the passé old man to her bright young thing. A stark contrast to the dismissive politician she met at the viewing the other night. She makes herself smile.

"Consul—"

"Cato, I insist."

"Cato," she amends, taking the proffered chair of handsome wood and chintz.

Out of the corner of her eye, she sees Tair take up position against the wall behind her, next to one of the other attending servae—eyes down, though she knows her ears are perked to hear every word. Her stomach lurches again. Servae at Breakwater don't behave like that. It's not what's expected. There's decorum, of course, but it's not the *same*. It can't be.

But it is.

She forces her attention back to her host.

"Cato," she says again, edging her mind into that particular kind of patrician propriety, that kind of cadence that always makes her think of Mima's friends. She's not a politico, but she's turning into an actor. Maybe it's not far from the same thing. "Thank you for receiving me on such unforgivably short notice. I'm sure you have your hands full."

"Not at all." He waves her away. "I'm really only in town still to address this terrible business with your father. And, as I recall, I *did* ask you to come visit me sometime."

"And I'm so glad you did. I feel you and I perhaps got off on the wrong foot. I'd very much like to rectify that."

"Lady Historian—"

"Selah. Please."

"Selah," he says, something of a purring cat in his manner. "You're young. You're going to have all sorts of high ideals that, while admirable, aren't exactly practical in context of the real world. That's only to be commended. I don't think we got off on the wrong foot at all."

"But that's just it. Everything I said, about the judicial system and education reforms and the like . . . you don't really think I *meant* it, do you?" Palmar's brows rise. Selah forces herself to keep her steady gaze on him, smiling. "My mother has a reputation to uphold, Cato. I take that seriously. But I'm not her, and I'm certainly not my father. I have very different ideas when it comes to what I want out of life."

"And what," Palmar asks, "might that be?"

"I should think that's obvious," she says, casting her eyes appreciatively around the room. "I'm here, aren't I? You demand the very best. The best parties, the best diversions. Why *wouldn't* I want to be part of that, now I've come into my majority?"

Palmar's eyes light up at that, that grandfatherly look not disappearing exactly, but becoming something altogether more predatory. "Well, then," he says, "you must be my guest at the Leontine Club soon. Perhaps next week?"

Selah has no idea what the Leontine Club is.

"I would *love* to."

"And your mother would have no objection?"

"My mother may object to whatever she likes. She isn't paterfamilias."

And at that, the look Palmar gives her is almost conspiratorial, though the predatory gleam hasn't faded. He laughs instead, stretching out again on his chaise, and gestures carelessly for a nearby serva. The young woman materializes out of nowhere to refill his cup of tea. Palmar barely glances at her. Selah has less success, not when she glimpses the butterfly burned into the flesh just below the woman's clavicle. A brand, out in the open for everyone to see. She nearly chokes.

"See something you like?"

Now Palmar is smiling at her in a way that she emphatically Does Not Like. A way that seems to recognize a kindred spirit. "Selah Kleios," he says, rolling her name between his wrinkled lips, glancing between her and the retreating woman. "What a delightful surprise you've turned out to be. There have been the rumors, of course. Your fine taste in women. It seems I'm not the only one who demands the very best of life."

What?

"I—"

"Oh, don't worry, your secret's safe with me," he says, and takes a sip of tea, utterly unaware of Selah's reeling. "You'll marry some proper familia's younger son, I'm sure, to keep tongues from wagging. I understand. My Cornelia was the same way. A sweet thing. A good wife. But they simply don't . . . scratch the same itch, do they? I hear you keep your crim girls very close indeed."

There is a very, *very* good chance that Selah's about to be sick. She prefers women to men, that much is true, that much only even becomes scandal if she doesn't eventually do her duty as paterfamilias to continue the Kleios line. But she'd had no idea that she had somehow become the subject of Luxana's rumor mill. No idea there were people out there— her friends, even, maybe, because who else could have told?—speculating about her private life like that. Except it's worse than that, even, because she has *never* . . . not *once* . . . *would* never force herself on anyone who didn't want it. The very concept, the very *idea* that someone out there has been poisoning her name with the suggestion . . . Patricians talk, of course they do, but Selah always considered herself firmly on the outside of the gossip mill. She's absolutely seeing red.

But Palmar isn't done, evidently taking her enraged silence for some kind of self-satisfied acquiescence. "Yes, very fine taste indeed," he says, and now he's looking at someone over her shoulder. "Girl, come closer. Let's have a look at you—"

"I'm sure I don't know what you're talking about," Selah snaps, a little harsher than she should, because that is *not* a road they're going down. Forget the bile that wants to rise in Selah's throat. Palmar does not get to touch Tair. He does not get to *look* at her.

So then, hating herself—"Certainly you don't expect me to believe *half* the rumors I hear about you?"

The baiting is intentional, the way her coy voice lilts as if to say, *Of course it's true. It's all true. I'll show you mine if you show me yours.* But she needs to steer his attention as far away from Tair as she can. She needs for this to have been worth it.

"If I did," she continues, "I'd be *much* more cross with you at the moment."

"Whatever for, my dear?"

"For all the noise on the street. Do you have any idea how far out of my way I had to go to avoid the rabble all but conducting martial law around the city? Evidently they're up in arms over the deaths of *your* clavaspher player and his sister."

"Are they?" Palmar asks, mildly interested, mildly amused. "Well, I couldn't imagine what that has to do with me. I'm certainly not the one who sent him into a poppam den."

A jolt of excitement thrills down Selah's spine, something cutting through the rage and disgust, though she knows from here on she'll have to play her cards very, *very* carefully. "Of course you weren't," she says. "I saw him play, you know. Those *muscles* . . . mmm. Divine. Marten, was it?"

"Miro. A fine specimen."

"And such a waste of an investment. Have you managed to recoup the loss?"

Oh, and she does *not* like the satisfied smile that curls across his powder-caked face when he says, "Quite nicely, in fact. So much so that I'm not quite sure I could be pressed to call it a loss at all. A . . . *metamorphosis*, perhaps."

"How intriguing."

"Indeed. He's being put to far better use."

Miro is alive. Miro is *alive*. Under a visage of vague yet carefully crafted interest, Selah's heart is racing. "Oh?" she asks, and quirks a casual brow.

"Oh, indeed. You would be interested in such a thing?"

Selah hasn't got the first idea what *such a thing* is, but the light in her eyes and the firm nod are no act. She's very, very interested in *such a thing*.

Palmar purses his lips. "Your father never seemed to think much of our circle—as though he had any right to judge, with the living proof of his own diversions walking around in plain sight for all the world to see."

Bastard. Like he knows anything about her family.

"I'm not my father."

It's not a lie. Not really. She misses Dad every day, would give anything to have him back. But he didn't fight for Tair, and he didn't fight for Arran. Not really, in the end. And he wouldn't be here, using lies and veiled truths and the power of his office to bring justice to a missing plebeian boy and his murdered sister. He had too much faith in the Imperium for that.

Cato Palmar regards her for a long, drawn-out moment, and Selah wills herself to regard him right back. Young and beautiful and vibrant, playing with the lives of others so casually you could forget they have wills of their own. He'll give her what she wants. She repeats these things back to herself, forcing herself to believe them, these truths belonging to the arrogant girl she could have been in another life. She waits.

Then he smiles—that cracked, horrible thing—and she knows she's got him. "No. You're not your father at all." And then: "Paper," he says, to no one in particular, and a moment later a serva is handing him a crisp vellum notecard and pen.

She doesn't look at whatever it is he scratches out on the card. Doesn't trust herself not to look overeager, not to glance back at Tair in anticipation, not to give herself away. Instead, she leans back, casual and beautiful and bored, and becomes very interested in the state of her nailbeds until a cough begs her attention again. Palmar is holding out the notecard between two knobbly pale fingers, appraising her with some strange mix of fondness and triumph. She takes the card.

"Keep that safe now," he tells her, picking up his teacup again. "That's your ticket inside. His next match is tonight."

"His next . . . match?"

"Yes, of course." His horrible lips curl into a smile. "I'll escort you there myself." Then, snapping his fingers as if he's just had the most ingenious idea, Palmar adds, "Speaking of your father's verna son, why don't you bring him along?"

It's only by the tiniest fraction of a second that Selah catches herself from freezing on the spot. Why in the savage Quiet would Palmar invite *Arran* of all people? But she's got him, she's so close, and Miro is *alive*.

"What an idea," she says faintly, noncommittal, and takes another sip of tea.

"I thought you'd like that," he says. "I heard about the boy's run-in with the Publica the other day. How very embarrassing for you. And on the day of your father's viewing, too. Shameful behavior. Maybe in the pits you'll find a better use for that fighting spirit."

This time, Selah actually does freeze.

No. No way.

"He's a freedman," she makes herself say, the only protest she can think of.

"I'm aware." The Consul leans back in his chair, rolling his eyes. "Your father's incessant whining saw to that. But he's dependent on *your* goodwill, isn't he? I'm sure he'll do as he's told." Cracked lips curl back into an unpleasant smile. "Oh, I admit I'm now rather looking forward to tonight. Our Miro will be making his thraex debut, you'll be pleased to know. No chest armor. Those muscles you so admire on full display."

There is a very distinct possibility that Selah has swallowed her own tongue.

Pit matches. Thraex armor. Missing athletes. And now her brother.

Gladiator games.

"Slow *down*," Tair hisses, the moment they've rounded the corner. Out of sight from Belamar, onto the main thoroughfare of the Arborem, and straight into the shaded cover of the trees where they can't be seen. Vaguely, Selah is aware of the number of Institute Civitatem sentries marching along the street, their numbers filled out by green-clad Publica. Normally, she might find this strange. Right now, she's too angry.

She shoves her, hard, and Tair stumbles back.

"What the fuck, Selah?"

"You *knew*."

Bewilderment colors the older girl's face. "I *knew*?"

"You *knew*." Her entire body is vibrating with rage. Not at Tair. Not really. A general rage, at the Arborem and Cato Palmar and everyone who ever propped him up to believe he was worth so much as a ceres. At reeducation and attollos and her own beloved Archives, fast crumbling to dust. "I don't know how, but you knew what kind of place that was. You knew . . . you *knew*."

Tair stares at her for a moment, face blank, then shrugs. "Yeah, obviously I knew."

"Why didn't you tell *me*?"

"Would it have made a difference?"

And Selah wants to scream. Because the answer is *yes*. Yes, it would have made a difference. But she wants to scream just as much because the answer is *no*. It wouldn't have made any difference at all. She still would have walked in there, forced herself to pretend to be someone she wasn't—only this time she would have known Tair was prepared for it. That nothing the Consul said could surprise or faze her friend, because it was a familiar world. Dress a serva up in a silk chemise or linen slacks, brand them where all the world can see or hide it away to pretend it isn't there, force them into service with impossible laws or at the end of a sword, at the end of the day it's the same result. And Selah had always thought that Breakwater was so different. So civilized. Her familia. Her *family*.

She wants to scream.

"Gladiator games," she says, stone faced.

"Apparently," Tair responds, grim.

"Gladiator games are ill—"

"Illegal. Yeah. That's why they're underground, Selah."

They can't call the Publica. Of course they can't. The Consul all but admitted to kidnapping Miro Ontiveros to fight in the pits, and the Publica isn't just letting it happen, they're actively covering it up. If they want to find Miro, they'll have to see this through themselves.

"I can't drag Arran into this," Selah says, a sinking feeling in her gut even as Tair purses her lips.

"You may not have a choice."

"What difference does it—"

"You said you would bring him," Tair cuts in before she can finish, a surprising urgency in her voice. "I know it seems like nothing, but I've spent my whole life watching people like Palmar, staying out of their way. Maybe he wouldn't care, but he'd definitely notice. You *don't* want that. You can't give him any reason to think you're up to something."

Selah wants to pull away from Tair's unexpected ferocity, tell her she's being overdramatic. But this is her world, and the fervor in her words is matched with absolute concern, and that, if nothing else, is enough to make Selah believe that they are true.

She cares about Arran's safety, of course she does, but she's also seen the way he fights. He's good. Better than good. He can hold his own. That's not what's making her feel like she could projectile vomit at any second now. It's what she said to him the last time they saw each other.

I'm paterfamilias, and you're a fragging client.

She hadn't meant it. She hadn't *wanted* to have meant it. She can hardly fathom that it's been less than a day since those poisoned words left her mouth.

Well, she won't do it. She can ask, but it's got to be his choice.

V

NEW DARK LIGHT

Can't write too much down here. Update you next time in person. There's been a change in power—turns out Griff's not actually his name, it's the pseudonym for whoever's in charge. Must keep an eye on this new one—I had no idea anything was happening until the coup was already over. She's subtle, but ruthless. And I have a feeling she's onto me. Thought I passed for pleb no problem but she keeps making little comments and I do have to wonder . . . no idea how a native knows half of what she does about life in the updistricts, to be honest. More when I see you.

—MEMO FROM AGENT GEORGIO EVERS TO CHIEF GENERAL QUINTUS KOPITAR OF THE COHORT INTELLIGENTIA. DATED MARCH 19, 772 PQ. EVERS'S BODY WAS DISCOVERED IN LUXANA HARBOR THE NEXT DAY.

TAIR

Seven Dials is overrun, when they cut back through this time around. Arran might be anywhere now, but Selah seems to think they're most likely to find him in a room over a Paleaside taberna. It's the first place to look, anyway, except that they can barely pass through Seven Dials in the first place to find out. The district's packed to overflowing with a furious buzz that grows and grows as they move south, and the avenues get narrower until they're standing there, Tair and Selah, and it's not a riot. Not yet. Not like they're murmuring about up in the Arborem behind their tall trees and private sentries, over their worried cups of tea.

They arrive where the crowd bottlenecks into the depths of Longewild Acre, one of the eponymous dials, and they're still far, much too far away from the center of the district, where they need to pass through. People are shouting, banging on tin kitchen pans and wooden boards and the red clay bricks of passing buildings—trying to move as one, up through Seven Dials toward the Regio Capitolio, up to where justice ostensibly lives. Only no one's moving, brought to a standstill by something loud and unseen up ahead.

"What's happening?" Selah asks the man in front of them, a wiry, muscular type with oil-stained hands that have probably never been this far updistrict. He shrugs, barely glancing down at her. Helpful.

"Come on," Tair says, and plunges into the fray, Selah's hand tight and sticky in hers.

At first it's a matter of weaving through bodies, ducking down to find the spaces between in that zigzag way Ibdi taught her not so many years ago, the clunk of both atlas and Iveroa Stone heavy against her hip. Then the bodies begin to break up, and Longewild Acre opens out to the central roundabout, and it becomes clear that *what's happening* is chaos.

Gone is the tranquility of the morning, because this is where the Cohorts have chosen to make their stand. This is where they've decided

to stop the influx of downdistrict rabble coursing upward from disturbing the north end's comfortable peace. The blockade of green uniforms stretches three dials across and several officers deep, while their
comrades-in-arms do what amounts to little less than battle with the
citizens of Luxana.

Here a Publica officer shoves a gray-haired woman to the ground,
and six strangers run to help her up. Here two men, teenage boys
really, smash the windows of a brownstone and are mown down by a
blackbag on horseback. Someone sets off a firework, a scatter of erratic gold, leaving a trail of black smoke in its wake.

All this for you, Xochitl, thinks Tair, rooted to the spot where she
stands amidst the violent fray. Then—*No. You were the final straw.*

"*Tair,*" shouts a voice that belongs to Selah, somewhere to her
right, somewhere cutting through amidst the yelling and the running
and the breaking glass. "Tair, we have to *move.*"

And then she's being pulled, running behind Selah, left hand clasped
tight once more in hers, and a flying bottle of something narrowly
misses her, and they can't go back the way they came. The crowd is
pressing in too thick and fast and they're being pushed toward the
barricade. Glass is flying, catching in her hair, and she doesn't know
which way they're darting or why they've changed directions, and
then a horse rears up out of nowhere and Selah's stuck to the spot,
staring upward like she's never seen anything like it in her life. So now
it's her turn to pull Selah away, she doesn't know where just *away,*
except then she turns and she's face to face with a blackbag and her
heart stops for that split second between realization and fear because
that unforgiving black baton is sailing through the air, toward her
head, about to crack into her skull and—

Someone barrels into her and she's stumbling sideways, but the
nightstick never meets its mark. It hits Selah instead, sending her
sprawling to the ground after taking the hit that was never meant
for her.

Tair can't think straight. She heaves her back up she can't stay
down there she'll get trampled down there there's blood there's *blood,*
and there's an opening just like Ibdi taught her to see, just there, and
she just realized she lost her cruiseboard somewhere in the fray but

Selah's hand is still in hers and that's more important, that's all that matters, they have to keep *moving* and—

They're out of the roundabout.

Back down one of the dials—not Longewild Acre, someplace else, veering east maybe.

Down one of those winding streets that connect the main roads.

It's darker here and older somehow and her heart is pounding so hard she can feel it at the base of her throat, and they can tuck themselves into an alcove as stragglers run past and Tair can finally get a proper look at Selah.

Blood trickles down in a steady trail, down from somewhere above her hairline, streaking her face and painting her once-persimmon duskra darkest red, and Tair can't see how bad the damage really is. She isn't trained for this. She doesn't *know*. She's completely useless. Completely helpless in the face of Selah's reckless nature, the part of her that will always run headlong into danger to push someone else out of its way.

Skin thrumming with it, Tair holds up three fingers and asks, "How many?"

"Three. I'm fine." Her voice is shaking.

"No, you're not," she snaps, anger mounting. "You're a godsdamn mess."

The stolen service blacks are still in her bag, alongside the Iveroa Stone—unmarked and unmarred, thank Terra—and she tears a strip away from the tunic. Selah hisses when she presses it to her temple. She wishes she had an antiseptic, water even. Something to wash the blood away. Some way to be more gentle. But it's not her nature. She only has what she has.

"Always the fucking hero," Tair grits out, wiping away as much of the red-black mess as she can and wondering if Selah understands, *actually* understands that she's capable of getting hurt. That she's capable of dying. That her perfect storm of ego and loyalty and sense of righteous justice can't protect her from nightsticks and charging horses and the million tiny things that threaten to tear the two of them apart. That she is confident, and kind, and *good*, and ridiculous, and still believes in the best in people, even after everything. That these are the things the world will always seek to destroy.

She rips another, longer strip from the stolen tunic, and it's satisfying, pouring this frustration and the growing tremor in her hands into something she can ruin, though she does try to exercise a bit more care as she winds it around Selah's head. It won't stanch the flow by much. Selah needs proper medical care before the blood dries and sticks to the makeshift bandage. But it's what she can do.

Selah is staring at her, she realizes. Has been watching her steadily all this time while she worked, something focused and intent in her gaze, and Tair suddenly feels wildly exposed.

"What?"

She shrugs, and says nothing.

"*What?*"

The corner of Selah's lip quirks upward and okay *no*. She doesn't get to do this. Doesn't get to sit there quiet and solid and *knowing* and Tair is angry she is so so angry and it's all Selah, it's *always been* Selah and she could have *died* and it would have been no one's fault but Selah's. And Tair would never have gotten to know for herself what this really was between them, with the long years stretching out behind. And it's the way that Selah's face is tilted up just slightly, the way the sun is slipping through the afternoon sky and her face is red with blood but there's also the wind and Tair *wants*.

She's used to wanting. She's not used to taking.

But here, in a back alley of Seven Dials in the midst of a growing riot, Selah is looking at her like she already knows, and Tair is done with denying herself.

So she takes her wrist and then Selah's mouth is hot against hers and it's instinct. Fragile and shaking and fierce, like all that anger was just waiting to turn, and she feels something in herself release, something that she never knew she was holding back. Selah's mouth is hot against hers and her hands are in Tair's hair and gripping at the back of her shirt like she might disappear otherwise and Tair thinks she just might.

But it's the way the leaving feels. Something she never let herself fully know. Something like how they can have lived like this for so long, and never said anything about how much it hurts sometimes. How a person can love and love from so far away, how they can muddle through this and come out alive and breathing and full of the world.

In the space between, they're just breathing against each other's mouths, and then Selah turns her head just a little so it's lips to the corner of her mouth. It's cold and beautiful. Strange and strong. And Tair's stomach twists when Selah smiles at her, just a little, their fingers still warm and entwined together.

All right, she thinks, forehead resting against Selah's, leaning into the arms that wrap Tair in against her smaller frame. *Here we go, then. Here we go.*

SELAH

She could stay here on this doorstep forever, wrapped in Tair's arms. Corded muscle and black tattoos, fierce anger and fiercer love, and Selah can't help but think that if she really is up there, somewhere, Tair can't help but be Terra's favorite. She'd thought, once, that the two of them were the same. That there was no marker divide for where one ended and the other began. She knows better now. *They're* better now. Not two halves of the same whole, but two wholes meant to find each other and bring storms to their feet.

"Selah."

She could stay here forever, but they're always on the move, she and Tair. If not one, then the other.

"Selah."

"Mm-hm."

She's here, and she's listening. She is, but she's also taken by the heat of Tair's chest flush against her own, the way she smells like sweat and dirt and star anise. Tair pulls away from her, looking clear above Selah's head, eyes blown wide and spine gone ramrod straight.

And then, from somewhere behind her, a familiar voice—*"Tair?"*

Selah whips around.

Halfway down the winding cobblestone street, standing stock still, hand in hand with Theo Arlot and staring in shocked disbelief at the both of them—*Arran.*

His eyes are bulging, flicking back and forth in rapid succession from Tair to Selah, up to the makeshift bandage at her hairline, then back to Tair again. It would be funny, if she weren't so acutely aware of the tension radiating from Tair. The pair of them set out to look for him, but he's stumbled onto them instead, and with only scant yards looming between her brother and the woman she would do anything to keep safe, it's only now that Selah realizes she has no idea what Arran is going to do next.

"What," he says, "the fuck?"

"Arran," Tair says, and warily stands.

They stare at each other a moment longer, the space between them hanging thick with anticipation. It's been five years, and Arran never had anything resembling what existed between her and Tair—what almost existed, anyway. But that doesn't mean that Selah hadn't been prone to mild fits of jealousy now and again whenever the two of them ribbed each other over inside jokes born in Gil's classroom, or that she'd ever fit in downstairs the way Arran and Tair did. They shared common ground in a way she never would.

But that was then. This is now.

Then, in barely four strides, Arran closes the length of cobblestone and pulls Tair into an enormous, all-encompassing hug. Tall as Tair is, she all but drowns in it.

At twenty-one, Arran had been lanky, and constantly looked like he was on the verge of apologizing for it. Maybe it's something to do with seeing him through unexpected eyes or the way Tair goes stiff in his embrace, but for the first time Selah realizes that now, at twenty-six, he's broadened out. And maybe it's also partway to do with the cut lip and dark bruising around his jaw, or just the inevitable result of a year spent in the legions, but there's a hardened ease with which he carries himself these days. Like if you don't get out of his way, he might just make you.

Gradually, Selah watches the tension release through Tair's body, and at last she lets herself give into it, awkwardly patting him on the back until he finally lets her go.

"I don't know why I'm surprised," he says faintly. "You look good."

"You have a split lip."

"I'm aware of that, thanks. This is—"

"Theo. Yeah. I'm aware of that, thanks."

"Are you?" Selah asks, surprised.

Tair shrugs. "We used to run in the same circles."

"Oh, is that what we're calling it now?" Theo asks, the ghost of a laugh at her lips. Arms folded across her chest, giving Tair a once-over that's nothing short of appraising. But rather than shrink away, Tair glares right back, cold regard incongruous with the spark of mischief in Theo's quirked brow.

"I didn't see you if you didn't see me," she tells her, and it sounds like a dare.

At that, Theo actually does laugh, and Selah finds herself gratified to see that Arran is clearly just as lost as she is. *The same circles*—that has to mean the Sisters of the First, right? She doesn't know why this surprises her as much as it does. Theo's a pleb, sure, but somehow Selah has always been under the impression she wasn't *that* type of pleb. More Seven Dials than Sinktown. Building a career in politics doesn't leave much time for volunteer work or mutual aid, and anyway, no.

Back up.

That makes no sense. That makes no sense at all.

"I'm sorry, *how* exactly do you two know each other?" she asks, because so far as she's aware, Theo has only even been in the city for three months. "You said you grew up in the Halcya province."

Theo blinks at her. "Did I?"

"Yes. You did."

A moment of hesitation then, the flicker of something strange passing between Theo and Tair both, and suddenly Selah understands. Of course. Of *course* that was a lie. Theodora Arlot, plebeian, can't rely on sheer grit and playing by the rules any more than Tair once could. Whether it was forged credentials or something else, she'd had to write her own rules to make a life worth living. Whether she knows Tair through a history of working together or because Theo herself was the recipient of much-needed charity, it isn't Selah's place to ask. It isn't Selah's place to feel any sort of betrayal for having been lied to. Theo did what she had to to survive.

"It's fine," she tells her, grave nod cutting through the strange tension. "I won't tell."

"Selah—" Arran starts, but she shakes her head.

"I won't. I swear."

Then Arran frowns, as if really noticing her there for the first time. Eyes flicking down to the deep red spattering her duskra, the make-shift bandage wound around her head, the crusted blood just beginning to form in her braids, and his face goes dark with concern. "What happened to you?"

"I'll show you mine if you show me yours."

She flashes him a grin. He doesn't return it, just pulls her to her feet and toward him, as though closer inspection could make the wound heal itself. "Arran, I'm *fine*," she insists, pushing him away.

The distant roar of the riot at the center of Seven Dials is growing louder, evidently not so distant anymore.

"That does look pretty nasty," says Theo. "Come on. My place isn't far from here."

Tair's hands are surprisingly gentle, the sting of needle and thread barely a bite as she works in the last stitch above Selah's hairline. She'd grabbed the medical equipment straight out of Theo's hands the moment they—*they*, and that's just one more private detail to stow away and out of sight from Mima or anyone else who decides to sniff around where Theo's concerned—emerged from the entryway closet of their little studio apartment. Now, Selah sits cross-legged at the table by the window, and barely feels the tug of thread. Arran is more important, and the way he still won't look at her even as she finishes speaking.

Clavaspher players and state-sanctioned murder and alchemical scientists and Quiet-damned gladiator games.

"I'm so sorry," she says, as Tair ties off the last stitch. Theo watches them from the stove, a kettle of tazine brewing in wafts of mint and almond. "I didn't know what he was asking, and by the time I put it together, it was too late. I didn't know how to say *no* without blowing the whole thing out of the water."

"Pleb fights go easy," Tair puts in. "That's what I've heard, anyway. And we figure this could turn out to be a good thing—if you can find Miro Ontiveros before the games start, maybe we can spring him out before you have to actually do anything. Pretend to change your mind, Selah acts all vexed off, we all get out of there before anyone's the wiser."

"I'm so sorry," Selah says again. "I wasn't trying to . . . I didn't know. But if you don't want to be part of this—"

"He can't."

The growing whistle of the kettle isn't enough to drown out Theo's voice, firm in a way that Selah's never heard it before. They're leaning against the green and white tile counter, arms crossed again, and it's with no small prickle of annoyance that Selah snaps back, "He can decide for himself."

She doesn't get to decide for him, and Theo—never mind their own secrets, never mind whatever they and her brother are getting up to behind closed doors—certainly doesn't, either.

But Theo just shakes their head. "There's no such thing as an easy fight down in the pits," they say, frustratingly calm, and takes the screaming kettle off the flame.

"And how would you know that?"

They don't dignify her with an answer. Instead, they cross to where Arran is still standing by the unmade bed, one arm braced against the other window and frowning out at the clear blue sky, like the answer might be waiting up there somewhere instead. Theo places a gentle hand at his wrist, some silent conversation passing between them as he looks down at it, then up to meet their gaze.

"They're right. I can't," he says at last, turning to face her, and Selah's heart sinks. "We've got something else to do tonight. Something important."

More important than her.

Of course.

It shouldn't feel as momentous as it does.

There's a breaking point that's been coming for a while. Since before last night and the words she can't take back, since before Dad died, maybe even since before Arran left for Fornia and the legions. She's known in her gut it was there and done her best to ignore it, putting it off with education initiatives and schemes to bring him in to work with her at the Archives, anything that meant keeping him with her.

It was never going to work. Arran couldn't live in limbo forever. Just because she's been able to overlook that until now doesn't make it any less true.

"All right," she says, gathering herself against the rejection. "That's all right."

"Like *hell* it is," snaps Tair, and Selah, having almost forgotten she was there, nearly falls off the chair.

Tair slams the needle and excess thread against the scrubbed wooden table, then snatches up her bag from where it lies crumpled at her feet. The three of them watch as she heaves the Iveroa Stone out and sticks it firmly under Selah's nose.

"Show him."

"Tair . . ."

"You didn't tell him everything. Show. Him."

Selah sighs, because Tair's right—whatever Arran's choice, she'll respect it, but that doesn't mean she gets to keep this from him. In spite of the growing schism between them, in spite of the harsh last words between him and Dad . . . this *could* change his mind. And even if it doesn't, he still deserves to know everything he's saying no to.

So she places the Iveroa Stone on the table between them as Arran and Theo gather round, then lifts the old, crumbling atlas out of her own bag and opens it up to the map of Luxana.

"Uh," says Arran. "What exactly am I looking at?"

"These belonged to Dad," says Selah. "He left them with Gil to pass on to me. Said they were classified. This is an atlas, and this . . . well, we're not entirely sure *what* it is, but we're pretty sure it's a so-laric light. It's called the Iveroa Stone."

There's a strangled cough as Theo chokes on their tazine. Selah ignores that, and flips the leather cover open to reveal the irradium surface as Arran's eyes widen in shock. He glances up, something unsaid and inscrutable passing between him and Theo as their honey face runs pale. And then Selah explains everything.

Everything she can, anyway. None of it connects, not really. But there are the corresponding languages, and the fact that both of these relics belonged to Dad. The fact that someone murdered him and they still don't know why. The fact that someone is blackmailing Tair to get at the Stone, and they don't know who or why that is, either. Selah explains it all, and traces her fingers along the flimsy, delicate pages of the atlas map, the one depicting a Luxana neither of them recognize. She tells him what they know, and watches as Arran's brows climb higher and higher on his forehead, watches as some unfathomable look passes between Tair and Theo, and tries to ignore the way it makes the hairs at the back of her neck prickle with discomfort.

Tair has had a life in the past five years, the same as Selah. She'll ask about it later. She isn't going to dwell on it now.

"So what next?" Theo asks, excitement spilling over at the edge. "What does it *do*?"

"They don't know."

Her brother hasn't said much yet, focused frown intent on the glyphs etched into the Stone's thin edge. But when he looks up at Selah, twin pairs of green eyes meet in a frank gaze.

"No," she admits. "We don't. It doesn't light up like Dad's lamps. But it *was* Dad's, and now someone's after it. Maybe multiple some-ones. So it's a guess, but I think he had to have known something. Something that other people are willing to commit murder and blackmail over. If we can figure out what the Stone *is* and how it *works*, then I think there's a chance he might have left other clues for us to find."

He raises a brow. "Like what, a letter?"

Selah rolls her eyes. "No, not a—I don't know, Arran, it could be anything. Or nothing. Maybe Tair's right, maybe I'm grasping at straws. But if there's a chance, then—"

"Then it might lead us to who killed him," Arran finishes for her. She nods.

Because there it is. She hasn't said as much to Tair, but Arran has known her from the moment she was born. The ravines and chasms in their family may be growing, but the rest of the landscape remains the same. On instinct he can understand what she's barely admitted even to herself, because it's where his mind goes, too.

"Why," he asks, glancing from her to Tair, "do I have a feeling you two already have a plan? And why do I have a feeling I'm gonna hate it?"

"Because it's the same plan as before," says Tair. "Diana Onti-veros is the *only* authority on solaric tech. If anyone can get this thing going, or at least tell us what the frag it is, it's her. And for the record, I don't think Selah's grasping at straws. I never did."

A slight pause, and in the heavy silence that sweeps through the single-room apartment, Selah glances up at her and smiles. Tair remains stone-faced, but slips her hand into Selah's, and that's enough. They are going to save two innocent lives, and maybe put the pieces of Dad's murder together in a way the Cohorts never could, and Tair has faith in her. That's enough.

Then the frown Arran's been wearing since they all but ran into each other twists itself into a rueful grin. "Pincer move," he says, leaning back against the tall window frame, and it's half a groan, half a laugh. "Well played."

"What?"

"Attack on two fronts. The two of you are fragging lethal."

"Is that a yes?" asks Tair.

He nods. "I'll do it."

A small shattering noise rings from the counter, where Theo has been pouring out more tazine. They've dropped one of the small earthenware mugs. They seem absolutely unconcerned, however, with the dripping pool of hot liquid or ceramic shards littering the floor where it fell. Instead, their eyes are blazing, fixed firmly on Arran.

"No," they say, and it's firm, but it's also a little bit wild. "You can't go down there."

"Theo—"

"Go easy, my ass. I know you can fight, Arran, but even pleb matches are fucking brutal."

"Theo."

"Those people *train* for it. They actually *want* to be there."

"*Theo.*"

It isn't all that loud, really, but it's final in a way Selah isn't used to hearing from Arran, and even she finds herself sitting up a little more straight in her chair. Theo, meanwhile, seems to snap out of whatever flight instinct came over them, and is now frowning intently at her brother, knuckles gone white where they grip against the tile counter.

Arran goes to them, hands cupped around their jaw, and suddenly Selah feels very hot. Like she's watching something she isn't supposed to. Arran's not a Vestal fragging Virgin, she does know that, but she's also never exactly *seen* him with anyone. He's never properly dated someone before, though she's not really sure if this even qualifies as that. She drops her gaze all the same, down to where Tair's hand is still clasped in hers, and keeps it there as Arran murmurs something in Theo's ear.

It comes to her, suddenly, that they haven't been exactly subtle. What's shifted between them happened so fast and so soon before their unexpected collision with Arran and Theo that there was hardly time to dwell on it. But it occurs to her now that Arran must have seen them together, even if he didn't immediately recognize who they were. So he's seen them kiss, and he's seen the way Tair took care of her, the way they stay in each other's space, and their hands clasped like this. He's seen these things, and he doesn't seem at all surprised. Like maybe it wasn't so fast or soon at all, just the natural destination to a road that they've been on for a very, very long time.

She rubs a thumb across Tair's knuckles, and gets a quick squeeze back in return.

Across the apartment, Arran and Theo finish their quiet conversation. They certainly don't look happy about it, but when Arran presses his forehead to theirs, Theo closes their eyes and finally nods.

"Okay," they say, turning to Selah and Tair. "If you really insist on doing this . . . then you're going to need to know the way out."

DARIUS

It's hardly damning evidence. Darius has to remind himself of that, has to stop himself from barging into Kopitar's office with the name in triumphant hand. If Persie's books are to be believed, then this Ynglot serva woman is acting entirely above the board, because the monthly order that this *Una* collects for Breakwater not only comes from the majordomo herself, but also includes about seventeen other parcels in addition to water hemlock. Still. She has access. And she knows who else might be dipping their hands in the well. She might be the very link Darius needs to the culprit himself.

That still presents a problem.

Because it's not like he can just bring her into the Ministerium of Intelligentia for questioning. He can't even ride up to Breakwater House and ask to see her there. Too many eyes and ears, even if he were to leave his uniform behind, and Darius knows better than to think that word wouldn't get back to Kopitar about someone bothering Kleios familia servae before he even had a chance to finish up his questions. So he has to be smarter than that. He needs a go-between who won't look out of place.

That presents a solution.

Getting her address isn't hard. The clerk at Naevia Kleios's office gives him a strange look when he asks. "You know she's first gen, right?" the clerk says, a judgmental brow raised, as though that should make some sort of difference. And then, "Word of advice, you're not the first man to ask me for this today."

He has no idea what to make of that.

Doesn't, anyway, until he's out the door and halfway across the Plaza Capitolio and has to bring his roan mare to an abrupt stop. Oh. *That*. Darius is halfway to turning around, riding back up to the Senate to correct the man's obvious assumption about Theodora Arlot's extracurricular activities, before he stops himself. It's a waste of time, and anyway, it's not . . . well, it's not the worst rumor in the world. He urges the horse onward.

She *is* first generation. She's hardly suitable for a wife. That doesn't mean he can't entertain the rumor mill, if the story spreads that they're more than just professionally involved. He wouldn't even mind stoking the flame. Nothing like dinners on the Boardwalk, of course, and he can never take her to social events. That's not the kind of rumor he's interested in, anyway. But maybe they can spend their meridiem hour together under the javhouse's blue tiles instead of in their separate corners, just close enough to get people talking about a different kind of attachment altogether.

It's not like it would be awful. Maybe she's a little wider than ideal, but objectively he can appreciate that she's attractive enough. And she listens to him. She can keep up. Moreover, she won't look down on him for his family. She can't. That, if nothing else, is a fragging breath of fresh air.

Except that when he does find Theodora Arlot, leaving the tiny apartment complex in the Fourth Ward as the sun goes down, she's already hand in hand with another young man. Annoyance flares hot in his chest.

"Deputy Miranda," she says, surprised, when he calls her name before they can get swept away in the crowd. "This is unexpected."

"Less so than you'd think," he says, eyeing the man at her side. So that's what the clerk was talking about.

She shifts uncomfortably. "Can I introduce Arran Alexander?"

Unbelievable. *Unbelievable.* Darius has to work very hard to keep the rising heat off his face.

He knows who Arran Alexander is, of course, but he's never seen him in person. Tall and broad as his father was, with the same intelligent green eyes, and nearly as pale. But his curling hair is dark where the Historian's was light, with scattered moles arrayed over a stronger jaw and fuller lips, something almost native to his features. Or maybe that's just projection. The boy is an abomination either way. Darius ignores his outstretched hand.

"A word in private?" he asks Theo, pointed. And then, once Arran Alexander's gone: "You've been busy."

"What's that supposed to mean?" she asks, brows shooting up as she lets him draw her away to the shade of a cobbled side street.

"Nothing."

Except that the scheming bitch is smart. Too smart. Sleeping with Alexander Kleios's mongrel son is a brilliant move. The boy's apparently considered a Kleios in all but name, but he is still and will always be a client. Half crim. Half-caste. A match with him would position Theo favorably within a powerful familia without her seeming to overreach herself. The very same familia Darius has got his eye on, he reminds himself with a stern nudge. The reason why he's here in the first place.

"I took your advice," he tells her instead, leaning against the brick wall as he offers her a cigarette.

"And?"

"And I have a lead."

"Good for you." She leans forward, lights her cigarette on his match. "I'm guessing you aren't here just to brag about it, though."

Despite himself, Darius rolls his eyes. She *is* clever, really. Maybe her attachment to Arran Alexander isn't a complete non-starter. Girls like that can be seen with multiple men. "No," he says, and moves a little closer in. "I was wondering, actually, if I could get your help." And then, leaning forward. "I could really use it."

Theo blinks at him, then exhales through a knowing grin. "Darius Miranda, are you about to bring me in on *top secret* Intelligentia information?"

He smiles, almost despite himself. "No, but I *will* tell you as much as you need to know if you agree to be . . . discreet about it."

"Not tell Senator Kleios, you mean."

"Yes."

"Hm . . ." She takes another drag. "I think I could be convinced."

Yeah, he just bets she could. Information is power to people like her, and if he can give Theo more power than the senator can, then he can turn her loyalty to him in an instant. He sees the politico game for what it is now, knows how that strategy goes into play. Take that, Naevia Kleios.

But he'll have to tread carefully. He can't play his hand too early, not before she's firmly on his side. "There's a serva at Breakwater," he tells her. "*I* can't go talk to her, obviously—"

"Obviously?"

"If I'm asking for forgiveness instead of permission from the Chief."

"Right."

"But no one's going to bat an eye if you're seen up there instead."

"And what am I talking to her about, exactly?"

This. This is where he has to be careful. "Between you and me?" he starts. "She has . . . access to some dangerous substances. Above the board, of course, but it's the water hemlock that worries me." He leans in close again. "Water hemlock is the primary ingredient in par-cae. That's the poison that killed Alexander Kleios."

Theo's eyes go wide. "You think that she—"

"I *think* she had access, yes, but something like poison? She's Yn-glot. They're exceptionally prone to violence, I'll grant that, but they aren't subtle about it. And anyway, it's not like she would have had the motive. So what I think is that she knows who else could have been dipping into the stores, and *those* are the names I need."

"Right . . ." she says faintly, eyes still wide as she processes what he's asking her to do. "Right, of course. That makes sense."

"This has to be *discreet*."

"I know that." She snaps back to herself then, back to attention. Good girl. "Not a word. I can go tomorrow."

Darius shakes his head. "No, we have to go now."

"I'm—"

"*Please.*" It's not in his nature to beg, and that's far from what's happening now, but he finds himself taking her hands all the same, the jolt of urgency in his gut, because this has to happen tonight. Before Theo has a chance to change her mind, before she can tell Naevia Kleios what he's asking her to do. Before Kopitar catches onto his movements or, even worse, the lead runs dry. "I know, you've probably got other things on your plate, but this is important."

"Miranda—"

"Darius. Call me Darius."

He holds her hands fast in his, and wills her to understand just how important this is. He may never get this chance again. And he's already put too much on the line to go back now. Dark eyes meet his, that thread of something suddenly back from last night, and they're the same, he and Theodora Arlot. He remembers that now.

"I've been missing from the Intelligentia already for a day," he tells her. Screw the political game and the rumor mill, it's integrity and honesty that have always gotten him where he needs to be. "I *have* to have something to show for it. If I don't . . ." He can't even think it, though the truth is he doesn't need to. Kopitar would never go through with it. Still, it looms like a noxious smoking cloud. "Say you'll help me."

There's a long moment then, with nothing but the ghost of his father's drunken shouts echoing in the space between. Quietly, at last, Theo nods, and Darius can fragging *breathe.*

"Thank you," he says.

"What's her name? The serva."

"Una. Her name is Una." A flash of something darts across Theo's face, something too quick to catch—but no, it's just a frown, like she's trying to place the name to a face. "Ring any bells?"

"Yeah," she says. "I think we've met."

THEO

For a brief moment when Darius Miranda first approached, Theo had actually been annoyed. They don't have *time* for this. They need to find Griff and update her on what's happening, Tair and the Iveroa Stone and this plan to find Diana Ontiveros in order to learn how this supposed weapon actually *works*. They need to tell her about all of that, and they need to arrange for backup. Then they've got to double back around to the Regio Marina to meet Tair, and do what they can in the meantime to make peace with a descent back down to that place where they swore they'd never return.

"Don't do this," they had told Arran quietly in their apartment, out of earshot of his sister and Tair, who—thank Terra—seemed to have no idea they knew anything about the Iveroa Stone, and evidently no intention of revealing their real identity to Selah Kleios.

"I have to," had been his response. "She has the Stone, but it's worthless if she can't activate it."

"Griff might know—"

"She doesn't. You said she doesn't." Damn him, but he was right. "And if Tair really is being blackmailed over it, that means someone else knows about it, too. We need to know who so the Revenants can cut off that loose end." And then—"You'll come with me, right?" The growing knot in Theo's chest had tightened. "You've been there before."

It wasn't a question, and saying *no* wasn't an option, because Arran was right. They have to go back. Theo feels bile rise in their throat at the prospect, but it *is* what needs to be done. That, at the very least, is grounding. So they had made their plans, and then made their excuses, because Griff needs to know what's happening before anything else.

So, yes, when Darius Miranda first materialized out of the bustle of the Fourth Ward like a pasty, self-important shadow, Theo had actually been annoyed to see him. Now, they're more than a little freaked out.

Because Una. Stubborn, freeborn, entirely-too-noticeable Una.

He doesn't *actually* know anything. Theo is clinging to that. Darius Miranda has no idea that Una is one of their canaries, or even remotely related to the Revenants. He's come to her a completely different way. But he knows who she is, knows her by name, and *that* is a fucking problem. It's one of the reasons servae make such good spies. No one's supposed to notice them. There's nothing more dangerous for a serva than being noticed, never mind the reason why.

So now it's Theo's job to make sure Darius Miranda forgets that Una exists.

Theo is a good actor, but they don't like trading the light jabs and smiles of comradeship with Darius fucking Miranda. They don't like entertaining that gleam in his eerily pale eyes, the one that says, *Yes. What an excellent choice I've made. What a good investment you'll be.* Others have looked at them that way before. But they need this. They need his trust. They need his utmost confidence for when they convince him that he's chasing the wrong lead.

Questions unasked and unanswered carry them from the Plaza Capitolio to the Arborem by hired rickshaw, Darius Miranda next to them, because he'll agree to stay out of sight but he won't be shaken from their side. These questions carry them up the winding road to Breakwater House and around the back to the kitchen entrance, where they send a preteen stableboy up to fetch Una. They carry them in small paces back and forth across the gravel, as Darius retreats to the tree line some thirty yards away, until the quick shuffle of steps alerts them to Una's arrival.

"What are you *doing* here?" she hisses, but Theo jerks their head and hopes the message comes across. *Shut up, for just once in your life.* Darius Miranda is out of earshot for the moment, but he may not stay that way for long.

"Relax," they hiss, and their mind has been working overtime on the way here, gears whirring hot to figure out the best way to play this off. "I have a cover here. If anyone asks, I got lost and you were giving me directions back to the main road. Just follow me and act natural, and do as I say."

"What's happening?"

"Blackbags." They glance sharply over at the tree line, because they don't dare anything more obvious than that, but it's enough. Una's shrewd gaze follows the line to its obvious conclusion.

"They're *here*?"

"One of them. He thinks you might have something to do with the Historian's death."

"*What?*"

"Don't worry, he's not accusing you. Just thinks you might know something, and I have to get him off your tail. Did you—?"

"I haven't done anything. Haven't even been off the estate since you saw me last." There's something mutinous in Una's expression, and it's only then that Theo realizes how terrible she looks. Cheeks hollowed, swaying slightly on her feet. "Stared at some fucker a second too long at the viewing. The senator told the domo to take care of it, and Imarry . . . took care of it. I've been on quarter meals all week."

Theo winces, because they've been there. But someone always tried, at least, to squirrel them away some extra food. It's what you're supposed to do. It's an unspoken rule—while the world may turn its back, you try to have each other's. But it doesn't surprise them somehow to know that Una hasn't had great luck making friends. She's always been more concerned with her own skin than looking out for anyone else.

"Fucking patricians," they say, and she looks gratified by that, at least. "Don't worry, this'll be over quick. Just play dumb and he'll move on to the next lead."

Una nods, and lets herself be led closer to the tree line. Theo can see the vague outline where Darius Miranda has knelt down amid the brush, but only because they know to look, and not for the first time they can appreciate that he is decidedly excellent at his job.

But this will be quick work, because he, like all blackbags, has one fatal, deadly flaw. He doesn't really believe that someone like Una is capable of using her brain in the first place. And that isn't his fault. That's the same inherent believed decency of a man who upholds the law. Darius Miranda is not a bad person because he is an evil one, a sadist who relishes in the pain and misery of others. Darius Miranda is a bad person because he has been taught to use his talents for the sake of bad works. Of the two kinds of bad people in this world, that's the one Theo has a harder time reconciling.

Evil men are so much easier to hate.

The two of them approach the tree line, and Theo opens their mouth, but Una gets there first: "He's not wrong, though."

Her voice rings loud and clear through the gathering dark, and Theo's heart nearly leaps out of their chest. Has she completely lost her mind? Darius Miranda is right there, and Darius Miranda is *listening*.

Deathly quiet, they whisper, "Una—"

"You fucked me over. You promised me freedom."

"Una, be *quiet*."

"*No*," she snarls, and that mutinous glare has become a storm, and Theo realizes with a plummeting jolt that it's not for some faceless majordomo, it's for *them*. "You promised me freedom in exchange for information, when you never intended to hold up your end. And now that the blackbags are onto you and the Revenants, you're just gonna let me take the fall instead? No. I don't think so."

Theo is falling, falling fast and hard and wild, so why are they still standing on their own two feet? This is going sideways fast. "That's not what this—"

"I *saw* you at the viewing, Theo Nix. I know all about your little cover story here, you goddamn thremid, and I *know* that blackbag in the trees has no fucking idea who you really are. But I do. I know you. I see you. And I am *not* taking the fall for you."

"*Shut. Up*," they hiss, bruising hands darting out to catch her wrists, and if Terra is actually up there somewhere, if she's listening, then she'll have placed Darius Miranda too far inside the brush to hear a thing.

This is bad. This is really, really bad.

"Una, you have *got* to trust me. Not Griff, not the Revenants, *me*. The blackbags don't suspect you. They don't even suspect *me*, that's not what this is. He just wants to know—"

"Like I can trust a fucking word you say."

"You *can*. I'll get you out of here, I swear. I will *get* you past the legionaries at the gate, and I will personally guard you along the Imperial Road myself, but *only* if it means you shut up *right fucking now*. He only even knows you exist because—"

Click.

"I think," says a voice, that smooth patrician cant gone glacial, "that the time for staying quiet is over, Miss Arlot. Or rather . . . Nix, was it?"

And there, taking shape from the trees, blond hair flying away at the temples, Darius Miranda is aiming an honest-to-god *pistol* dead straight at the pair of them.

Theo's heart catches somewhere in their throat.

Gunpowder is an Imperial-regulated substance. They've never seen it in their life. Not outside the random distant firework. But they've heard the stories, the warnings of destruction, how a single shot from a handgun can burrow a narrow path clean through a person's brain in under a second, and they have never stared down the barrel of one before. They understand the phrase, now.

But Una just raises her chin. "Officer."

He nods, curt and courteous, and they could be meeting for a meridiem date. "Una. Thank you for your candor. I think your companion there was going to lead me on a fool's chase, but that confession just sped up my investigation by a considerable amount."

"They're not my *companion*," she spits, like the word could be poison. "And of course I confessed. I'll confess to whatever you want."

A curious smile seems to edge at the corner of Darius's lips, something hollow and ugly haunting the edge even as his eyes dart briefly to Theo and back. But he doesn't lower his pistol. Simple, he must think. A simple native savage. But Theo is starting to get a terrible feeling they know what Una's playing toward. *He's not wrong, though.* That's what she said, at the start of this fucking mess.

They don't know how to get themself out of this. They don't know how a gunfight works.

"Accommodating of you," Darius says, and gets straight to it. "Are you a Revenant?"

"No. But I pass Griff information, sometimes."

"Could you lead me to him?"

"Her. And no. But I could point her out if she's around."

Theo wants to scream. Wants to take the knife strapped inside their duskra and slash Una's traitorous Ynglot throat and watch the blood pour out. *They* brought her into this. *They* recruited her. *They're* the one who found a captive in enemy territory and offered her the chance to work her way back home. It would be an adventure, Theo had thought. Once Griff gave the go-ahead. There are no free Ynglots in Sargassan cities, but Theo would find a way to smuggle Una through the city gates and past the legionary checkpoints of outlying agricultural villages all the same. They'd stay with her until the terrain began to look familiar, or until they came upon more Ynglots who might know where her family were. The Imperial Road would be too dangerous to just abandon Una to it, noxious mists and tales of rabid hybrid wildlife still a threat even to a solo Ynglot raider. Theo had planned on that. They had made a promise and they had *meant* it. And here Una is, repaying Theo by throwing all sense of self-preservation out the window, and both their lives out with it.

"Did you buy water hemlock from Tobin Persie's apothecary?" Miranda asks. The questions just keep coming.

"Every month to the day."

"And did you use a portion of those orders to distill parcae?"

"No."

"Then who else had access to—"

"I just crushed it up as is. You Sargassans make everything so much more complicated than it needs to be. And yes, I used it to kill Alexander Kleios, too, if that was about to be your next question."

For a moment, Theo thinks they hear a small sound come from somewhere in the trees, something like a strangled halfway hiss. But they must have imagined it, it must have come from their own heart skipping a beat, because *Una killed Alexander Kleios* and wait, *what?*

Darius Miranda is regarding her now with an air of solid triumph, and Theo wonders how quickly they could draw their blades and bury them in his chest, but they have no idea how fast he can cock and shoot that gun.

"Why?" It's simple, the final question. "Why confess so freely?"

"Because," says Una, smiling now, "you can't arrest me. The Consul wouldn't let you."

Darius Miranda cocks a brow in perplexed surprise, but Theo feels their heart jolt. Because if the sinking feeling in their gut is at all on the right track, then Una hasn't lost her sense of self-preservation at all.

Here is the bad news, what Theo has always known: no one is coming to save you.

Here is the good news: you can always save yourself.

Except when a gun's involved, it turns out, because Theo is frozen where they stand and they don't know what to *do* to get out of this mess, but in the end it doesn't matter.

He comes out of nowhere.

So this is what it feels like, they recognize dimly, as he comes barreling out from the trees and slams a granite rock over Darius Miranda's head with a sickening crunch. *This is what it feels like to be saved. This is what it feels like to have someone come back for you.* The Deputy Chief of the Cohort Intelligentia drops like limp dappham to the ground, and Arran Alexander turns to face the woman who murdered his father.

This is how it is, to be Theodora Nix at twenty-seven. This is how it is, to have been on their own for a very long time.

It's to never have guessed someone would stay all along, moving unnoticed and unseen at a distance, through crowded limestone plazas and quiet wooded brush. It's to feel the natural rhythm of two separate minds working as one, their hands scrabbling for Darius Miranda's gun as he bleeds out from the skull, dying fast where they roll him inside the tree line, Arran's own hands working to pin Una's wrists behind her back even after she's gotten a solid punch in.

It's their thumping heart and thumping footfalls running through the forest in the falling dark. It's to know that this is a stolen freedom, and they'd accept no other kind. It's their eyes meeting his, a quiet *thank you* unsaid but loudly heard.

No one has ever come back for them before.

ARRAN

Una killed Dad. Una, who taught him to swear in Ynglotta and roughed out bits of grit and gravel from his scraped knees when he was eight.

This makes no sense. This makes no sense at all.

This, says that horrible voice in the back of his mind that sounds uncomfortably like his own, *makes all the sense in the world.*

He wants to scream. He wants to hit something again.

Instead, he watches Griff pacing the floor beneath Amphitheater Messalina, and her face is an impassible mask. Una watches her, too, bound at the wrists to a crumbling arch, held at gunpoint by the pistol Theo liberated from the dying Darius Miranda. Long-since shut down under the pretense of renovation, the abandoned steps and inner allées of the Amphitheater are a haven for the unhoused and the ill, the abandoned youth and poppam addicts, the black marketeers and those—like them—with business they'd rather went unheard.

Finally, she kneels, level with the other woman. "Why?"

Una shrugs, and looks away. Like a crack of lightning Griff's hand darts out to snatch her chin, to force her back to look at her, and it's with a low simmer like an earthquake that she repeats herself—"*Why?*"

Arran doesn't understand this rage, not coming from Griff, but he does understand *it*. It roots him down where he stands, infecting every pore and vein.

This time, Una answers, but it's barely more than a sneer. "Did I need a reason? I was his prisoner. I was his slave."

His gut sinks as confirmation floods in. Griff lowers her hand, but this time Una keeps her gaze, daring her to refute it. A long, searching moment passes between them, and then Griff says, "No." Her voice is level once more, but a roil of some turbulent, unknowable thing stirs beneath the surface. "I don't think that's it. Revenge is sweet, but you wanted more than that."

"I did," she agrees, calm like she knows there's no getting out of this now. "I wanted you to keep your word. You said you'd find my family. Get me home safe. You *promised*. But it was taking too long, so I found someone else who'd do it."

Arran understands the bewildered sort of disbelief as Griff shakes her head. "I'm sorry," she says, unexpectedly.

"Sorry's not good enough any—"

"No, I *am* sorry," says Griff, and that roil is closer to the surface now, and *oh* is she angry. "Sorry that I put my trust in someone too blind to see the bigger picture without needing it spoon-fed down her throat like a godsdamn child."

He takes a step back. He's furious too, but the anger of a quiet woman is a terrifying thing.

"I'm not a child."

"You're right. That was an insult to children, and I owe them an apology. You're a grown woman. A cowardly, self-serving, Ynglot *bitch* who—"

"Who wasn't working alone," Theo's quiet voice breaks through.

Una doesn't bother denying it. But neither does she say anything else.

"You told Darius Miranda that the Consul wouldn't let him arrest you," says Arran, speaking for the first time in what feels like days. "Why would Palmar care? Why would Palmar even know who you are?"

Una has been doing a commendable job of pretending she doesn't know him up until now, pretending he doesn't exist, pretending she didn't just give him a black eye. And she doesn't respond to him now, either, but she doesn't have to say a thing for Arran to know his hunch is right. The answer is written in her silence.

He and Theo told Griff everything the moment they arrived, Una hauled in between them—told her all about how Selah has the Iveroa Stone after all, and how Tair was with her, and their plans for finding Diana Ontiveros because without her the Stone is just a pretty piece of rock. They tried to explain about the glyphs and the atlas and how it could all be connected, but Arran isn't entirely sure they've done it justice.

In one fluid motion, Griff slips a short blade from her gray jacket sleeve and brings the tip to rest just under Una's chin. The entire echoing allée seems to hold its breath.

"How long?" she asks, calm efficiency returned. A moment passes, then two, and the blade presses *in*, just enough to dig pressure into the soft skin. "How long have you been working for Cato Palmar?"

"Why should I tell you?" asks Una, barely daring to move her throat. "You'll kill me either way."

"She won't," Arran hears himself saying, and doesn't back down from Griff's steely glare, from the way Theo's slight jerk of the head seems to say *shut up*.

"That's not your—"

"She wants to go home? Fine. We dump her outside the city after this. Find her own way back in the wilds. Good luck with that. But you said it yourself, you don't kill unless you don't have another choice."

"I was speaking about your father," says Griff, and he can hear the danger percolating there. "Not some backwater bitch."

"So, what, you're just going to *kill* her?" he asks.

Because that's not good enough. Yes, Una murdered Dad. She poisoned him, took him away from everyone who loved him because *she* wanted to, *she* felt like it, left Arran here with too many questions and not even a map to the answers, and he knows why she did it.

Alexander Kleios was two different men. He wasn't the man who sang off key to his children, not to her. He wasn't the man who taught Arran how to sail and got overexcited about Ante Quietam poetry and forgot to eat until Gil threw a sandwich at him. Arran's seen too much in too short a time—children torn from their mothers and underground singers and tattoo ink burned into skin—and he knows why she did it.

He still hates her. Hates her with every fiber of his being. But he understands.

A moment passes, then two, and then a small sort of smile tugs at the corners of Griff's lips as she snaps the knife back into its handle, then stands.

"All right," she says, and pulls something small from the pocket of her coat. "You do the honors, then. Straight from the horse's mouth, and then we'll decide."

The bottle is tiny, nestled in the dip of her palm, so tiny it barely makes a dent as she slaps it into Arran's hand. He's only seen this in illustration before, but from the pale blue tonic twinkling through the dark, the laurel sigil of Cato Palmar's Consulate, he has a strong feeling he knows what this is. But he's never seen it used.

"It won't hurt her," says Griff, as if she could hear his thoughts out loud. "Truth tonic my ass, flumene's just a relaxant. Fucking strong one. It'll make her more susceptible to the power of suggestion. Makes people compliant as hell, though you have to be willing to put up with whatever random thoughts come through their head."

She doesn't need to tell him any of this. He knows what flumene does. He wants to ask instead how in the savage Quiet she got her hands on it, highly regulated as it is, near-impossible alchemy for even the most skilled hands. But even without the warning in Theo's eyes, he has a feeling he's already tested the woman's patience more than enough for one day.

There's a calm efficiency to Theo's hands wrenching open Una's protesting mouth, and as Arran pours the meager contents of the tiny bottle down her throat, he tries not to wonder if this is really any less of a violation. Within moments, the Ynglot woman goes slack.

"Better," says Griff, nudging the woman sitting in the dirt allée with the toe of her boot. "It should kick in right away. What's your name?"

"Montana," comes the answer, halfway between a mumble and a sigh. "They gave me a different one, but it's not my name. Names are important. Mine's Montana Satterfield."

Arran doesn't know what to make of that. It's the strangest name he's ever heard. But Griff just rolls her eyes. "I've heard weirder," she says. "Ynglots aren't indigenous, not really. Not like my people. Ynglots are settlers, same as the Romans, they just don't see it that way because they got here first." She crouches, then, and grips Montana-who-was-Una by the jaw. "Why did you kill Alexander Kleios?"

Montana Satterfield's mud-brown eyes gaze easily into Griff's. "Because Cato Palmar told me to," she says, monotone, and Arran locks eyes with Theo as the final puzzle piece slides into place. *You can't arrest me.* There's only one thing that would make a serva say those words to the Chief General of the Cohort Intelligentia with so much certainty. "He said if I did it, then he'd find my family, help me go home. I was supposed to give the Historian small doses over time, make it look like his health was going downhill on its own. Palmar didn't want anyone to suspect. . . . Kleios must have done something to make him angry, want him out of the way." Through the flumene haze, her lip curls. "But I just wanted him dead. I gave him too much. An overdose on water hemlock looks the same as parcae, you know."

"Palmar must not have been happy about that."

"No. That's why I told him about the Iveroa Stone."

And the world seems to freeze.

Because *that* has no part in this puzzle at all.

"What," asks Griff, ice singing in her voice, "do you know about the Iveroa Stone?"

"Only what you told Theo," Montana answers, completely unconcerned. "I stayed behind, that morning in the Regio Marina. Right before the viewing. I heard what you said. A weapon that could overthrow the Imperium." And, somewhere from the depths of her relaxed mind, "I'm a canary. I'm good at listening in."

"Why? Why tell the Consul?"

"He was so angry with me. He wasn't going to help me get home. I thought about leaving on my own, I thought about it so many times. But I wouldn't last a day alone out there. I don't remember how to fight, and other bands don't care if you're Ynglot, too, not as long as you have something they can take. But the Stone . . . I needed Palmar back on my good side. I thought handing him something that powerful would change his mind. So I went and told him all about it and he agreed that if I got it for him he would hold up his end of the deal. But Imarry would have found it in my things if I'd taken it myself. So I got someone else to do it for me."

"Who?"

"Tair. You remember that skittish thing? You had me run her out of Breakwater a few years ago. Her and not me." A shot of anger slides through Montana's lazy eyes.

Through the murky dark, Theo catches his eye, and the answer to a question he hadn't even known to look for clicks into place. The thief, that night of the viewing. That had been Tair. She must have taken the Iveroa Stone from Breakwater, and he watched as Selah went tearing after her into the Hazards. Those two have been attached at the hip for seventeen years. Once the Stone brought them back together, once they decided to work out what it was for themselves, Montana and Palmar never really stood a chance of getting it back.

But Montana isn't done. "She was perfect for the job—knows Breakwater House better than I do, probably, and I have the right dirt on her. And the Consul, he knew what the Iveroa Stone looked like, so he knew how to describe it. He must have read about it somewhere." Griff frowns hard at that. "I went straight to the Kirnaval. Paid a kid to deliver the message. Tair has no idea it's me. Got a beating for being late, but it was worth it. Once she hands it over, all I have to do is bring it to the Consul. He's expecting me. He'll have to kidnap Selah, after that—you said you needed her. I told him about that, too."

"No," says Theo, sharp. "No, Griff said we *didn't* need to kidnap her. She wanted—fuck, never mind, but she didn't fucking say that."

"Oh," she says, still hazy. "Well, maybe I'm not that good at listening in after all."

Arran had thought once, only earlier that day, that he might very well be facing down the woman who murdered Dad. He was wrong then. He isn't now. And now she's dragged his sister into this mess, too. Cold fury trails down his spine. Fury and panic, because Selah is in danger, and Selah is headed to Cato Palmar's house *right now*.

Griff stands and looks straight at him, as if to say, *This is what you get for being soft.*

"I'm not surprised to see you here," Montana says, and with a jolt he realizes that she's looking at him now. "I thought maybe it was a matter of time. Out of respect for your mother, at the very least."

Okay, no. They're not doing this. She's already put his sister in danger. She's already taken his only parent from him. She doesn't get to drag the other into this. "Keep my mother out of your mouth," he says, deathly calm even as his heart races. He needs to get to Selah before Palmar does. "You never even knew her."

"No, but servae talk. We know the truth."

The truth. The truth was buried, like Alex Kleios buried her, and barely spoke her name again. Like he buried a nineteen-year-old infatuation, because nineteen-year-olds are always in love, but that doesn't mean it matters. *Wouldn't even look at the kid,* the whispers said. *Ended it herself.*

"The truth is postpartum depression," says Arran, pulsing with the memory of the day he forced Gil to sit down and explain what it meant that he didn't have a mother. He doesn't have time for this. "It happens."

"It does. A good story for when you're trying to cover something up."

He's highly aware of Griff and Theo. Highly aware of the thrumming beneath his skin. Highly aware that Montana, or Una, or whatever her name is, is a proven liar. Highly aware that the flumene makes that fact utterly irrelevant.

"So, what?" he asks, eyes narrowing. "You're saying *my dad* killed her?" It's the most far-fetched thing he's ever heard in his life. Dad used to trap spiders under teacups and escort them to the window of his study.

Montana shakes her head, and somewhere beneath those glazed and easy eyes is pity. "No," she says. "But maybe that would've been better. He sold her."

Two options occur to him in that moment. The first is to take the heavy hunting knife in his hand and shove the blade directly into the center of Montana's pale, sagging, lying face. The second is to laugh. He does neither. Because Montana's a liar, but flumene is not.

Arran stares, breathing in, then out, then in again.

His mother is dead. She's *dead.* He knows so little about her, outside the bare facts, outside the occasional story slipped from Gil, stories that belong to a stranger, no matter how much he wants to hear some mirror of himself in them. She was a serva, an orphaned thief picked off the streets at the age of nine. She dyed Imarry's teeth blue once with dogwood bark and cornflower in her tea. She had his dark hair and his high cheekbones and his constellation of moles and beauty marks. She was funny and ferocious and not at all *nice.*

Her name was Qaia.

Her name was Qaia and she was a serva and she must have liked Dad enough for Arran to have been born because otherwise Gil would have *told* him, right? But Gil is Dad's oldest friend and Dad's client and used to be Dad's verna, and maybe there are some things you just keep quiet about to keep the peace. These are the things Arran has pushed down ever since he learned what it is to bring a child into the world against your will, the things he's refused to entertain because she killed herself she *killed* herself and he's never thought to question that before because wasn't postpartum depression explanation enough?

"Talk," he says through gritted teeth, and it doesn't mean he'll believe her.

"It's not a long story. After you were born, your father started bothering the Consul about reform. Citizenship for all at birth. Very utopian." She leans back, quirking a corner of her lip. "Funny how patricians start to care when it touches their lives. *Their* kids."

Arran doesn't bristle so much at that. Doesn't startle so much at this new information—the idea of his father as a reformist, an *idealistic individualist*. It doesn't add up, but it's not the most ridiculous claim Montana's made so far. And he's waiting for the part that matters.

"He wasn't the Historian then. Not yet. Delena was still around, so Palmar didn't really pay much attention to him. That's what they say at Breakwater, anyway. But then she hacked her way to death from smoking fever, and Alexander got some power, and he started getting loud. Trying to rally others in his crowd to back him up. Not that anyone took him very seriously. But I guess the Consul *did* take him kind of seriously, because this is the part we're not supposed to talk about.

"He gave your father a choice, in the end. Get what he really wants out of all this—freedom for his son, but give up the girl and shut up about it. Marry a nice patrician lady and move on. *Or* keep on how he's going, and lose you to the system instead. He chose you. Obviously."

Vaguely, Arran is aware of a ringing in his ears.

Desperate. She's desperate, and she's drugged. Pulling at his frayed heartstrings, unasked questions and a history of loose threads and stories that just don't add up, grabbing onto one last hope of getting out of here alive. Trying to turn his anger around, away from her, back toward her victim. Another story, that's all it is. Cruel and inventive and *sick*, but a story all the same.

And yet.

Flumene relaxes inhibition but it doesn't addle the brains. He studied it, once, briefly in school with Gil.

Gil.

The stories just don't add up. The way Gil always talks about her—Qaia, his mother—like a sister, a best friend he and Dad both had loved and lost. The way Dad barely said anything about her at all. But in Gil's stories, Dad is always there, the third of some wayward trio forever protected by the magic of childhood—and that too, just doesn't add up. Dad never had those stories. Gil was just a client. Qaia was just a ghost.

Everyone protects their heart in different ways. Some learn to fight, in body and in mind. Some learn to perform, to endear themselves to a hostile world. And some retreat entirely. Unable to escape their physical circumstances, they spin a new narrative so tight around themselves that it becomes inextricable from reality, even to their own mind. They have to, to survive that kind of pain. Suddenly Arran feels sick.

"Gil," he hears himself saying. "Gil knows."

Montana nods. "I think he's probably the only one that knows all the details anymore. Aside from Qaia, wherever she is."

Because that's what this means. Because if he can entertain this, if he can comprehend the notion that his mother didn't actually die, and make that fit into his understanding of what's true and real, then logically the only alternative is that she's still alive. Somewhere. Maybe.

He has to put that away. He has to, because Theo is closing their hand around his, steadying or comfort or a reminder that they're running late, they have to *go*. Because Griff is staring at Montana, stonefaced and ready and all but done with this particular diversion. Because he can't do this. He needs to talk to Gil, he needs to sit somewhere and *think* because his mother could be out there somewhere, alive and waiting and *alive*, and that means Dad lied he *lied* he *sold her* but wasn't it her or Arran? A zero-sum game. An impossible choice.

Arran grips tight to the handle of the hunter's knife, heart beating so fast he thinks it might just tear itself out from under his buzzing skin, and grabs Montana Satterfield by the throat.

He wants to kill her. He's never wanted something like that before. With Darius Miranda it had been different—that was an accident, the heat of the moment as he came to Theo's rescue, and he hadn't realized his own strength. He hadn't let himself look as the blood seeped from the blackbag's head. But now . . . now, Una—Montana, whatever—hasn't stirred. No protest. No fight. She can't. She's still high on flumene.

Arran releases his grip.

"Do whatever you want with her," he says, venom dripping from his voice, as he cuts her bonds and pushes Una toward Griff. "Just leave me out of it."

His sister is more important. He needs to get to Belamar before she does.

DARIUS

When he comes to, Darius's head is throbbing. A sharp jab cutting through, and it takes a moment for his mind to catch up with the rest of his body, remember the cause for that rush of adrenaline that's asking what in the savage Quiet he's *doing*, staying still like this?

"Kopitar," he groans, mouth dry, unsure who he's even really talking to. "Get me Kopitar."

"Calm down, officer. You need to rest."

The room swims into focus, and so does the nausea. White sheets. The golden blaze of a setting sun through long windows. A medicus about ten years his senior, all golden hair and dimples. Hospitium Luxana.

"No," Darius tells him, urgency rushing in, and pushes the bedsheets off his legs even as the room still swims. "Kopitar. I need to speak with the Chief General right now."

Fragging *Quiet*, his head hurts.

"What you *need*," the medicus responds, infuriatingly, "is to let yourself heal. You got lucky—that's a nasty skull fracture, but it missed your vital centers. You've got a brain bleed, though, so—"

"Are you *deaf*? This is Intelligentia business. Send word for Kopitar *now*."

"No need for that, Miranda."

Thank Terra. Kopitar stands in the doorway of the room, long black overcoat and salt-streak hair, arms crossed over his chest. Darius wets his chapped lips, pushing down the nausea still swimming in his sinuses. They haven't got time to lose.

Theodora Arlot is a Revenant. A *spy*. The thought curdles, a rancid addition to the very real nausea, because he'd thought they were the same. He'd thought they understood each other, understood how a person could rise in the world, the duty they owed to the Imperium in return. She'd been playing him for a fool the whole time.

The betrayal stings so much more than it should. They aren't the same. They never were. She's a Revenant *spy*. So, it would seem, is Arran Alexander, the late Historian's own bastard son. A veritable nest of deceit buried in the heart of the Kleios familia, and more than that—this serva woman Una. Alexander Kleios's self-confessed killer. Darius doesn't know where to start with that, the new information swimming groggily in his mind alongside the nausea and the pain like a knife and the way he can't fragging seem to make the room stay *still*.

"Chief," he says, and tries to push back his sweaty hair. His fingers brush against bandage, and come away tinged red. "The Revenants, they—" But the words won't order themselves. He takes a deep breath, tries again. "Theo *Nix* . . ."

"You're confused, Miranda."

"No. *No*, I'm just—"

"Concussed, and confused." Kopitar sits, concern at the furrow of his brow. "Perhaps you could start by explaining what, precisely, you were doing on Breakwater Estate."

Yes, of course. Because he very explicitly was not supposed to be there. But Kopitar will understand. Once Darius tells him what he's discovered, Kopitar will set the Cohort to action, scour the city until Una and her co-conspirators are found and brought to justice. So Darius breathes in hard, and speaks through the searing pain in the side of his head. He tells him everything. The water hemlock. Tobin Persie's apothecary. Theodora Arlot—no, Theo Nix, deceitful bitch that she is. Una, who confessed her loyalties and her crime, clear as day. And Arran Alexander, revealing his true colors at the last minute before dealing the blow that's landed Darius here in the first place.

"If we act quickly, there should still be time to catch them before they leave the city," he says, then, heart beating fast. "Shut down the ports, both the Western and Southern gates. Rouse the Publica, the reserves, the legions stationed on the walls. We'll flush them out and—"

"I thought I told you to leave the Kleios familia alone."

Darius falters. Because Kopitar hasn't moved from where he sits, but there isn't a trace of ease or that usual vague amusement Darius knows how to look for. Something hard, instead, like concra falling into place. Disappointment where he'd thought there was concern. His heart sinks.

"I," he starts, but that's no good. His mind is racing fast. Hadn't Kopitar understood? "Persie's tip-off about water hemlock. I felt it would be a dereliction of duty not to pursue that link."

"Despite strict orders *not* to?"

"You told me not to investigate the senator, not to ignore a perfectly good—"

"I explicitly told you to investigate Avis Tiago-Laith's trail in pursuit of the Revenants."

"And I *found them.*"

It comes out sharper than he means it to, practically a bark, but Darius is so nauseous he thinks he's halfway to being sick, and he doesn't understand. He doesn't see how Kopitar can't grasp what he's saying. How the Chief could be more concerned with a minor break in order and decorum than in the very real and urgent threat of three known Revenants—*murderers*—at large in Luxana, their chances of disappearing growing more and more with every second the two of them waste here talking about it.

He breathes in through the pain. "I'm sorry, Chief. I'll answer for my insubordination. I understand I acted against orders. But . . ." And then he stops, because he forgot something. In the picture of reality swimming in and out of focus, the thoughts and words fighting to arrange themselves, he forgot one vital, uncanny piece of information. Darius breathes in sharp. "Consul Palmar," he says.

Kopitar's dark eyes narrow. "What about him?"

"The serva woman. She said . . . she tried to claim that she was acting under the Consul's orders." A lie. It has to be a lie. Low and dirty and underhanded, an Ynglot savage undermining the very integrity of the Imperial soul. "We need to find her before she has the chance to discredit him further."

He's halfway out of the bed again, but then a strong hand is at his shoulder, the Chief General pressing him back.

"You're not well," Kopitar says.

"I'm well enough to—"

"You're not. Well. You'll need rest before your journey."

Darius falters. "My . . . what?"

Then Kopitar is standing, straightening the black overcoat over his uniform. "I believe I was clear about the consequences of pursuing this suspicion of yours," he says. "We'll have an escort put together once you're well enough to ride. They'll see you back to Ithaca in one piece."

No.

No.

This can't be happening. This isn't.

He didn't disobey orders, not really. He had been right about the Kleios familia, but he hadn't touched Naevia. He'd left her alone, her and the Lady Historian both. He had been wrong about the senator, but he had been right to follow his gut. He had been *right*.

He must be more concussed than he thought.

"Chief, you can't—"

"I certainly can. Your last month's pay will find you there, but don't expect a reference."

Darius is falling. Fast and endless through some terrible abyss, with nothing to grab onto to make it stop. The bottom of his stomach an endless pit where his esophagus has fallen through, and he can't find his tongue to speak. Doesn't know how to form words even if he could.

He's spent his life doing the right thing. He's prided himself on that. His gut has never led him astray. It's the reason Kopitar took him under his wing. The reason their correspondence blossomed into a mentorship. Late-night conversation and necessary introductions and professional references and those words of advice that showed Darius how to open the door to a brighter future. Kopitar was his rock, the way his own father never could have been. Alcohol on his breath and bruises the size of a grown man's fist against Darius's cheek, and the cold and run-down manor in Ithaca looms like a haunted house in the nauseous dark.

So this isn't happening. It *can't* be. He can't go back.

But it is. It's happening, and he can do nothing but watch as Kopitar leaves the room without so much as a look back his way.

VI

KATABASIS

The genesis of classic comoediae theatrum *stems, of course, from the seat of art and civilization itself—Roma. Theater arts of the lesser provinces and client empires have gone in and out of fashion over the years, but* comoediae *is considered evergreen due to its signature plotlines and stock characters—the lecherous old man, the forbidden lovers, the trickster crim. Audiences are at ease knowing already where the play will end, and so naturally it becomes the getting there that matters.*

—CHAPTER 4 INTRODUCTION, OCTAVIAN TITANIS'S *THE DEFINITIVE IMPERIAL THEATER ARTS (3RD EDITION)*

TAIR

S he was eighteen years old the day her life ended.

Tair remembers it like a dream, like something underwater. Something happening to some other girl, because there was no way to make herself understand that this was real. The words passing through air, and the voice sounded like Gil's, sounded like concepts that should make sense. *Sentenced* and *magistrate's decision* and *eligibility revoked*. None of them mattered. None of them were real. Not until hours had passed and she saw Selah's face. Something about that had brought her reality crashing in with alarming clarity.

It wasn't anger. It wasn't blame. Nothing about what had happened was either of their fault, not when it came down to it. Not when Tair could see it now, how slim her chances had ever really been. She'd just gotten closer to it than most.

So when Una woke her in the middle of the night, a hand over her mouth and vague, hushed promises on her lips, Tair hadn't been as suspicious as she probably should have.

"The people I work for, they can help you disappear."

"What? Who are they?"

"You'll find out soon, but we have to leave now, while everyone's still asleep. No, don't take anything. They'll give you a new life. They'll protect you. You'll be free."

Free. What a fucking word. It hadn't occurred to Tair before then that she was anything but. Of course there were rules and chores, laws she had to abide by, but didn't everyone? Wasn't that the price you paid for living in the Imperium's civilized embrace? It wasn't like she was a serva, after all, locked for life into menial labor as consequence for her own bad decisions. She had a future. She had a *purpose*. One that was gone forever now, wiped away in an instant with a magistrate's shrug, and in that tiniest of moments Tair could see the lies for what they'd been. Even as a verna, she'd never had a future at all. Not one with anything but the flimsiest illusion of choice. A little wooden house next to Gil's and the name Alexander and a head full of knowledge-organization systems to assist Selah in her work and for as long as she could remember Tair had wanted that. She had wanted it so, so badly, but she had never actually *asked* for it. It was handed to her with a reminder to be grateful she had been given anything at all. Was it what she had ever really wanted? How could a person know the difference?

Now, with that one word *freedom* on Una's lips, Tair could feel it like a buzzing in her skin, all the tiny pieces of her body reaching out to meet all the tiny pieces of the world. Endless possibility. Boundless creation. True freedom meant that she could do anything at all, and savage Quiet was that a terrifying thought—terrifying but intoxicating, that capacity to invent beyond what she had ever dared to imagine.

Tair had hesitated, both Selah and Gil making a place for themselves in the space between, but only for a moment.

Why me?

Una hadn't had an answer to that.

Truth be told, she'd been half expecting Una's mysterious employer to turn out to be the Revenants. Maybe it was childish, a byproduct of news headline and urban legend, because you can't get three blocks in this city without hearing some Imperial street orator blame the burning of an apartments complex in Paleaside on Revenant terror. They are the Enemy that loom large in the popular imagination of Roma Sargassa, and Tair had been shocked at first to find that there were only four of them total.

Griff had been quick to correct that assumption.

"Most of us still have the cover of our regular lives," she'd told her over a mug of tazine in that little network of underground halls that was now her home. "What you've got down here are those of us who've been compromised. Or have nowhere else to go."

Griff. Pa'akal Zetnes. Theodora Nix. Izara Charis. And now Tair.

"So what's the end goal?" she'd asked, very early on. "If you're not actually responsible for half the crap the Cohorts pin on you."

The older woman had smiled, too warm and open to be the monster in the night. "Self-rule, Tair. On our own terms. A true people's representation, never mind who your parents were. A direct democracy of the people by the people."

What an absolute concept.

It was exciting, at first. For all Tair was ready to embrace her new-found freedom, her sudden and completely novel ability to wake up when she liked and eat what she liked and tag after who she liked asking whatever questions popped into her head, it was overwhelming, too. The problem with *choice* is that it's endless. Turns out there actually *is* such a thing as too much. So she was glad for the routine. The communal breakfasts and close combat training with Theo and afternoons spent with Griff answering question after endless question. Details about the Archives and its classified contents and even the personal lives of the Kleios familia, and Tair had learned to ignore the Selah-shaped guilt in her gut that told her this was a betrayal.

She learned to ignore a lot of Selah-shaped things.

Then the novelty wore off.

Tair, if asked, would never be able to pinpoint the exact moment she realized what was wrong. Maybe there wasn't one. Maybe it began small, a seed that took root and grew over the two months she spent with the Revenants until it was just too big to ignore anymore. The way that no one ever questioned Griff. The way that all she had to do was say the word and her foot soldiers leapt to obey. Orders couched as requests are still orders, after all, and the more she watched Griff the more Tair had trouble picturing the Revenant leader ever willingly handing over that kind of power to a people's self-rule. And then one day it occurred to her, watching Izara abandon her dinner halfway through to follow Griff into the city at the drop of a word—just as no one ever asked if she wanted to be a verna, no one had ever asked if she wanted to be a Revenant, either.

The bad taste in her mouth lingered from there, and it didn't go away. Because she had done this before. She had been through this already. Blind obedience to what she's been told she's supposed to want. *A true people's representation, never mind who your parents were. A direct democracy of the people by the people.* It sounds good in theory, but if the very people who are fighting for it can't demonstrate that in the way they operate among themselves to get there, then what hope could Sargassa ever have to see it on a grand scale?

Tair was done with being told what to do. She was done working for a goal someone else told her she was supposed to have. She was done with following orders when she doesn't understand *why*.

A new life was promised to her. Freedom. She had left behind too much to deny herself that.

Leaving had been surprisingly easy. She waited until the others were gone on some mission no one had bothered explaining, and slipped back aboveground. Even Theo, who had returned early and sent her on her way with a black eye, had ultimately let her go. Tair has always wondered about that.

Tair was eighteen years old the day her life ended. She was eighteen years old the day her life began.

"Why didn't you just kill me?" she asks now, when Theo finally shows up in the brick alley behind Neptune's Folly. String music and rowdy singing spills from inside the taberna, laughter and lamplight. They're half an hour late.

"Trust me, the thought occurred," they say. "But I had a feeling Arran and Selah might not be too thrilled."

"You know that's not what I meant."

"Do I?"

Infuriating. Fucking infuriating, but that's on Tair, honestly, for getting herself mixed up with Theo or anyone from that crowd again. Not that it was *her* decision, mind, they all but ran into each other in the road, unable to speak freely thanks to the brother and sister they'd somehow each managed to collect. Tair doesn't like it, keeping the whole truth from Selah. It's only been a day since they crashed back into each other's lives, after all, and maybe that means that Tair doesn't owe her the whole truth yet, but it still feels wrong. Lying, even by omission. But it's only been a day, and the Sisters of the First are one thing. Admitting that she was briefly a Revenant is another one completely. The sooner this is over, the better.

The plan, in theory, is a simple one.

Theo, it turns out, has a surprisingly thorough knowledge of the layout of the fighting pits, and Tair has her suspicions about that but she hasn't pressed. According to them, there are multiple entrances secreted around the city where you can find your way down to the pits—a nondescript cellar door behind Neptune's Folly being one of them. That's Tair and Theo's way in.

Selah, on the other hand, is Palmar's guest. She and Arran are meeting him at his estate and will go with him from there. Selah will stick with him the entire time, making sure he's happy and distracted and, if possible, preferably drunk. Meanwhile Arran will be sent to wait for his match with the rest of the fighters, which should give him enough time to find Miro Ontiveros if he's actually there. Once he's found him, he'll meet Tair and Theo behind the cells where the servae fighters are kept and hand off Miro from there. According to Theo, there should be a secret way out back there, unknown even to the handlers who make their living down in the pits, where they can smuggle Miro back above the ground.

From there, it should be easy. Arran sends word via a handler that he's changed his mind. He doesn't want to fight. Selah will make a scene about it, yell at him or whatever else it takes to throw off Palmar's suspicion, and later on they'll all meet up at Theo's apartment again. After that, if Miro knows where Diana is, if he has even a hint of an idea, they'll follow her trail from there.

Easy. Right.

Except for the part where she knows Theo. She knows they don't do anything without good reason, and that reason more than usually has to do with Griff's orders. So she needs Theo for now, Theo and Arran both, but Tair still knows she'll have to be ready for the double-cross when it inevitably comes.

There's something Ibdi says now and then, whenever the Sisters of the First find themselves working with surprising allies. District prefects, that sort of thing. *No permanent friends, no permanent enemies.* Something about how, if you're waiting around for pure ideological alignment, you're going to be waiting for a very long time. And in the meanwhile, you'll get nothing done at all.

Tair feels for the Iveroa Stone in the bag at her side, a solid reminder that it's still there. All this for the hope that Miro knows where his mother is. All this to protect the Sisters from her blackmailer. If nothing else, all this so that a man will go free.

At least she knows why she's doing it.

SELAH

The existence of the fighting pits may be technically against the law, but in Roma Sargassa, Cato Palmar *is* the law. Subtlety isn't exactly in his nature, except where the illusion of deference to the Imperium and Ovidii princeps are concerned. Selah arrives back at Belamar just as he's preparing to climb into his coach, an ostentatiously ornate thing crested with the Palmar familia sigil and flanked by two sentries on either side.

Arran isn't here yet. He was supposed to meet her at the gate, after she stopped home to wash up and change into clothes free of sweat and bloodstains and riot debris. He didn't, and it's done nothing for Selah's rattled nerves.

"You didn't bring your girl with you," Cato Palmar remarks.

Selah shakes her head. "My mother has too many eyes and ears at Breakwater. I'm still learning which ones I can trust."

The truth is, with Arran and Theo around to back her up this time, Selah did what she's been unable to do since they were ten and eleven years old, and successfully argued Tair down. She didn't want her to come at all, but Tair had pointed out that the Iveroa Stone was in *her* possession, after all, and Selah was forced to give in. She's coming with Theo through one of the back ways they seem to inexplicably know about, along with the rest of the crowd.

"Yet you trust *him*?"

His eyes rake over to where Arran has just run into view around the corner of the winding drive, and she sees her brother stop short, tense beneath the scrutiny. Relief washes over her at the sight of him, even as Selah wants to rip Palmar's eyes out.

Instead, she makes herself smile, and lets him help her up into the waiting coach, and hopes he can't hear her heart pounding in her throat. She doesn't let herself look at her brother, who's left to lift himself up next to the driver.

"Arran knows it's in his best interest to stay on my good side," she says, feeling disgusting.

When the coach pulls to a stop twenty minutes later, Selah blinks, and for a moment thinks there must have been some kind of misunderstanding. She had been expecting to end up back in Paleaside or the Third Ward, dark alleys and shady warehouses. Instead, they're somewhere in the Financial District, stopped right outside what looks like a perfectly respectable brownstone home.

By now, she thinks she should stop being so surprised.

A serva—just a teenager, just a boy—lets them in, and Selah has the distinct impression she's stepped into some sort of patrician social club. Lacquered wood, easy conversation, the smell of cigar smoke. Men, mostly, but a few women here and there that nod their welcome to Palmar and raise their surprised brows at her, and the serva boy shows them through the crowded foyer hallway down to the wine cellar.

Underground, indeed. Arran bumps slightly against her, and Selah has to stop herself from glancing back to make sure he's all right as the kid slides open the door to what looks like some sort of subterranean cellar. Their party steps inside.

Down here, the world is quiet, and Selah feels her heart drop into her stomach as she realizes exactly where she is. It's not a cellar.

The ancient catacombs that run beneath Luxana's busy streets are wide and sloping things of smooth and maintained concra, lit every now and again by the odd mourner's candle flickering its last—little pools of weak firelight piercing the heavy dark. A final resting place for the dead. Selah was here not so many days ago, a few miles north beneath the Imperial Archives where they lay Alexander Kleios to rest beside his parents in the familia crypt. She had said nothing then, at the mourner's vigil that night after the viewing. Mima's hand held tightly in her own, Arran's presence heavy behind and somewhere to her left, and she watched the last of her father's pale skin melt from his face, his salt-streak auburn hair curl and burn away to dust.

That will be her someday. Sacrificed to the flames lest her deathtoxins poison and choke All-Mater Terra's sacred soil. Nothing but an effigy left, a poor shadow of the person who once ran barefoot along the Sargassan shore. That will be all of them, erased into stone and ash. Selah shivers, and tries not to think of the souls too poor and immaterial to receive a likeness, whose faded memories watch her now from row upon row of dusty burial plates set along the catacomb walls, made anonymous by long years of wear and obscurity.

This is a sacred place, now defiled.

"Will all of those people be coming to the games?" she asks Palmar. "Back at the house?"

"Some may, some may not. Some prefer to look the other way. The Leontine Club isn't the only entrance to the pits. Just the most exclusive."

The closest, too, it turns out. It doesn't take long for them to arrive, the muffled echoes of shouts and jeering curling their way into her ears long before one of the Consul's four flanking sentries raps on the hard, curved door—and it's not concra, but neither is it any other stone or metal Selah has ever seen—and she steps into chaos.

It's an arena.

A pit.

You could fit the whole of Breakwater House down here.

Paraffin lamps illuminate a cavernous room the size of several warehouses, yawning wide and high even as it seems to be carved out from the earth itself. Risers loom in a huge circle around the center, and from the top of the high stone stairs where she entered, Selah can see that the fighting ring within sinks into the not-concra floor, too deep for even a full-grown man to climb out. On the far left end of the enormous space, a row of latticed cells, secured and locked, that somehow seems to go on forever. And everywhere she looks, *people*. Salt-worn plebs with weathered faces shouting over each other to place their last-minute bets. Well-dressed women greeting each other with a kiss to each cheek. Laughing, waiting for hops at the bar, arguing over their favorites to win. Just . . . people. Regular people, out for a good time. Selah feels sick.

Don't they realize what's happening here?

She doesn't let it show, though, as a hatchet-faced man in gray materializes out of the crowd, and Palmar says, "There you are. Selah, this is Wieler, our chief handler. Wieler, the Lady Historian."

Wieler inclines his head, an awkward bow. "He'll take the boy down to the staging area, get him armed up and such."

"Armed?" she asks quickly. "He fights bare-knuckle."

"Oh, I only mean in the general sense of preparation."

"Good," Selah says, and, aware of the relief in her voice, makes herself add, "I'd hate to lose an investment so quickly."

"Naturally." The Consul inclines his head, his white teeth glistening in an all-too-pleasant smile. "The opening matches are just a warm-up to the real blood sport. We'll want to see what he's capable of before entering him into anything truly lethal."

Palmar's assurances don't go very far to sway her unease. She watches as the man Wieler fingers the heavy baton in his belt and at long last lets herself turn to look back at her brother.

He's gone. Well, no, he's still *there*, but Selah's never seen him like this. How he holds himself away from her, a quiet shadow of himself. If she looks hard enough, she can see him glance at her for just a fraction of a second, something hard and urgent in his gaze that she doesn't understand. But then the green eyes they share flick back to train themselves steady somewhere just over her left shoulder.

"Ma'am," he says, and his voice sounds *flat*, it sounds *dead*, and they're back at the cobblestone banks of the Third Ward canal but this time there's no wink, no smirk, nothing *Arran*. He still won't meet her eyes.

Just an act. It's just an act.

Be careful, she thinks, desperate, willing him to somehow hear. And then he's gone, for real this time. Disappeared with Wieler into the press of people.

"Come," says the Consul, his sentries parting a way for them through the crowd. "I'll show you to my private pavilion. There are some friends I'd like to introduce you to."

ARRAN

The pasty, thick-set man called Wieler pokes him from behind with his nightstick, and Arran turns around and glares.

"Let's get something straight," he says, pent-up anger and panic fraying at the edge. "I'm not one of your serva fighters you can bat around. I'm a free man, and I'm pretty good at what I do. Touch me with that thing again, you and I are going to have a problem."

It's almost a relief, letting some of it out. He got to Belamar too late to warn Selah about Palmar, and now she's out there with him, none the wiser to the danger and completely unprotected. Finding Miro and getting out and away from Palmar as soon as possible is the only option left.

He's needed somewhere to put this heat since long before the unending coach ride, and people talking about him like he wasn't even *there*, and being forced anywhere in the vicinity of the man who tore apart his family like it's nothing at all, and having to remind himself all the while that he *chose* to do this. He's needed it since long before then, since the moment he watched Montana Satterfield disappear into the darkness of Amphitheater Messalina, bound to Griff in the long march back to Revenant headquarters.

It was the right thing to do, he does know that. Doesn't mean he wouldn't prefer to just hit something. Wieler, preferably.

The handler blinks at him now, then grunts his assent. Bullies respond to strength, and between that little speech and Montana's surprisingly strong uppercut, Arran apparently fits the profile.

Wieler shows him to the long row of iron cells at the leftmost end of the pits, just where Theo said it would be. Most are shut tight and locked, spectators gathered to ogle at the men, women, and themed on the other side. Servae, Arran realizes grimly, the state of them confirming anything the locked gates left in doubt. While toned and trained and on the whole a pretty terrifying bunch, that doesn't make up for the grisly sight of missing limbs and burn scars, crushed hands and gouged eyes. Here and there are slighter figures, attending servae. Most show clear signs of malnourishment, even those who aren't outright emaciated. No rations wasted on non-fighters, then. They're not the ones who bring in the coins.

Three cell doors at the very end are wide open, however, revealing a connecting network amongst them once inside. That's where the plebeian fighters are getting ready.

"First-timer, right?" Wieler asks, grabbing some kind of schedule off the rough concra wall. Arran nods, ignoring the whispers and threatening glare one man flexing on a bench is sending his way. "Okay. You're on with Nameed over there, third match. Ground rules for opener fights: no weapons, no killing, you get five minutes to knock him out or you don't get your cut."

"That's it?"

"That's it. People don't pay to see pleb boys rough each other up. Questions?"

"Yeah," he says, eyeing the little corridor that seems to sneak its way from the open cells along behind the back of the closed ones. Theo told him to look for that. "There a toilet that way I can use?"

He doesn't have much time, not if he's supposed to change his mind before the third match and get Selah the hell away from Palmar. Wieler points him in the right direction down the dark, narrow hall carved into the bedrock, and the moment his back is turned, Arran is at the cell bars asking, "Miro? I'm looking for Miro Ontiveros."

The first person to notice him, when he finally gets her attention, just shrugs. Doesn't know who he's talking about. He has better luck with the next, an older man with a nasty scar running down his neck that's taken his whole ear off. Arran tries not to stare as he points him further along. Heart beating against his chest, he slides down the long, cramped hallway, passing gate after gate and savage Quiet, how many *people* are down here?

Quite suddenly and without warning, he thinks of Pina Bema, the corner-store owner a day late on rent.

Fabian, the cook at Breakwater, whose parents took out loans he inherited and could never hope to repay.

Tair, dumped on the steps of the Servile Children's Asylum at only a few days old, just another mouth to feed.

Theo, who Griff said spent nine years down here, and Arran still doesn't know why.

It doesn't matter why. No one deserves this. The names and crimes spin through his head, and Arran passes face after anonymous face, exhausted and worn and scratched and burnt. The burdens on society. The ones left behind. Any moment of his life, that could have been him, and he's never appreciated as clearly as he does now how much of a shield Dad's money and name were for him. When you have influence, the rules don't apply.

He can hear Dad's voice now, clearly in his mind. *We live for the many.*

Not the few.

He can do that. That is what it is to be a Revenant. These are his people now.

Finally, at the second to last gate, he grabs a bald thremid's shoulder and hisses, "I'm looking for Miro—"

"Yeah, I heard."

The voice comes from somewhere to the right.

Miro Ontiveros is tall, taller even than Arran, which doesn't really come as a surprise. He *is* a clavaspher player, after all. But his long braids have been buzzed to the root, and there's a just-fading scar split across the bridge of his now-broken nose. That silver cuff clasped around his left ear. The wide, friendly face from Tair's sketch is gone, replaced by one that's seen far too much in too short a time. He eyes Arran from a wary distance, scanning him up and down before asking, "What do you want?"

"My name's Arran. I'm here . . . I'm here for your sister. I came to bust you out."

The distrust doesn't leave his eyes. "You know Xochitl? She's here?"

"No—I . . ." And here Arran's mouth runs dry. He doesn't like lying. He doesn't like lying by omission. But there's a time and place to grieve, and this isn't it. He'll mourn the man's sister with him later.

"She's not, it's just me and some friends. Is there a way out of there from your side?"

Miro shrugs, grimacing at the metal bars between them. "No. They lock us in during matches, meals, nighttime. Anything that's not training, really."

"All right," says Arran, thinking very fast. That wasn't supposed to happen. Theo said the cells were closed off, but not locked. "All right. I'll try to find, I don't know, a pin or something. Do you know how to pick a lock?"

"No. And even if I did, I wouldn't."

Arran stops. "What?"

"I don't know you," he says, his face hard. "I don't know that you know Xo. And even if I did, I step out of line and my mima's fragged. So I'm staying right where I am, thanks."

THEO

Theo knows, in an intellectual sort of way, that the chances of being recognized down here are slim to none. They have eleven years and a good hundred pounds on them since the last time they were here, their hollowed face made full by three reliable meals a day, black hair short and thick and glossy with health.

That doesn't mean they can't suspend disbelief for a moment of fantasy. The satisfaction of hailing Kyrie or Wieler or one of the other handlers over to answer some question or other away from the crowd. The realization in their eyes just in the shuddering moment before Theo takes their trusted blade and puts it right through his or her shocked face. That they would know they were meeting their end at the pleasure of little Theodora. Jarol's kid. The one that got away.

It's a pretty thought, revenge, but it isn't one that belongs to tonight.

They come through the back alley behind Neptune's Folly, Tair close behind. They've made it a point since escape to know each and every entrance to the pits, for when the time really does come. So there's something reassuring in knowing that there's a Revenant stationed at each one, ready and waiting to act if things down here go south. Griff in the Regio Marina. Pa'akal in Paleaside. Any number of other operatives elsewhere whose names Theo has never known.

Griff wasn't thrilled about it, but she agreed in the end that there was no way they were letting Selah Kleios and the Iveroa Stone go down into the pits alone. Especially not in the company of Cato Palmar and his designs on both the girl and the weapon itself. And she also agreed that the Stone and its potential are useless to them without the knowledge of how to operate it. Finding Diana Ontiveros is a priority.

"Timeline's moving up." Griff had drawn Theo to the side before leaving the amphitheater, an urgent warning on her lips. "I wanted to give you more time to work on Selah, let it happen naturally. But I don't think we have the time for that anymore. Things are developing faster than I expected."

"What do you mean?"

"He shouldn't know. Palmar. Una said he knew what the Stone looks like. He shouldn't."

"She said he probably read about it somewhere."

"Not possible."

"How do you kn—"

"Later. Keep your eyes sharp on him down there. He knows more than he should, and I don't like it. Leave through the Regio exit with Selah once you've found the Ontiveros boy, and make damn sure she has the Stone with her. I'll meet you there."

Kyrie's taken point at this door, checking for weapons and collecting the entry fee, and Theo freezes as the enormous woman pats them down. The last time she touched them, they'd been unconscious for two days after. Theo was fifteen. This time, she manages to miss all three weapons concealed amongst Theo's boots and clothes. Tair drops two ceres in her palm, and nudges Theo along.

"What was that?" she hisses. They ignore her.

Their head is buzzing slightly, which is more disconcerting than anything, as they move through the thick press of the crowd. Through laughter and drinking, arguing and betting, and the purpose that Theo has carried with them all these long years feels dangerously close to converting right back to wild, unconfined fury.

Breathe, they think, and hold their head up high. *Just breathe.*

At the far end of the pits is the little corridor carved into the earth, the one that leads to the fighters' living quarters. If you can call it that. A damp, cold hallway where darkness presses in, and if you happen to take a right instead of veering left toward the holding cells, you might just stumble across the same crack in the earth that Theo found, all those years ago. That innocent crevice where they hid from a drunk and violent Wieler, and found that it just . . . kept going, all the way out to the world above.

Theo glances around to make sure no one's watching, about to slip inside, when Tair says from behind, "Wait. Stop."

At the urgency in her voice, they just barely suppress the well-honed instinct to grab for the knife hidden against their ribcage. "What?"

"What are you doing with Arran?" Tair asks, unexpected.

"Making out, mostly."

Tair doesn't laugh, doesn't budge from where she's glowering like some red-headed little gargoyle. "You're undercover at the Senate?" It's less a question than a statement of fact.

"This is true."

"You're spying on Senator Kleios?"

"Mm-hm."

They have to wonder where this is going. Tair's stone-faced, like someone just died and it's all Theo's fault. Which is unfair, really. If anyone has the right to be pissed, it's *them*. Tair's the one who took advantage of the Revenants' generosity only to throw it back in their face, the one who nearly derailed Griff's plans for the Iveroa Stone, and now, because of Tair, Theo is standing in the one place they swore they'd never return.

Now, Tair is still glaring at them, but there's something else going on as she twists her lips. "Look," she says. "I know Arran seems . . . fun. A good time or whatever. But I've known him my whole life. Stop fucking around with him."

"Savage Quiet," says Theo, suddenly realizing what this is really about. "Is this a shovel talk?"

"No."

"It fully is. You're giving me a shovel talk."

"I just don't want you messing him around and then disappearing. He's had enough of that. And he's not like you and me. He tries to hide it, but he's sensitive."

Theo rolls their head back, pushing back the laughter that wants to escape. "If that's him trying to hide it, he's doing a pretty terrible job." And then, because Tair is still glowering—"Babes. This is sweet. But you have *got* to give him more credit than that. When it comes to me, Arran knows exactly what he's getting into."

And Tair's eyes go wide. She stands up straight, arms uncrossed. "No."

"Yep."

"Griff—"

"Gave him the seal of approval and everything. Sorry to break it to you, but it looks like we're all on the same side again."

"We're not on the same side," Tair growls. "Not until you tell me why the Revenants want the Stone."

Ah. Clever girl. Theo thought they'd done a pretty good job, back at their apartment when Tair pulled a slab of rock out of her bag and casually declared it was the Quiet-fucking Iveroa Stone, of keeping their reaction to themself. Apparently they were wrong.

"We don't want the Stone," they lie, and again there's that kernel of truth. "We want Selah to have the Stone."

"And why the fuck would you want that?"

Theo's lip quirks, just a little. Then there's a blade in her hand, pressing just slightly into Tair's side, and they've angled themself just there so that anyone in the passing crowd would assume that they're a pair of lovers taking a moment in quiet talk. Tair's eyes go wide, her pale brown face flushing with something between anger and fear, but Theo gets there first.

"You asked me why I didn't kill you five years ago."

"Don't dodge the question." Tair's voice is a hiss.

"I'm not. You were right to ask. I've killed for less, never mind a runaway verna brat who knows way too much about Griff and the Luxana cell. But the thing is, you were never a loose end. Griff was onto you. She knew you weren't going to stay, and she had a feeling you might be useful down the line. And she was right. Look who you've brought together. Look at the present you brought us." Theo leans in, a whispered caress blowing against the frizzing red hair around her ear. "That's what you never understood, Tair. The long game. I don't follow Griff like a stupid fucking dog blindly obeying its master. I have faith because she *earned* it. And it hasn't steered me wrong yet."

A long moment passes then, the angry inhale and exhale of the girl in front of them, and Theo's never been one to play with her food. Still, they don't put the knife away just yet. "While we're on the subject," they say, conversational now. "How long exactly are you planning on lying to Selah about how we know each other?"

Tair's face darkens. "Don't you dare—"

"It's just a question. Your secret's safe with me."

"*What* is taking so long?"

Speak of the Quiet. The blade is gone in an instant, tucked safe back in Theo's sleeve.

It's Selah, hands on hips as she materializes through the crowd. Tair shoots a worried glance their way, but it's a wasted gesture. Theo isn't about to drop that sort of major payload on Selah—not here and now, anyway, never mind how much fun the fallout would be to watch. Instead, they just roll their eyes. "It's been barely twenty minutes."

"That's forever and a half for her," says Tair, nudging the other girl's hip with disgruntled fondness, hard suspicion still ghosting at the edge of a glare. "You get used to it."

When the three of them arrive at the dark corridor's crossroads behind the fighters' cells, Arran is there as planned. Miro is not.

"What the hell are you doing here?" he hisses at Selah, eyes wide. "Where's Palmar?"

"He's talking with someone from the Intelligentia, it's fine. He won't even notice I'm gone."

"That might be a good thing." Arran purses his lips. "Palmar is—"

"Where's Miro?" Theo interrupts.

Of the four of them, Theo is the only one with real covert mission experience. So they don't mind taking the reins, steering the others back on course, and the simple fact is that they don't have the time for this. Palmar's done some real damage to Arran and Selah's family, yes, but right now they have the advantage on him. If they're going to keep it, they have to stay working on a tight schedule.

"He's here," says Arran, eyes suddenly blazing. "I found him. Locked in the holding cells."

"Fuck."

Pit fighters weren't allowed to roam free, exactly, when they were a child, but neither were they locked up in pens like cattle. Still, they should have planned ahead. They should have slipped Kyrie's keys from her belt just in case, instead of just standing there useless. Theo knew some things would have changed since they were here last. This puts a dent in things.

"Yeah," says Arran, looking grim. "And there's another problem, too."

Miro Ontiveros is waiting at the back edge of his cell when Arran leads them to him, anxiously glancing now and again over his shoulder. His cellmates seem to have realized something's going on, and are doing their best to obscure him from the view of gawkers and handlers up at the front.

"These your friends?" he asks Arran, when they come to a stop.

"Selah, hi."

"Tair. Your sister was my—"

"I'm Theo. I grew up down here."

Miro stares. So does Selah. But they don't have the time to build up the man's trust. They need it *now*.

"Sure you did," he says.

Wordlessly, they unbutton their duskra, shaking arms out of sleeves to reveal keloid tattoos, then hike up the back of their undershirt as they turn around, leaving their back exposed to his view. They can't see Miro, but they can see Tair, jaw set firm. Tair will know what this means, has felt the burn of fire and ink herself, and the searing pain mixed with gentle humming as Ody worked. They can see Selah, too, utterly confused. And then there's Arran, curiosity and a dawning realization mingling as one. He's seen them naked twice now. He just didn't know to look. That crude shield and spear at the very base of their spine, the same one the handlers will have given to Miro when they dragged him down here, Theo's own nearly faded now beneath the scarification they underwent to declare themself free.

Nearly. It's still there, underneath.

"My dad. He owed a lot of money," they explain, shrugging the duskra back down. "And my mima . . . wasn't well. No one knew where she was. So they just processed me with him. I was three."

"So you were verna?"

It's Selah who asks, dark brow furrowed hard. Theo just shakes their head. "No."

Verna are born, not made. There's no limit to how young a serva can be.

"Dependents have to stay with parents, so." They shrug. "Anyway. I was too little to fight at first, too scrawny after that. Believe it or not. But someone's got to polish armor and clean the cells and feed the fighters and everything."

Something's struggling to pull together behind Selah's eyes, some pieces falling into place that make her dark cheeks go pale, and it occurs to Theo then that they've done this before. Sitting across jav during the humid meridiem hour while they laughed and joked and Theo spun tales about some invented childhood while Selah listened along with rapt attention. Those had been outright lies. These aren't, but they wouldn't really blame Selah for not believing them. But she says nothing, and when Theo turns back around, Miro is silent, too. He just nods. He's spent enough time down here to understand the way things are.

"There's a way out back down that way," they go on, nodding in the direction of the crevice escape. "If you keep going straight instead of turning toward the arena. It's how I got out last time. It's how we can get you out, too, but first—Arran says you know where your mother is."

Miro takes a deep breath. "I don't know *where* she is, not exactly. But the sentries took her somewhere in that same direction when they brought us here, and I see the Consul heading down that way all the time. There's . . . noises, too. I can't explain it. We all hear them. Booms and that. Like fireworks, but worse, coming from somewhere below. I know she's still alive, though. Or . . ." and here he blinks, the alternative too awful to consider. "That's what he tells me, anyway. The Consul. She's alive, and if I step out of line, he'll hurt her. He already has."

He's glaring again, this time at the floor, like it's offended him somehow.

"It's my fault," he says through gritted teeth. "It's my fault she went into that Quiet-damned house in the first place. My fault for getting cocky—I was so excited. The *Consul* wanted to sponsor me. I—"

"Yeah, I'm sure it's all fully tough for you, but we don't really have time for the self-flagellation right now," Tair cuts in, eyes shining with the news that Diana is alive—that she's *here*—and Theo could kiss her. "You're fighting tonight, right?"

"Second-to-last match."

"Okay, that's a lucky break." The gears in Tair's head seem to be working double time, and her eyes slide over to Arran and Selah. "If Diana's down here somewhere, we may not get another chance at this. I'll go."

"I'm going with you," Selah says at once.

"*No.*" Tair grabs her hand, urgent. "Palmar can't suspect anything."

"Tough. Booms and explosions? You're not going down there by yourself."

"I can—" Theo starts, but Selah cuts them off.

"*You* can keep an eye on Palmar and make sure he behaves himself. But I'm going with Tair."

This is ridiculous. Selah isn't a fighter and Palmar will be wondering where she's gone. If anyone should be going with Tair for protection, it's them. Theo opens their mouth to tell her exactly that, but before the words come out, Arran steps down lightly on their foot.

"I think that's a great idea," he says, firm, and all at once Theo remembers the very real threat that Palmar poses to Selah. He isn't just after the Stone. He thinks he needs her, too. And it isn't just that Griff wants them both on their side and safe from Cato Palmar, who somehow knows more about the Iveroa Stone than he should—it's that Arran will do what he has to in order to protect his sister. Theo isn't used to thinking in those terms.

"Sounds good to me," they find themself agreeing, through barely gritted teeth, and there's a ghost of a twitch at the corners of Arran's mouth.

"Fine," Tair snaps. "Fine. But Palmar can't think anything's off.

Not until we're all well clear of this place. Theo, you're on Palmar Watch. Arran . . . you're actually not too bad with those fists, right?"

Arran catches up to her at exactly the same time Theo does.

"Not too bad, no," he says, and their heart sinks at the determination in his eyes. *Non-lethal,* they remind themself. *Opening matches aren't to the death.* "I can buy you time."

DARIUS

If someone had asked the Darius Miranda of a week ago, he'd have called this career suicide. Even just the thought of going over his direct superior's head would have been unthinkable, but the simple fact is that, if Kopitar gets his way, Darius's career has already come to an abrupt and screeching halt. So there's nothing for it. Nothing left to lose, and everything to gain, because whether the Chief General wants to hear it or not, there are at least three terrorists at large who have conspired to kill before, and will likely kill again.

So he brushes off the protests of the overbearing medic, and he ignores the pounding nausea and searing pain slicing through his head as he pulls on the black uniform of the Cohort Intelligentia for what could very well be the last time. He tries not to think about that. Instead, he holds his shoulders back and his head high, never mind the mess of blood and bandage. Kopitar's damnation or no, *this* is what he joined the Cohort to do. This is what it means to be an officer of the Intelligentia.

Except that Cato Palmar isn't at his office in the Senate. He isn't at his home in Belamar, either, and Darius thinks his guts are about to revolt at the thought of getting back on his roan horse when the young serva boy who answered the door says, "He's gone down, sir."

"Down?"

"Yes. To . . . you know."

Darius most certainly does not know. He raises an expectant brow, but the boy—strikingly beautiful, it has to be said, almost feminine even—just flushes and fetches a sentry to answer for him instead. "Ask for him at the Leontine Club," the sentry tells him, before providing an address.

It isn't the done thing, showing up at a private social club without an escort or an invitation. But by now Darius is so far past the *done thing* that he hardly stops to think about it, too intent on working through the unsteadiness of his own body and the hundred thousand acts of chaos and violence that Theo and her ilk could have already committed in the time since he saw them last. He bangs on the door to the Leontine Club, a townhouse in the Financial Quarter, and barely waits for the door to open before he's barging in.

The uniform, thank Terra, actually does wonders in a place like this.

"Oh, he's already gone down," says the majordomo when he asks again for Cato Palmar, and Darius is so ready to strangle these inarticulate fragging servae for their vague insinuations. Furthermore, he's aware he must look half insane. He's made a cursory attempt to slick back his hair, but his head is shaved where the stitches went in, and a trail of blood crusts dry down the high neck of his velvet uniform collar. So whether it's that or the fact that he isn't bothering to mask how Quietdamn impatient he is anymore—or maybe some combination of the two—Darius doesn't have to say another word before the domo signals for another serva to, apparently, *take him down*.

Down, it turns out, means underground.

Down, it turns out, means something he never could have imagined.

Screaming plebs and a jostling crowd and ceres dropping into palms and near-naked whores plying their wares and down there, down in the carved-out guts of this forsaken place, two bloody men slamming into one another with nothing more than their fists. It's not the head wound this time, but still, Darius is almost positive he's about to be sick.

This can't be right. This can't be *down*. This can't be where Cato Palmar, the Consul of Roma Sargassa herself, is well known to be. Plebs in the press of crowd go ashen quiet at the sight of him, and that's as it should fragging be. This place, this *pit*. This is the height of illegal, the height of disorder and mayhem. The serva must have gotten it wrong. That, or he misunderstood in the throes of his head wound, and took a wrong turn somewhere, because this can't *possibly* be where he'll find Palmar.

Then he sees it. The raised platform pavilion at the top of the fighting pits' makeshift amphitheater. Gleaming tiled tables heavy with wine and oysters. Fine wooden chairs and lush velvet chaises on which to recline. Soft carpet, a far cry from the rock floor below, sticky with hops and blood and Quiet knows what else. Darius launches himself through the crowd toward the stairs, up into the mingling chatter. Men and women he knows by name, some only by face. Patricians all. Helen Briago clinging to her suitor of the week, a few men and women he recognizes vaguely from the Horace College. And then he sees him. Cato Palmar, holding court near the pavilion's edge.

Darius's stomach doubles.

A mistake. This was such a mistake.

He's never spoken to Cato Palmar before, never had an introduction. He doesn't *know* him. And the Consul, it turns out, is even more corrupt than any of the lesser politicos he holds domain over. His very presence in this place attests to that, his ease in reclining back to watch the bloodsport, laughing and jeering as one of the fighters' arm breaks with a horrible snap.

Darius can still leave, still turn away and slip back into the crowd. Still . . . but no. No, that's no good, because if he does that, then his life is well and truly over. Never mind Theo Nix and the Revenants, there'll be nothing left of Darius but a putrid corpse still somehow living, left to rot in a drafty Ithaca manor house. This is the only option left.

How in the savage Quiet has his life so quickly come to this?

Dazed, Darius moves forward to make himself known.

At the sight of the uniform, Palmar's eyes go wide. "What in Terra's name—" the Consul blusters, cheeks turning red as he stands to pull Darius aside. "Explain yourself, officer."

"I—"

"How dare you wear that uniform down here? Do you *want* to start a riot?"

"No, sir, I only—"

But then the fury's melting away, replaced in an instant by a broad smile across the old man's face. "I'm just messing with you, officer. Your name?"

"Deputy Chief Miranda, sir." It's not a complete lie. He hasn't yet been officially stripped of rank.

"Well, I'll be having a word with Kopitar, Deputy—I've told him his men are to come in plainclothes if they want to join the fun."

"Kopitar . . . the Chief *knows* about all this?"

"You're funny, Deputy. Why don't you pour yourself a—" The Consul frowns, evidently only just noticing the extent of the injuries he's looking at. "What in Terra's name happened to you, man?"

But Darius is still trying to catch up. Still reeling. The Consul, here . . . these pits . . . and it's not only Kopitar who knows about this place but the rest of the Intelligentia, apparently, and. . . . He slams his eyes shut, does his level best to pull his thoughts together.

Kopitar, who he had trusted as a father. Kopitar, who is a good man. Kopitar, who enables this kind of corruption and threw Darius away like a used-up mutt without a second thought.

"The Revenants." He finds his voice, somehow. "The Revenants happened to me."

The effect is immediate. Color draining from the Consul's face. "Why haven't you gone to your Chief?" he demands.

"I tried. He didn't want to hear it."

"That's preposterous."

"I don't like to . . ." But that's no good. He's here, isn't he? Going over Kopitar to Palmar himself. He breathes through the pain. "That's why I came to you. There's a serva in the Kleios familia, a Revenant creature called Una. She confessed to the murder of Alexander Kleios, although of course she claimed to be acting under different orders."

"Whose?"

"Yours, sir."

A lie. It had to be a lie. That's what Darius had thought, at least, in the clear air of the Breakwater grounds, so maybe it's just the haze of concussion that's curdling his thoughts. But the stink of corruption is everywhere in this pit. Palmar stares at him for a long moment, face utterly unreadable, and it isn't hard to wonder. It isn't hard to think it. And that, more than anything, makes Darius want to crack open then and there.

It shouldn't be easy. The Consul *is* the Imperium. The Consul *is* Sargassa. Nothing about the thought that Una could actually have been telling the truth should be *easy.*

Then the Consul laughs. A snide, predatory thing that doesn't meet his eyes, a shot of ugly disquiet through Darius's gut. "I can see why Kopitar turned you away," he says, and Darius freezes at that. "A desperate lie told by a crim savage looking at a death sentence, obvious to any child with half a brain. You're better than this, man. I'll put this slip-up down to that head wound." And then—"Where is the girl now?"

"She . . . got away."

"She got away." The Consul's lip curls.

Darius bristles. "I didn't have backup. She did. That's how I ended up with these." He gestures to the stitches in his shaved head, and he is *not* going to mention Theodora Arlot—or Theo Nix, whatever the Quiet-damned woman's name is. Guilty or not, corrupt or not, Palmar is his only chance to keep his life here, and the most he can do now is try to claw back some of Palmar's fleeting esteem, for whatever that filth is worth. "But her accomplice. Sir, I recognized him. Turns out the Kleios familia is a nest of Revs."

"Another serva?"

"No. Alexander Kleios's son. The freedman, Arran. He was present to overhear the woman's . . . delusions." Had Theodora Nix radicalized him, or had Arran Alexander been the one to radicalize her? It's a nasty thought, the idea of the two of them laughing behind his back.

Cato Palmar, however, keeps perfectly calm. "He heard me accused of collusion?" he asks, with an air of almost academic interest.

"Yes, sir."

"Interesting," he says. "Thank you for letting me know, Deputy. You did the right thing." Then he's turning toward the staircase that descends down into the packed rabble surrounding the ring, calling for someone called Wieler, and that's no good. Darius stumbles forward.

"Sir," he starts, because he needs him. It grates, disgust and fury at this man who may or may not be guilty of murder but most certainly is guilty of allowing and, even worse, presiding over all that Darius knows to be wrong. This man, who should be setting the highest of examples and spits on them instead. Who holds the power over Darius's future, crumbling fast to dust even when Darius has always done the right thing.

"I don't suppose," he tries again, "you could put a word in with Kopitar for me? He wasn't happy with how I came by all this, he—"

"As it happens," Palmar says, turning back from the stone-faced handler below, "Kopitar has mentioned you to me, Miranda. I hesitate to say *Deputy*, as I'm given to understand that's no longer your proper rank. You should know that the order to keep away from the Kleios familia came down to your Chief from me, so no, I actually don't think I'll be putting in a word for you. Now, I'd see about getting yourself back to the hospitium. I have to say, you do look terrible."

Palmar waves him away, finished with the conversation, and Darius feels the world around him fall away, crumbling to dust.

TAIR

There's only one way to go. At the dead end of the dark subterranean corridor, just past the crevice where Theo thinks they can smuggle Miro out, Tair's foot catches against the dip in the floor. Behind her, Selah breathes in sharp, and Tair knows she's seen it, too.

So this is where Cato Palmar's been disappearing off to.

The small, circular trapdoor is little more than a pothole, set into the stone at their feet in a perfect circle. Tair sinks to her knees, skims her fingers along the grooves that run around the pothole's unbroken edge, the five-point holes sunk into the door lid. It's made of some filthy stone-metal something that's not concra and not iron, and she regards it for a moment, frowning. Then, with a little laugh, "Oh. Of course."

She sinks her fingers into the lock—what had seemed to be a lock, anyway, those five-point holes—and *twists*. A little circle laid in around the holes, barely perceptible before, gives way to shift counterclockwise, and then the entire trapdoor swings down with an enormous bang, left swaying great and heavy on a groaning hinge.

Below is nothing but darkness, and the little rungs of the not-concra ladder that disappears into pitch black.

"Come on," Selah says, already lowering herself down. "With our luck, someone definitely will have heard that."

It's not a long way down. Not as long as she thought at first glance, anyway, closing the trapdoor above her head. The darkness isn't a bottomless pit, just the natural result of emerging down to a double sub-level in the middle of a tight and lampless tunnel. By the time she steps off the last rung, Selah has already felt around enough to take stock of their surroundings, and she throws her arm across Tair's chest just in time to stop her from stepping off the little lipped edge and falling onto the tracks below.

"Mines?" Selah asks, as Tair's eyes readjust to the new and thicker dark. It's still almost impossible to see, but she can just make out the murky outline of some filthy maybe-silver rail-path snaking the length of the tunnel. The tracks are wide, far too wide to belong to a cart.

There are no mines in Luxana, not as far as she knows. No valuable deposits of Terra's wealth sitting below the city, and no chance the Imperium would ever compromise their precious catacombs like that.

Tair shrugs, unnerved, and she doesn't think she's imagining it, the way that far in the distance the looming dark seems to give way to a lighter, grayer gloom. She leads the way, the pair of them feeling along the high lip of the tunnel, grappling semi-blind at the sloped wall, tiled and filthy and unnaturally smooth. It would be so easy to get lost in the dark, Selah's hand clasped tight in hers, accidentally scuffing against Tair's feet every now and again, and she can practically hear the echo of her heart ringing out in the silence.

This can't be right. There's no sign of Diana Ontiveros. No sign of any life at all.

But this *has* to be right. They've come too far for this to be a dead end.

The tunnel does open out, in the end, making itself first known in the dark when Tair slams directly into a safety gate at the edge of the lip, followed by a small flight of stairs.

"Safety, my ass," she grumbles, rubbing at the pointy part of her hip, and sees that they've stepped onto a platform of some kind.

It's easier to adjust to the darkness here, more a deepening gray than true pitch black, and soon she can see the motes of dust and decay floating lazily through the air. The tracks still run here, sunk deep into the ground until they disappear in the far distance, off into another tunnel. But while the two of them had to press against the wall to tread the narrow lip of the tunnel behind, here it has opened out to something that could easily accommodate ten or fifteen people deep. Small benches scattered every thirty feet or so, the twin of the platform across the deep-inset tracks. Cords and tile and broken apparatuses hang in ruin from the low ceilings, dotted here and there with unlit and shattered solarics. Tiled walls and concra floors and graffiti covering every inch of it, a thick layer of dust disturbed in little breaths with each step they take. And sitting there on the tracks, some fifty yards away—

Selah breathes out low. "What in the savage Quiet . . . ?"

Tair's inclined to agree.

Some sort of mammoth carriage-cart, all rusted metal and broken glass windows and the same faded graffiti that covers the platform's walls and floors. Tair finds herself moving, drawn as though hypnotized, fear and wonder and curiosity mingled all together, and she reaches out to touch the first set of doors, smashed in and leaning sideways on their hinges. There's something not right about it. The precision welding, the shine too smooth to have been made by artisan hands. She can practically hear Selah in the back of her mind, *And I'm supposed to be the reckless one.*

But this isn't reckless. Her heart is thumping so hard she half expects it to burst clear out of her chest. Her mind is whirring at six hundred miles a minute. But this is not reckless.

And then the faintest thump from somewhere behind her, like a distant frustrated boot against concra.

"Tair."

She turns, fingers an inch still from the carriage doors. Selah isn't where she left her, some ways down the platform instead, where the dust motes rise and dance in puffs of breath, illuminated by the faintest cracks of light.

It's a doorway. Small and rounded slightly at the corners, the door itself is tightly shut. Only the tiny crack around the edges allows a silhouette of light to escape.

Tair's heart catches in her throat. Right. Signs of life. Okay, then. This is either a good sign, or very, very bad.

She stands back on instinct as Selah takes the lever that seems to function as a knob and *twists*. The metal lever, solid and unyielding and still definitely not made of concra either, gives her nothing. Tair glances around in the murky dark, making sure no one's around to hear.

"Savage . . . Quiet," Selah groans, leaning into it, trying to find some kind of twist, although it's clearly locked or rusted shut. "Gods-*damn it*."

"Selah, wait. Stop that."

Eyes alight, Tair snatches up a piece of debris lying on the ground some ten yards away. Some kind of pipe or bar segment, maybe iron or that same not-concra as the door, rounded and thick but thinned to a fine edge at one end. Tair slots it into the door's rusty middle hinge, and it pops off with a satisfying *plink*. The top comes next, then the bottom hinge, and at last the door groans wide open.

"You're brilliant, you know that?" Selah asks, mouth agape.

"I've been told."

Lit by candles and paraffin gaslight, the strange little room swims into focus as the two of them step inside. Broad boards of not-concra metal inset with too many tiny knobs and levers and little pulleys to count. Mountains of papers and coiled parts sprawled across a collection of tables, a blackboard covered in chalk scribblings of proofs and equations. A single cot bed pushed into the corner, blankets neatly tucked in. Looming over it all, wide windows overlook a pitch-black abyss. Some kind of observatory-turned-makeshift lab. A mirror world—twisted, somehow, and wrong. And in the center of it all, a middle-aged woman stares back, arms firmly folded across her chest.

"Well," she says, observing the pair of them with an alchemical scientist's critical gaze, "that explains why you didn't just knock."

"Professor Ontiveros?" Tair asks cautiously. The woman in front of them certainly *looks* like Xochitl and Miro, with her black braids and skin as dark as jetstone.

The woman snorts. "I guest-lecture sometimes when they need a little color in the curriculum, that hardly makes me a professor. It's *Doctor*, if you'd rather stand on ceremony, but Diana will do fine. Who are you?"

"I'm Tair. This is Selah." Diana raises a brow. "Your son told us where to find you—we've come to get you out. Both of you."

"That's sweet," says Diana, uncrossing her arms to jab a thumb over her shoulder, toward the wide windows. "How about them?"

Frowning, Tair follows Selah over to the window, and she nearly forgets to swallow her gasp when she sees the room below.

No, not a room.

Mines, for real this time.

And she had thought the fighting pits were huge.

Below, far far below the observation window where she and Selah and Diana stand, paraffin ghostlight casts a weak beam across one end of the underground cavern, enough to illuminate two more platforms, just as unnaturally made as the one above, another row of deep-set tracks—and beyond that, the cavern has been blown out wide, opened up to the point that it could comfortably house the Sisters' headquarters on Naqvi Row five times over. Slivers of shining black stone glimmer in the earthen bedrock.

Mouth after mouth after mouth, tunnels blasted deep into the earth, disappearing in every direction, deep into the dark. A crude set of latrines dug along one side. And row after row of cells sunk into the long tracks, latticed bars secured and locked from above like some grotesque patch job, their inhabitants crouched and shoved together underneath.

There are hundreds of them. Thousands, maybe. Men, women, themmed. Grandparents so old their limbs have faded to nothing but wrinkle and bone. Children so young their hair barely brushes past their ears. And even this far away through the open dark, Tair feels nausea bubbling up in her gut at the sight—because emaciation and poking-out ribs are far from the worst of it. Festering stumps at shoulder caps and purple, shining burns covering necks and torsos and limbs. Faces half melted off. A little girl without a foot. Less than half still have any hair to speak of. A dozen or so enforcers, indistinguishable from the handlers above, patrol past the locked cells, banging batons against the bars every now and again whenever they hear a murmur. Or maybe just because they can.

Tair drops out of sight into a crouch, heart pounding in her ears, a violent lurch threatening somewhere in her stomach. Beside her, Selah's pushed herself away from the windows, away from the view of unfriendly eyes.

"What is this place?" she hisses, rounding back on Diana Ontiveros, grabbing a coil of copper off the workstation—though how, exactly, she thinks she's going to be able to threaten the scientist with it is both a mystery and deeply endearing. "Who are all those people? They need a *medic*. Why are they chained up?"

Tair climbs to her feet, in case she needs to hold Selah back. Diana, far from being rattled, sets herself down in the chair at her makeshift worktable. "Can't have them making noise during the entertainment upstairs, I imagine. It wouldn't be good for business."

"Explain."

"And here I thought you two were the ones with all the answers. Here to rescue me."

"*Explain.*"

"It's an irradium mine."

Both Selah and Diana snap their heads toward Tair, who's staring at the alchemical scientist's chalk blackboard scribblings. Some equations, yes, but closer up she can see now more notations than numerals, more hypothetical questions posed than proofs to solve. The sketch in the corner gives it away, even without the glittering black stones on Diana's worktable, safely locked up inside glass observation cases, serving as confirmation.

Tair eyes one of them, roughly the same size of her palm, and she's willing to bet it's the same as the glints of black embedded in the gray stone below. She doesn't dare touch it. Untreated irradium is notoriously volatile. A potential explosive.

"Clever," Diana says then. "And I'm sure you know irradium's predominant usage."

"Even if I didn't, it wouldn't be hard to guess. You're the expert on solaric tech here."

She hasn't spent much time studying solarics. There was never any point, not when it was assumed to be a dead technology. The domain of quacks and dreamers. Even Diana's own texts suggest more hypothesis than verifiable fact. But she *saw* those black bulbs of Alexander Kleios's prized lamps, the one time Gil showed them to her. And she knows the look now, that endless dark shine of the stone on the worktable just the same as the Iveroa Stone in her messenger bag.

"So Palmar's mining irradium," she says, and meets Selah's widening eyes. "This place, these tunnels, whatever they are. He figured out it's an irradium deposit. And all these arrests . . . he needs the manpower."

"But why?"

"Good question," mutters Tair, and glances down at Diana. "Follow-up to that—what does he have *you* doing with it?"

One corner of the woman's mouth quirks into a smile, and it isn't at all pleasant.

"No," she says, flat, although somehow it doesn't feel like an answer to Tair's question. "No, I don't think we're going to do this again today. You say you know my son. How am I supposed to trust that this isn't another of the Consul's tricks?"

"Do I *look* like I'm friends with the Consul?" Tair snaps. She and Selah both are covered in dust and debris from the tunnel they came through, as if her oversized wrap pants and tattoos don't scream low-caste as it is.

"No," Diana answers, "but neither did the last idiot he sent to pry information out of me."

And all at once, it locks into place—the woman's wariness, her haughty demeanor, her unwillingness to share anything that the two of them haven't already confirmed first. She'd put it down to Diana being Seven Dials, eager to align herself with the same patricians who'd never have her over Tair's low-class patois. She realizes now it isn't that at all. Cato Palmar's been playing games with her.

Tair crouches down, eye level with Diana, and hopes she can see that she's sincere.

"I'm a Watcher with the Sisters of the First," she tells her, doing her best to keep her patience in check. "You're a donor, right? Ask me anything you want about them, I can tell you. The chairman's Artemide Ekagara. We're based out of Naqvi Row in the Kirnaval. And I'm working with your daughter, Xochitl. She . . . she was arrested, because she knew something was wrong. They spread a story about you and Miro, faked your deaths. She *knew* it wasn't right. So that's why I'm here. For Xochitl."

Diana regards her silently, but slowly Tair begins to see the cracks in her carefully constructed mask. The rapid blinking, although no tears follow.

"Is my daughter all right?" she asks finally, voice thick with the unsaid. "Is she safe?"

Tair hesitates, if only for a split second. She can't do this, not right now. Can't be the one to deliver this kind of news. But she's never been much good at lying, either.

Selah rescues her from herself.

"Yes," she says, bewilderment and anger vanished into the air, replaced by a kind of world-weary compassion. Selah is a fearsome actor, Tair is beginning to understand, and she doesn't know if she finds that more admirable or worrying. "She is. And your son's alive, but he definitely isn't safe. So let's get the three of you reunited as soon as possible, yeah?"

Diana, now shaken from her position of defense, seems to slump. She clasps her hands together, leans forward to brace her forearms against the worktable. And then she shakes her head. "I can't leave this place," she says, deathly quiet.

"Yes, you really, really can."

"*No.* I can't. The Consul was under the impression I was close to . . . reviving solaric technology," she says, voice small. "He was wrong, of course. I've spent my life studying the chemical and alchemical properties of irradium, but I'm no closer to discovering the conduit for solaric power than I was my first day as a junior scholar at the Universitas."

"Then what . . . ?"

"I made some suggestions." She grimaces. "When I first came here. I thought . . . I thought I could find a way to make it safer for them, the laborers down there. If Palmar wouldn't provide them with adequate protection, then I thought maybe a change in methodology . . ." Diana's face goes dark. "I was wrong. Only there *was* an increase in production, so the changes stayed. The poor souls who meet their end in mineshaft explosions are the lucky ones."

"What do you mean?" Tair finds herself asking, morbid curiosity getting the better of her.

A dark shadow crosses over Diana's face. "You saw them, down there," she says. "The effects of interacting with untreated irradium are . . . horrific. And my strategy only made it all the worse. Two days ago I watched third-degree burns spread across a young man's body in under a minute. Skin, organs, all of it." A shudder ripples through

Tair's skin, raising goosebumps in its wake. Diana's mouth hardens into a line. "Through it all, that boy never made a sound. The Consul has his people dose them with flumene to ensure compliance. He robbed that boy of everything, even his own death screams. I could see them, though, there in his eyes. At the very end." She shakes her head once more, determined. "I can't abandon these people, not when I'm responsible for so much of their suffering."

Selah takes her hand. "You're not to blame for—"

"I am, though." She chuckles darkly. "I am. I told you Consul Palmar thought that I was close to discovering the conduit, and I told you that he was wrong. But I wouldn't be so far away, not if I had the right tools to work with. The right materials to treat the irradium. The theory's sound enough. All I'd have to do is ask. I'm sure he'd be happy to provide."

Tair stares at her.

"You've been stalling."

She shrugs, and doesn't bother to deny it. "Solaric technology is a wonder. I've devoted my life to bringing it back to the world. It doesn't belong in the hands of someone like him."

"But you had to know that would only work for so long," Tair points out. "Eventually he's going to want results."

"You think I don't know that?" Diana snaps. "You think I've just been sitting here twiddling my thumbs? That man has less patience than a toddler waiting for dessert. And I only just survived raising two of those. It's been barely a month and he's already threatening to bring Miro down here." She breathes in, heavy through her nose. "I'll find a way to tear this place apart before it comes to that. He's safer up in the pits."

A groan of frustration rips from Tair's throat, and she pushes herself from the workbench before she can say something she'll regret. This isn't Diana's fault, intellectually she knows that, even if she's a holier-than-thou updistrict pleb. This is Cato Palmar's fault, and putting the blame on anyone else is playing exactly into his hands.

Then she sees it.

Just in the corner of her eye.

Something small, a minute detail, yet something she can't stop seeing lately, like it's been hiding in plain sight.

The eight-point Kleios sun, set into the metal board between the two large observation windows, is old and fading, but it's unmistakably there. The same one she's seen delicately etched into the lamps in Alexander Kleios's office. The same one she's seen somewhere else, and much more recently than that. The memory of Gil Delena's voice seems to fill the air, one of his oft-repeated mantras during their forays into the Archival stacks on some research project.

Once is an incident. Twice is a coincidence. Three times is a pattern.

Because what other possible reason could there be for it to be down *here* of all places?

Tair can appreciate, now—the realization clicking into place like it was always there, just waiting for her to open her mind to the possibility long enough for the pieces to fall into the right order—that the all-too-distinctive eight-point sun may well be the Kleios familia sigil, but it also means something else entirely.

She doesn't stop to second-guess herself, just dives into her messenger bag for the leather-bound Iveroa Stone, ignoring both Selah and Diana's curious eyes. She flips it open so that its shining surface of flat irradium gleams in the low lamplight, and there it is—the one imperfection on the Stone's brilliantly cut surface.

"This," she says to Diana, jabbing her finger at the eight-point sun etched deep in the otherwise unmarked black expanse, then up to the one on the wall. "We thought it meant that this belonged to the Kleios familia. It doesn't, does it?"

"No," Diana says slowly. "The symbol is found repeatedly in writings pertaining to solarics. This isn't a well-studied area, you have to realize that. It isn't respected and the Imperium isn't inclined to grant us funding and access. But so far as we understand, this particular emblem does indicate a presence of solaric power."

"So far as you understand?" asks Selah.

"Well, yes. Most surviving literature is written in Ynglotta. That, for example." And she points at the tiny glyphs etched along the

Iveroa Stone's thin edge. Tair's stomach does a loop on itself as Selah's eyes go wide.

"That's Ynglotta?"

"It is."

"I didn't realize Ynglotta had a written language."

"Most people don't, but there *are* some remaining examples from before the Great Quiet. A very considerable part of my research isn't even in alchemical science, but linguistics. Trying to decipher the meaning of a dead language."

"But it's not dead," Selah points out. "Ynglots still exist. Why didn't you just ask one?"

"Oh, certainly, of course I should have just tracked down a band of bloodthirsty raiders and—"

"There are plenty of Ynglot servae right here in—"

"But you *can* understand it," interrupts Tair. They're wasting valuable time, and who knows what Arran and Theo are facing above their heads, to saying nothing of Miro's upcoming death match.

Diana nods. "Well enough."

"And?"

"And that says *Property of Antal Iveroa.* How in the savage *Quiet* did you two get your hands on it?"

Tair doesn't answer. She can't. She's too preoccupied with her own sinking heart, and with the distinct feeling that she's swallowed her own esophagus. Across from her, Selah's face goes ashen gray.

"No," Selah says, barely a whisper. "No, it has to say something else."

"Well, it doesn't," Diana replies.

"But we already *knew* that." It explodes out of her, out of patience and out of hope, and Tair shoves herself away from the long worktable that separates her from Diana Ontiveros, because this can't be a dead end. She's let herself believe too much for that. "This thing doesn't *do* anything and we don't know what the fuck it is, and everyone and their mima's out for blood over it. And you're really going to sit there and tell me that our only lead—"

"Well, of course it didn't work for *you.*"

Tair stops. "What."

Diana raises a brow, evidently unimpressed with her outburst. A knot works itself in the older woman's jaw. "If this did in fact belong to Antal Iveroa," she says, like it's the most obvious thing in the world, "it will be protected by thumbprint recognition technology. Someone of that status? No question. Unless you're the Historian or someone deep in her trust who was granted explicit access, there's no way in the Quiet it's activating for you."

Thumbprint recognition technology.

A very real part of her wants to laugh at the concept.

Sure. Why not?

But the roar of her thumping heart is deafening as Selah's wide eyes meet her own, and the memory rests clear in its irony between them—last night in an empty clinic, and Selah's pointer finger jammed against the Stone. Not her thumb. Her *pointer*.

They were wrong. The Iveroa Stone doesn't need to be recharged. It doesn't need to be explained. All it needs is the right part of the right person, and Alexander Kleios left Gil with explicit instructions to see that this ended up in Selah's hands.

Tair has no idea what it's going to do. But there isn't a doubt in her mind that it *will* do it. Because that's the thing about solarics. The real reason the Imperium keeps them so highly regulated, forget volatile untreated compounds. Solarics are powered by the sun, and the sun is an infinite source of power. The sun, too, is ancient. The sun is never too old to work. And neither is solar-powered tech.

Wordless, Selah snatches the irradium slate off the table and smashes her thumb against the small sun that means *power*.

And the Iveroa Stone turns on.

THE HISTORIAN REVISITED

*H*e *doesn't have much time.*
     When the tremors first began, Alex had put it down to the well-warranted punishment of pulling yet another all-nighter. He'd batted Gil away hours ago, told him to go home and get some sleep before he gets cranky. He can already see him, arms crossed and glasses askew in the doorway of his home office, holding two mugs of steaming black jav and telling him, "You're getting too old for this." It's a well-practiced routine by now, though he's starting to think Gil may have a point. Not that he'll ever give him the satisfaction of admitting it.

     Only then the tremors got worse, and the floor beneath him began to rumble and sway like the rolling deck of a ship at sea, and it didn't take long for him to realize. Swollen blue-veined tracks at each wrist. A sinking sensation deep in his gut, like the world was falling away beneath his feet, and he's been drinking that whiskey all *night. Alex had allowed himself about thirty seconds to panic before pushing away those unhelpful thoughts of* unfair *and* please All-Mater no *and* I don't want to die.

     He is going to die.

     And he doesn't have much time.

     It wasn't easy going, making his way to the private attollo that took him from the top floor down to the sub-level stacks. Dusty sheafs and towering shelves and unsorted fraying tomes, and the door in back to which only he holds the key. A forgotten and barely used office workspace within, and that long hallway playing home to vault upon vault of restricted texts. Restricted, that's a polite word for it. Red code–regulated. Not supposed to exist.

     The tablet is in its case, inconspicuously shoved between two books in the seventh vault lest someone come looking. There's only one person who would, of course, only one person who knows that it exists, and only then if she's even still alive. He'll have to change the privacy settings once he's done—dig out the flimsy little sheet of see-through parchment from his desk, the one he's kept his daughter's thumbprint on since the day he inked it there as she slept, her calculus textbook repurposed into a pillow in the corner of his office.

For now, Alex presses his own thumb to the power button, locks the vault back into place behind him before setting himself down heavily on the hardwood office work chair up front, its wheels rusted from disuse and squeaking in protest. He used to spend so much time down here, losing himself in page after page after page of written Ynglotta. Alan Watts and bell hooks and Hildegard von Bingen and Ta-Nehisi Coates. So many ideas. So many could-have-beens. So many still-could-bes.

He was younger, then. He knows better, now.

The Stone flickers to life in the glowing pixels he'd once thought must be magic, the first time Mima showed him, back when she was fading fast and it was her turn to hand over the torch to him. "Not magic, Alex," she had laughed, wheezing slightly through the smoking fever. "Just technology." Call it what she liked, even his mother couldn't deny there was something akin to magic about the knowledge and histories of countless forgotten years, all held in one small solaric tablet, ready and available with the brush of his fingers. Delena Kleios had lamented that their time to cover his training—his real training—would be so haphazard and cut short by her illness. (Radiation poisoning, that's what she called it. That's what smoking fever is. Courtesy of a rogue west wind on her way to Halcya.) Her own mother had worked with her over the course of five years, and the same for her grandfather in his day, and so it went all the way back to Antal Iveroa.

In the end, they only had two months.

Right now, two months feels like unimaginable luxury.

There's an image of some long-forgotten receiver in the upper left-hand corner of the Iveroa Stone's touch-screen. His thumb hovers just above it, and he still hasn't decided.

She's the only one who knows, the only one who can deliver this to Selah, the only one who can make sure it doesn't fall into the wrong hands. But what if she, too, is the wrong hands? He doesn't know

*who she is, not anymore. He doesn't know where she is. He doesn't
even know if she's still alive. They had never seen eye to eye about
what to do with the responsibility he bears, back when they were
young and foolish and he had made the mistake of letting her in on
the secrets he had been entrusted to keep.*

*If she's still out there, somewhere, one touch of that button will
signal the alert straight from him to her. It was the only piece of tech
he had ever released from his grasp, because at the time Alex had
thought that maybe, one day, she would find her way back. It was a
moment of weakness. He had resolved, long ago, never to use it. But
he's broken that promise once before, and the situation then was far
less dire than this.*

*He presses his thumb against the receiver's image, and the dial
tone begins to ring. It rings and it rings and it rings, bouncing its
signal off a solaric satellite still floating four thousand miles above
his head. No one answers on the other end, and he does not know
that he could leave a message. He's not a digital native, after all.*

*Somewhere in a repurposed atomic fallout shelter far beneath the
Third Ward, a stout woman with black tattoos and a sea of beauty
marks in a warm bronze face wakes to find a missed call from someone who's contacted her directly only once in twenty years. He asked
her to spirit away a verna girl from his home once, five years ago. She
doesn't know what he could possibly need now. But he didn't leave a
message, and she has no way to call him back.*

*She's aware that it's three in the morning. She's aware that there's
a hurricane brewing. She calls her followers to her all the same.*

*But back in the here and now, because this is a matter of memory and
history, a matter of life and death:*

*He scribbles a note instead, one he'll shove inside the neat stack
of Gil's inbox on his way back up. Only Gil knows the secret cache
in his office where they used to pass notes and hide bugs to scare
Mima with back when she still sat in the Historian's chair. The one*

that's empty now except for an ancient atlas, one that he's been exploring in his spare time—a good joke—but normally belongs down here with the rest. Gil may not know its true nature, but he's the last hope for getting the Stone to Selah. He's the last hope for keeping it out of the wrong hands. He'll know where to find it.

Alex picks a different symbol then, because he has only one option left. He waits for the screen to load, and presses the round red circle that means record.

"Selah," he says, and hates the way his voice breaks. "My Selah. I wish we could do this in person. I wish you never had to do this at all. I would have you happy and unburdened and free. But my time's come sooner than I'd hoped, and there are things . . . things I must tell you. Secrets of the highest order. Secrets that can't be allowed to pass out of knowledge. Because we almost killed ourselves, last time. It's the Historian's duty to remember that. To put a stop to dangerous ideas before they start, ideas that could make us go so very wrong again."

Alexander Kleios inhales a shaking breath, then says, "I have so much to tell you, and I don't have the time. But I'll have to try. So then. To start at the start. Eight hundred years ago, in the calendar year 2113 AD. In this land called North America. When the Imperium won the war."

TAIR

Tair considers herself ravenously well-read, but there are words and phrases that even she has never heard before.
Global warming.
Nuclear holocaust.
Mass extinction event.

History is written over by the victors. That much has always been clear. Those in power get to say what really happened, and everything else passes into some jumble of story, legend, and myth. Who can say, after a certain point, where legend ends and history really begins?

Alexander Kleios, evidently.

Alexander Kleios, whose echo is still here, in a form that should not exist.

Alexander Kleios, who knew the truth, and kept it to himself.

Roma died.

Not seven hundred seventy-nine years ago. Not some nebulous time before that, because the Great Quiet never happened. The Great Quiet itself is the myth.

Roma died two and a half millennia ago, became something else, and the world moved on. New ways of doing old things. Empires to kingdoms to nations. Feudalism to chattel slavery to capitalism and the prison industrial complex. Oil to coal to electricity to solarics. The world moved on, until it didn't.

Until the shorelines eroded and the weapons grew too terrible and the technology used up All-Mater Terra's resources and choked the air in her children's lungs in revenge. Until too many people died, starved and flooded and bombed and overheated from their homes, with nowhere else to go. Until someone won control, and reset the clock to save them from themselves. To regulate who could learn this and innovate that.

By then, Roma itself was little more than myth, and the Imperium could pick and choose the creation of a new world order as they pleased, pretending it was simply an extension of what had come before.

Tair doesn't know what the word *fascist* means. Or *social media algorithms* or *alternative facts* or *pan-corporate military conglomerate*. She doesn't have to, to understand.

How do you convince entire civilizations to forget what they once were? How do you so profoundly alienate them from themselves? Is it desperation? Did they partake willingly, hoping for a better tomorrow? Or were they choked off at the source?

The question feels too big, but the answer is so small.

The Imperial Historian.

Antal Iveroa was never meant to preserve the world's true history. He was the only one meant to remember it at all. He was meant to help everyone else forget.

Alexander Kleios was a thief, but Tair's the one people will call a crim.

SELAH

H er father is speaking to her.
        Her father is dead, but her father is speaking to her, alien and
preserved and faintly glowing within the rectangle frame of this
Terra-touched relic, this marvel of technological work.

These are the things that Selah will remember later:
    Dad's voice, halting and breaking.
    Tair's face, intent and unreadable.
    The Stone's glow, a pool of too-bright light.
    And the beat of her own heart thrumming loudly in her ears,
somehow steadfast for all that she should be screaming.

Information. There's more of it, her father tells her, contained within
the Stone, from the world that came before.
    Ynglotta. She'll have to learn it, to understand.

It's getting harder for him to speak now, coming out in choppy shivers. Selah is watching her father die, and she can hear the gathering
rumble of a hurricane that began two and a half weeks ago, and she
does not know how to process what she's hearing.
    Why didn't he tell her? Selah has dedicated her life to study,
thrown herself into history and academia with a ferocity she knows
had shocked even her parents. Not just because it was expected of her
but because she is *good* at it. Because she *loves* it. Drawing the lines
of how we got from here to there, the movements like poetry, the
rhyming stanzas that dictate the cause and effect of wars and praxis
and social change. Dad knew that. He should have known, anyway.
Should have known that beneath that first flush of anger and raw,

reeling shock, he could trust her with this. Should have known that whatever else she felt, wonder and awe and excitement would eventually come to the fore.

Did he ever really know her at all?

Did she ever really know him?

For all the years of her life, Alexander Kleios had been nothing if not a staunch Imperialist. Unwilling to throw his weight around to ensure preferential treatment for Arran, not since that scandalous first transgression. Unwilling even to help Tair in court. He believed so deeply in duty, familia, empire. That the individual matters only so much as the role they play in Roma's continued survival. Roma, which *is* civilization and always has been. Roma, without which they would all be lost. A cog in the great machine. And all that time, he was the cog at the very heart of everything. The one that knew it was all built on a lie.

She doesn't understand how that could make sense to him, and now she never will.

They could have had years.

"Selah," Dad is saying now. "This is your burden to bear. No one else's. No one else can know, you understand?"

The irony of both Tair and Diana Ontiveros standing there, next to Selah, listening to him saying this, is not lost to her.

"I made that mistake, and now it's up to you to fix it. I'm . . . I'm so sorry. Cato Palmar, the Consul. You mustn't trust him. He's building something, building it on a mass scale. Solaric technology, he's . . . he's trying to produce it again. He intends to become dictator. To break away from Imperial rule, perhaps even overpower the Imperium itself. And if he succeeds . . . with solaric power like that . . . the Imperium doesn't stand a chance.

"I threatened to expose him. But I made a fatal error. I showed him the Iveroa Stone. I thought it would persuade him, if only he could see the horror of nuclear war for himself. You can't even imagine, Selah . . . I tried to warn him, but it backfired. He wants the Stone for himself now. He wants the secrets it contains, the secrets to recreating nuclear power. Solarics are one thing, but nuclear . . . He'll be looking for it, Selah. He can never get his hands on it. Promise me. It would be the ruin of us all."

Selah's grip on the Stone tightens, her knuckles going pale, an unwelcome shiver running down her spine.

"I should have known better," Dad is saying. "After everything Palmar has done to this family, I should have known. . . . It was such a mistake. He wants the Stone, and I was going to tell the Imperium about his plans. . . . I made myself a loose end. I can only imagine this poison is his doing. There's so much else I want to say, so many secrets I should have . . . But I have to go now. I love you, my girl. Give your mother a kiss for me, and tell Arran . . . tell him I'm sorry."

Then Dad's face disappears, a soft gray glow left where he had been.

Her imagination is good. Her capacity for abstract thought, even better. But they're not this good. The sheer enormity of it, compressed into a few square inches of solaric-powered stone, and the hundred thousand questions that come with it. Eight hundred years of it. The truth written in Ynglotta, secreted away in a piece of technology that by all rights should not exist. And if the Consul gets his hands on it, he'll plunge the entire world into destruction.

Why, Selah wants to scream, wants to rage. *Why did you never tell me?*

It's too big, too sudden, too new. Too much responsibility for just one person to hold. She doesn't know where to begin.

She misses her father, *so much.*

She hates him, too. Just a little bit.

Selah forces herself to look up, forces herself to meet Tair and Diana's equally bewildered gazes, the deafening sound of silence and the collapse of everything she's ever known to be real ringing in her ears. The seconds slip by, feeling like eternity, because what do you say now? What can possibly happen next? When the bedrock of reality has just crumbled beneath your feet, anything that follows can only be freefall.

Cato Palmar can't have the Iveroa Stone. That's the only real thing left in the world.

ARRAN

Arran's barely returned to the holding cell where the pleb fighters wait before Wieler and another handler approach, faces grim, hands ready on the nightsticks at their hips.

"Problem, gentlemen?"

"You need to come with us."

"Yeah, no time, unfortunately. Gotta limber up before my round."

"There's been a change in the schedule," says Wieler, and grabs him by the arm.

"Hey, man, I *told* you—" But then the other handler grabs his upper arm, and Arran finds himself seeing stars as the blunt end of a nightstick meets the backside of his head.

So it isn't a choice, exactly, to let himself be steered down a stone staircase, but more a matter of the time it takes for the world to stop spinning. When they reach the bottom, Arran is shoved down on a bench and, still fighting to pull his head together, doesn't notice the irons being slipped around his wrists until it's too late.

When the world finally rights itself, leaving Arran with a full-on bitch of a headache, it becomes immediately apparent that the large cell he's now sitting in is much like the one above, with one major glaring difference.

It's an armory.

Not the kind of sleek, modern blades and weaponry he grew used to in the Teec Nos Pos fort. This stuff belongs in the history books. Rough wooden spears and curved, rusting swords, and a good array of downright evil-looking spiky things he wouldn't even know where to begin with trying to name. That isn't the most disconcerting part. No, that honor goes to the men, women, and themed sitting along the bench on either side of him, wrists chained to the wall just the same.

What. The fuck.

"Hey," he shouts again, this time at Wieler's retreating back. "The hell is this?"

The stone-faced handler sneers down at him. "You deaf? Told you there was a change in the schedule."

"This is a mistake." A hot, angry laughter bubbles up inside him. This has to be a joke. "My patron's upstairs, she wouldn't have agreed to this. Go ask her."

"No need—you're a crim. That's what the Consul says. And what he says goes."

The laughter dies on his lips.

Palmar. This is Cato Palmar's doing. And why why *why* in the savage Quiet does it always come back to him? Arran is so ready to never hear about that man ever again in his life.

Well, a dark voice whispers in the back of his mind, *you might get that wish.* It's certainly looking like his life is about to be cut pretty short just about now. And that, more than anything else, is what does it.

Because suddenly Arran can't breathe.

He shouldn't be here. He isn't supposed to be here. He isn't supposed to die this young, and he has *some* weapons training but not the kind that's going to get him out of this, and yes, believe it or not, he's fully aware that he's descending into a full-blown panic attack in the middle of a room full of scarred and hardened gladiators, thanks.

Frag it. If he's going to die anyway, might as well get one last good one in.

The drowning in his chest and throat is nothing, because Cato Palmar has decided he is going to die, so he is going to die. Because Cato Palmar knows who he is, because Cato Palmar gave him his freedom on the condition that Dad send his mother away. Because he is going to kill him the way he killed his father and as good as killed his mother, and Selah's out looking for Diana Ontiveros, she's not upstairs at all, and idiot fucking Una got it wrong and told Palmar he needed his sister to operate the Stone, and if he has this planned for Arran, what in the savage Quiet does he have planned for her?

Selah and Tair are who-knows-where chasing a missing alchemical scientist, and Theo's meant to be watching his back, but what can they do from the crowd, realistically, and Griff and her backup are still waiting above the ground for them to come back out with Selah and the Iveroa Stone, and here he is—chained to an armory wall with his head thrown back and eyes squeezed shut, absolutely useless to anyone.

It might have continued that way for a while, or at least for as long as it took for someone to come take him away to his fate. Only then a heavy hand is resting on top of his and squeezing tight.

"I've got you, brother."

Arran opens his eyes to find Miro Ontiveros sitting next to him, dark eyes full of concern, offering as much physical pressure as he can given both of their constraints.

"I've got you," he says again. "Just breathe with me, okay?"

"Easy," Arran just makes out, "for you to say."

Somehow, Miro manages a smile, white teeth shining. "You can breathe, come on. Where's the panic coming from? You know, physically?"

Arran frowns through the hitching gasps of breath—he's never really thought about that before, but in an instant the answer comes to him all the same. "Chest. A ball in my chest . . . and throat."

"Okay, good. What's the ball look like? Is it moving?"

"Yeah," he gasps, closing his eyes, and lets out a dump of air. "Circling . . . sort of forward . . . really fast."

"You can see it?"

"Yeah."

"All right," Miro says, the calming tenor of his voice worlds away from the suspicious young man Arran met upstairs. "It's a good thing, you know. It's trying to keep you alive. No wonder, in this place. So just take a second and sit with it, yeah? We've got the time. Say thanks, then send it on its way."

Well, when you put it like that.

The ball in his throat doesn't seem to be moving as quickly anymore, and after a moment something jolts loose in his chest. He takes a long, shaking breath. *Thanks,* he thinks quietly, as it breaks free. Then, opening his eyes, he turns to Miro and thanks him, too.

"No problem. Xochitl has them all the time."

Arran has to look away.

"So," Miro continues, "this wasn't really part of the plan, huh?"

The handlers come for Miro first. When they pull him away, Miro looks back just the once, and nods. Arran returns it, glad at least that if Miro lives long enough to find out his sister is in fact dead, he won't be around to see it. Palmar will make sure he's dead by then, too.

It isn't long after that they come for him.

He doesn't make it easy for them, spitting and cursing and pulling away as they yank some cursory greaves up his legs that bite into the soft skin behind his knees, and shove a sword, shield, and spear into his hands—weapons that, for all they look impressively ancient and savage, with their fraying bindings of dyed leather and angry, serrated teeth, are as blunt as the message behind them. This isn't a fight—it's an execution.

He doesn't know what he's done to bring the Consul's ire down beyond generally existing, but neither does he really have the time to dwell on that. Before long, he's being frog-marched down a long underground hallway, the growing cheers and shouts of the crowd above making the hair on his arms stand on end.

Oh shit. This is happening.

Arran makes himself put one foot in front of the other.

Maybe he can still find a way out of this.

Maybe Theo can still do something from the crowd.

Maybe Selah and Tair are on their way back.

Maybe he can *win*.

Doubtful, that last one, but he'll still have to try. It's the only option Arran has full control of at this point.

One foot in front of the other, and the light at the end of the underground tunnel where the latticed door leads to the arena pit looms closer.

One foot in front of the other, and Arran can see the harsh and unwilling face of his intended executor in his mind's eye—that woman with the shiny, twisting burn scars along both arms that he saw from across the lower cell, maybe, or the thremid missing half a cheek.

One foot in front of the other, and his heart threatens to pound itself right out of his chest. If he can make himself believe, then this is just the cobblestone banks of the Third Ward, the fort training yard at Teec Nos Pos.

One foot in front of the other, until Arran steps out into the light.

The roar of the crowd is deafening, and this is definitely not the Third Ward. The deep, circular pit is made of rough, unforgiving concra, stained with decades and maybe even centuries of faded red. And standing on the other side of the sunken arena, eyes wide at the sight of him, is Miro Ontiveros.

THEO

Theo chews at the inside of their lip, slipping through the wild throng to reach the guardrail at the ring's edge. Sour bile rises in their mouth as one deceptively short fighter runs, leaps, and locks his legs around his opponent's neck. Then, taking advantage of the position, he latches his teeth around the taller man's ear and *rips*. The crowd roars and shrieks with disbelief and ecstatic thrill as the ear tears off, blood pouring out the side of the man's head.

"Great Terra!" a man exclaims at their side, then nudges them and adds with a sly wink, "Just goes to show. Never put your money on size alone."

Theo bites down at the inside of their lip, hard, because the alternative is wresting the man's pint of hops out of his hand and splashing it back in his face. Satisfying as that would be, they have to stay focused.

Up in the pavilion, a clear view directly across from where they stand, Cato Palmar reclines on the lush couch set in pride of place. They've never seen him before, but it isn't hard to guess who he is— sagging into the cushions as well-dressed patricians drink crisp white Fornian wine and vie for favor around him. With his enormous white mustache and powder-crusted jowls, Theo's first impression is that of an emaciated, silk-robed walrus, something rotting and sick at its core.

Down below in the pit, a serva is mopping up blood, clearing the way for whatever pleb match comes next. The victor is taking a lap, brandishing his defeated opponent's ear like a spoil of war as the crowd roars their approval.

Theo is no stranger to pain. No stranger to careless cruelty. Most hurts have no imagination, not down here in the pits where Theo was raised. The discipline, the malice, the casual, petty boredom. Never a fighter themself, that doesn't mean they weren't thrown into the ring sometimes as an interesting way to up the stakes. The coyote—just as scared and trapped as they were—who threw its weight across their tiny body in the ring, shattering their femur so that white bone poked through on both sides. The hops vendor who pinned Theo's hand to the counter with a knife until Wieler coughed up what he was owed. Jarol's drunk and stinking corpse tossed out with the rest of the waste. Tile biting hard and sharp into knees and bile rising in their throat, ringing in their ears and jeweled fingers twisting in their hair, pressing down *down* until they choked, robbing them of breath. They've known since age seven that people are expendable, only worth what they produce. Growing up here made that abundantly clear.

"Ladies and gentlemen." The thunderous voice of the ringside emcee booms above the clamor of the crowd, his echoing reach aided by a bullhorn. "That brings an end to the first part of the night's entertainment."

What?

"Let's have another round for our champion prizefighters! Brave plebs, all, but I'll say they're going to have to keep an eye out for that Malakai from now on if they want to win—or indeed, if they want to keep both ears!" Appreciative laughter ripples through the crowd, anticipation building for the main event, what they've all *really* come here for, but Theo isn't listening. Not anymore.

The pleb fights are over. So where in the savage Quiet is Arran? Heart pounding, Theo turns to fight their way through the thick mass of the crowd. Something has definitely gone wrong. Only then a hand clasps cold and unforgiving around their upper arm.

This is what happens, apparently, when you don't finish the job. This is what happens, when you were sure Darius Miranda was dead.

He looks terrible. Hair half-shaved, his pale face is tinged green, a vaguely crazed look in his eye. Theo would take more satisfaction in this if it weren't for the cold thrill of panic forcing their heart to beat overtime. He's dead. He's *supposed* to be dead. They would have taken the corpse with them if they didn't have Una to deal with, but there was blood pouring from the base of his skull and a fast-weakening pulse and they wouldn't have just left him there in the woods buried under a pile of leaves if they hadn't been absolutely sure he was about to be *dead*.

"Theodora," he says, voice as cold as the blue of his eyes, and there's something entirely unhinged behind them. Something unnerving. "Nix, wasn't it? Nix . . . *Nothing*. Clever. Did you come up with that yourself?"

Theo wrests their arm away from his grasp. "Darius Miranda. You look like shit."

They've hurt him. They can see that now, up close, without the distraction of Montana Satterfield sitting between them. Hurt his pride, anyway, and for a man like Darius Miranda, that is all the more dangerous.

There's a screech as the grilles of the passage to the fighter cells slide up, and a fighter walks out into the pit. He holds a short, curved sword in one hand, a small shield in the other. Armored greaves on shins and sword arm, a belt above a loincloth. That's it. Shield arm, chest, thighs all naked, exposed to the elements, vulnerable. It takes a moment for the roaring crowd to make sense, the name on people's screaming tongues to really hit Theo's ears, because they're a little *busy* right now and they might not have otherwise recognized him from this far away.

Miro.

Miro, who isn't supposed to be fighting until close to the end.

Fuck. Something is very, very wrong.

So here they are—staring down Darius Miranda's unfocused, furious face, a wounded animal threatening to strike, his left hand sneaking down to where the pommel of his sword rests at his side and the swarming crowd around them none the wiser, when Miro's opponent walks out into the pit. He's only marginally more armored—greaves covering his entire legs, armed with sword, shield, and spear, and Theo freezes where they stand. Because even from this far away, they would recognize Arran anywhere.

An iron vise clamps around their heart, squeezing it until it stutters and skips a beat. So this is what it means, then, to let yourself care. It means opening yourself to the possibility of losing it all just as fast.

This is what they've known, since the age of seven:

That a person is only worth what they can contribute. That no one is coming to save you, but you can always save yourself.

This is what they know now, twenty years later:

That there is no such thing as good people and bad, just the circumstances you're given and what you choose to do with them. That sometimes someone, somewhere, might not *need* to save you, but they will choose to anyway because they can. Because they are good. Because they want to. That maybe saving everyone is impossible, but you can still choose to try.

Arran needs them. That's the only thing that matters now.

So in one swift move, Theo grabs the pommel of Darius Miranda's sword where it sits at his waist, pulls it out of its sheath, and smashes the hard, blunt end across the shaved and tender side of his head. He staggers back, falling into a group of unsuspecting revelers, and Theo turns on their heel, disappearing into the crowd.

TAIR

Somewhere down beyond the wide windows of the ancient control room, a brighter light turns on, followed by an angry shout.

Tair grabs Selah and pulls them both to the floor, and her heart is caught somewhere between ribs and throat. She's almost grateful for the low murmur of conversation now drifting up from the taskmasters in the mines below, an excuse not to give voice to the thousands of questions and angry thoughts buzzing through her head. Selah, too, looks like she's on the brink of saying something, so Tair slaps her hand over the other girl's mouth. Diana Ontiveros, eyes wide but at least *meant* to be here, sinks slowly into the chair at her desk.

A long moment passes, then another, and every measured breath Tair takes is a gamble.

The light goes off.

She crouches there very still for thirty, forty-five, then sixty seconds. They can't stay here.

"Fuck," she whispers, barely a breath, into the air. *"Fuck."*

"Tair."

Selah is still holding the Stone, frowning down at its gray glow. Where Alexander Kleios's face had been, speaking impossible words, are now a myriad variety of symbols lit from within and arranged in neat rows, most of which Tair couldn't begin to understand. One of which she knows all too well. Another Kleios sun, tiny and glowing gold. And under that, the tiniest label—not Ynglotta, but Sargassan Latin, written clear as day.

Urban Power Grid—Central Hub

A quick glance followed by a nod, then Selah taps a thumbpad lightly against the sun. The tablet screen shifts again, illuminated images of the irradium surface dancing to rearrange themselves, and Diana Ontiveros leans forward to watch with the eager, hungry eyes of an alchemical scientist witnessing a paradigm shift in her life's work.

There are more images, now, each with its own accompanying label. A lamppost—*Street Lights*. A spray of water—*Reservoir*. A shield—*Armory*. And a long, metal carriage cart, the identical twin to the one just beyond the doors on the track outside. The one she'd be willing to bet once belonged to a larger fleet, traversing the path built by some long-ago architect in the mines below. Beneath that—*Metro Rail*.

Alarm bells ring in Tair's mind, more pieces falling into place now she's allowed herself to entertain the impossible. She has to, now. Alexander Kleios made sure of that.

Urban Power Grid—Central Hub. Some previous Historian must have translated from Ynglotta to make the emblems easier to read, but there's more than just history and information left behind here.

Urban Power Grid—Central Hub. If another world existed in this place before Luxana, then it must have run on the sun's power. And maybe, long ago, before it was a patrician familia's heirloom, the Iveroa Stone was something else entirely. Something vital to the infrastructure of the city that became Luxana.

Her gaze lifts, runs up to the solaric sun carved into the wall, and across the instruments set into the control boards. Then her eyes are drawn even further upward, to long strips of black irradium running the length of the ceiling, quietly unlit overhead. Duplicates, too, of the smashed and ruined panels of the platform where they came through, and Tair doesn't imagine for a moment that there aren't more to be found in the mines. If the rest of it mirrors up—subterranean train tracks, tiled arched ceilings, metalworks too precise for human hands—then this, too, is the only logical result.

"Diana," she whispers. "You said you've been trying to destroy this place. It runs on solarics."

"It should," the woman says. "But it doesn't. I've looked high and low—there's no mechanism for turning on the power. More thumbprint recognition tech, I'm sure."

"Maybe. Or maybe the mechanism routes through somewhere else." And she points to the glowing image of the long carriage on the Stone's screen, a twin of the real one that sits gutted and abandoned just beyond the control room's doors. *Metro Rail*. "Maybe it only works when the source is live."

Selah frowns. "You think pressing that thing will let us turn on the lights?"

"No," she says, eyeing the overwhelming foreign array of long-ignored buttons and pulleys and dials spanning across the control room, this place belonging to a murdered world. "If I'm right, then pressing *that thing* is gonna let us do a fuck ton more than just turn on the lights."

From the look on Selah's face, she's caught up to Tair's line of thinking. There's a glint of something slightly manic in her eye, yet something reassuring all at once, and Terra help her but this is why she loves her, after all. Selah has a crazy streak all her own. Selah has never needed to go running for help.

Selah nods once, decided, and slams her thumb against the carriage on the screen.

Brilliant light pours in from all sides, solar panels of black irradium stone at their full charge. The light is blinding, but there's no time to panic, no time to do anything but work *fast*.

Dials turn, knobs twist, switches flick. Little black squares set along the wall burst into life, the same ethereal glow as the Iveroa Stone. She doesn't know precisely what to do with that—instead, she grabs three tiny levers in each hand and pulls them all the way up.

The worst thing that could have happened is nothing. No effect whatsoever, nothing happening down in the mines, just two fool-headed girls up in the control room messing around at random with technology they could never begin to understand—that is, up until someone below noticed the bright light coming from above and caught them in the act.

What happens, instead, is chaos.

And that's the best thing they could have hoped for.

Down in the mines, solarics blare on overhead. Locked doors and grilled cells slam open. Alarmed enforcers stumble haphazard into the temple-sized cavern, only to be met by the roars and fury of prisoners climbing out of their dirty cells. The enforcers are armed, and the imprisoned miners are weak from work and torture and abuse. It doesn't matter. They're angry, and Tair knows from hard experience just how dangerous that can be.

A red-haired woman with one arm wrests the club from one of her captors and bashes a crumpled dent into his head. A barrel-chested teen with no teeth and a rotting eye slams a hatchet-faced man against the spike of an open cell door, running him clean through. The bare flesh of a naked child flashes through the crowd, and Tair wants to grab them to safety, wants to yell at someone to *watch out*, but she's too far away and then the child is gone, disappeared back into the melee.

Selah twists another dial, and a sluice groans open on the far end of one deep-set track, liberating the rush of water it had held at bay. Tair can't see how many people are swept away in the roar.

This is chaos.

This is reckless.

And this is working.

Then Selah shouts, "Tair, we have to *move*."

"But they're still—"

Selah jabs a finger down to where the fighters—captive and captor alike—have converged, a platform metal staircase snaking against the wall, up and up and around and leading straight to the control room where they stand, and Tair sees her point.

"Get Dr. Ontiveros to safety," she yells to Selah over the noise. She had to leave her combat knife behind before the weapons check upstairs. She'll figure something else out. But Selah, she doesn't know how to defend herself. She has to get out of here now.

"But—"

"I'll find you up there, I promise, but you have to *go*."

Selah isn't a fighter. Not this kind, anyway. As for the scientist, Tair's willing to bet she's never touched a weapon or thrown a punch in her life. And she doesn't have time to be worrying about the pair of them in the middle of this. Selah, apparently thinking along the same lines, nods—she grabs Diana by the arm and yanks her toward the open door. The moment the two of them are gone, Tair wrenches open the side door, the one that opens out to the metal staircase leading up from the chaos below. A few dozen meters off, across the rickety platform, an enforcer is at the lead of the murderous mob, only steps ahead of his own doom.

She grabs the copper coil off the table where Selah left it. The end is sharp enough.

Come on, then.

But then a creak of metal squeals out from behind her and she turns to see Selah, hands clasped around the end of the metal prybar she'd used to pop off the door's hinges, wielding it like a bat.

"Oh, come *on*," Tair yells at her, half panic, half exasperation. "Do you even know how to use that thing?"

"No," Selah answers. "But you do." And she sends it flying like a pole vault across the control room.

The enforcer comes barreling through the side door just as Tair reaches up to snatch the prybar out of the air. She steps forward in two elegant moves, hands widening on the metal pole the way Jinni Jordan taught her, and bashes him upside the head. He crumples, a tiny spray of red blood and pink brain matter flying upward as he falls.

Selah stares at her, awe and admiration and something like *okay, gross* shining from her eyes. The barest twitch of a smile makes it to the corners of Tair's mouth.

"I love you," Selah says, and an eruption of something wild and free loosens from her chest.

"You—"

Then the melee bursts into the control room, and Selah is gone, and Tair throws herself into the fray.

ARRAN

Miro Ontiveros stands across the arena, jaw set, and suddenly the concept of *winning* doesn't just seem impossible—it isn't an option at all. Arran doesn't want to fight him. He needs him alive, and preferably not too pissed at him, if it turns out Selah and Tair aren't able to find Diana down below. That said, he isn't particularly thrilled about the idea of letting Miro kill him, either.

"Still planning on busting me out?" Miro murmurs beneath the din, grim, passing Arran as he paces the circular ring.

"Haven't really had a chance to think about it."

"Well, you'd better make up your mind, because I don't plan on dying here."

"I had a feeling." He breathes in through his nose, hard, and tries to push out the roar of the crowd. He really doesn't like how close Miro's getting with that sword. "Give me a second to think, yeah?"

He scans the faces jeering down from the stands above, and he can't find Theo in the crowd. Up in the raised pavilion, some feet above the rest, Cato Palmar has two ring-encrusted hands gripped tight to the railing's edge, a deeply unpleasant expression of utter triumph spread across his face. Something tight and horribly familiar begins to clench in his chest, and through it, somehow, *somehow* Arran manages to breathe.

Hello again, he thinks, and the spinning ball of panicked chaos in his chest stays where he can hold it. *Here to keep me alive?*

"Ladies and gentlemen," the booming voice of an emcee rings out from above his head, and oh shit, this is really happening, and Arran still hasn't worked out what to do. He can't kill Miro, but he can't let Miro kill *him,* and Theo's nowhere to be seen, and Selah is the only one in his corner with the power to end this, but Selah isn't here. He's well and truly on his own. "Now the sport you've been waiting for!"

Their circular pacing around the pit crosses paths once more, and out of the corner of his mouth Arran asks, "What happens if I refuse to fight?"

"I'll probably stab you."

"Okay, don't love that. New question. What happens if *we* refuse to fight?"

Miro shakes his head. "Bad idea. They'll throw a mountain lion in with us or something."

Right, okay, not doing that either.

But before he has the chance to come up with anything else, the resounding boom of an enormous horn sounds out across the cavernous pits, the clamor of the crowd swells to a breaking point, and they're out of time.

"You know how to use that thing?" Miro asks, beneath the dull roar.

"The basics, yeah."

"Good," he says, and brings his short, curved sword down.

It happens so fast Arran nearly forgets to react. He swings his own blade up to meet Miro in a parry, and the elated shouts of the mob rise as the match begins in earnest.

Fuck. *Fuck.* This is happening too fast. He wants to stop, wants to shout, "What are you *doing*?" but there's no point, not when he already knows the answer. Miro's just trying to stay alive. He brings his sword down again, and again, and *again*, and Arran has no choice but to parry, then bring his shield across, then parry again—all the while able to think of nothing but the next move, the next step to survival.

It goes this way for a while, with Miro on the offensive and Arran doing the very best he can not to find himself spit on the pointy end of his opponent's notably sharpened blade. Arran may have some cursory legionary training, and the experience of bare-knuckle street brawls, but Miro is a professional athlete. What's more, he's been trained to use the weapon in his hand. He isn't fumbling to catch up, to get accustomed to it the way Arran is. There's strength in each blow, but precision, too, and that's what turns out to be all the more deadly. With each strike, it's all Arran can do to raise his shield in time, and in the correct angle to make sure that the force of the sword ricochets back off the way it came.

Yet, for all that skill, it doesn't take long for Arran to realize that Miro is holding back.

Screw it. Throwing caution to the wind, he takes advantage of a momentary gap to press his advantage. Their swords meet high above their heads, and under the screams and jeers, he grits out, "Hoping they'll just tire out and get bored?"

Miro pushes him back, feints to the left, and then meets him again in another pass.

"Got any better ideas?"

Despite himself, Arran feels a rush in his chest. Miro isn't trying to kill him at all. Not yet, anyway, and he can work with that. This crowd wants blood, but they also want a show, and if it means stalling, then he can give them that. He might not know the rules of combat as well as Miro, but he knows how to fight dirty. No one asked him if he wanted to be here—that means he gets to play by his own rules. Miro shifts to retreat into a short guard, and in the split second between sliding his boots along the rough-stained concra and assuming the intended position, Arran kicks him hard in the groin. Miro stumbles back, swearing.

There was a plan here, and it was a good one, but it becomes moot fairly quickly as the surprised shouts of the onlookers veer into something altogether different. This may not be the Third Ward, but it's eerily reminiscent of a time—only scant days ago—that a distinct shift had ripped through the cobblestone banks and Arran, in the midst of heady action, had caught on a half-second later than everyone else.

Cries of bloodlust turning into confused yells. Thrilled jeers giving way to screams of real panic. And in the split second between Arran yanking the sword away from Miro and throwing it to the side, a screeching woman falls into the pit.

Arran looks up.

Up above, the crowd has descended into bedlam. Men, women, and themed shoving at each other with alarmed shouts, desperately pushing at each other to get around the rim of the sunken pit, toward the exits. Almost like they're trying to get away from something. Whatever's happening to cause the mass panic, however, is too far from away Arran's view to make out. All he can see from down here is the chaos, and another man falling down into the pit, and no one seems to be paying much attention to the two of them at all anymore.

The moment's now.

"*Miro!*" he shouts urgently above the clamor. "Shield!"

It's a desperate act, but he has to try. Miro braces himself and kneels, shield raised, and Arran drops his own shield and spear to the ground. With a running start, he propels himself off the offered shield and *leaps*, willing himself to make it.

With only one hand free, the other still clenched tight around the pommel of his sword, he just barely catches the pit's crumbling upper rim. Pulling together his last reserves, he swings his other arm up and heaves himself out. He pulls himself to standing, and only just avoids being trampled by the hysterical mob.

All around him are screaming, stampeding spectators, and he's nearly knocked back down into the sunken pit when he crouches to throw a hand back down and pull Miro out after him. When he stands back up, it isn't just the mob pushing and shouting to reach the exits. At their backs, there's a new mass of people pouring in from the crevice of a corridor set into the back wall, and they are *definitely* not paying customers.

They look like the stuff of nightmares. Emaciated and deformed, burnt and bruised and bald and amputated, they hardly look human. Rags hanging from ribcages and cheekbones poking through ashy and sallow skin, and all the more frightening for the fact that they are, for the most part, absolutely incandescently wild with rage.

Over the top of the swarming mass's heads, Arran catches sight of Wieler scrambling out from the looming horde's direct path. He adjusts his grip on the blade in his hand, hot fury in his chest, but it's too late. Theo—*there*—appears through a split-second gap in the melee, seizes the hatchet-faced handler by the arm, and shoves one of their blades right through his chest. Smooth and clean as butter, if not for the burst of crimson blood. He doesn't have time to dwell on the satisfaction on Theo's face, however, because some yards behind them is Tair, raising some sort of shining metal pipe and smashing it down on the thick chain links keeping the fighters' cells locked tight. The chain-link snaps apart, and the fervent throng of servae pit fighters spills out to join the fray, itching for blood.

Cold thrill shooting through his heart, Arran turns away. *Selah.* If Tair's back, then that means she has to be somewhere, too. He has to find her.

He pushes through the frenzy, throwing elbows where he has to, bringing down the blunt end of his pommel only once on some man who decides to put up a fight, but for the main part the crowd has the good sense to steer clear of him. Another glimpse of Theo, dodging a blow from one of the ghoulish mob this time, and—*Miro,* was that Miro? Hand in hand with an older woman who looks so much like him, who has to be—Then the flash of a blackbag uniform, maybe, but he doesn't care, he has to find his sister, and for all the injured and dead falling to the ground, still the crowd doesn't seem to be thinning out, and people run this way and that, shoving each other in a bid to make it to one of the exits, and *there*—

Selah is putting up a good fight, he'll give her that, thrashing and digging her nails into the arms and chest and *face* of Cato Palmar's sentry. But the Consul's man has her firmly around the waist, and is dragging her toward the exit, and to anyone else it might look like the Consul protecting her escape, but Arran *knows* better because Palmar wants her and he wants the Stone and she's too far away, he won't make it to her in time, the press and rush of the mob is too thick, and they're almost out a back exit door.

Then the sentry drops, and Tair is standing there, breathing heavy, hands clasped around the metal pole she just used to bash the man across the head.

Arran presses the last length to reach them, where Tair is now standing between Palmar and Selah, weapon raised, blood shining from a cut along her bicep. Palmar's lip curls, and if he intended to say something, to call for new sentries, to *whatever*, it doesn't matter. Arran arrives just as he takes a breath, wrests a dangerously gleaming blade from a passing thremid's grip, and runs it straight through the Consul's throat.

And, just for that brief moment, time seems to stop.

Because all Arran can think is, *Good.*

Cato Palmar is dead. He's dead, and he didn't deserve the dignity of last words. Last breath. A poignant moment of clarity where he knew it was all being taken away and why. He deserved a careless end, the way he used others carelessly in life.

"Tair," he yells over the crowd. "Did you find Diana?"

"Saw her and Miro go out the back way."

"Good. Get Selah out of here."

Tair doesn't need to be told twice. She grabs Selah by the hand and drags her away, and Arran turns back into the melee. He isn't going anywhere without Theo.

SELAH

"Wait!" Selah shouts, but her brother's retreating back is already disappearing into the crowd.

"He can handle himself," Tair answers. "Selah, we have to *go*."

And now Tair is pulling at her arm, and in the distance Theo is throwing a pitmaster over their shoulder, and crumpled at their feet is the bloody corpse of Cato Palmar, and all around them gladiators and mine servae from even deeper under the earth are wringing necks, running people through, making no distinction between handler and spectator, patrician and pleb, and Selah can see her point.

"Right," she says. "Go go go go *go go go*."

Through the thrashing mob, Tair's prybar gleaming as it swings.

Past the gate.

Through the exit, slamming it closed, though the echoes of the fight behind them still ring in her ears. Tair grabs her hand and jerks her along in an all-out sprint down the dim-lit catacombs, and Selah's heart is pumping so hard she doesn't know how it hasn't already pumped clean out of her chest, and this isn't the way either of them came, and this doesn't matter, and did Arran and Theo and Diana and Miro make it out all right, and did any of them make it out all right, and she doesn't know how long they've been running now, and Arran *killed* Cato Palmar—

They round the corner, Selah and Tair, straight into a mourners' vigil. Sheer-gold veils and flickering pyre-light, and fervently hissed apologies are not enough to spare them the bereaved family's scornful glares. But when they retreat back the way came, no one comes after them.

She beckons Tair over to someone's familia crypt, holding open the white stone gate so they can conceal themselves into the little natural-formed alcove in the rock. So they can stop to take a breath. So they can hide, hands clasped tight, tucked between two effigies, and Selah thinks the dead won't mind. So the blood pumping furiously through her heart can calm itself, and her lungs can even their heaving, and she can stop to think properly for the first time since turning on the Iveroa Stone. So she can sit there in her own drying sweat, Tair's hand clasped tight in her own, and wonder how it is that they can no longer hear the battle raging below.

"Diana," Tair's quiet voice says, next to her. "We have to find her and Miro."

"Do you think it even matters now? With Palmar gone . . ."

"She knows about the Stone. She heard your father's message. We should find her before someone else does."

This is your burden to bear now. That's what the ghost of her father had said. *No one else's. No one else can know.* Well, it's too late for that now as a hard and fast rule, but Selah's inclined to agree that they can still mitigate the damage. Whatever else she might think about the secrets Antal Iveroa buried, or the morality and rightness of that choice, she *does* see Dad's point. The more people know about this, the more they'll be fighting tooth and nail to use it to their own ends. And Diana knows too much.

"Well, fuck."

Adrenaline still coursing through her veins, it just slips out.

Tair snaps her head around so fast it's a wonder she doesn't give herself whiplash. "Did you just . . . ?"

"Yep."

Tair eyes her for a moment. "How'd it feel?"

"Honestly?" asks Selah. "Really fucking good."

And Tair bursts out into laughter. An inelegant cackle that is so purely *Tair*, and then she straight-up snorts, and it's that more than the adrenaline, or the violence and the death, or even the absurdity of the last hour—or maybe some combination of everything—that has Selah joining her. Like a release of steam from a pressure valve, it all comes pouring out. Selah, a hand clamped over her mouth as she throws her head back against the wall, trying to stay quiet. Tair, having less luck, doubled over into Selah's chest and shaking with bursts of barely contained giggles.

She takes Tair's hand, and presses their sides more firmly to each other. Silver and blue beads from Tair's ocher hair glint in the dark, and she tucks her head into the crook between Selah's shoulder and chin as her laughter finally dies.

"Selah," Tair says suddenly, into the dark.

"Hm?"

"Did you turn it off?"

"Turn what—*Oh.*" She scrabbles for the Stone, still glowing faintly, and jams her thumb on the icon reading *Metro Rail*. Presses it a second time against the etched sun at the bottom, and the Stone itself goes dark.

"What happens now?" Tair turns to her, wonder and terror and something deeply unsure mingling in her voice. Mourning vespers rise around them from the nearby vigil, deep and haunting and strong, beseeching All-Mater Terra receive her child back to the earth. Tair's quiet voice beneath it could be the wind. "We just took out an irradium mine and maybe even the *fighting pits.* Liberated thousands of people, just with a couple buttons and levers. That kind of power . . . you could do so much good with it. And so much damage. It just depends on who's controlling it. It's amazing. And it scares me."

Tair sets her jaw, and Selah's lungs are slowing but her heart won't stop pounding and suddenly she knows precisely the reason why. Brown fingers laced with browner ones, disappearing entangled into the dark, she turns her head and meets Tair's lips with hers.

They are alive, and they are here, and they have the Iveroa Stone. Whatever comes next, they'll figure out how to meet it together.

They emerge with the dawn, just as the first spectacular purples shot with orange climb up into dark blue. Selah has always loved Luxana's sunrises. She's not as well-traveled as she would like, but somehow she knows this in her bones: they're like no other in the world.

They've come out somewhere in the Regio Marina, and it feels friendlier, this time around, despite the steady fisting heartbeat caught firmly in her throat. Maybe it's something to do with the warmth of Tair's hand in hers. Maybe it's the reassurance that this is, after all, where they agreed to meet back up with Arran and Theo, should something go wrong. Or maybe it's just the emptiness of the early-morning piers. At the docks, schooners in their berths hang their paraffin lamps, the transition from night to day still some ways off. Just ahead, a half-repaired sloop sags lower than it should in the waterline.

Darting between the growing shadows, Selah follows after Tair. They discussed this, in the dark hours of the night. They don't know what the fallout of the last few hours will be yet, and while Selah has the plausible deniability of having been present for the massacre in the pits as Palmar's guest, anyone might have caught a glimpse of Tair in the fighting and recognized her. Until they know more, Tair has to lay low, and Selah is staying with her. In the meantime, she thinks, they'll have to decide what to do about the Stone.

There's a flicker of lamplight, just up ahead, and a hushed conversation where they can make out two silhouettes in the waning dusk. Tair grips Selah's hand tighter, wary eyes darting toward the sound as they creep along the side of some half-rigged boat, and pulls her safely out of sight behind a cluster of barrels.

Somewhere in the distance, the ancient bells of the Plaza Capitolio clocktower echo out across the rooftops of Luxana.

There are no lanterns here, not even a sailor's meager candlelight for a game of desktop cards. Whoever's approaching, they're well and truly shrouded in the midnight gloom, keeping to the shadows of the ramshackle sloop. A schooner passes in the water some meters away, a leisure cruise at the end of its tour, filled with Fornian wine and the latest Roman fashions, laughter and light and gently lapping harbor waves spilling out in its wake. A beam of paraffin lamplight passes over the pier, and for the smallest of moments one shadowed figure is illuminated in stark relief.

It's enough. Selah knows those clever eyes. That warm, amber-glow skin. The hand held tight in Arran's, who she can see clearly too once another light from the schooner casts briefly across the pier.

The pair of them look terrible, frankly, with blood and sweat and bits of matter she does *not* want to know the origin of, thanks, matted in their hair and spattered across their clothes. Selah can't imagine she looks much better herself. None of that matters. She's never been happier to see her stupid big brother.

"*Oof*," says Arran, as she launches herself at him and latches on. She is never letting go of him again.

"You're such an idiot."

"Glad to see you, too."

Selah buries her face in his shoulder, and he squeezes her tight. The reality of what's happened comes down to bear full weight at last. Arran killed Cato Palmar. Arran killed the Consul of Roma Sargassa in just about the most public manner he could have. It doesn't matter that Palmar killed their father, though Arran couldn't know about that. It doesn't matter that he was acting in her defense. It doesn't matter that chaos rained down around them as it happened. Someone will have seen.

"Where will you go?" she asks, pulling slightly away. Tair isn't the only one who has to hide now.

Arran smiles down at her, a little sad, then glances over at Theo. "I have some people to lay low with," he says, and by now Tair has joined Selah at her side. "But I could use your help."

It's on the tip of her tongue—*Anything*. She has plausible deniability, and she'll do whatever it takes to protect him. But before she can speak, a soft thunk on wood heralds the arrival of another set of footsteps. Next to Selah, Tair goes stiff.

The woman's gait is both heavy and brisk, an easy thunk on the dock's sea-worn boards. Selah hears her well before she emerges from the wharf-side end of the pier.

"So, you're Selah Kleios," the woman says.

Long black hair twisted into two thick braids, small and sturdy and somewhere vaguely middle aged. Selah thinks that if she passed her on the street, she'd never have given her a second thought. Here in the Regio Marina, however, in the early hours of the dark morning, every breath of air seems to gravitate toward her, this strange woman commanding the attention of all who fall into her orbit. There's something vaguely familiar about her. It sends a chill down Selah's spine.

"You look like him," the woman says, now. "Your mother's there, of course, but your face is all Alex."

"Arran . . . ?" she starts, because she doesn't understand.

But neither her brother nor Theo look in the least surprised. They know this woman.

"Don't worry," says the woman. "I knew your father well. He was . . . well, I wouldn't go as far to say *one of us*, but we worked together when it made sense."

"Who exactly is *us*?" Selah asks, wary, but bolstered all the same. Because Tair's hand has slipped back into hers, and it's like rediscovering solid ground.

"She's lying," Tair says, a whispered mix of confused warning in her ear. "Your father wouldn't have trusted them. That's Griff. They're the Revenants, Sel."

And Selah wants to laugh, because that has to be a joke. This woman—*Griff*—maybe, she could see. But Theo? *Arran? Her* Arran, who runs away at the first sign of responsibility, who never puts up a fight. Who mostly sticks with jav for breakfast because he can never make up his mind. A Revenant. One of the ghosts who haunt children's stories. It's too ridiculous to conceive.

But there are the things.

The way Griff crosses her arms, brass knuckles shining over the fingers of her left hand.

The way Theo isn't who they said they were from the start.

The way Tair wouldn't lie to her, not after all they've done and seen.

The way Arran meets her eyes, daring her to deny it.

"Two out of three, Tair," the woman called Griff says. "I *am* a Revenant. But Alex was a canary, too. I wouldn't lie about that. You, on the other hand . . . I wonder if you've been entirely honest with your paterfamilias here. I wonder, did you tell her who helped you escape from her house?"

Tair grits her teeth. "That doesn't mean I was ever one of you."

"No. All it means is that Alex called in a favor. I'm not in the business of freeing every verna who asks for it. Especially not ones that go crawling back to their patrician girlfriend looking for protection. I don't waste my time with lapdogs."

She can recognize the warning signs, the way Tair grits her teeth.

The way she stands a little taller, her shoulders pulling back. Like she
wants to punch Griff right in the face. Like she knows doing so would
be a death sentence. Like she'd do it anyway. So when Selah steps in,
it's not to save Tair from herself.

Tair doesn't need a champion. But Selah needs answers.

"He called in a favor," she echoes, the gears of her mind already
whirring to the inevitable conclusion. Five years ago. Tair's sentence
of a lifetime spent in service. *It's not my place to interfere.* That's
what Dad had said, in his home office as the setting sun streamed
through the windows and Selah's heart had felt like it would give out
on itself from the unfairness of it all. *We all have our parts to play.
Someday you'll understand.*

"He couldn't overrule the magistrate," Selah says now, the incon-
ceivable realization grabbing hold, "but he had another way to give
Tair her freedom. The Revenants. You."

Griff nods her head once, curt, like the merest act of acquiescence
causes her pain.

"But if you hate patricians . . ."

"We had a complicated relationship, Alex and I. He was a valuable resource, but he only passed us the supplies and information he
thought we should have. Like I should have expected anything else
from a Historian. We believed in the same things, but we disagreed on
the means to get there."

"He was a pacifist," Selah says.

"Yes."

"But he had a weapon that you wanted. A weapon that he'd shown
you before." A weapon he'd shown to Cato Palmar, too, for which he
had paid the ultimate price. *This is your burden to bear. No one
else's. Don't make the same mistakes I did. No one else can know.*

Who *is* this woman, with whom her father risked sharing his life's
work? This woman, with whom he had a falling-out? This woman,
nodding humorlessly now, saying, "Yes. He had something that didn't
rightfully belong to just him."

Like I should have expected anything else from a Historian.

It rankles on instinct, but somewhere deep in her gut Selah knows that's only because she's been raised since birth to revere the work of the Imperial Archives. They all have, but her most of all. The collection and preservation. The curation of what's sent back out. Inexplicably, she thinks of Jankara and the Shikibu team, and the curdling acid trying to hold back the words. *Censorship. Propaganda.* Is that really what the Archives are for?

The proof of it is there in the Iveroa Stone. The Imperial Historian's work, deciding who gets to know what. Shaping the narratives of how they're allowed to understand it at all.

And then she thinks of Linet. Caught in the narrative they wrote for her, the one that even Selah and her supposed authority couldn't save her from. Because it didn't matter if she was a criminal, or what her crime even was. Selah used to think it did. She understands now that it's an excuse, a convenient way of shuffling more people through the great machine. The machine that's working perfectly as it's meant to. Tair helped her to see that.

"So," she says slowly, "you were waiting for it to pass to the next Historian."

"I was hoping you might share our views."

"Or that I'd get my hands on the Iveroa Stone and learn a few hard truths."

Griff smiles at that, a sly and broad thing. "Clever girl," she says. "You've already worked out how to turn it on."

Selah shrugs, but her heart is pounding.

Her father, in league with terrorists. Her father, an anarchist. No. Her father, who believed in a better world, but was too paralyzed by the mistakes of the past. Too mired in the misery of what he knew, who did his best in small acts of kindness but would never allow himself to dream beyond the world he'd inherited. The world that worked for some, but not for many. Her father, who alone held the keys to possibility, yet willingly put a leash on his own imagination.

"And if I have?" she asks, voice quiet among the lapping waves. She needs to know just how much this woman Griff knows. "What good is it to you?"

"You're Alex's daughter, don't play dumb with me. Information is knowledge—"

"—and knowledge is power. Yeah, I know. And I also know the Stone doesn't just have my dad's far-fetched conspiracies about world wars and a lying Imperium, I know it controls dormant solaric systems all throughout the city. And I know *you* know that, so what else does this thing *really* have that you people want?"

For a fraction of a second, Selah thinks that Griff is going to slap her. She doesn't. Instead, the older woman regards her for a long, drawn-out moment. Appraising. Selah feels naked under her eye, but she doesn't back down. She can still see Arran in the periphery of her sphere, hard gaze crinkling beneath a divoting brow. Did he know about Dad all along? Is that why he joined the Revenant cause? Either way, the sinking disappointment of betrayal shivers its way into her gut, even as she knows full well why he wouldn't have trusted her with this.

Finally, Griff nods, apparently decided on something, and gets right to the point. "It's a weapon of the mind," she says, "that much is true. That tablet contains unimaginable histories, going back millennium on millennium. Textbooks, sure, but photographs too. Something called films. Songs. Novels. *Culture.* The *ideas*, Selah Kleios. The medicine. The science. The political theory. The statecraft. The warcraft. The technology. And if you dig deep enough, if you know where to look . . . the location of where to find more."

TAIR

More.

More.

"More," says Selah, at her side. "More of what?"

"Weapons," says Griff, eyes gleaming. "Real ones. Physical ones. I'm not talking about gunpowder, I'm talking about the kind of weapons you couldn't begin to imagine. There's a cache of them somewhere—that tablet holds the location. And whoever holds that kind of power holds the power to shape the world to their will. The Imperium couldn't stand a chance."

Tair sucks in a breath. A single *on* button of solaric tech was enough to free the pits. A single loaded gun from the distance of the control room and Tair could have ended every one of the pitmasters forever. With the kind of weaponry Griff's talking about, what kind of good could *more* of that do? What kind of disaster could it wreak?

"So what do you want?" Selah is asking now. "You want me to join you, you want the Stone and the weapons cache. But what do you *want*?"

"Democracy," Griff answers, simple. "On our own terms. Roma, gone. The people of Sargassa in charge of their destiny, free of the great machine." Tair's eyes snap up. Selah's, too. The echo of Alexander Kleios's own words ringing in the purple pre-dawn. But there's a soft smile on Griff's face when she says, "I don't think that's so much to ask."

Selah bites the corner of her lip, and Tair knows that look. It sends a cold thrill of dread straight into her heart.

"I thought I could really make a difference from the inside," Selah says slowly. "Education reform and everything, but . . . I don't know if that's true anymore. Even the Archives aren't what I . . . Well, I wonder if it just makes more sense to build something else. Something better. Something honest." She levels her gaze at Griff. "You said he showed you the Stone."

"Yes."

"What did you think?"

"I think," says Griff, "that people deserve to know the truth. When the time is right. And furthermore, I think that having the Imperial Historian behind us will go a long way toward gaining popular support. Changing people's minds about the Imperium. They trust you. They trust the Archives, and what comes out of there. I'll be honest, that's why I put Theo in your mother's office, to get close to you. We need you, Selah. Will you work with us?"

No.

No.

It screams in Tair's mind, the protest.

When the time is right. People deserve to know the truth, but only when the time is right. What a load of shit. Tair knows Griff too well for that, and it shouldn't be down to any one person to decide what's best for everyone else. Not when the world belongs to all the people living in it. She can't keep quiet another minute longer.

"And then what?"

Griff and Selah and Theo and Arran all turn to her, mildly surprised, so enthralled in the Revenant leader's spell they might have entirely forgotten she was there, part of this conversation, too. They probably had. Tair pulls her shoulders back.

"What comes next?" she asks Griff again. This shouldn't be a difficult question, but she knows it isn't one she'll get a straight answer to. All the same, it has to be asked. "After you've waged your war and broken away from Roma and are responsible for millions of lives?"

"Like I said, direct dem—"

"Bullshit. You can't even run four people as a direct democracy."

"There's a difference between peacetime and—"

"*Bull. Shit.*" Blood pounds in her ears. "Why should she trust you? Why should any of us believe you'll take that Stone and this big cache of weaponry it's supposed to lead you to and then actually give Sargassa back to the people instead of just naming yourself dictator? Or better yet, why not queen? Why should I believe for a *second* you wouldn't do that?"

Those heavy hooded eyes bore mercilessly into her own, and Tair fights the urge to look away. No. She doesn't do that anymore.

"That's a fair question," Griff says at last, but her gaze slides over to Selah. "I don't need to be the one in control of the Iveroa Stone. I'll leave that to you if it's what it takes to build trust between us. We can be equal partners in this revolution. I *wanted* to work with your father, Selah. He was just too afraid to say yes."

"Afraid of what?" Selah asks, and Tair grits her teeth because she knows what Griff is doing.

"Of seeing everyone he loved suffer as a result. He knew what the cost could be, and he decided his family was more important. But me . . . I wanted to use his mind, his resources, the languishing potential of two thousand years of forgotten civilization. It *won't* just be me. We'll build it together. But we have to get rid of the Imperium. You can't grow new life until you've pulled out the weeds that are strangling you."

Slowly, Selah turns to face her, and Tair feels her heart plummet to the bottom of her gut. "No," she says urgently, holding her hand tight. "There are other ways."

"If you can't trust her," says Selah, "trust me?" Her green eyes are wide and pleading, and Tair thinks this must be what drowning feels like. "You were the one who said it—I have to do better. We all do. And if this is a chance to build something new . . . a Sargassa where people are in charge of their own destiny, their own *truth* . . . then I think it's worth it."

She turns back to Griff, Arran and Theo on either side, and before Tair can say another word, Selah holds out her hand.

THEO

Theo is a keen observer. It's how they've survived this long.

It's how they know what Griff is doing, harsh words and tougher truths to entice Selah Kleios over to their side. It's how, despite her historically loose relationship with things like facts and the truth, they know somehow that Griff isn't lying about what the Iveroa Stone really contains. It's how, an instant before the throwing star would have hit its target, they know to throw their body across Arran's and pull him to the ground. The bladed star whirrs overhead, burying itself deep into the side of the berthed sloop instead.

"What—" he just starts to say, but by then the answer is already clear. The Intelligentia must be doing patrol on exits from the underground in the wake of the massacre, and they've lingered here too long.

At a glance, Theo counts seven blackbags in all. Seven—no, nine. Two on the water, silent shadows on skiffs. Two more on the wharf, to block any retreat. Four more still, clopping down the dock, the Chief General Blackbag himself at their head.

Shouts break out around them, the opening scuffles of a fight just getting underway. Griff, her concealed blades and brass knuckles at the ready. Tair, flipping the prybar from the underground into her hands with extraordinary grace. Quintus Kopitar, shouting, "Arrest them! No casualties! *Take them alive!*"

Oh, that's how he wants to play this?

Game on.

One of the blackbags off the skiff makes the jump across the gap onto the dock, and Arran turns around to land a fist square against the man's jaw. Theo winces. That's how knuckles get torn. But now Arran's landed two, three more blows and the blackbag keels back into the water with a satisfying splash.

Tair, taking on two blackbags to one. Griff, holding Kopitar himself at bay with a smile on her face, like she's been waiting for this moment all her life. That leaves a blackbag still for each of them, the two on the wharf and the one still on the water too far out of reach. Theo shifts their weight, and reaches for the familiar comfort of their favorite ring knives. But their target is looking up, and then an angry shout rings high above the fray.

Because Selah Kleios doesn't know how to fight, and Selah Kleios has sought higher ground.

The abandoned sloop is lower in the waterline than it should be, but it still looms high above the skirmish. She's pulled herself up the rope ladder rotting against its side, and a sharp-featured woman with a bright orange bun is now halfway to following suit.

Arran lurches forward, but they grab his hand. "I've got this," they shout, and shove the pistol they took off Miranda back in the woods of Breakwater into his hand. They had to stash it before going down to the pits, but seeing it now in Arran's hand makes them feel better, somehow. "You take the one on the water. We're gonna need that skiff if we want to get out of here." And at his hesitation, eyes still fixed high on his little sister—"*Go!*"

They don't need to tell him again.

Arran elbows an incoming officer out of the way and swings himself across to deal with the one on the skiff. Theo forces themself to tear their eyes away, to grab onto the fraying rope ladder and climb up after Selah and the orange-haired blackbag. They make it to the top of the waterlogged deck just in time to find themself at one point of a three-way stand-off.

Selah, hands wrapped in the foredeck rigging, like she might try escaping further up. The officer, sword in hand, daring her to move another inch. And Theo, ring knives at the ready, who'd like to see her try.

"Wait!" they call across the deck to Selah. "Don't move."

Because more wooden boards have cracked and fallen away than they had anticipated from the pier, and more want to give way underfoot. One wrong step and any one of them could go crashing down through the structure beneath. Theo scans across the deck, eyes squinting in the dark, searching for the telltale signs of a board that's still structurally sound.

There.

Got it.

"Listen to your friend," the blackbag says, and creeps forward slightly, testing out the board in front of her. "The boss wants you alive, but he didn't say a thing about unharmed."

One more step, that's all they need, and . . . *there*.

The blackbag steps onto the board, the one that'll carry them both, and Theo doesn't waste a moment. They launch themself forward in an instant, balanced on the mere space of half a foot, and fast enough to hope their velocity will make up for it if they're wrong. A half-second of falling through air and they have the woman caught in a lockbind, her throwing stars falling through the skeleton of the sloop along with the rotten boards to either side.

But not the board they're standing on.

That one holds.

Theo doesn't give her the satisfaction of last words. They pull her close, back flush against their chest, and drive the knife *up* from under the blackbag's chin. It's easy. It's not personal. It's the most personal thing in the world. Retching on her own blood, the woman shudders, then stills, and Theo pulls the blade back out from her skull and lets her fall away, crashing through the sloop and down into the water below.

"Come on," barks Theo, and throws out their hand.

Selah doesn't hesitate. She takes it, and they pull her close, and edge down the single wooden board back to the dock-side rail of the boat deck. Griff is still down there, surrounded by fallen bodies—Kopitar there among them, his own sword through his throat—and taking on the final two blackbags with her bare hands. Arran's got control of the skiff, is steering it around closer to the pier. And Darius Miranda is climbing over the side of the sloop, another Cohort regulation sword acquired from somewhere and pointing right at their heart. Where in the savage *Quiet* did he come from?

Theo backs up on instinct, putting themself between him and Selah. They have to hand it to him. He might look like death, but the man just refuses to die.

"You brought friends this time."

"I learn from my mistakes," he says, and for a man with a concussion, his gaze is remarkably sharp. They still wouldn't trust him with that blade. "So. This is where we stand, is it? Theodora Nix."

They hesitate, just for the briefest moment. Because Darius Miranda is a man who stands for everything Theo finds abhorrent in this world, who defends it as infallibly right. Because they hate him, but they can't shake the itch that there's something else hiding in the barest tremor of his voice—Respect. Regret.

"Yes," they answer, one eye on the fight below where Arran is coming around, one eye on the wounded animal in front of them. "This is where we stand."

And they grab Selah around the middle, pulling her bodily to the side as a single, clear shot rings out. Darius Miranda goes down hard, for the third time that day, and in the space across his shoulder blades, dark blood seeps in generous blooms.

ARRAN

The force of the shot reverberates through his arm, ringing up into his skull, and Arran hadn't thought it would take such physical strength to shoot a man. A pistol is so small, in the grand scheme of things. But neither had he thought it would be so easy. A gun is still a weapon. And he's never shot one in his life.

Had never, not till now.

Arran watches Darius Miranda drop out of sight on the deck above, and only then does he lower Darius Miranda's own pistol. It still rings in his ears, but life goes on around him, as it tends to do.

Griff, punching her brass knuckles into the last of the blackbags' face with a satisfying crunch, leaping over the half-foot space into the skiff, shouting, "Let's *go*." Theo, hand in hand with Selah on the deck above, jumping into the water below. Griff, taking charge of the bow-line rigging as he veers the skiff around to meet them, and he doesn't ask how she knows what to do. Selah, her hand in solid in his, as he pulls her out of the water. Theo, their eyes meeting his, and he doesn't know where to start to say, *Thank you.* Griff, who doesn't have time for this, yelling at him to steer out into the fast-lightening dark. And then Selah, suddenly frowning, looking wildly around.

"Tair," she says, panic coming in at the edge. "Where's Tair?"

THE BEGINNING

Here is where one world ends, and another world has to begin. Here is where a girl must make a difficult choice.

Here is where a girl stands on a half-sinking pier, as the last of her enemies fall to the makeshift staff she fashioned out of the debris of a dead world. Several feet away, the Revenant queenpin does glorious, gritting battle of her own. Out on the water, an overlooked son takes control of a boat. Up on the deck of a crumbling ship, the Historian will be fine. Theo is the best protector she could ask for.

Three things, Tair knows now:

One. Another world is possible.

A world where gladiators can be set free with the single push of a button.

The key to that world is a tablet sitting in her bag.

Two. Alexander Kleios was right.

Too many people have their own ideas about what to do with the Stone. Too many people would want to use it for their own personal power. And Tair doesn't know who to trust.

Three. Selah loves her.

She *loves* her, and in the moment between hearing those words and the violence that followed, Tair thought her skin might catch fire, because she loves Selah, too, more than she ever thought it was possible to love a person.

Through all the days of Tair's life, love has had to be earned—that is, if it's come at all. It has always come with a cost, and the cost was making herself small. So no one prepared her for this. For the way it feels to have someone creep into the narrow crevices of your soul, for the overwhelming desire to know every inch of them in return. For a person to grow and change for you without asking for anything in return. To witness you in all your mess and darkness, and affirm that you still and will always matter.

Tair loves Selah so much, the thought of what needs to happen next might break her in two. Because no one prepared her for this, and they didn't prepare her for the fact that sometimes, maybe, love just isn't enough.

By now, Tair is good at disappearing.

In the dark and crumbling underground bunker deep beneath the Third Ward, Griff busies herself making tazine. Theo sits across the way, wringing water out of their hair, eyes alight with fire now Selah's explained everything that the message from her father contained. Arran drops a heavy blanket around Selah, cold and dripping from the sea, and she doesn't let him take her hand.

"I'm sorry," he says.

She doesn't look at him. She can't. She doesn't know where she could have gone so wrong.

"The good news," he tries again, and Selah wishes that he would just *stop*, "is that she has to come back for you. If she ever wants to actually *use* the Stone."

At long last Selah looks at him, and the salt tracks that run down her cheeks are not the lingering remnants of the Sargasso Sea. "It's my fault," she whispers into the dark, and here's the thing. Selah is not just heartbroken. She's ashamed. She's afraid. "I made a mistake."

Two girls sit in the catacombs beneath a city, waiting for the dawn. The city is old, but more ancient than they know. Even further beneath their feet, a battle rages in an abandoned subway station, dozens on dozens of men, women, and thremed taking back their lives.

Here, the world is quiet, and dark, and Selah brushes a finger lightly over Tair's eyelid. The scar there is faded, lit with silver, and she does not ask where it came from. She ghosts a gentle kiss against it, and Tair smiles, more relaxed than she has ever been in her life.

So she chooses this because she wants to.

She chooses this because she can.

Selah wants her, and she wants Selah, and they move together in the dark. A thrumming in Tair's spine that shoots all the way down, and her heart has never beat so fast. She has never been touched like this, like she is mortal made divine. Like each press of Selah's mouth on her throat her breasts her belly her lips is an act of tribute, an offering of lapis lazuli and gold.

"You look like starlight," Selah whispers, tracing the heavenly bodies beading across Tair's brow.

She takes Selah hard, against the reliquary to someone's forgotten ancestor, and the familia should consider themselves lucky to be consecrated with such an act. Selah sucks a purpling bruise into the soft skin beneath her ear, and the mourning vespers rise around them as she hisses into Selah's hair. There is no space between them, now, no place where one ends and the other begins, and Tair did not know it was possible to have someone else under your skin. Did not know it was possible to leave your body for pleasure, not just to escape the pain. Did not know she could be this, a hurricane colliding with a rainstorm, sticking together into one great destroyer of worlds.

Thank you, she says to no one, after.

"Here," Selah says to her. She parses the instructions left inside, Sargassan Latin mixed in just enough to follow, and presses Tair's thumbprint to a cool Stone. It will open for both of them now. Just her and Tair and no one else. "Whatever comes next, we face it together."

"No," she tells her brother, Theodora Nix holding his hand. "She doesn't need me. She doesn't need me for anything at all."

There's a clang at the makeshift kitchen sink, and Griff is holding the remnants of a broken ceramic mug, eyes closed, breathing in heavily through her nose.

There was a time, not very long ago, when Selah used to define herself by her duty to other people. Paterfamilias of the Kleios familia. The caretaker of the world's knowledge. Naevia and Alexander's daughter. Arran's sister. Tair's . . . something. But that time is over. The time for shaping something new has come.

Dropping the blanket behind her on the chair, Selah stands. "I'll find her," she says.

Griff doesn't look at her. It's Theo who answers, instead. "She won't go back to the Sisters," they tell her gently. "How do you—"

"I'll *find* her," Selah repeats, louder this time, and it comes out a snap.

Because this isn't about Tair. Not anymore. Tair ripped her heart out, and stomped on it for good measure, but Tair also has something that doesn't belong to her. It's not about duty, and it's not about Dad leaving what he knows to Selah and Selah alone. It's about what they can make with it when they get it back.

"I meant what I said." She moves to meet Griff where the older woman stands. "Up in the Regio, I meant it."

Finally, she meets her eyes. "I know you meant it," she says. Then—"Go home."

"But—"

"Go *home*. Cry to your mother. People will have seen you in the pits, no point pretending otherwise. I hear you're a pretty actress, so here's what you're going to do: You're going to go home. You're going to be traumatized. You're going to miss your brother but accept that he's a criminal on the run for an egregious offense all the same. And then you're going to get to work."

The steadiness of Griff's voice beats nearly in tandem with the thump of Selah's heart, so much so that she nearly doesn't notice as Arran moves to her side. She straightens up. "What do I do?"

"Spread the right story," Griff answers with a small smile. "Whatever happened in the massacre down in the fighting pits, the Revenants weren't involved. You spread that story, and you have a look around to see if there's anything else your father was keeping from us.

Meanwhile, we'll look for Tair. But if you happen to use your advantage of position to find her first, then I'd appreciate it if you bring her to me."

A shudder ripples down her spine. But Tair made her choice, and she didn't choose her.

"We'll see each other again soon, Selah Kleios," says Griff, and at their perch across the room, Theo sheathes their knives. "We're partners in this now."

A girl crouches low in the dripping allées of Amphitheater Messalina, arms wound tight around her satchel, pressing the hard and solid weight of the Iveroa Stone within to her erratic beating heart.

Tair can't go back to the Kirnaval. She can't go back to the little apartment she shares with Ibdi, or the headquarters at Naqvi Row, or the Watchers' warehouse by the Tenant's Gate. She can't go back to Gil's tired smile, or the warm flush of Selah's cheek against her own. Once again, Tair is well and truly alone.

But the thin tablet pressed against her chest is a miracle. It is wondrous, opportune creation. It's dangerous, of course, but isn't any shift in the status quo? A chance either for catastrophe or change. And that's the old promise. That at the crux of catastrophe and change, rage brings the former and focus brings the latter, and that she will always choose change.

Tair meant what she said to Selah in the catacombs beneath the city. This power scares her. But it also does not belong to her alone. Maybe Griff thinks people need to wait to know the truth. Maybe she's no better than anyone else who thinks they know better than others, and have to tell them what to do. Tair knows better than that. The truth is in her arms, and the time for people to know about it is now. One person alone shouldn't get to hold this kind of power. One person alone shouldn't get to decide what to do with it. Not even two, together.

Maybe she'll pay Artemide and Ibdi and the Sisters of the First a visit after all. Maybe it's time to stop running away.

So Tair stands, bag heavy at her hip, and walks out into the rising sun.

AN OFFICIAL HISTORY OF ROMA
& HER CLIENT EMPIRES

1547 AQ—The foundation of Roma by the twin brothers Remus and Romulus.

1303 AQ—The last king of Roma is overthrown. The city-state reorganizes into a Republic.

821 AQ—Augustus Caesar becomes the first *princeps* of Roma.

746 AQ—Marcus Aurelius passes over his son Commodus to adopt Ovidian as his successor. Ovidian creates the first colleges of the Imperium.

618 AQ—Roma consolidates power over Caledonia to Armenia in the north, and Mauritania to Arabia (Maghreb-Anatolia) in the south.

599–590 AQ—Rome begins the annexation of Serica from the Parthian Empire. The first consul and senate of Roma Serica are established, answerable to the Imperium.

535–528 AQ—The Caesarian explorers cross the Sargasso Sea and arrive in Aymara. They defeat the Maya and Quimbaya and annex the continent as a client empire. The first consul and senate of Roma Aymara are established. The province of Arawaka and the Taino Territories is established.

478–473 AQ—The Caesarian explorers move north to Sargassa. They defeat the Ynglots and annex the continent as a client empire. The first consul and senate of Roma Sargassa are established.

11–6 AQ—Plague sweeps through Italia, decimating the population. Grain shortages in Egypt and Sicilia further severely weaken the import-dependent Romans.

5 AQ—The second sack of Rome. What begins as grain riots turns into all-out civil war in the heart of the city.

1 AQ—A general breakdown in law and order within the mother empire leads to Roma losing contact with her client empires and provinces. The Great Quiet begins.

QUIETAM MAGNA (THE GREAT QUIET)—The intervening years during this period are unknown and the events are pure folktale and speculation.

Historians estimate the duration of the period to be around 300 years. *(Note: Much of written history, literature, and technological advancement was destroyed or lost during this period. This is where the legend of Roman antiquity ends and the verifiable facts of history begin.)*

1 PQ—After years of rebuilding, Roma is reestablished. The Imperium sends legions to reestablish contact with client empires through both diplomacy and force. The Great Quiet ends. The Imperial Age of Enlightenment begins.

2 PQ—The Imperial Charter of Roma Sargassa is created. Luxana is established.

9 PQ—Antal Iveroa is appointed the first Imperial Historian.

31 PQ—Construction concludes on the Imperial Archives in Luxana.

120 PQ—The Third Aksumite War ends with the Roman and Aksum Empires signing an alliance treaty.

382 PQ—Serican sailors discover Pacifica, numerous islands to the southeast unconquered by any of the world powers.

383 PQ—Roma attempts to invade Pacifica. They can't get anywhere close to the islands, however, without their ships being sunk via underwater guerrilla attacks. They decide to leave the islands alone.

410 PQ—The second attempt to invade Pacifica. The second failure.

549 PQ—Gladiator games are abolished in Roma and all client empires.

577–579 PQ—The Twelfth Servile War breaks out and is quelled in Roma Sargassa.

753 PQ—Delena Kleios dies of smoking fever. Alexander Kleios becomes Imperial Historian.

779 PQ—Alexander Kleios is assassinated. Selah Kleios becomes Imperial Historian.

Acknowledgments

This story was written on the lands of the Wampanoag, Narragansett, and Tongva peoples, rightful custodians of that land and of storytelling traditions far older than this book.

None of this would have been possible without my agent, Maria Napolitano. Thank you for your friendship, for your practical advice, for my sourdough starter, and for your unending generosity. I also have to thank everyone at kt literary for welcoming me into the fold.

Next, a massive thank you to my phenomenal editor Navah Wolfe, as well as to Joshua Starr, Laura Fitzgerald, Madeline Goldberg, and the rest of the team at DAW and Astra Publishing House. To Rebecca Yanovskaya and Adam Auerbach, my endless appreciation for making the jackets look so damn good. I thought this book was done. I was very, very wrong.

Thank you, thank you, *thank you* to Christina Sweeney-Baird, Lia Ryerson, and Leo Goodyear for beta reading my mess of a second draft long before I even had publishing rep. Christina, thank you so much for your sensible Capricorn braying and for getting to wake up to your fantastic voice notes. Lia, thank you for holding my hand through the querying process and for text messages proclaiming your undying love and support. Leo, thank you for your industry advice and for letting me help pick out your first drag fit. It was an honor.

Thank you to Petie Sjogren for asking the best questions. To Stitch for ensuring that both Selah and Tair came to life in the way they deserved. To Erika Lynn-Green, Daniel Packard, and Liv Adams for letting me pick your brains about various gruesome injuries and hypothetical medical emergencies. To Ammy Ontiveros for graciously letting me steal your last name—occupational hazard of being friends with a writer. To Lela Barclay de Tolly for childhood days spent climbing around apothecaries and warehouses and farmstands, and for being my chosen family.

Thank you to the amazing community at Stories Books & Cafe, where most of this was written, and to the folks at Riffraff and the Providence Public Library, sites of many a long editorial fugue state. Please support your local libraries!

To my trio of champions: Miguel Angel Parreno, Bernadette Greaney, and Adam Kantor. You all believed in this project with passionate—and loud, Adam—enthusiasm right from the start. To Kira Mason and Alexis Ames, the most esteemed Cursed Book Club. And a profoundly heartfelt thank you to Ashley Ellis and Lauren Davila.

In no particular order, there are a few other people I have to thank for helping to birth this book into being, whether they're aware of doing so or not: Sam Blinn, Abdi Yazdi, Kyle Bass, Linda McDonough, Iniki Mariano, Tyler Spicer, Malcolm Ingram, Zora Moynihan, and Flavia Viotti.

At last, my family. A huge thank you to my dad John, who taught me the elements of style and, when I threw them out the window, very generously got over it. To my mom Rachel, who showed me that a life dedicated to passion and art is not only possible but necessary. To Isabel for keeping me grounded, to Sebastian for keeping me laughing, and to Olivia for your love of stories—and for your love of this one in particular.